MEAN STREAK

SANDRA BROWN

GRAND CENTRAL
PUBLISHING

NEW YORK   BOSTON

Copyright © 2014 by Sandra Brown Management, Ltd.

Grand Central Publishing
Hachette Book Group
1290 Avenue of the Americas
New York, NY 10104

GrandCentralPublishing.com

Printed in the United States of America

RRD-C

Originally published in hardcover by Grand Central Publishing.
First trade edition: February 2015

10 9 8 7 6 5 4 3

Grand Central Publishing is a division of Hachette Book Group, Inc.
The Grand Central Publishing name and logo are trademarks of Hachette Book Group, Inc.

The Hachette Speakers Bureau provides a wide range of authors for speaking events. To find out more, go to www.hachettespeakersbureau.com or call (866) 376-6591.

The publisher is not responsible for websites (or their content) that are not owned by the publisher.

Library of Congress Cataloging-in-Publication Data
Brown, Sandra
Mean streak / Sandra Brown.
pages cm
ISBN 978-1-4555-8112-2 (hardback)—ISBN 978-1-4555-3008-3 (large print hardcover)—ISBN 978-1-4789-2742-6 (audio download) 1. Couples—Fiction. 2. Missing persons—Fiction. 3. Kidnapping—Fiction. 4. North Carolina—Fiction. I. Title.

PS3552.R718M43 2014
813'.54—dc23
2014017848

ISBN 978-1-4555-8114-6 (pbk.)

MEAN
STREAK

Prologue

Emory hurt all over. It hurt even to breathe.

The foggy air felt full of something invisible but sharp, like ice crystals or glass shards. She was underdressed. The raw cold stung her face where the skin was exposed. It made her eyes water, requiring her to blink constantly to keep the tears from blurring her vision and obscuring her path.

A stitch had developed in her side. It clawed continually, grabbed viciously. The stress fracture in her right foot was sending shooting pains up into her shin.

But owning the pain, running through it, overcoming it, was a matter of self-will and discipline. She'd been told she possessed both. In abundance. To a fault. But this was what all the difficult training was for. She could do this. She had to.

Push on, Emory. Place one foot in front of the other. Eat up the distance one yard at a time.

How much farther to go?

God, please not much farther.

Refueled by determination and fear of failure, she picked up her pace.

Then, from the deep shadows of the encroaching woods came a rustling sound, followed by a shift of air directly behind her. Her heart clutched with a foreboding of disaster to which she had no time to react before skyrockets of pain exploded inside her skull.

Chapter 1

———◆———

Does it hurt this much?" Dr. Emory Charbonneau pointed to a drawing of a child's face contorted with pain, large teardrops dripping from the eyes. "Or like this?" She pointed to another in the series of caricatures, where a frowning face illustrated moderate discomfort.

The three-year-old girl pointed to the worst of the two.

"I'm sorry, sweetie." Emory inserted the otoscope into her right ear. The child began to scream. As gently as possible, and talking to her soothingly, Emory examined her ears. "Both are badly infected," she reported to the girl's frazzled mother.

"She's been crying since she got up this morning. This is the second earache this season. I couldn't get in to see you with the last one, so I took her to an emergency center. The doctor there prescribed meds, she got over it, now it's back."

"Chronic infections can cause hearing loss. They should be avoided, not just treated when they occur. You might consider taking her to a pediatric ENT."

"I've tried. None are accepting new patients."

"I can get her in with one of the best." It wasn't a misplaced boast. Emory was confident that any one of several colleagues would take a patient that she referred. "Let's give this infection six weeks to heal up completely, then I'll set her up with an appointment. For now, I'll give her an antibiotic along with an antihistamine to clear up the fluid behind the eardrums. You can give her a children's analgesic for the pain, but as soon as the meds kick in, that should decrease.

"Don't push food on her, but keep her hydrated. If she's not better in a few days, or if her fever spikes, call the number on this card. I'm going away for the weekend, but another doctor is covering for me. I doubt you'll have an emergency, but if you do, you'll be in excellent hands until I get back."

"Thank you, Dr. Charbonneau."

She gave the mother a sympathetic smile. "A sick child is no fun for anybody. Try to get some rest yourself."

"I hope you're going someplace fun for the weekend."

"I'm doing a twenty-mile run."

"That sounds like torture."

She smiled. "That's the point."

Outside the examination room, Emory filled out the prescription form and finished her notes in the patient file. As she handed it over to the office assistant who checked out patients, the young woman said, "That was your last of the day."

"Yes, and I'm on my way out."

"Did you notify the hospital?"

She nodded. "And the answering service. I'm officially signed out for the weekend. Are Drs. Butler and James with patients?"

"They are. And both have several in the waiting room."

"I hoped to see them before I left, but I won't bother them."

"Dr. Butler left you a note."

She passed her a sheet from a monogrammed notepad. *Break a leg. Or is that what you say to a marathon runner?* Emory smiled as she folded the note and put it in her lab coat pocket.

The receptionist said, "Dr. James asked me to tell you to watch out for bears."

Emory laughed. "Do their patients know they're a couple of clowns? Tell them I said good-bye."

"Will do. Have a good run."

"Thanks. See you Monday."

"Oh, I almost forgot. Your husband called and said he was leaving work and would be at home to see you off."

"Emory?"

"In here." As Jeff walked into the bedroom she zipped up her duffel bag and, with a motion that was intentionally defiant, pulled it off the bed and slid the strap onto her shoulder.

"You got my message? I didn't want you to leave before I got here to say good-bye."

"I want to get ahead of Friday afternoon traffic."

"Good idea." He looked at her for a moment, then said, "You're still mad."

"Aren't you?"

"I'd be lying if I said I wasn't."

Last night's argument was still fresh. Words shouted in anger and resentment seemed to be reverberating off the bedroom walls even now, hours after they'd gone to bed, lying back to back, each nursing hostility that had been simmering for months and had finally come to a boil.

He said, "Do I at least get points for wanting to see you off?"

"That depends."

"On?"

"On whether or not you're hoping to talk me out of going." He sighed and looked away, and she said, "That's what I thought."

"Emory—"

"You should have stayed and finished out your day at the office. Because I'm going, Jeff. In fact, even if I hadn't planned this distance run for tomorrow, I'd still want to take some time for myself. A night spent away from each other will give us a chance to cool off. If the run wears me out, I may stay up there tomorrow night, too."

"One night or two won't change my mind. This compulsion of yours—"

"This is where we started last night. I'm not going to rehash the quarrel now."

Her training schedule for an upcoming marathon had been the subject that sparked the argument, but she feared that more substantive issues had been the underlying basis for it. The marathon wasn't their problem; the marriage was.

Which is why she wanted so badly to get away and think. "I wrote down the name of the motel where I'll be tonight." As they walked past the kitchen bar, she tipped her head down toward the sheet of paper lying on it.

"Call me when you get there. I'll want to know you made it safely."

"All right." She slid on her sunglasses and opened the back door. "Good-bye."

"Emory?"

Poised on the threshold, she turned. He leaned down and brushed his lips across hers. "Be careful."

"Jeff? Hi. I made it."

The two-hour drive from Atlanta had left Emory tired, but most of the fatigue was due to stress, not the drive itself. The traffic on northbound Interstate 85 had thinned out considerably about an hour outside the city, when she took the cutoff highway that angled northwest. She'd arrived at her destination before dusk, which had made navigating the unfamiliar town a bit easier. She was already tucked into bed at the motel, but tension still claimed the space between her shoulder blades.

Not wanting to exacerbate it, she'd considered not calling Jeff. Last night's quarrel had been a skirmish. She sensed a much larger fight in their future. Along every step of the way, she wanted to fight fairly, not peevishly.

Besides, if the shoe had been on the other foot, if he had left on a road trip and didn't call as promised, she would have been worried about his safety.

"Are you already in bed?" he asked.

"About to turn out the light. I want to get an early start in the morning."

"How's the motel?"

"Modest, but clean."

"I get worried when clean is an itemized amenity." He paused as though waiting for her to chuckle. When she didn't, he asked how the drive had been.

"All right."

"The weather?"

They were reduced to discussing the weather? "Cold. But I planned on that. Once I get started, I'll warm up fast enough."

"I still think it's crazy."

"I've mapped out the course, Jeff. I'll be fine. Furthermore, I look forward to it."

It was much colder than she had anticipated.

She realized that the moment she stepped out of her car. Of course the overlook was at a much higher elevation than the town of Drakeland where she'd spent the night. The sun was up, but it was obscured by clouds that shrouded the mountain peaks.

A twenty-mile run up here would be a challenge.

As she went through her stretching routine, she assessed the conditions. Although cold, it was a perfect day for running. There was negligible wind. In the surrounding forest, only the uppermost branches of the trees were stirred by the breeze.

Her breath formed a plume of vapor that fogged up her sunglasses, so she pulled the funnel neck of her running jacket up over her mouth and nose as she consulted her map one final time.

The parking lot accommodated tourists who came for the nearby overlook. It also served as the hub for numerous hiking trails that radiated from it like the spokes of a wheel before branching off into winding paths that crisscrossed the crest of the mountain. The names of the particular trails were printed on arrow-shaped signposts.

She located the trail she'd chosen after carefully reviewing the map of the national park and researching it further online. She welcomed a challenge, but she wasn't foolhardy. If she wasn't certain she could make it to her turnaround point and back, she wouldn't be attempting it. Rather than being daunted by the inhospitable terrain, she was eager to take it on.

She locked her duffel bag in the trunk of her car and buckled on her fanny pack. Then she adjusted her headband, zeroed the timer on her wristwatch, pulled on her gloves, and set out.

Chapter 2

Emory came awake gradually but didn't open her eyes, fearing that admitting light would make the excruciating headache worse. It had jarred her out of a deep sleep with pains so piercing it was as though a nail gun were being used inside her skull. She was hearing a noise not ordinarily heard in her bedroom, but even her curiosity wasn't enough to embolden her to lift her eyelids.

In addition to the sharp pains inside her head, her right foot was throbbing constantly. She'd run too hard on it this morning.

The aroma of food was making her queasy.

Why was she smelling food in her bedroom, when it and the kitchen were on opposite sides of the house? Whatever Jeff was cooking—

Jeff didn't cook.

Her eyes sprang open, and, when met with nothing she recognized, she sat bolt upright.

The alien scene before her blurred and spun. Scalding bile gushed into her throat. She barely managed to choke it down before spewing it. Dizziness thrust her back down onto the pillow, which she realized wasn't her pillow.

And the man looming at the side of the bed wasn't Jeff.

She blurted, "Who are you?"

He came a step closer.

"Stay away from me!" She held up her hand, palm out, although she had no chance of fighting him off. She was as weak as a newborn. He was a giant.

But on her command, he stayed where he was. "Don't be afraid of me. I'm not going to hurt you."

"Who are you? Where am I?"

"You're safe."

That remained to be seen. Her breaths were short and quick, and her heart was pounding. She willed herself to calm down, knowing that panicking wouldn't benefit her.

"How do you feel?" His voice was low and rusty, as though he hadn't used it in a while.

She just stared at him, trying to piece together the disjointed stimuli and form an explanation of where she was and why she was here.

"How's your head?" He hitched his chin up.

Tentatively she felt the area indicated and groaned when her fingertips touched a knot behind her left ear. It was like she'd struck a mallet to a gong, sending waves of pain through her head. Her hair was sticky and matted with blood, and her fingers came away stained red. She noticed blood on the pillowcase.

"What happened to me?"

"You don't remember?"

Her mind backtracked. "I remember running. Did I fall?"

"I thought maybe you could tell me."

She was about to shake her head, but the motion made her ill and caused another sunburst of pain. "How did I get here?"

"I'd been watching you through binoculars."

He'd been watching her through binoculars? She disliked the sound of that. "From where?"

"A ridge on another peak. But I lost track of you and thought

I should check it out. I found you lying unconscious, picked you up, brought you here."

"Where is *here?*"

He made a motion with his hand, inviting her to see for herself.

Every movement of her head meant a fresh agony, but she pushed herself up onto her elbows. After giving the vertigo several moments to subside, she took in her surroundings, specifically looking for a possible means of escape should one become necessary.

There were four windows. Only one door. Only one room, in fact.

The bed on which she lay occupied a corner of it. A screen of louvered panels, probably meant to separate the sleeping area from the rest of the room, had been folded flat and propped against the wall, which was constructed of split logs.

Other furnishings consisted of a brown leather recliner and matching sofa. Both had creases, wrinkles, and scratches testifying to decades of use. Between them stood an end table, and on it was a lamp with a burlap shade. These pieces were grouped together on a square of carpet with a hemmed border.

The kitchen was open to the rest of the room. There was a sink, a narrow cookstove, an outmoded refrigerator, and a maple wood table with two ladder-back chairs painted olive green. A large stone fireplace comprised most of one wall. The fire burning in it was making the crackling sound she'd been unable to identify when she first woke up.

He'd given her time to survey the room. Now he said, "Only one of your water bottles is empty. You must be thirsty."

Her mouth was dry, but other matters concerned her more. "I was unconscious when you found me?"

"Out cold. I've tried several times to wake you up."

"How long have I been out?"

"I found you around seven thirty this morning."

She looked down at her wristwatch and saw that it was twenty past six in the evening. She bicycled her legs to kick off the layers of covers. Throwing her legs over the side of the bed, she stood up. Immediately she swayed.

"Whoa!"

He caught her upper arms. She didn't like his touching her, but she would have fallen on her face if he hadn't. He guided her back down onto the side of the bed. Her head felt as though it was about to explode. Her stomach heaved. She covered her eyes with her hand because everything within sight was alternately zooming close and then receding, like the wavering images in a fun house mirror.

"Want to lie back down or can you sit up?" he asked.

"I'll sit."

He gradually withdrew his hands from her arms, then left her. He went into the kitchen and took a gallon jug of water from the refrigerator. He filled a glass and carried it back to her.

She regarded it suspiciously, wondering if he'd drugged her. The date-rape drug was odorless, tasteless, and effective. It not only debilitated the victim, it wiped clean the memory. But if this man had some nefarious purpose in mind, what would have been the point of drugging her if she was already unconscious?

He said, "I tried to get some water down you earlier. You kept gagging and spitting it out."

Which explained why the front of her shirt was damp. She was fully clothed except for her jacket, gloves, and headband. Her running shoes had also been removed and placed on the floor beside the bed, lined up evenly side by side. She looked up from them to the man extending her the drinking glass. "I'm certain I have a concussion."

"That's what I figured, since I couldn't wake you up."

"My scalp is bleeding."

"Not anymore. It clotted quick enough. I've been dabbing it with peroxide. That's why the blood on your fingers looks fresh."

"I probably need stitches."

"It bled a lot, but it's not that deep of a gash."

He'd made that assessment himself? Why? "Why didn't you call nine-one-one?"

"I'm off the beaten path up here, and I can't vouch for the quality of the emergency services. I thought it best just to bring you here and let you sleep it off."

She didn't agree. Anyone who'd sustained a blow to the head should be seen by a physician to determine the extent of the damage done, but she didn't yet have the energy to argue the point. She needed to get her bearings and clear her head a bit first.

She took the glass of water from him. "Thank you."

Although she was desperately thirsty, she sipped the water, afraid that if she drank it too quickly, she'd only throw it up. She was feeling a mite less anxious. At least her heart was no longer racing and her breathing was close to normal. She would take her blood pressure soon—her wristwatch allowed for that—but she didn't feel up to doing it yet. She was having to white-knuckle the glass of water to keep it steady. He must have noticed.

"Dizzy?"

"Very."

"Head hurt?"

"Like you wouldn't believe."

"I had a concussion once. Didn't amount to anything except a really bad headache, but that was bad enough."

"I don't think mine is serious. My vision is a little blurry, but I remember what year it is and the name of the vice president."

"Then you're one up on me."

He'd probably meant it as a joke, but there was no humor either in his inflection or in his expression. He didn't come across as a man who laughed gustily and frequently. Or ever.

She sipped once more from the glass and then set it on the

small table at the side of the bed. "I appreciate your hospitality, Mr.—"

"Emory Charbonneau."

She looked up at him with surprise.

He motioned toward the end of the bed. Until now, she hadn't noticed her fanny pack laying there, along with her other things. One of the earpieces on her sunglasses was broken. There was blood on it.

"I got your name off your driver's license," he said. "Georgia license. But your name sounds like Louisiana."

"I'm originally from Baton Rouge."

"How long have you lived in Atlanta?"

Apparently he'd noted her address, too. "Long enough to call it home. Speaking of which…" Not trusting herself to stand again, she scooted along the edge of the bed until she could reach her fanny pack. Inside it, along with two water bottles, one of them empty, were two twenty-dollar bills, a credit card, her driver's license, the map she'd used to mark her trail, and, what she most needed right now, her cell phone.

"What were you doing up here?" he asked. "Besides running."

"That's what I was doing up here. Running." When she tried unsuccessfully for the third time to turn her phone on, she cursed softly. "I think my battery is completely out of juice. Can I borrow your charger?"

"I don't have a cell phone."

Who doesn't have a cell phone? "Then if I could use your land line, I'll pay for—"

"No phone of any kind. Sorry."

She gaped at him. "No telephone?"

He shrugged. "Nobody to call. Nobody to call me."

The panic that she had willed away earlier seized her now. With the realization that she was at this stranger's mercy, a baffling situation became a terrifying one. Her aching head was suddenly packed with stories of missing women. They disappeared and often their families never knew what their fate had been. Religious fanatics took wives. Deviants kept woman chained inside cellars, starved them, tortured them in unspeakable ways.

She swallowed another surge of nausea. Keeping her voice as steady as she was capable of, she said, "Surely you have a car."

"A pickup."

"Then could you please drive me to where I left my car this morning?"

"I could, but it—"

"Don't tell me. It's out of gas."

"No, it's got gas."

"Then what?"

"I can't drive you down."

"Down?"

"Down the mountain."

"Why not?"

He reached for her hand. She snatched it back, out of his reach. He frowned with annoyance then walked across the room to the only door and pulled it open.

Emory's distress gave way to dismay. Supporting herself on various pieces of furniture as she slowly made her way across the room, she joined him at the open door. It was as though a gray curtain had been hung from above the jamb.

The fog seemed impenetrable, so thick that she could see nothing beyond a few inches of the doorframe.

"It rolled in early this afternoon," he said. "Lucky I was there this morning, or you could've woken up to find yourself stranded out there in this."

"I *am* stranded in this."

"Looks like."

"I don't have to be." Once again, her respiration sounded and felt like panting. "I'll pay you to drive me."

He glanced over his shoulder at the open fanny pack on the bed. "For forty bucks? No way."

"Charge whatever you want. I'll pay you the balance as soon as you get me home."

He was shaking his head. "It's not that I doubt you'd pay me. It's that no amount of money will entice me. The roads up here are winding and narrow, steep drops on the outside. Most don't have guard rails. I won't risk your life, or mine, to say nothing of my truck."

"What about your neighbors?"

His face went blank.

"Neighbors? Surely someone living close by has a phone. You could walk—"

"No one lives close by."

It was like arguing with a fence post. Or a telephone pole. "I need to let my husband know that I'm all right."

"Maybe tomorrow," he said, glancing up toward the sky, although there was absolutely nothing to see. "Depending on how soon this lifts." He closed the door. "You're shivering. Go stand by the fire. Or, if you need the bathroom..." He pointed out a door on the other side of the room near the bed. "It can get cold in there, but I turned on the space heater for you." He went over to the cookstove where a pot was simmering. "Are you hungry?" He removed the lid and stirred the contents.

His casual dismissal of her situation astounded her. It frightened her. It also made her mad as hell.

"I can't stay here all night."

Even though her voice had carried a trace of near-hysteria, he remained unruffled as he tapped the dripping spoon against the rim of the pot, set it in a saucer, and replaced the lid. Only then did he turn toward her and gesture toward the door. "You saw for yourself. You don't have a choice."

"There's always a choice."

He looked away from her for several beats. When their eyes met again, he said, "Not always."

Uncertain of what to do next, she stood where she was and

watched as he began gathering utensils to set a place at the table. He asked again if she was hungry. "No. I'm sick to my stomach."

"I waited on you to eat, but since you're not going to, do you mind?"

Not that she believed her answer would matter to him, she told him to go ahead.

"I have something for your headache. And a Coke might settle your stomach. Or maybe you should go back to bed."

Lying down would make her feel all the more vulnerable. "I'll sit for a while." Moving unsteadily, she walked over to the dining table. Remembering that she had blood on her fingers from her head wound, she said, "I need to wash my hands."

"Sit before you fall."

Gratefully she sank into one of the chairs. He brought her a plastic bottle of hand sanitizer, which she used liberally, then blotted her hands on a paper towel she tore off the roll standing in the center of the table.

Without any ado or hesitation, he took the blood-stained paper towel from her and placed it in a trash bin, then went to the sink and washed his own hands with hot water and liquid soap. He opened a can of Coke, brought it and a bottle of over-the-counter analgesic pills to the table, along with a sleeve of saltine crackers and a stick of butter still in the wrapper. At the stove, he ladled a portion of stew into a ceramic bowl.

He sat down across from her, tore a paper towel from the roll and placed it in his lap, then picked up his spoon. "I hate eating in front of you."

"Please."

He spooned up a bite and noticed her looking at the contents of the bowl. "Probably not what you're used to."

"Any other time it would look good. Beef stew is a favorite of mine."

"It's venison."

She looked up at the stag head mounted on the wall above the fireplace.

He could smile after all. He did so, saying, "Not that particular deer. He was here when I moved in."

"Moved in? This is your permanent residence? I thought—" She surveyed the rustic room and its limited comforts and hoped that she wasn't about to insult him. "I thought this was a get-away, like a hunting cabin. A place you use seasonally."

"No."

"How long have you been here?"

With elbows on the table, he bent over his bowl, addressing it rather than her as he mumbled, "Six months or so."

"Six months. Without even a telephone? What would you do in an emergency?"

"I don't know. I haven't had one yet."

He opened the packet of crackers, took out two, and spread them with butter. He ate one alone and dropped the other into his bowl of stew, breaking it up with his spoon before taking another bite.

She watched him with unabashed curiosity and apprehension. He'd placed a paper towel in his lap as though it were a linen napkin, but he ate with his elbows on the table. He served his butter from the wrapper and had crumbled a cracker into his stew, but he blotted his mouth after every bite.

He lived in an outdated log cabin, but he didn't look like a mountain man. Particularly. He had a scruff, but it wasn't more than a day or two old. He wore a black-and-red-checked flannel shirt tucked into faded blue jeans, but the garments were clean. His hair was dark brown, collar length in back, longer than most men his age typically wore. It was laced with strands of gray at his temples.

That frosting would make another man look distinguished. It only made him look older than he probably was. Late thirties, possibly. But it was a lived-in face with a webbing of creases around his eyes, furrows at the corners of his lips, and a watchful wariness behind his eyes, which were a startling aquamarine. The cool color contrasted with his suntanned, wind-scoured face.

He was an odd mix. He lived ruggedly, without even a telephone or TV, but he wasn't uncouth, and he was well-spoken. Open shelves affixed to the log walls held dozens of books, some hardcover, others paperback, all tidily arranged.

The whole place was neat, she noted. But there wasn't a single photograph in the room, no knickknacks or memorabilia, nothing that hinted of his past, or, for that matter, his present.

She didn't trust his casual manner, nor his explanation of why he hadn't taken her to a medical facility as soon as he found her. Calling nine-one-one would have been even more practical. If he'd wanted to.

A man didn't simply pick up an unconscious and bleeding woman and cart her to his remote and neighborless mountain cabin without a reason, and she couldn't think of one that didn't involve criminality or depravity or both.

He hadn't touched her in any untoward way, but maybe he was a psychopath who drew the line at assaulting his victims while they were unconscious. Maybe he preferred them awake, aware, and responsive to his torment.

Shakily, she asked, "Are we in North Carolina?"

"Yes."

"I ask because some of the trails in the park stretch over into Tennessee."

She remembered parking in a designated area, doing her stretches, clipping on her fanny pack. She remembered hitting her stride, and she recalled the stillness of the woods on either side of the trail and how the cold air had become thinner as she gained altitude. But she had no memory of falling and striking her head hard enough to cause a concussion.

Which led her to wonder if that's what had indeed happened.

She helped herself to one of the crackers and took a sip of Coke, hoping that the combination of them might relieve her queasiness. "What's the elevation here?"

"Close to five thousand feet," he replied. "Difficult terrain for running."

"I'm training for a marathon."

He stopped eating, interested. "First one?"

"Fifth, actually."

"Huh. Hoping to improve your time?"

"Always."

"So you push yourself."

"I don't see it that way. I love it."

"Quite a challenge, distance running at this altitude."

"Yes, but it makes running at a lower level easier."

"You don't worry about overdoing?"

"I'm careful. Especially with my right foot. I had a stress fracture last year."

"No wonder you favor it."

She gave him a sharp look. "How do you know I do?"

"I noticed as you were hobbling from the bed to the door."

Possibly, she thought. Or had he noticed it before when he was watching her through binoculars? From just how far away? From a far ridge as he'd claimed, or from a much closer distance?

Rather than confront him with those questions, she continued making conversation in the hope of gaining information. "My foot gave me fits last year after Boston. The podiatrist advised that I stay off it for three months. I hated being unable to run, but I followed his instructions. Once he gave me the green light, I began training again."

"When's the marathon?"

"Nine days from today."

"Nine days."

"Yes, I know." She sighed. "This concussion comes at a most inconvenient time."

"You may have to pass."

"I can't. I have to run it."

He didn't ask, just looked at her.

"It's a fund-raiser. I helped organize it. People are counting on me."

He spooned another bite, chewed, and swallowed before continuing. "Your driver's license identifies you as *Dr.* Emory Charbonneau. Medical doctor?"

"Pediatrics. I share a practice with two OB-GYNs."

"You take over the babies once they arrive?"

"That was the plan when we formed the practice."

"Do you have kids of your own?"

She hesitated, then shook her head. "Someday, hopefully."

"What about Mr. Charbonneau? Is he a doctor, too?"

"Mr. Surrey."

"Pardon?"

"My husband's name is Jeff Surrey. When we married I was already Dr. Charbonneau. For professional reasons, it seemed best not to change my name."

He didn't remark on that, but his eyebrows came together in a half-frown. "What does he do for a living?"

"He's a money manager. Investments. Futures."

"Like for rich people?"

"I suppose some of his clients are well-to-do."

"You don't know?"

"He doesn't discuss his clients' money matters with me."

"Right. He wouldn't."

She bit off another corner of the cracker. "What about you?"

"What about me?"

"What do you do?"

He looked across at her and, with all seriousness, said, "Live."

Chapter 3

———◉———

*L*_{*ive.*}

He wasn't being glib, and Emory sensed that he didn't intend to elaborate. He held her gaze for a moment, then set his spoon in his empty bowl and pushed back his chair. He carried his utensils to the sink. Returning to the table, he politely asked if she wanted any more crackers.

"No, but I'll keep the Coke."

While he set about washing dishes, she excused herself. Treading carefully to keep the walls in place and the floor from undulating, she made her way into the bathroom. The space heater was the old-fashioned kind like her great-grandmother had had. Live blue flames burned against blackened ceramic grates.

She used the toilet, washed her face and hands, and rinsed her mouth out with a dab of toothpaste squeezed from the tube she found in the medicine cabinet above the sink. Also in the cabinet were a bottle of peroxide, a razor and can of shaving cream, a box of Band-Aids, a jar of multivitamins, and a hairbrush.

The shower stall was made of tin. The wire rack hanging from the shower head contained only a bar of soap and a bottle of shampoo. She longed to wash the blood out of her hair but didn't for fear of reopening the cut on her scalp. The goose egg beneath it hadn't gotten any larger, but any pressure she applied caused blow darts of pain.

She couldn't resist peeking into the small cupboard. On the shelving inside it, folded towels and washcloths were neatly stacked. It also stored rolls of toilet tissue, bars of soap, and cleaning supplies.

Out of the ordinary were the boxes of bullets.

They were on the highest shelf, labeled according to caliber. She had to stand on tiptoe to lift one down. She raised the lid. In the glow of the light fixture above the sink, the shells looked large, long, and lethal.

She quickly closed the box and replaced it exactly as she'd found it, wondering where he kept the guns that corresponded to his arsenal of ammunition.

She left the bathroom to find the main room dark except for the flickering light of the fireplace and the fixture above the kitchen sink. He was folding a dishcloth over the rim of it. Hearing her, he turned his head, speaking to her over his shoulder.

"I figured you'd want to turn in early."

She glanced toward the bed, where the covers, which she'd left rumpled, had been straightened and, on one side, folded back at a precise ninety-degree angle. The bloody pillowcase had been replaced with a clean one.

"I'll sleep in the recliner."

"You'll sleep in the bed." He yanked on a string to extinguish the light above the sink.

The action had a finality to it that strongly suggested arguing over the sleeping arrangements would be futile. Emory sat down on the edge of the bed. She'd been in her running tights all day. Her jogging bra felt uncomfortably tight. But there was no way in hell she'd be removing so much as a single thread, and he was in for a fight if he intended to take her clothes off.

Her breath caught when he started toward the bed, but after setting the bottle of analgesics and the can of Coke on the nightstand, he walked past and went into the bathroom, returning within seconds with the bottle of peroxide and an applicator formed of folded toilet paper squares.

"I don't have any cotton or gauze," he said as he poured the solution onto the toilet paper. He set down the bottle and leaned toward her.

"I'll do that."

"You can't see it. If you start feeling around, you might reopen the cut."

She knew that to be true, so she lowered her hands.

"Turn your head…" He nudged her chin with the back of his hand. She complied and sat there, strained and nervous, while he dabbed at the wound.

"Does that hurt?"

"A little." It hurt a lot, but she couldn't think of a proper way to complain without sounding critical of his technique. In fact it was hard to think of anything with him standing so close, bending over her. The proximity of her face to his middle was unsettling, and she didn't breathe until he said "There" and stepped away.

"I hate to dirty another pillowcase."

"Blood washes out. Most of the time." He picked up the pill bottle and shook two into his palm, then extended his hand to her. "They'll help with the headache."

"I'll wait to take them. See how I do."

He looked prepared to argue but returned the tablets to the bottle and replaced it on the nightstand. "They're there if you change your mind. Let me know if you need anything else."

"Thank you. I will. But I'm sure I'll be fine."

"Maybe I should wake you up at intervals. Just to make sure you're all right, to make sure that I can wake you up."

"That's a good idea. But rather than disturb you, I'll set alarms on my wristwatch."

Mouth set with disapproval, he said, "Suit yourself," and turned away.

She lay down and pulled the covers to her chin. Although she closed her eyes, her ears were on high alert as she listened to him moving about the room, adding logs to the grate, scooting the fire screen back into place.

Blood washes out. Most of the time. Spoken like someone who had experience with that dilemma.

She shuddered to think how exposed she was. She couldn't even stand alone for more than a couple of minutes. If she had to protect herself, what would she do?

While in college she'd taken a self-defense class, but that had been a long time ago. All she recalled of it now was not to think of the assailant as a whole, but to focus on individual parts of him that were vulnerable to counterattack. Eyes, nose, ears, testicles. She feared that rule wouldn't apply to a man who appeared as solid as a redwood.

She wished she'd secreted one of those deadly looking bullets. The tip of one jammed into an eyeball would do serious damage. It would stop even a giant long enough to slip past him.

She heard what sounded like boots hitting the wood floor muffled by the carpet, then the squeak of leather as he settled on one of the pieces of furniture. She opened her eyes to slits and saw that he'd chosen the recliner over the sofa. He was leaned back in it, a quilt pulled over him to midtorso.

Disconcertingly, he was looking straight at her, his eyes reflecting the firelight like those of a predatory animal.

His voice rumbled across the distance between them. "Relax, Doc. If I was going to hurt you, I would have by now."

Reason told her that was true. She'd been sleeping defenselessly all afternoon and he hadn't harmed her. Nevertheless...

"Why did you bring me here?"

"Told you."

"But I don't believe it's the truth. Not completely."

"I can't control what you believe. But you don't have to be afraid of me."

After a time, she asked, "Is Drakeland the nearest town?"

"No."

"What is?"

"You've never heard of it."

"How far is it?"

"As the crow flies? Twelve miles."

"And by road?"

"Fifteen."

"I could easily run that. Going downhill, that wouldn't be a challenging distance for me."

He didn't say, *Oh, for God's sake, lady, you've got a concussion and can't even walk a straight line, much less run one.*

He didn't say anything at all, which was more unnerving than if he'd cited how illogical that prospect was. His silence was also more menacing than if he'd told her flat out that she wasn't going anywhere anytime soon, that he'd brought her here to be his sex slave, and that upon pain of death, she had better not be plotting an escape.

However, she did escape his opalescent gaze by closing her eyes. For five minutes, they shared nothing but a thick tension and the snapping of the logs in the fireplace.

In spite of her fear, her body was exhausted. On their own, her muscles began to relax. She sank deeper into the mattress. Her concussed brain dragged her toward oblivion. She was just this side of it when she jerked into full awareness. "You never told me your name."

"That's right," he said. "And I won't."

Before going to sleep, Emory had set her alarm to go off two hours later, but the precaution proved to be unnecessary. Minutes before the alarm jingled on her wrist, he was at the bedside, his large hand lightly shaking her shoulder. "Doc?"

"I'm awake."

"Have you slept?"

"Catnaps."

"Does your head hurt?"

"Yes."

"Want to take a couple of pills?"

"Not right now."

He stood there for a moment without saying anything, then, "Do you need to use the bathroom?"

"Maybe."

In this case, *maybe* meant yes, because nausea had awakened her a half hour ago. She'd been lying there, trying to talk herself out of it. At the risk of waking him, she didn't want to get up and stagger into the bathroom. She didn't want to ask for his assistance, but, worse, she didn't want to throw up in his bed.

So when he asked if she needed the bathroom, although she committed only as far as *maybe*, she was grateful to him for taking it as a definite, emergency-level yes. He pulled back the covers. She slid her legs to the side of the bed and set her feet on the floor. He cupped her underarms and helped her to stand.

Knees wobbly, she took a tentative first step. "Steady." He placed one arm around her waist and secured her against his side.

"I'm sorry for the inconvenience."

"No bother."

The distance to the bathroom was a matter of steps, but it seemed longer than the Great Wall of China. When they got to the door, he reached around her and flipped on the light, then pulled the door closed, saying, "Take your time."

But she didn't have time to do anything except drop to her knees in front of the toilet bowl. There wasn't much to throw up, but the spasms were intense, wracking her whole body, and she continued retching even after her stomach was empty. When at last it stopped, she flushed and, using the sink as a handhold, weakly pulled herself up.

He spoke from just the other side of the door. "Okay?"

"Better."

She'd never felt water as cold as that which came out of the faucet, but it felt good when splashed against her face. She washed her mouth out several times. Her vision was still a bit blurred, which was just as well. She was glad she couldn't see her reflection in the mirror above the sink with 20/20 clarity. Even fuzzy it was dreadful.

She was sallow. Her lips all but colorless. She had bedhead of the worst sort. The blood in her hair had dried to an unsightly black crust. But she was too wrung out to care how frightful she looked.

She was more concerned about the headache. The pain was no longer like the nail gun. It was blunter than that. More like a baton being beaten against her cranium from the inside. The light made it worse. She turned it off and then shuffled to the door and opened it.

He was right there. She was eye level with his sternum. "After that, I think I'll feel better."

"Good." He reached out to help support her, but when he touched her shoulder, his hand moved around to the back of her neck under her hair. "You're sopping wet."

During the bout of vomiting, she'd broken a cold sweat that had left her skin drenched, her clothes damp. "I'll be fine." She barely got the words out. Her teeth had begun to chatter.

He guided her back to the bed and eased her down onto the side of it. "I'll get you something to change into."

"No, really, I—"

"You can't spend the rest of the night in wet clothes."

He left her, went to a bureau tucked under the sloped ceiling, and pulled a flannel shirt much like the one he was wearing from a drawer. When he handed it down to her, she met him eye to eye.

"I'm not going to undress," she said, meaning it.

He watched for her a moment, then went back into the bathroom and came out with a fresh towel, still folded. Although the gesture was kind, his expression wasn't. His lips had thinned into a cynical line. "Your virtue is safe, Doc. I meant to set up the screen to give you some privacy."

He dragged it away from the wall and unfolded the panels. When it was balanced, he stepped around it, leaving her feeling like an ungrateful idiot.

Whatever modesty she'd ever possessed had been abandoned in med school. She and fellow interns had practiced procedures on one another, usually amid ribald joking, but in any case it had been impossible to remain maidenly skittish about nudity and bodily functions.

As she unzipped her running shirt, she told herself she hadn't protested undressing because of modesty, but rather self-preservation. He'd been caring and considerate, a gentleman. But how trustworthy was a man who wouldn't even share his name?

She undressed as quickly as her uncontrollable shivering allowed. Rid of everything on top, she hastily dried her torso with the towel, then pulled on the shirt he'd loaned her. The flannel was old, soft, and it felt wonderful to be free of the binding, clammy jogging bra.

Last to go were her running tights. In the morning, she'd put them back on, but for now, it felt good to slide her bare legs between the sheets.

He couldn't see her, but he must have been listening to the rustle of clothing and bed covers. Once she was settled beneath them, he said, "Is the coast clear?"

"You can leave the screen."

He began folding up the panels.

"I prefer having it," she said.

Apparently what she preferred was immaterial. He returned the screen to its place against the wall. "I need to be able to see you."

"I'll tell you if I need anything."

"You didn't tell me that you had to throw up, and we almost had a big mess on our hands." He bent at the waist and pulled a small metal wastebasket from beneath the table beside the bed. "If I don't get here in time." He placed the trash can where she couldn't miss it if she hung her head over the side of the bed.

"I think I'm over the nausea."

"If not, don't be prissy about it, okay?"

She gave one terse bob of her head.

"Anything else you need now?"

"No."

"You sure?"

"Yes."

Looking doubtful, his eyes scanned down her form beneath the covers, making her extremely self-aware. To avoid looking at him, she closed her eyes. Eventually he took her at her word and moved away.

His stocking feet were mere whispers against the floor, but something as large as he couldn't pass through air without creating a disturbance. She mentally followed his movements, heard the *thunks* as he added two logs to the low-burning fire, then the squeak of leather as he again settled into the recliner.

A few minutes elapsed. The new logs made popping sounds as they caught. She watched the flickering patterns of firelight and shadow cast onto the ceiling. She noticed something she hadn't before. A metal rod about two inches in diameter extended horizontally between two of the exposed rafters, each end fitting into a borehole. She couldn't imagine what the rod was for. As for the rafters, they looked as roughly hewn as he.

Roughly hewn perhaps, but thoughtful.

She cleared her throat. "I didn't thank you before."

"Don't mention it."

"I'm thanking you now."

"Okay."

Another while passed, but she knew he wasn't asleep. "I'd like to know your name."

The fire crackled. One of the rafters groaned under the weight of the roof.

He didn't make a sound.

Chapter 4

——◦◉◦——

Y ou're not worried?"

Jeff Surrey stretched and yawned and then turned onto his side and propped himself up on his elbow. "Not in the slightest. This is a ploy to get attention. Emory wants me to be worried about her."

"It's not like her not to call."

He frowned. "And at the most inopportune times. Like last night."

His cell phone had vibrated across the bathroom vanity just as he and Alice were climbing into the shower after a round of strenuous sexual activity. Talking to his wife had actually added a bit more excitement to the soapy afterplay. Even so, he'd resented Emory's interruption, which had almost seemed deliberately timed.

Lately, she'd been calling him often throughout the day, more likely than not for something mundane. Did he want to eat in or out? Was she supposed to pick up the dry cleaning, or had he volunteered to run that errand? Had he called the gutter company to schedule a cleanout, or should she?

The ruses were laughably transparent. She thought she was

being oh-so-subtle, when it was clear that she was keeping track of his schedule. For the past few months he'd had to account for everywhere he went and how long he'd been there. Her constant monitoring had become increasingly tedious, and he was running low on plausible excuses for the time he spent with Alice.

"Hasn't it been terrific? Two days, virtually undisturbed."

"You're spoiling me. Breakfast in bed this morning."

"More like lunch," he said, nuzzling her neck.

She groaned. "I can't believe we slept so late. How much did we drink last night?"

"I don't think it was the wine, I think it was the weed. Very high grade."

She covered her face with her hands and laughed. "It had been years since I'd indulged. My tolerance had lapsed."

"It was naughty fun." He trailed a finger between her breasts. "It made you very sexy. Not that you need help in that department."

Alice wasn't a head-turner. Her dark hair and eyes complimented her olive complexion, which some might consider striking. She could be called a handsome woman. But even the most forgiving critics would rate her no higher than a five.

However, there were advantages to being involved with a plainer woman. Fear of rejection made her grateful; gratitude made her easily pleased and effortlessly malleable.

A vertical line of concern formed between her eyebrows. "Do you think Emory knows about us?"

"No."

"Honestly?"

"Honestly, no. She doesn't."

His firm denouncement was basically truthful. He could truthfully say that Emory hadn't accused him of having an affair, which wasn't to say that she didn't suspect it. But to alleviate his lover's concern, he rubbed the space between her eyebrows with his index finger, smoothing out the worry line. "She's pouting, that's all."

"Did she say anything to you before she left?"

Mildly irritated by her persistence, he sighed. "Yes. She said good-bye."

"You know what I mean. Did she say anything to indicate that she was on to you?"

"I went home to see her off, and put up token resistance to her going. But frankly I didn't look a gift horse in the mouth. The sooner she was out of town, the sooner I could get you into bed." He placed his hand on her breast and began reshaping it with gentle squeezes.

"Nothing else was said?"

"I asked her to call me when she arrived at the motel, and she did." Near her ear, he growled, "And delayed the fulfillment of my shower fantasy. For which I'll never forgive her." He bent down and gave the tip of her breast a love bite.

But she wasn't so easily distracted. "That was over twenty-four hours ago, Jeff, which is a long time without hearing from her."

"She said she might spend another night up there, depending on how tired she was after her run. Apparently that's what she's doing."

"How do you know she hasn't come home while you've been here?"

"Because if the house alarm goes off, it beeps my phone. Thank God for apps."

"Wouldn't she let you know if she was staying over?"

He sighed with resignation. "Not that I enjoy discussing this, especially during foreplay, but, if you must know, we were angry with each other when she left. She's miffed and is punishing me by not calling tonight."

"What were you angry about?"

"That damn marathon she's running."

"What do you have to do with her running a marathon?"

"Exactly!" he said with heat. "That's what I asked her. It's not my thing, so why should I always have to tag along?"

"To cheer her on?"

"I've done that. Every frigging marathon. For hours I jostle for space at the finish line, waiting for the ten seconds it takes her to run past me and receive my applause for her outstanding achievement. I refused to do it again. But this is a special race for her, so she got her feelings hurt, and... Why the hell am I talking to you about my marital woes, when I'd rather be doing this?" He slid his hand between her thighs. "Isn't this a better plan?"

She sighed and squirmed against his hand. "A much better plan."

He rolled on a condom and settled between her thighs, which felt entirely different from Emory's. That was, from how he remembered Emory's open thighs feeling. It had been so long since they'd had sex, his memory of it had grown dim.

He was unsure who had cooled first, her or him. Was he cheating because marital sex had become so infrequent and unexciting, or had it become infrequent and unexciting because Emory intuited that he was finding fun in another woman's bed?

Not that he was accepting all the blame for his unfaithfulness. Oh no. A large portion of it lay with Emory. Every day, she was up and out before dawn, never home before dark. She worked endless hours at the clinic, then took calls at all hours of the night from frantic parents asking her what to do about their kid's runny nose, or fever, or diarrhea.

Her free time was devoted to training for her damn marathons. She ran. All. The. Time.

She'd been a runner when they met. Initially he had admired her athleticism, stamina, and self-discipline. As well as, of course, her trim form and shapely legs. For a couple of years they'd run together. But then she'd gone fanatic on him.

Fine. He had let her indulge in her hobby, while he'd indulged in his, and right now his was clenching her soft thighs against his pumping hips. He gave one last push and came. He wasn't sure Alice did, but she was better than Emory at faking it.

Chapter 5

Almost immediately upon waking, Emory realized that she was alone.

She sat up. The cabin was empty.

Throughout the night he had kept vigil. Each time she'd stirred, he'd left the recliner and had come to the bedside, asking if she was all right, did she need anything, was she feeling sick again?

She'd had no more nausea, so at about two o'clock she'd taken a few sips of Coke. It had stayed down. Two hours later, she'd switched to water. He'd urged her to, telling her what she already knew: that dehydration was a concern. She'd run hard, slept all day without taking fluids, then had vomited what little she'd drunk.

Now, according to her wristwatch, it was just after nine o'clock, Sunday morning. She'd slept for five hours without waking or without his waking her, and now he was gone.

Moving tentatively because of the residual dizziness, she got up and went into the bathroom, taking her running tights with her and pulling them on after using the toilet.

When she returned to the bed, she tested her other clothes. Her shirt, jacket, and bra were still damp and cold. She dragged one of the dining chairs nearer to the fireplace and draped the garments over it to speed up the drying process.

Now what?

She took another canned Coke from the refrigerator. It actually tasted good. She used a swallow to wash down two more analgesic tablets because the headache, like the dizziness, had hung on. It wasn't as blinding as before, but it was definitely still there and impossible to ignore.

She pushed aside a muslin curtain and was disheartened to see nothing except cottony fog beyond the windowpanes. She opened the door and called out a hello, but the fog absorbed her voice. She took a few steps forward and when she'd covered about a yard, the planks dropped off to a step six inches below, and that to another. Beyond the lowest step was a large, flat rock embedded in the soil.

She couldn't possibly feel her way like this for fifteen miles without either dropping off a cliff or becoming hopelessly lost in the mountain wilderness. Retracing her steps back through the door and into the cabin, she took a thorough look around.

There was a wall hook adjacent to the door. The set of ignition keys that she'd noticed hanging on the hook last night weren't there now. Even if she were able to find his pickup in the fog, she wouldn't be able to start it. And if by some miracle she could figure out how to hot-wire it, she wouldn't know in which direction to go. She'd probably drive herself right over an edge and down a mountainside.

Which meant that her solution to getting back to civilization must be found inside the cabin.

She started her search in the most logical place, the bureau from which he'd taken the shirt she was wearing. She found socks, underwear, T-shirts, flannels. One drawer contained nothing except folded blue jeans.

The closet had a rickety door made of what looked like barn wood. In their earlier life, the planks had been painted a dull red. It was no larger than a telephone booth, with a single rod from which hung jackets and coats and a pair of coveralls like a hunter would wear.

Lined up on the floor were several pairs of boots of varying kinds, from scuffed hiking boots similar to those he'd had on yesterday to a pair of fleece-lined rubber lace-ups. She moved them aside to search for a hidey-hole underneath the floorboards, but there was none.

The shelf above the rod held folded blankets, bulky sweaters, and a shoe box in which were several pairs of gloves. She aligned her fingers to the palm side of one. The glove outsized her hand by an intimidating degree.

She replaced everything and slammed the closet door in agitation. Dammit, he had guns stored somewhere.

She discovered the locker underneath the bed.

Jeff had never served in the military, but she'd seen enough movies to recognize a foot locker for what it was. The metal trunk had reinforced corners and substantial brass fastenings. Fortunately they appeared to be unlocked. If she could manage to slide the locker from beneath the bed, she'd be able to open it.

It wasn't going to be easy. She was weak from not having eaten for over twenty-four hours and spending most of that time in bed. Simply the act of bending down to inspect under the bed had brought on a surge of dizziness and rockets of headache pain. She took deep breaths to stave off both, and when they decreased to a tolerable level, she grasped the handle at one end of the locker and pulled on it with all her might.

She was able to move it no more than an inch or two at a time before having to rest. By the time she got it clear of the bed, she was damp with perspiration and her arms and legs were aching from the effort.

She flipped open the fastenings and raised the lid.

The moment he cleared the door, she launched herself at his back, leaping onto it piggyback, reaching around his head to dig her fingers into his face.

She got a thrill from hearing his grunt of surprise and pain when one of her fingernails peeled a good two inches of skin off his cheek. But her success was short-lived, lasting all of ten or fifteen seconds.

Then his gloved hands closed around her wrists and forced her hands away from his face. While before, she'd been holding on with fierce determination, she was now fighting just as hard to free her wrists from his iron grip. She kicked against the backs of his legs but that was a waste of valuable energy.

She acknowledged the futility of trying to work herself free at the same time her reservoir of strength ran dry. She sagged against him, draped over his back like the flag of the vanquished.

"You done?" he asked.

"Not by a long shot."

"I'm going to let you down. No more nonsense, all right?"

"Go to hell."

"In due time, Doc. It's a sure thing."

Stretching his arms behind him over his shoulders, he dangled her until she could touch the floor, then he let go.

She'd planned for this. Before he was fully turned around to face her, she jerked free the butcher knife she'd stuck into one of the wall logs and made a swipe with it across his middle. He bowed his back and sucked in his belly just in time. She missed completely. The second swipe nicked the material of his coat but did negligible damage to the tough fabric.

"Damn you!"

She raised the knife high and arced it downward toward his neck. The tip of the blade caught in the wool of his scarf, but never found flesh before he grabbed her hand and, with humiliating ease, unarmed her. He tossed the knife across the room, where it skidded across the hardwood floor before banging into the baseboard.

"*Now* are you done?"

She stumbled back against the wall, fearing retribution. He looked huge and indomitable. Blood trickled from the deep scratch on his face. He brushed it with the back of his hand, leaving a red smear on the chamois leather glove.

He looked at the fresh bloodstain, then at her. "I guess you're feeling better."

She pulled herself up to her full height and glared at him, despising her own weakness and infuriated by his composure.

"Want to tell me what the hell that was about?" he asked.

He followed the direction of her angry gesture and looked over his shoulder toward the dining table where she'd placed the incriminating laptop and its charger, which she'd found in the locker beneath the bed. "You lied to me."

"No I didn't."

"You said you didn't have a charger."

"I said I didn't have a *phone*. Which I don't."

"Well I found the charger, and it's been plugged into my cell phone for two hours, and the phone is still dead. What did you do to it?"

"I took the battery out."

His calm admission rendered her speechless. As she stood there gaping, he clamped the end of his middle finger between his front teeth and used them to pull off his right glove, then began unbuttoning his coat.

"Why?" she wheezed.

"So it couldn't emit a signal."

She'd been entertaining a sliver of hope that she'd let her imagination get the best of her, that she'd seen too many TV shows, read too many books, fiction as well as true accounts, about women who were captured, tortured, abused, murdered.

She'd held on to the diminishing hope that he wasn't actually keeping her in this isolated place against her will and with evil intent.

But he'd just dashed that slender hope all to hell. He'd disabled her phone. On purpose. Her location couldn't be tracked using GPS, which is one of the first things the authorities would try to do when Jeff reported her missing.

"Why did you bring me here?"

"Haven't we already established that?"

"We haven't established a damn thing except that you're a kidnapper and a—" She broke off, not wanting to plant ideas in his head.

He seemed to read her mind, however, because he arched one dark brow inquisitively. "And a what?"

She'd had a slim-to-none chance of incapacitating him, either by gouging his eyes out or plunging the knife into him. Since both attempts had failed, the only weapon left to her was reason.

"Listen, I don't care what you've done in the past. You haven't hurt me yet. In fact, you've been exceptionally kind. Which I appreciate. Things could have gone a lot worse for me if you hadn't been there to . . . to find me and bring me here."

He waited several beats. "But?"

"But I need to leave now and go home. You must let me go."

He raised his shoulders slightly and motioned toward the door. "It's unlocked. But I warn you, I don't believe you'll get very far. I walked a couple of miles down the road, thinking that the fog might not be so thick at a lower elevation. I never walked out of it."

"You walked."

"Yes."

"Why didn't you drive?"

"For the same reason I wouldn't drive you last night. There are dozens of switchbacks. I could miss a curve and go over a three-hundred-foot drop."

"But you took the keys to your truck."

"Because I didn't want you driving it."

"It occurred to me."

"I figured. I didn't want you wrecking it and possibly killing yourself in the process. Which is why I took the keys."

He stuffed his gloves, bloodstain and all, into the pocket of his coat and hung it on a wall peg. He unwound the scarf from around his neck. Static raised his hair when he pulled off his watch cap. It and the scarf were added to the peg.

He went to the fireplace, hunkered down in front of it, stirred the embers with a poker, and then added several logs. Coming to his feet and dusting his hands on his seat, he asked if she'd eaten anything.

"No."

He went over to the refrigerator and opened it. She marched up to it and pushed the door shut with enough force to rock the appliance and rattle bottles inside. He turned, looking like he might kill her then and there, but she didn't let his murderous glower intimidate her.

"My husband will be frantic to know where I am and what's happened to me. He'll have the police out searching."

"Well they won't find you today. Not the way things are socked in."

"I can e-mail him. But I need the password for your laptop."

He glanced at the laptop, then turned back to the fridge, bumped her hip with his to move her out of the way, and re-opened the door. "I don't do e-mail."

"That's okay. I can contact him through Facebook. Even if Jeff doesn't see my post, a friend—"

"Sorry, Doc, no."

"But—"

"No."

"I won't mention you. How could I when I don't even know your name? I'll just let Jeff know that I'm okay."

He shook his head.

"No details, I promise. You can approve the post before I send it."

"No."

It was like hitting the dreaded twenty-mile wall of a marathon. One had to press on, power through it, or be defeated. "You're committing a crime, you know."

"I haven't laid a hand on you."

"But you're keeping me here against my will."

"Circumstances are keeping you here."

"You could change the circumstances if you wanted to."

"I can't change the weather."

"I wasn't referring to the weather. You're refusing to let me use your laptop to—"

"The laptop is off-limits."

"Why?"

"That's my business."

"Whatever that is, it can't be good."

"I didn't claim it was good. It's just the way it is."

"Tell me why you're holding me here."

He advanced on her and bent down to bring his face almost on a level with hers. Speaking in a rasp more sinister than a shout, he said, "I'm not keeping you in, Doc." He hitched his chin toward the door. "I'm keeping them out."

Chapter 6

J eff let himself in through the garage door and disengaged the house alarm. No lights were on inside. The house was cold and empty.

Before leaving Alice, she'd again expressed her fear that Emory was onto their affair. "You're certain that she doesn't know?"

"She's feeling neglected and playing the wounded wife to the hilt," he assured her. "She's in a sulk, that's all."

But the fact remained that Emory hadn't been heard from since Friday evening when she'd called from the motel where she'd spent the night. This was Sunday afternoon, which added up to a significant amount of time not to have heard from one's wife, even a miffed one.

There wasn't a married man in the world who wouldn't understand his waiting out Emory's little rebellion and letting her get over her huff in her own good time. But doing nothing made him look like a heel, even to his extramarital lover.

It's not like her not to call, Alice had remarked more than once during their weekend. *You're not worried?*

He wasn't, but he supposed he should be. He called Emory's cell phone, and before it even rang her voice mail greeting requested the caller to leave a message. "I thought you would be home by now. Call me."

She often worked at the clinic after hours and on weekends, using that time to catch up on paperwork. He called the main line and then the private number reserved for family use only. Both were answered by recordings. He left messages asking her to call him. He then phoned the hospital where she practiced and asked to be put through to the pediatric floor.

The nurse who answered recognized him by name. "How can I help you, Mr. Surrey?"

"Is Dr. Charbonneau around?"

"I thought she signed out until tomorrow."

"She did. But I was expecting her at home by this afternoon, and I've been unable to reach her on her cell. No one answers at the clinic. I thought she might have stopped there to check on a patient and had gotten tied up."

"I just came on duty, so I don't know, but I'll ask around."

"Thank you. If anyone's seen her, please ask them to call me. And if she shows up, tell her that her phone is going straight to voice mail. She needs to check the battery."

He disconnected, dropped his cell onto his desk, stood up, and began to pace, trying to decide what he should do about this. He debated it for another several minutes, but there was only one logical option.

Ten minutes later, he was speeding north on I-85.

Emory picked at the grilled cheese sandwich, feeding herself small bites, testing her stomach to see if it would reject solid food. She'd had no more nausea today, only a sick feeling in the pit of her stomach that she might not leave this cabin alive.

After his refusal to let her use his laptop, she'd retreated to the bed, but not before defiantly setting up the folding screen. She lay down on top of the covers, pulling only one corner of the bedspread over her legs.

She'd lain there, tense and wary, but he ignored her and busied himself around the cabin. She'd smelled the coffee he brewed and the egg he fried. He washed the dishes, then went outside for only a couple of minutes. She'd dropped off to sleep while listening to him moving around in the living area.

When she woke, hours had passed. It had grown dark. Through the louvers in the screen, she could see that the lamp with the burlap shade was on.

She'd worried that maybe her lame and unsuccessful attack on him had jostled her brain and left her even more enfeebled. But when she'd sat up, she noted that the dizziness was actually better. Her headache, however, persisted.

She'd gotten up and used the toilet; then, although she'd sworn that hell would freeze over before she left her flimsy sanctuary, that he would have to drag her out from behind that screen by her hair, she stepped around it.

Just as she had, he'd come in from outdoors, bundled up as he'd been before. He'd been carrying an armload of firewood. Seeing her, he'd paused on the threshold, then closed the door with a backward kick of his heel, wiped the soles of his boots on the jute doormat, and carried the wood over to the hearth. He was conscientious about keeping the wood box filled.

Once he'd added the fresh logs to it, he removed his outdoor garments, shaking ice pellets from his coat before hanging it on the peg. "It's started to sleet."

"What a lucky stroke for you. The worse the weather, the easier for you to hold me prisoner."

Matching her wryness, he said, "Look on the bright side, you won't starve. I have enough food to last us for several days."

After that exchange, he'd gone about preparing canned

chicken noodle soup and the cheese sandwiches, which up till now she'd been picking at. But, in fact, that simple fare tasted delicious, and the more she ate of it, the hungrier she became. Following her run yesterday, she'd been carb-depleted. The soup replaced sodium. She finished the meal.

He noticed her empty dishes, but didn't comment on them as he carried them to the sink. "Coffee?"

"No thank you. Do you have any tea?"

"Tea." He repeated it as though he'd never heard of it.

"Never mind."

"Sorry." He carried his mug of coffee to the table and sat back down across from her. "I'm not a tea drinker."

"You should keep it on hand. You never know when a captive will request it."

"You're my first."

"First captive or first tea drinker?"

"Both."

"I don't believe you."

With supreme unconcern, he raised one shoulder and blew on his coffee before taking a sip. When he returned his mug to the table, he caught her looking up at the metal bar suspended between the rafters. When she looked back at him, and their eyes connected, she felt a jolt like a sock in the belly. She wasn't about to ask him about that bar, afraid of what the answer would be.

Feeling the weight of his stare, she traced the wood grain on the tabletop with her thumbnail. "What did you do?"

"When?"

"Your crime. What was it?" She held off looking at him for as long as she could stand it. When she dared to meet his eyes, they glittered like multifaceted gemstones. She would have thought them beautiful if she hadn't been afraid of them. " 'I'm keeping them out.' That's what you said."

"Uh-huh."

"The police? You're hiding from the authorities?"

"You're batting a thousand, Doc."

"Stop calling me that. It sounds like a pet name. And I'm not going to be your pet."

"Not a docile one anyway. You scratch."

She'd tried to avoid looking at the long, bloody mark across his cheekbone. The blood had clotted, but it looked painful and nasty. "You should put some of your peroxide on that to keep it from getting infected."

"Yeah, I should. But I didn't want to breach the wall of Jericho over there to get into the bathroom." He tilted his head toward the screen. "I was afraid of being set upon again."

"I didn't hurt you that badly."

"I wasn't afraid of you hurting me. I was afraid of hurting you." At her shocked expression, he clarified. "Not on purpose. But if I have to defend myself from you, you could wind up hurt because I'm so much bigger than you are."

His size would have been intimidating if she'd been standing behind him in the checkout line at the supermarket, or sharing an elevator, or sitting beside him on an airplane. He didn't have to work at being imposing, his height was sufficient. Today's cream-colored cable-knit sweater was form fitting and emphasized the breadth of his shoulders and chest.

His hands, folded around the earthenware coffee mug, made it look as delicate as a cup from the china tea service she'd played with when she was a little girl. Even dormant, his hands intimidated her. From the knob of his wrist bone to the tips of his long fingers, they looked capable of doing...

Lots of things.

She remembered how gently those fingers had explored the skin on the back of her neck. *You're sopping wet.* Her cheeks grew hot over the thoughts that flickered through her mind. She drank from her glass of water, then picked up her interrogation where she'd left off. "Were you in the military?"

"What makes you ask?"

"Your tidiness. Everything folded uniformly, stored neatly. Boots lined up in pairs."

"You must've given the place a thorough search."

"Didn't you expect me to?"

"Yeah." He stretched his long legs out in front of him, at an angle to the table. "I knew you'd snoop."

"So what did you hide in advance of my search? Handcuffs? Leather straps?"

"Only my laptop. Not well enough, as it turns out. But I didn't think you'd have the strength to move the locker out from under the bed."

"It took every ounce of energy I had."

"You had enough to pounce on me."

"But not enough to hold on."

"You should have thought of that."

"I did."

"Oh, right. The butcher knife."

"Little good that did me."

"It poked a hole in my best scarf."

He had the gall to look amused, which irked her. She tried to catch him off guard. "Tell me about the war."

Her probe had found a sore spot. He pulled his legs in, sat up straighter, took a sip of coffee. Normal, inconsequential actions, but in this case, revealing.

"Well?" she said.

"What do you want to know?"

"What branch of the service were you in?"

Nothing.

"When did you serve?"

Nothing.

"Where?" When he didn't answer that, she said, "Nothing to say on the topic of warfare?"

"Only that I don't recommend it."

They eyed each other across the table. In his steady gaze she read a warning that he wanted the discussion to end there. She didn't press her luck. "The boxes of bullets on the shelf in the bathroom..."

"I thought they'd be out of your reach."

"I had to stretch on tiptoe. If you have bullets, you must have guns."

"My arsenal didn't turn up during your search?"

She shook her head.

"Too bad. Otherwise you could have shot me instead of attacking with your fingernail and a butcher knife. It would have taken less energy."

Again, he was making fun of her. She struck back. "Was yours a violent crime?"

His grin dissolved. No, not dissolved, because that denoted a gradual fade. His levity vanished in an instant, that corner of his mouth dropping back into place to form the firm line it usually was. "Extremely."

His blunt reply filled her with desperation and a wrenching sense of despair. She wished he had denied or mitigated it. Still clinging to a vain hope, she said, "If it was something you did during wartime—"

"It wasn't."

"I see."

He gave a harsh laugh. "You don't see a bloody thing."

He stood up so suddenly, she nearly jumped out of her skin. In reaction, she shot to her feet, sending her chair over backward. When it crashed to the floor, she cringed.

He stepped around the table, picked up her chair, and set it upright with angry emphasis, banging the legs against the floor. "Stop jumping every time I move."

"Then stop scaring me."

"I'm not."

"You are!"

"I don't mean to."

"But you do anyway."

"Why? I'm not going to hurt you."

"If that's true, then let me call my husband—"

"No."

"—and tell him that I'm all right."

"No."

"Why?"

"We've been through this. I'm tired of talking about it. I'm also tired of going outside to pee against a damn tree, which I've been doing all afternoon so I wouldn't disturb your rest. But now I'm going into the bathroom to use the commode and grab a shower. Make yourself at home. Snoop to your heart's content," he said, spreading his arms wide at his sides. "The place is all yours."

He collapsed the screen with several loud claps of wood against wood and set it in its original position against the wall. "It stays here."

At the door of the bathroom, he switched on the light, but before going in, he turned back. "You wouldn't make it ten yards beyond the door before getting lost, and I don't feel like going after you tonight. So deep-six any plans you have to bolt."

Then he went into the bathroom.

As soon as he'd closed the door behind him, she retrieved the laptop from the sofa, where he'd placed it when he set the table for their supper. She sat down with it at the dining table, raised the top, woke it up, and placed the cursor in the box for the password.

Her fingers settled on the home keys. And stayed there. How could she possibly guess what his password was when she knew absolutely nothing about the man? Not his name, birthday, hometown, occupation, hobby. Nothing.

She tried dozens of combinations anyway, some with military themes, most of them ridiculous, but, as expected, none was successful in unlocking the computer.

"Damn it!"

"No luck?"

Startled, she turned around in the seat of the chair, not having heard him leave the bathroom. He was wearing only his jeans and was carrying his boots, socks, and sweater. If she'd thought he was intimidating before, he was even more so like this. Damp hair. Barefoot. Bare-chested.

Flustered, she turned back to the laptop, none too gently lowered the cover, and stood up. "Go to hell."

"You said that already."

"And I meant it."

She walked around him and headed for the bathroom.

"I saved you some hot water."

She slammed the door and went to flip the lock, only to discover there wasn't one.

Longing for a shower, lured by the clean smell of his soap and shampoo but afraid of being naked, she settled for washing out of the basin with one of his damned neatly folded washcloths. She dabbed it against her blood-matted hair, but it did little to break up the scab and, besides, it hurt.

Hanging on a hook on the back of the door was the flannel shirt she'd slept in last night. She'd changed back into her running clothes before he'd returned that morning, but now she couldn't resist replacing them with the shirt.

She also yielded to the temptation of using his hairbrush on the parts of her head not affected by the sore goose egg and scab. However, the intimacy implied by that was unsettling. She cleaned her teeth with her index finger.

She switched out the light before opening the door. He was sitting in the recliner, reading a paperback book by the light of the lamp. In her absence, he'd put on a plain white T-shirt and white socks. He didn't raise his head or otherwise acknowledge that she was there.

She slipped between the sheets and removed her tights, then rolled onto her side to face the wall.

A half hour later, he turned out the lamp. She was still wide awake and acutely aware of him as he approached the bed. She squeezed her eyes shut and held her breath.

Wild with fear, she mentally chanted, *Please don't, please don't, please don't.*

But alongside that silent plea for him not to molest her, not to kill her, was another, equally strong, that he not disappoint her. It was stupid and inexplicable, but there it was. For reasons that had nothing to do with fear, she didn't want him to be a degenerate, a rapist, a murderer, or in any way deranged or evil.

"I know you're awake. Look at me."

Except for her heart hammering against her ribs, she lay unmoving.

The mattress dipped when he placed his knee near her hip. Alarmed, she rolled onto her back and gasped when he planted his hands on either side of her shoulders, bridging her body, blocking her view of the rafters, that worrisome metal bar, everything except his face.

"When the weather clears, I swear to you that I'll take you down the mountain. I'll see to it that you're safe. Until then, I won't hurt you. Understand?"

Incapable of speech, she bobbed her head once.

"Do you believe me?"

With absolute honesty, she whispered, "I want to."

"You can."

"How can I, when you won't answer the most basic questions?"

"Ask me a basic question."

"What's your name?"

"What's it matter?"

"If it doesn't matter, why won't you tell me?"

"Trust me, Doc, you go meddling in my life, you won't like what you find."

"If you didn't want me to meddle you shouldn't have brought me here."

He came as close to smiling as he ever did. "You've got me there."

She analyzed his features, searching for clues into the terrible thing he'd done. It was a strong face, unrelievedly masculine, but evocative of mystery more than menace. "Why are you hiding from the authorities?"

"Why does anyone?"

"So they won't get caught."

"There you have it."

"As a law-abiding citizen, I can't simply—"

"Yes you can," he said insistently. "You can *simply* leave it alone."

Suddenly she was tired of his veiled threats and decided to challenge him. "Or what? What will you do? You've promised not to hurt me."

Even had she not been able to see his eyes in the darkness, she would have felt them, taking in her mouth, throat, the open neck of the shirt. They moved as low as the vee of her thighs before coming back to hers.

She held her breath.

He whispered, "It wouldn't hurt."

Chapter 7

Emory let the curtain drop back over the window. "It's hopeless out there."

The weather had worsened overnight. It had begun to snow, and it was accumulating over a thick layer of sleet. Which, of course, was in his favor.

He was seated at the dining table, tinkering with the toaster that had failed to pop up the slices of bread at breakfast.

"How old is that thing?"

Her cross tone of voice brought his head up. "I don't know. It came with the cabin."

"Why don't you just buy a new one?"

"This one can be fixed. Besides, I enjoy working on things." He'd already glued the broken piece of stem back onto her sunglasses. He'd set them carefully on the table for the glue to dry.

"You're a born handyman?"

"I manage."

No doubt he was being modest and that he was, in fact, a good fix-it man. He would have to be to live the way he did, alone in an isolated area, relying on no one except himself.

Jeff wouldn't know how to set the controls on a toaster, much less repair one. Although to think so uncharitably of him was unfair. He'd never been required to fix a household item and would have been surprised to know that she would find such an effort endearing even if he failed at it.

To her recollection she had never asked him to help her with something around the house. Perhaps she should have. If she hadn't been so self-reliant, and had instead asked small favors of him, maybe they would be happier.

The rift between them had started a year ago when he had failed to make partner in the investment firm in which he was an associate. He had assumed an air of indifference, but she knew that being passed over had been an enormous disappointment to him and a blow to his ego.

Wanting to reassure him of her support, she'd made a concerted effort to call him throughout the day, sometimes for something silly, just to let him know that she was thinking about him. However, rather than buoying his spirits, the extra attention seemed only to irritate him. At one point, he'd even asked her, with chilly politeness, to please stop patronizing him.

In an effort to get them back on track, she had switched tactics, suggesting weekend getaways, pursuing things she thought he would enjoy. A wine-tasting weekend in Napa. An indie film festival in Los Angeles. A bed-and-breakfast in the French Quarter.

Her ideas were met with lukewarm responses or outright derision. Their sex life dwindled until he complained about the infrequency, while at the same time, he stopped initiating it. Her pride wouldn't let her attempt to entice him. They reached a stalemate. The gap continued to widen. Months of increasing tension culminated in an argument over his indifference to the upcoming marathon. It was a charity fund-raiser that she had initiated and helped to organize. Beyond showing a lack of interest, he had developed a hostile attitude toward the event and what he called her "obsession" with it.

His rejection of something so important to her was symptomatic of his emotional withdrawal in general, and when she had cited that last Thursday evening during their stilted dinner conversation, the situation quickly became combustible.

What she hadn't said, what she'd held back, was that she suspected him of having a lover. Customarily, when a man's ego had been trampled, wasn't more adventurous sex the restorative he sought?

But lacking evidence to support her suspicion, she'd kept it to herself. She'd left on Friday afternoon, angry but hopeful that spending a night away would realign her perspective and, if she was being honest, ignite a fighting spirit to keep their marriage intact.

She hadn't counted on falling and getting a concussion and being "rescued" by a nameless man who, without even touching her, had aroused more sexual awareness last night than Jeff had aroused in more than a year.

"Are you cold?"

His question jerked her out of her reverie. "What?"

"You're chafing your upper arms. Are you cold?"

"No."

He left the eviscerated toaster and got up to go to the fireplace. When the logs he added began to flame, he replaced the screen and motioned her forward. "Move closer. Warm up."

"Who supplies your firewood?"

"Nobody. I chop it myself."

"You go into the woods and cut down trees?"

"People do, you know."

No one she knew did. They bought firewood from someone who delivered it to their house and stacked it, or they picked up a small bundle at the supermarket along with their bread and milk.

Satisfied that the new logs were catching, he returned to the table, picked up her sunglasses, and passed them to her. "Glue dried. I think it'll hold."

She tested the strength of the repair. "Thank you."

"You're welcome."

"Your hands seem too large to work on something so small and delicate. I wouldn't think you could be that dexterous."

"I can be dexterous when dexterity is called for."

She could tell he was amused by the unwitting setup she'd given him and self-satisfied with his suggestive comeback. Turning away from him, she slipped the glasses into the shirt pocket. He sat down at the table and resumed fiddling with the toaster, seeming to be perfectly content. She felt like her skin had shrunk.

"Doesn't it drive you crazy?"

"What?"

"The silence. The loneliness."

"I have music on my laptop."

"Can we play some music?"

"Nice try, but no soap, Doc."

She paced the width of the room and back. "Doesn't the boredom drive you to distraction?"

"I'm never bored."

"How could you not be? What do you do all day? That is, when you're not repairing small appliances."

She had meant the remark as a putdown, but he took no offense. "Projects."

"Like what?"

"I'm building a shed for my pickup."

"By yourself?"

"It's not hard, but I'm particular, which makes it time-consuming. I had hoped to finish it before winter set in." He glanced toward the window. "Didn't quite make it."

"What else?"

"I built the bookshelves."

"That's it? That's all you do? Putter around here making home improvements?"

"I've hunted. Not much, though. I fish occasionally."

"When you get tired of venison."

"No, I don't like fish, so I always throw my catches back. I hike. Gorgeous scenery up here. Sometimes I camp, but I prefer my bed to a sleeping bag on the ground."

"So you're not completely opposed to creature comfort."

He gave a half grin. "No. I prefer my showers and my coffee hot."

She looked around, trying to gauge the sparse square footage in which he lived. "I can't imagine being cooped up in here with nothing to do."

"I've got something to do. I'm doing it."

"Repairing an old toaster?"

This time he did respond to the putdown. He sat back in the chair and stared at her thoughtfully while tapping a small screwdriver against his palm. "There are other things that need fixing."

"And what happens when they run out?"

"I don't see that happening."

More than a little subdued by his "do not trespass" tone, she made a circuit of the room, went to one of the windows, and moved aside the curtain so she could look out again. The snowfall was thicker than earlier. "How far are we from Drakeland?"

"Farther than a marathon, if you had in mind to run all the way."

"I spent Friday night there. I didn't see much of the town, though. Is it nice?"

"It's almost civilized. Has a Wendy's, a Walmart, a multiscreen movie theater."

She ignored his sarcasm. "How often do you go?"

"To the movies?"

"To town."

"When I need something. When I feel like going."

"Do you see friends?"

"The lady at Dunkin' Donuts always speaks. She knows my face."

"But not your name."

He didn't say anything.

"No friends. No..." At a loss for words, she went to the hearth and sat down. "How do you make your living? What do you do for money?"

"I get by."

"That's not an answer."

"I keep myself clothed and fed, but I don't have gobs of money." He paused, then added, "Not like you."

"I don't have gobs of money."

He raised an eyebrow.

"Wealth is relative," she said irritably. "Besides, how do you—" She stopped and looked over at the laptop on the end table beneath the lamp. "You looked me up?"

"The afternoon I brought you here."

"You got my name off my driver's license."

"The rest was easy. A few keystrokes. Charbonneau Oil and Gas popped up. You're an heiress."

She wasn't prepared to talk about anything this personal with him. Yet she heard herself say, "I hate that word."

"Why's that?"

"Because it means that my parents are dead. I guess you read about that."

He set down the screwdriver and gave her his undivided attention. "Your dad's friend was flying the plane."

"He was an experienced pilot, had flown his own plane thousands of miles. The two couples—best friends forever—were on their way to Oklahoma for an LSU football game. Tigers versus Sooners." She picked at the cuff button on his flannel shirt, which she'd put on over her running clothes for an additional layer. "They didn't make the kickoff."

Behind her, the fire blazed, warming her back, but not reaching the cold void caused by the reminder of the sudden loss of her parents. "For a long time, I was in a really bad place. I prayed to God and cursed him, sometimes in the same breath. I exhausted myself with weeping. In a fit of anger, I chopped off all my hair. Grief was an illness with me. Unfortunately it's incurable. I've just learned to live with it." When she realized how silent the room had become, she turned her head and pulled him into focus.

He was sitting perfectly still, watching her intently. "No other immediate family?"

"No. Just me. We were well known in Baton Rouge. I couldn't go anywhere without running into someone who wanted to talk about Mom and Dad and extend condolences. The reminders got hard to take. It seemed that my survival depended on leaving, starting fresh somewhere else. So, after finishing my residency, I sold the family home, my shares in the company, and relocated. New city. New state." She slapped her thighs, ran her palms up and down them. "There you have it. Did I leave out anything?"

"How you met your husband."

"A mutual friend set us up."

"Love at first sight?"

She came to her feet. "All you need to know about Jeff is how frantically worried he is right now."

"How long have you been married?"

"Three years plus a few months."

"Have they been happy years?"

"Yes."

"Does your scalp hurt?"

"What?" Then, realizing she'd been rubbing the wound, she lowered her hand. "No. The bump has gone down. The cut itches."

"Means it's healing."

"It means I need to wash my hair."

"Why don't you use the shower?"

"Why do you think?"

"Because you don't want to get naked."

His definitive answer didn't call for elaboration.

He gave one last turn of the screwdriver, then set the toaster upright in the center of the table and tested the ejection lever several times. It was no longer sticking. He got up and carried it to the counter, replacing it in its spot. He returned the screwdriver to a drawer.

"What about you?" she asked.

"I don't mind being naked."

"That's not what I was talking about."

He braced his hands on the counter behind him and crossed his ankles with more languor than she would have thought a man his size could achieve. He looked supremely at ease with himself and his surroundings, with the bizarre situation, with everything that was driving her mad, especially the mystery that was *him*.

"Then what were you talking about, Doc?"

"Family. Do you have a wife stashed somewhere?"

Last night his expression had practically dared her to pry. His hard gaze had warned her to proceed at her own risk. He was looking at her that same way now. "No."

"Ever?"

"No bride. No wife. Not ever." He let several seconds lapse, then said, "Anything else?"

Yes. A hundred things, but she shook her head.

"Then excuse me, please." He walked past her and went into the bathroom.

The conversation had left her feeling more disturbed than ever. She had bared her soul about the tragic death of her parents and its effect on her, a topic she was usually reticent about because it was so painful.

He had continued to dodge questions that could have been

easily answered with one or two words. Instead, he was keeping her in the dark, and it was a shadowy unknown that made her uneasy.

Feeling chilled again, she wandered over to the fireplace. The logs recently added had burned quickly. She moved aside the fire screen, took one of the smaller logs from the box, and carefully placed it on top of those aflame, then reached for another. As she pulled it out, others shifted, revealing something at the bottom of the box.

It was a brown paper bag, larger than a lunch sack, but not as large as a grocery bag. Curious, she worked it out from beneath the logs, which took an effort because it was heavy.

To keep the sack closed, several folds had been made in the top of it. She unrolled them and opened it.

Inside was a rock, eight inches in diameter at its widest point, with jagged points that formed a miniature mountain range across the top of it. Those peaks were stained dark red with blood. It had run into the network of minuscule crevasses like a macabre lava flow. Stuck in the dried blood were several strands of hair, exactly the length and color of hers.

She gave a sharp cry of realization just as hands, which she had noticed specifically for their size and strength, caught her upper arms from behind, spun her around, and yanked the sack away from her.

"You weren't supposed to see that."

Chapter 8

FBI Special Agent Jack Connell climbed the steps of the brownstone, checked the box at the door, and pressed the button beside the name Gaskin. She was expecting him and answered almost immediately. "Mr. Connell?"

"Here."

She buzzed him in. He opened the main door and stepped into a small vestibule, then went through another door with etched-glass panels set in heavy, carved wood. She had warned him that the building hadn't been modernized to include an elevator, but fortunately her apartment was on the second floor.

He rounded the elaborately carved newel post at the landing. Eleanor Gaskin was standing in an open door, through which she extended him her right hand. "You haven't changed."

"Can't say the same for you."

She laughed with good nature and patted her distended tummy. "Well, there is that."

Now in her early thirties, she was striking, with widely set brown eyes and straight black hair worn almost in 1920s flapper style. She had on black leggings, ballet flats, and an oversized shirt to accommodate her pregnancy. There was no artifice in her smile. After shaking hands, she moved aside and motioned him in.

"Thank you for calling me," he said. "We leave our cards with people but rarely expect to hear back from anybody. Especially not after so much time."

"Four years, if I'm not mistaken."

It had been four years since the mass shooting in Westboro, Virginia. He'd interviewed this young woman two months after that dreadful day but hadn't spoken to her again until her unexpected call last night.

"Have a seat," she said. "Can I get you anything?"

"No thanks."

He sat down on the sofa indicated. The room was awash with sunlight coming in through the bay window that overlooked the street. It was a tree-lined, strictly residential block, situated between two of the busy boulevards of New York's Upper West Side.

"Nice building," he said. Apartments like this, which seemed to encompass the entire second floor of the brownstone, came with a hefty price tag.

As though reading his mind, she said, "My husband inherited it from his grandmother. She'd lived here for over forty years. We had to update it, of course. New baths, new kitchen. Best of all, it had a spare room for the nursery."

"First child?"

"Yes. It's a girl."

"Congratulations."

"Thank you. We're excited."

They exchanged the smile of polite strangers who had something important but uncomfortable to discuss. She launched the conversation. "Did you watch the video I e-mailed you?"

"No fewer than a dozen times. But I'd like to watch it with you to verify that I'm looking at the right woman."

She went over to a cabinet that housed a stack of audiovisual components. She turned on the necessary ones, and a recording began playing on the flat screen TV mounted on the wall above the fireplace. She stood just to the side of it, remote control in hand. The call letters of a TV station were superimposed at the bottom of the picture.

"I've got it cued, so it will be coming up…there." She paused the video and pointed out to him a woman, a face in a crowd. It had been a national news story, broadcast last evening. Protestors in Olympia, Washington, had marched on the state capitol building over the repeal of a gun law. The woman in question carried a picket sign.

"That's who I thought you meant," he said. "She looks some-what like Rebecca Watson, but…I'm not a hundred percent." Jack walked over to the TV to take a closer look. He studied the face, which was in the midst of dozens. "You picked her out of this?"

"The instant I saw her."

He regarded her doubtfully.

"I knew Rebecca well. I moved to the city straight out of col-lege, wet behind the ears. She took a chance on me. People don't forget their first employer. We'd worked together at Macy's for almost five years before the incident in Westboro, and not just as casual acquaintances. I was her right-hand assistant.

"We spent hours of each workday together. I was single then. She was recently divorced. Sometimes we'd go to her place after the regular business day and continue working, then share a bot-tle of wine. We were friends."

She was repeating what she had told him four years earlier, when Rebecca Watson had gone missing and he'd questioned Eleanor about her friend's sudden disappearance. The young woman had been upset and concerned. And truthful. He would stake his career on her veracity. But she'd had nothing useful to tell him then. He'd left her his card and asked that if she ever saw or heard from Rebecca Watson again to please contact him immediately.

Last night, she had. But he wouldn't allow himself to get too excited over this development. Yet. For four years he'd followed leads that had looked promising. All had met with nothing but dead ends.

"She's changed," he remarked. Four years ago, he'd also spent time with Rebecca Watson, but they'd never split a bottle of wine. Their exchanges had been contentious. He'd questioned her at length. For hours. Days. She had told him from the very start that she would never give up her brother's whereabouts to him, and she hadn't.

"Her hair is different," Eleanor Gaskin conceded. "But that's easily changed."

"She wore glasses then."

"Large, horn-rimmed ones." She smiled. "She thought they made her look more businesslike and gave her an advantage when driving a hard bargain. And, believe me, she could drive a bargain."

"I believe you," he said, remembering Rebecca Watson's stubborn silence on the subject of her brother. Jack had never worn her down, and that failure still rankled. "I know we covered this territory back then, but maybe I missed something. Would you mind refreshing me?"

They returned to their seats and, with a gesture, Eleanor invited him to ask away.

"Did Rebecca talk to you about him, Mrs. Gaskin?"

"Her brother, you mean."

Jack nodded.

"She talked about him a lot. Their parents had died, so there were just the two of them. I was almost as worried as she that he would be wounded or killed in Afghanistan. I didn't think she could bear losing him. They were that devoted.

"When he got home, Rebecca was relieved, overjoyed. They

had some really good times together. He doted on Sarah, sort of stepped in as a father figure. She adored her uncle. Then..."
She looked at him ruefully and raised her shoulder.

"Westboro."

"Yes."

Jack remembered the date of the deadly event. It was stamped on his memory as indelibly as the name of the man he still sought. Then, fifty-five days after the shooting, his sister also had disappeared.

Jack had spent the past four years exploring every possible avenue in trying to locate Rebecca. Because, as Eleanor had said, the siblings were devoted. Finding Rebecca would bring him one step closer to finding her brother. Unfortunately, each seemed to possess an uncanny talent for vanishing.

Rebecca had been a buyer of housewares for Macy's, a well-paying position with incentive bonuses. Without giving notice, not even so much as a voice message, she had abandoned her job. She had vacated her apartment overnight, leaving a check in the super's mailbox that bought out her lease. That was the last check she'd written on the account. As of today, it still had over two thousand dollars in it. She had taken her daughter and pulled a David Copperfield, proving herself to be as elusive as her brother.

"She didn't show up for work one day," Eleanor said in sad reflection. "I called her all day, left messages that went unanswered. I thought maybe Sarah was sick."

Following her divorce, Rebecca Watson had retained full custody of her daughter. After their disappearance, the ex-husband had made some noise, put out feelers of his own, but he gave up the search after only a few months. In Jack's opinion he hadn't tried all that hard. By then he'd remarried. His new wife was pregnant. He had other priorities.

"I got nowhere with Rebecca's ex," he told Eleanor now. "And I followed up with him for years. I knew he wouldn't care much about Rebecca's exit from his life, but I couldn't believe he would let his daughter go so easily."

"He's a self-centered bastard, and an ass."

Jack smiled over her candor. "I couldn't agree more. His child was gone, but he seemed more concerned about how much a private detective would cost him to track her."

"He was relying on you to find them."

"Hmm, not exactly. He told me I couldn't find a stinking pile of shit on a white rose."

"Charming." After a beat, she said, "The brothers-in-law hated each other. Did you know that?"

"Rebecca told me as much."

"It was a mutual and passionate dislike."

Jack had soon eliminated the ex-brother-in-law as a person to whom a seasoned war veteran and sharpshooter would turn for help. They'd been hostile toward each other from the outset of Rebecca's marriage.

Jack said, "Eleanor, tell me true. After her brother disappeared, while I was chasing my tail trying to track him down, did Rebecca know where he was?"

"She swore to me she didn't. I told you that four years ago. I also told you that I believed her."

"Everybody lies," he said gently, as though dispelling a myth to a child. "They lie to good friends. They lie especially to the authorities, and particularly when they're trying to shield someone they love. And Rebecca's sudden abandonment of her life here didn't earn her any marks for trustworthiness. Not in my book."

"No, I'm sure it didn't." The mother-to-be gave him a small smile. "But where her brother was concerned, she was trustworthy to the extreme, wasn't she?"

When Jack Connell arrived at the Bureau's Manhattan office after his visit with Eleanor Gaskin, he bypassed anyone looking for conversation, went straight to his cubby, and shut the door. At his desk, he replied only to the e-mails and phone calls that were time-sensitive but did nothing that wasn't mandatory to catch him up on a typical Monday morning.

Putting everything else on hold, he opened the desk drawer reserved for a file with a well-worn cover, on which was stamped a name in red ink. As he dropped the file onto his desk, he cursed the name and the man who bore it, then opened the file and, after some rifling, located a photo of Rebecca Watson that had been taken four years ago by Jack himself, while surveilling her apartment, hoping her brother would show himself there.

The resemblance to the woman in the broadcast video was remarkable, but he couldn't be positive they were one and the same, and he didn't believe that Eleanor Gaskin could be either, although he didn't doubt her conviction.

He was still comparing the two faces five minutes later when someone tapped on his door and then his associate, Wes Greer, a data analyst, poked his head in. "Now okay?"

"Sure, come in."

He'd called Greer to ask a favor on his walk between the brownstone where the Gaskins lived and the nearest subway station. Greer was soft, pale, undistinguished looking, but brilliant. And he could keep his mouth shut, which, in Jack's estimation, was a major asset.

He sat down across from Jack. "I called the TV station in Olympia and talked to the reporter who covered the story. Hundreds of protestors formed the picket. But that particular group was bussed to the capitol from Seattle. Reason they made it on camera? He said they were the most vocal and demonstrative."

"Did you follow up in Seattle?"

"Found one Rebecca Watson in the county. She lives in a nursing home. Born 1941. Making her—"

"Too old. *Dammit!*"

"I'll keep trying. Widen the net."

"Thanks, Wes."

He got up and made it as far as the door. "Oh, almost forgot. Late Friday—you'd already gone for the weekend—I got more info on the soccer coach in Salt Lake City. He'll walk, but he'll never kick another soccer ball. Coaching days are history."

"The coach tell you that?"

Greer shook his head. "I tracked down the osteo specialist who pieced his femur back together. Took a lot of Super Glue, he said."

"Was he being euphemistic?"

"I'm not sure. He said the bones were splinters."

"What did the coach have to say?"

"Nothing. Soon as I identified myself, he hung up. Just like the others."

Jack looked down at the file. "Can't blame them. They're afraid to talk."

"I would be, too."

"Any idea who's next?"

"Working on it," Greer said. "But you know, things stack up."

"For now, stay on Seattle."

Greer left him. Jack stared absently at the closed door for several moments, then his eyes moved down to the folder. Pushing aside the photo of Rebecca Watson, he looked at the one beneath it, the one of her brother.

The picture had been taken before the man had grown angry and bitter and had lost his will to smile. In the photograph, there was a suggestion of a grin at the corner of his mouth. But if one studied it as often and as closely as Jack did, one would detect the faint lines already there, bracketing his lips, virtually foretelling the curse he would place on himself at Westboro.

Jack muttered the question he'd asked a thousand times. "Where are you, you son of a bitch?"

Chapter 9

Jeff, who'd been channel surfing, dropped the remote to answer his cell phone. "Hello?"

"Jeff? It's Dr. Butler, calling from the clinic."

Dammit! "Uh-huh."

"I'm on speaker phone with Dr. James. We're calling to check on Emory. She didn't come in this morning, and we haven't been able to reach her either on her cell phone or at home. Is everything all right?"

He sat up and swung his legs to the side of the bed. "She went out of town for the weekend."

"We're aware of that. But our understanding was that she would be back by this morning. She had appointments scheduled. At first we thought she was just running late, which isn't like her, but the receptionist juggled appointments, trying to cover. It worked for a while, but now the waiting room is overflowing. The receptionist will have to start rescheduling Emory's appointments if she doesn't come in soon."

"You'd better do that. Reschedule, I mean."

"For tomorrow?"

"On second thought, you might want to hold off until... until we know for sure when she'll be back."

He could hear Emory's two colleagues in whispered conversation, but he couldn't catch what they were saying. Finally, Dr. James said, "We don't know how else to ask this, Jeff, except to come right out with it. What's going on? Emory's personal life is none of our business, but not showing up for work, standing up patients, that's not like her. We checked at the hospital to see if she'd made rounds this morning. We were told you'd called there yesterday asking for her and expressing some concern. Have you spoken to her yet?"

"No." Realizing he could no longer put this off, he imparted the troubling news. "The truth is, I haven't heard from her since Friday evening. But," he rushed to say, "we'd had an argument Thursday evening. A doozy, actually. When she didn't call over the weekend, I figured that she considered us not to be on speaking terms. Foolishly, I decided to wait her out."

"Oh."

One syllable, and Neal James applied it like the blade of a guillotine. He'd always been a prick toward Jeff, having an air of superiority that was as obvious as his honker of a nose.

Trying not to sound defensive, Jeff continued. "I wasn't alarmed because Emory hadn't been specific about when she planned to come back. She mentioned staying over Saturday night, too. So I didn't become worried until yesterday afternoon when I still hadn't heard from her."

"You've had no contact since Friday evening?"

"That's correct."

Dr. Butler's shocked response was to ask if Jeff had reported Emory's unexplained absence to the police.

"Yes. I drove up here—the town is called Drakeland— yesterday and started looking for her at the motel where she spent Friday night. She ate an early dinner at the café next door. She called me from her room telling me that she was in for the night. The trail stopped there."

"She was doing her run on Saturday morning, right?" Dr. Butler said. "Did anyone see her leaving the motel?"

"No, but you know her. She likes to get an early start, so she probably left before daylight. The desk clerk had imprinted her credit card the night before when she checked in, so there was no need for her to stop there before leaving."

"And she didn't return to the motel Saturday night?"

"No. She didn't plan to either. She took all her stuff with her when she left."

Dr. James said, "That's even more cause for concern."

"I agree," Jeff said. "As soon as I learned that, I notified the sheriff's office."

"And? What did they say? What are they doing?"

"Nothing yet. I was told that it was too soon to panic, but, as you said, this is out of character for Emory. I impressed that on the deputy I talked to. Even if she's angry with me, she wouldn't stand up her patients."

"What can we do?"

He could tell by Dr. Butler's voice that she was deeply concerned but trying not to think the worst. He said, "For the time being, hold down the fort there. Emory would hate having patients inconvenienced. I'll let you know as soon as I know something. I'm supposed to report back to the sheriff's office an hour from now."

"Maybe you should go immediately. Another hour is an hour wasted."

He hadn't asked for Dr. James's advice and resented it being so sanctimoniously dispensed, but he responded in a neutral tone. "I was on my way out when you called." After promising to keep them informed and exchanging good-byes, he checked his appearance in the dresser mirror. His flannel trousers and silk sweater would stand out here in overalls country, but God forbid that he blend in.

He dreaded this mission but welcomed a reason for leaving the motel room, which left a lot to be desired.

Drakeland was the seat of a large and mostly rural county. The sheriff's office was busy despite the inclement weather. Actually, because of it. While Jeff waited his turn in the lobby, trying to keep the hem of his long overcoat off the dirty aggregate floor, there was a steady stream of official personnel and civilians going out, coming in, dealing with weather-related problems such as the jack-knifed eighteen wheeler that had brought highway traffic to a standstill in both directions.

One woman was noisily carrying on about the collapsed roof of her barn and the horses trapped inside. The manager of a hardware store was filing a complaint over the shoplifting of a kerosene lantern.

It was a zoo.

Finally the deputy Jeff had spoken with the night before came through a set of doors and motioned Jeff forward. "Hate to see you here, Mr. Surrey."

"I told you she hadn't just run off."

"Come on back."

Deputy Sam Knight was preceded by his big belly as he walked Jeff through a squad room, where harried-looking personnel were handling the overflow from the lobby. Knight motioned Jeff into the chair facing his cluttered desk as he sank into a swivel chair. The name plate on the desk designated him as *Sergeant Detective*. Jeff thought Knight was a bit too homespun for the title.

He said, "My wife is a responsible individual. She wouldn't—"

Knight held up a hand as large and pink as a ham. "Bear with me, Mr. Surrey. We gotta get the basic stuff first." He slid on a pair of reading glasses and pecked at his computer keyboard until a blank form appeared on the monitor. "What's Mrs. Surrey's full name?"

Jeff explained why Emory used her maiden name. "And it's doctor."

"How do you spell *Char-ban-o?*"

Using the hunt-and-peck method of typing, Knight filled in all Emory's pertinent information—Social Security number, age, height, weight.

"Five feet six. One twenty. So she's…slim?" the detective asked, peering at Jeff over the smeared lenses of his glasses.

"Yes. She's in excellent physical condition. She's a distance runner. Marathons."

"Yeah, you mentioned that last night." He then asked the color of her hair.

"Blondish. Actually very light brown, with highlighted streaks. About to here." Jeff touched his collarbone.

"Eyes?"

"Hazel."

"Last seen wearing what?"

"I don't know." Knight's hands stilled on the keyboard. He turned his head to look at Jeff, who explained somewhat impatiently. "The last thing I saw her wearing was a pair of jeans, brown riding boots, and a camel-colored sweater. She was carrying her coat. But as I told you last night, she planned a long-distance run on Saturday. I assume she left the motel dressed in running clothes."

"What kind does she usually wear?"

Jeff described them by brand name. "They're high quality, designed for serious runners. She'd counted on it being cold. She would have a zip-up jacket. Something thermal underneath. Gloves. She usually wears one of those bands around her head to keep her hair back and her ears warm. Sunglasses, maybe."

"Got any pictures of her?"

"At home. But there are numerous ones of her on the Internet."

Knight used a search engine and immediately got a couple dozen hits. "That her?" Jeff nodded when the deputy pointed to a picture of Emory, taken at the ribbon cutting when she and Drs. Butler and James opened their clinic.

"Pretty lady."

"Thank you."

"What kind of doctor?" Knight asked.

"Pediatrician."

"These two still her partners?"

"Yes. I talked to them half an hour ago. They haven't heard from her either."

"They all get along okay?"

"Of course."

"No professional rivalry?"

Jeff blew out a breath of exasperation. "You're barking up the wrong tree. Her colleagues are very concerned."

"Okay. Just asking. I'm gonna be asking a lot of things that might seem irrelevant, or just downright nosy. But, unfortunately, awkward questions are sometimes necessary. It's about the worst aspect of my job."

Jeff doubted the accuracy of that statement but didn't dispute it.

Knight scanned through some of the other links. "She's an active lady."

"Very."

"You sure she's not off doing one of these charity things?"

Jeff drew a deep breath and let it out slowly. "She came up here Friday afternoon so she could run on a mountain trail on Saturday. For conditioning."

"You know which mountain, which trail?"

"Not offhand. She showed me a map. If I saw it, I might remember."

"You know which park?"

"There's more than one?"

Knight just looked at him for several seconds, then said, "In this region of North Carolina alone we've got four national forests, and they merge with Great Smoky and Cherokee over in Tennessee. Then if you go south into Georgia—"

"I'm beginning to get the picture," Jeff said, cutting off the geography lesson. "I don't know which park, or which mountain. But she stayed the night here in Drakeland, so the logical place to start looking for her would be the nearest hiking area."

Knight looked pessimistic. "That still gives us a lot of choices, a lot of square miles to cover."

"I'm sorry I don't know more about her destination. However, what I *do* know is that she wouldn't be 'off doing one of these charity things' without telling me."

Unfazed by his impatience, Knight said, "No, probably not. What about family members?"

"I'm her only family."

"Nobody else she could've gone to see and decided to stay?"

"No."

"Friends?"

"I've called everybody I could think of, but nobody has seen or heard from her. Which I'm afraid means…means something's happened to her."

The detective leaned forward and propped his arms on the edge of his desk. "You're fearing the worst, Mr. Surrey. Don't blame you. I probably would be, too. But I can tell you that, in all my twentysomething years in this sheriff's office, I've wadded up and thrown away every single one of these missing persons' reports I've filled out. People turn up ninety-nine point nine percent of the time. It's the one-tenth of a percent that makes the evening news and gives us all nightmares. So stay positive, okay?"

Jeff nodded. "I'll try."

"First thing, we'll start looking for her car." He called over a deputy he addressed as Maryjo and gave her the make, model, and license number of Emory's car, which Jeff had provided. "ASAP," he said. Maryjo promised to get right on it but cautioned him that the weather was going to be a major obstacle.

"We've got cars sliding off icy roads everywhere. Most of the less-traveled mountain roads were closed yesterday, but I'll get the state troopers on it. 'Course, we're talking *three* states, unless you throw in South Carolina, too, and then it's four."

Jeff was impressed. She knew the sum of three plus one.

As she moved away, Knight called over another deputy and introduced him as Buddy Grange. He shook hands with Jeff and pulled up a chair to join them. "Sam shot me an e-mail of the missing persons' report on your wife. I'm up to speed."

"Wonderful," Jeff said, trying not to sound too droll. "When do we actually start looking for her?"

"A few more questions first," Knight said. "Would Emory have been carrying a weapon?"

"Weapon?"

"People hiking in the mountains usually carry some form of protection. Pepper spray. Bear repellent. Which in my opinion is a rip-off, but if it makes folks feel safer…"

"It's winter. Wouldn't bears be hibernating?"

"In theory," Knight said, flashing a smile. Then, "Does your wife carry a pistol?"

"Lord, no. Nothing else you named either. Not to my knowledge anyway."

"Do you?"

"Yes. And I have the license to carry it." He extracted his wallet from his hip pocket and showed them the issue from the State of Georgia. "I'm happy to show you the pistol. It's in the glove compartment of my car."

"Okay. Later." Knight glanced at Grange before coming back to Jeff. "You said she left Friday, but you didn't come see us till last night. That's what, around forty-eight hours?"

"Which was bad judgment, *terrible* judgment, on my part. I realize that now."

"Why'd you wait?" Grange asked. The name Buddy didn't suit him. He was younger, leaner, sharper than Knight. Not as folksy.

"Emory had remarked to me how grueling it might be to run

this trail. She mentioned the altitude as a factor. She also suffered a stress fracture in her right foot last year. She was worried about it.

"For all those reasons, she knew it was going to be strenuous and told me she might not want to drive home on Saturday, that she might stay over an extra night and rest. When I didn't hear from her, I figured that's what she'd decided to do."

Grange asked, "Would you describe your wife as conscientious?"

"He called her responsible," Knight supplied.

"She is," Jeff said. "Very conscientious and responsible."

Grange frowned. "Then it seems to me you would have been worried when she didn't call to let you know she wouldn't be coming home Saturday night."

"I was worried."

"But you waited another twenty-four hours before making the trip up here to look for her."

"I've acknowledged the delinquency as poor judgment. But I told *him*," he said, pointing to Knight, "*last night*, that I feared something had happened to Emory. He dismissed my worry. If you and this..." He looked around the squad room, his gaze pausing on the lady with the collapsed barn who was now weeping over a dead horse. "If this mismanaged department sat on her unexplained disappearance for another twelve hours, the fault is yours, not mine."

With maddening composure, Knight said, "Nobody's blaming you, Mr. Surrey."

"That's not what it sounded like to me. What he said sounded like an insinuation."

Grange, unfazed, asked, "What did I insinuate?"

"Negligence on my part. Indifference. Neither of which is true or accurate."

Knight leaned forward again and gave him that folksy smile. "Detective Grange wasn't insinuating anything, Mr. Surrey."

Jeff eyed them both coldly but didn't say anything.

"Only...the thing is..." Knight shifted in his chair and winced as though he'd inflamed a hemorrhoid. "That one-tenth of one percent of missing people I mentioned earlier? Usually the person who reports them missing is the very person who knows where they're at."

Chapter 10

Any trust he'd won vanished the instant she saw that damned rock and drew the logical conclusion.

Her freak-out had lasted several minutes, during which she had fought like a wildcat. He'd tried to restrain her without injuring her, but she continued to claw, kick, and beat at him. One of her fists connected with the scratch she'd inflicted yesterday. It reopened and started bleeding. She hadn't stopped flailing at him until sheer exhaustion overcame her. Otherwise she wouldn't be even as docile as she was now.

Docile, maybe, but wound as tight as a harp string. He had deposited her on the edge of the sofa where she sat hugging her elbows, literally holding herself together. He went over and extended her a glass of whiskey. "Here. Drink this."

"Like hell." She pushed the glass away, sloshing the bourbon on him.

"Waste of good liquor." He sucked it off the back of his hand.

"You'd like me to get drunk, wouldn't you? Make me more manageable?"

"I didn't pour enough to make you drunk, just enough to take the edge off."

"I don't want to take the edge off, thank you." She threw her head back and glared up at him. "Why didn't the rock work?"

"It did. It knocked you out."

"And then you dragged me here."

"Actually I carried you to my truck. You rode here slumped over in the passenger seat. Seat belt kept you from falling onto the floor of the cab."

"Why did you bring me here?" She studied him with what seemed to be as much bafflement as fear. "If you wanted to kill me, why haven't you just smothered me in my sleep?"

"No sport in that."

She gestured toward the ceiling. "Can I expect to be strung up on that bar and gutted like a deer?"

He looked up at the bar and frowned. "Too much sport. Lots of heave-ho-ing. Big mess to clean up after. Instead, why don't you just drink the poison-laced whiskey?" He extended the glass toward her again, and when she didn't move, he said, "No? Okay then."

He shot the drink. She might not want the edge taken off, but he sure as hell did. Setting the glass on the end table, he said, "That was all bullshit, you know, meant to be a joke."

In no joking mood, she continued to hug herself, rocking back and forth, obviously distraught. "I was beginning to believe..."

"What?"

"That you didn't mean to harm me."

"I don't."

She gave a short laugh and glanced toward the incriminating sack sitting on the dining table. "Despite evidence to the contrary."

Huddled there, she looked small, helpless, frightened. He admired the grit it took for her not to cry when her eyes shimmered with tears. Her evident fear affected him much more than her flailing and kicking ever could.

He sat down beside her, ignoring that she recoiled to keep

their shoulders from touching. "I never wanted you to see the rock."

"Then you should have had a better hiding place."

"Temporary. In the meantime, I never thought you'd go digging around in the wood box."

"One would never expect such a gruesome find at the bottom of it."

"Gruesome, yes. With your blood and hair on it. I knew seeing it would upset you."

"You're damn right it did," she said with heat. "I actually believed you when you said I fell."

"I didn't say that, you surmised it. I said I found you lying unconscious."

"Because you clouted me in the head with that rock!"

"No, Doc. I didn't."

"Did you keep it as a trophy?"

He didn't honor that with a reply.

She moaned. "I wish you'd just get it over with."

"What?"

"Whatever it is you're going to do to me. I wouldn't have to go on dreading it, fearing it. The suspense is killing me. Is that part of the torture?"

Her hands were on her knees, clenched into fists so tight that all the blood had been wrung out of them. They were bone white and cold to the touch when he placed his hand over them.

When she tried to pull them from beneath his palm, he held on. "Look at me."

She turned her head and looked directly into his eyes. Hers were hazel, more green than brown. The orange specks in them, which he'd first thought were a trick of the light, were real. This close, he could have counted them.

"I didn't hurt you. I *won't* hurt you. How many times do I have to say it before you believe it?"

"I'll believe it when you let me contact—"

"Not yet."

"When?"

"When I can deliver you safely."

"But in the meantime, people are worried about me."

"I'm sure they are. But they don't need to be. And you don't need to be afraid of me. Why would you be?"

"You can ask that when you won't even tell me your name, or anything about you?"

"All right. If I tell you one thing, will you stop fighting me and trying to get away?"

She nodded.

He knew she was making a false promise, but maybe it would calm her down if he told her something that revealed nothing. "I lost both my parents, too."

"You loved them?"

"Yes."

"Did they die before or after...whatever it was you did?"

"Before. For which I'm glad."

"What did you do?"

"Don't ask again, Doc. I won't tell you." He looked down to where his hand still covered hers and realized that his thumb was reflexively stroking the back of it. His mind began to spin with erotic images of other patches of her skin that he'd like to caress. "If I told you, you truly would be afraid of me."

Moving quickly, before he invalidated every promise he'd made her, he lifted his hand off hers and stood up. Keeping his back to her, he retrieved the sack from the table and tucked it beneath his arm. Then he went to the door and took his coat, scarf, and cap off the peg. "During your fit, you reopened the cut on your scalp. There's fresh blood in your hair. You might want to rethink that shower."

He closed the door soundly behind himself and stayed on the porch until he'd put on his outerwear. The wind was strong enough to bend treetops. It blew snow and ice pellets into his eyes as he crossed the yard toward the storage shed.

He placed the sack on a high shelf and pulled a spool of wire in front of it. He then dragged a wooden pallet from the shed out to the stout chopping block on the far side of the structure. Loading recently split logs onto the pallet was mindless work, so he could do it without thinking.

Which left his mind free to concentrate on Emory Charbonneau.

It bothered him that her instinctual distrust was so strong.

It bothered him even more that it was valid.

Nothing else, no one else, had ever distracted him from his resolve. She did. His preoccupation with her was foolhardy, potentially dangerous, and could be ruinous. He struggled with it, but he felt himself losing ground each time he looked at her... and each time she looked back.

He made three trips between the woodpile and the cords of firewood stacked against the exterior south wall of the cabin where they were semiprotected from the elements. When done, he returned the pallet to the shed.

Pausing there inside, sheltered from the weather, his breath ghosting in the cold air, he removed his glove and took from his jeans pocket the silver trinket.

Emory hadn't noticed it was missing, and he hoped she wouldn't and ask for it back. Rubbing it between his thumb and finger, he acknowledged how juvenile and foolishly sentimental he'd been to secretly collect a token from her. In his life, he'd never kept something to remember a woman by, not even if she'd given him the souvenir herself. *Especially* if she'd given him the souvenir herself.

He wasn't a romantic. Never had been. When he'd failed to order flowers for his prom date, Rebecca had been incensed.

"Who cares about crap like that?" he'd grumbled.

In a temper, she'd said, "I do! I care about being the sister of a complete and total asshole," and had ordered the flowers for his date herself.

He would never hear the last of it if she knew...

But she would never know about Emory Charbonneau. No one would. Her time with him would be a secret he would take to his grave. He had to let her go. He *would* let her go. But at least he'd have this trinket as a keepsake.

He put it back in his pocket and pulled on his glove. Before leaving the shed, he looked up at the shelf where he'd stored the sack to make certain it was well hidden this time, then went out and latched the door behind him. On the porch of the cabin, he stamped his feet to shake loose the snow and sleet that had stuck to his boots, then pushed open the door.

As he stepped inside, he was greeted by the familiar scents of his bar soap and shampoo. Emory was standing in front of the fireplace, draping wet clothes over the back of one of the dining chairs that she'd situated near the hearth. Her hair was damp. In place of her running clothes, she was wearing another of his flannel shirts and a pair of his socks.

And that appeared to be all.

Between the hem of the shirt, which struck her midthigh, and the socks bunched around her ankles, was nothing except smooth legs. They were a runner's legs, lean and long, calves and quads well delineated under taut skin.

She finished placing her running tights over the top rung of the chair back, straightening the garment to her satisfaction, and scooting the chair a mite closer to the fire screen before turning to him.

"I took you up on the offer of your shower." She motioned down toward the socks, then ran her hand over the placket of the shirt where only a few of the buttons had been done up. "I hope you don't mind that I borrowed these."

With difficulty, he pulled his gaze up from the hem of the shirt. In reply, he shook his head no.

"It feels wonderful to be clean."

He gave a nod.

"I washed out my clothes, too."

He looked at the articles of wet clothing, but didn't comment on them.

"My scalp stopped bleeding."

He mumbled a gravelly sounding, "Good."

He took off his coat, cap, and scarf, turned around to hang them on the peg, then kept his hands there, his fingers sunk deep in the yarn of his scarf, holding on to it as though for dear life, because all the blood in his system seemed to have collected in one critical place, and the concentration of it was so thick, it was painful.

He went into the kitchen area, took the bottle of whiskey from the cabinet, and poured another shot. Halfway to his mouth, he halted and glanced at her from over his shoulder. "Change your mind about this, too?"

"No. Thank you."

He tossed the drink back. It burned on the way down and fizzed like a cherry bomb in his belly, but it gave him something else to think about instead of clean, smooth skin and how soft and warm it would feel under old flannel. Under *him*. *Moving* under him.

"You said you'd been watching me through binoculars."

"What?"

"That morning when you...when I fell. You said you'd been watching me."

"When you were—" *Stretching. Arching. Bending.* "There by your car. Before you set out."

"What were you doing out there?"

"Hiking."

"Nothing else?"

"No." He gripped the edge of the counter and continued to stare out the window above the sink. He didn't trust himself to face her.

"What caused you to notice me?"

Your legs in those black tights. Your ass. God, your ass. "I was just, you know, sweeping the area with the binocs, taking in the view. Saw motion, I guess."

"Why didn't you call out a hello?"

"Too far away. But I was curious."

"Why curious? Didn't I look like somebody just out for a run?"

"Yeah, but I wondered why you were alone. Most people, whatever they're doing in rugged country, are doing it with somebody else."

"You weren't. You were alone."

"But I'm used to it."

The faucet had a drip. For a while, those *ka-plunks*, coming at fifteen-second intervals, were the only sound in the room. In the world.

Then she said, "That's the one thing we didn't talk about."

He twisted the taps to see if he could stop the drip. "Sorry?"

"This morning I asked you how you could bear the silence, the boredom, and the loneliness. We talked about the other two, but not the loneliness."

The faucet stopped dripping, but he kept a tight grip on both taps as though he would pull them out of their moorings.

"Don't you get lonely?"

Was it his imagination or had her voice dropped in volume and pitch? "Sometimes."

"What do you do about it?"

No, it wasn't his imagination. Her voice vibrated with an intimate undertone. It was gruff, as though she had drunk the whiskey after all, and it had seared her throat. He pried his hands from the water taps and slowly turned around. She'd come only as close as the dining table, where she stood as though poised for a signal from him of what she should do next.

"I don't think you're referring to loneliness in general, are you, Doc?"

She made a rolling motion with her shoulders that could have meant anything.

"Are you asking if I get lonely for a woman?"

"Do you?"

"Often."

"What do you do?"

"I go get one."

His blunt answer had the effect he'd meant it to. It shocked the hell out of her.

"Like you got me?"

"No. You were different. You were a lucky find."

She hovered there indecisively for easily half a minute, her eyes darting to this and that but staying off him. He could tell the instant she decided to soldier on, because her eyes stopped that restless search for...what? Courage, maybe. Anyway, they returned to him.

She asked, "Did you mean it?"

"What?"

"When you said you wouldn't hurt me."

"Yes."

She waited, as though expecting him to recant, then said, "Thank you for taking such good care of me."

"You've already thanked me."

"Yes, but those other times don't count."

"Why not?"

"Because I was only trying to placate you."

"Placate me?"

"Because I've been very afraid."

"Past tense? You're not afraid of me anymore?"

"I don't want to be."

She took a step toward him, then another, and kept coming until she was within touching distance. She stuck out her right hand. "Friends?"

He looked down at her hand but didn't take it. Instead he

placed his hands on her shoulders and pulled her to him. She bowed her head, so as not to look him in the eye, but she didn't throw off his hands, or back away, or flinch as she'd been doing any time he got too close.

She took baby steps to shrink the distance between them, then pressed her forehead against the center of his chest. He slid his hands over her shoulder blades onto her back, drawing her incrementally but inexorably closer, and when their bodies were flush, she turned her head and rested her cheek directly over his heart.

He lined his fingertips along the groove of her spine and moved them up and down until one hand came to rest in the small of her back. And stayed. And rubbed circles there and applied enough pressure to tilt her up and form a fit with him in the notch of her thighs that caused her breath to catch.

Then they both stopped breathing.

She tilted her head back and looked up into his face with those limpid eyes, and, when she did, all bets were off. He had to have her. He would go through hell to be inside her. He was sinking, sinking, sinking...

His mouth was almost on hers—so close to kissing her, he could feel the moisture of her breath on his lips, taste it—when he caught himself. He whispered, "You almost got me, Doc."

She jerked her head back and blinked up at him. "What?"

"I almost fell for it."

"I don't know what you mean."

"Hell you don't. Smelling good. Nothing but sexy you under that shirt." He dragged his fingers across the top curve of her breast that swelled in the open collar. "Looking soft and sweet enough to make my mouth water."

He rubbed against her suggestively. "You know what I want, and you thought that if you gave it to me, then I'd be *placated* and would take you home. You had just as well have climbed up onto an altar and laid yourself out."

He made a derisive sound. "I appreciate the gesture. Truly. To say nothing of the view." He angled his head back so he could see down her entire length. "But I'm not into sex with a martyr."

Angrily, she pushed against his chest and tried to worm out of his grasp.

But he held on and, in fact, yanked her closer, grinding against her open thighs with unmistakable implication. "But here's a warning, Doc. You give me another opportunity to put my hands on you, and I'm going to put them all over you. Got it? I'm not gonna imagine you naked, I'm gonna *see* you naked. Offer up yourself again, and I'll ignore every reason why I shouldn't fuck you."

Later, he wondered what would have happened in the next few seconds, if the truck hadn't slid off the road and crashed into the tree.

Chapter 11

———◆◆◆———

Brakes squealed.

He released Emory and made it to one of the front windows in time to see the rattletrap in a fishtail skid before it plowed into a tree across the road from his gate.

In the same instant he recognized the pickup, Emory streaked toward the door. "Shit!" His hand shot out and caught a handful of flannel shirttail, bringing her up short.

She gave a small cry, but he turned her around, jerked her up hard against him, and clapped his hand over her mouth. "Listen to me. Stay quiet and out of sight."

She wiggled and tried to throw off his hand.

"Goddamn it, listen to me! Those men? You don't want them messing with you. They would hurt you bad. Trust me, please. Okay? I'm serious, Doc. You think I'm a threat, you can't imagine the party they'd have with you."

Somehow, he got the message across. Her eyes remained wide and fearful, but she stopped struggling.

"I've got to go out there, but can I trust you to stay inside?"

She nodded.

"I'm not bullshitting you. They're bad news. Okay?" She bobbed her head again, and he removed his hand from her mouth. "Don't let them see you."

Moving quickly, he snatched his coat off the peg, opened the door, and stepped out onto the porch, hollering, "Stay where you are."

The two men had crossed the road to his gate but stopped when he shouted at them. He covered the distance in long strides, smelling them before he got halfway to the gate. They reeked of wet wool, stale tobacco, sour mash, and body odor.

Scraggly, unkempt beards covered the lower two-thirds of their faces. They wore stocking caps pulled over their brows. Dressed almost identically in heavy coats and canvas pants tucked into rubber boots, the only features distinguishing one from the other were the couple inches' difference in their heights and the double-barreled shotgun cradled in the shorter one's left arm.

They were his nearest neighbors but they'd never spoken, and the only interactions he'd had with them had been contentious.

On more than one occasion he'd had to clear his yard of empty liquor bottles and beer cans that had been chucked out the window of the pickup as it jounced past. Twice the wall of his shed had been peppered with buckshot, possibly fired from the shotgun the shorter of the two was holding now. One day he'd returned home to discover a dead raccoon on his porch. It hadn't died of natural causes. Its head had been severed.

Meanness for meanness' sake. He detested that.

He figured the pair were trying to provoke him into retaliating. He didn't give them that satisfaction. Instead, he'd ignored the incidents and had looked the other way whenever they drove past.

He'd been biding his time.

Now, he'd almost reached the gate when the one with the shotgun leaned forward and spat tobacco juice over the fence in his direction. The stringy mess landed just shy of his boots. The other was somewhat more polite. He touched the rolled edge of his cap in a mock doffing motion.

"Hey, friend. I'm Norman Floyd. This is my little brother, Will."

Norman waited for him to introduce himself.

When he didn't, the elder Floyd hitched his thumb over his shoulder. "We got a bit of a problem."

"I see that."

The pickup probably hadn't been road-worthy to begin with. One of the front fenders was missing. All four tires were bald. The camouflage paint job looked as though it had been applied by an amateur hand. The loose tailpipe had been attached to the rusted rear bumper with a strand of barbed wire.

Now the front grill was wrapped halfway around the trunk of an evergreen that had been partially uprooted upon impact and was listing thirty degrees. The truck's busted radiator was emitting steam.

"You shouldn't have been on the roads today. Too icy."

"Well, yeah, you're pro'bly right." Norman shrugged and gave him a goofy grin, which he would have to be a fool to trust.

Meanwhile, the other, Will, was looking beyond him into the yard, curiously taking stock of his pickup, the shed, the cabin. He hoped to God that Emory had taken his advice and was staying out of sight.

He would kill the two Floyd brothers if he had to, but he'd rather not have to today.

Norman said, "We're neighbors, you know."

"I've seen you drive past."

"You know where we live?"

He did but thought it best not to let on that he did. He nodded toward their wrecked truck. "You shouldn't try to tow it until the roads are clear."

"What we figured."

"Well, be careful. You should be okay if you stick to the shoulder so the gravel can give you some traction." He disliked turning his back to a man holding a shotgun, but he hated even worse the idea of the brothers thinking that he was afraid of them. He made to turn, but Will spoke up for the first time.

"You figuring on us walking home?" He expressed his opinion of that plan by spitting again.

"What we thought," Norman said in a whine, "was that you might give us a lift. It ain't but a mile, mile and a half, up the road to our place."

"If it's no farther than that, you can easily make it before dark. If you start now."

Beneath his beetled brow, Will's eyes turned even more hostile. He shuffled forward a few inches and assumed a more combative stance.

Ordinarily, the subtle threat would have amused him. He would have been thinking, *Go ahead, you hillbilly jackass, dare me.* He would have waited for one or the other to come at him, and then he would have mopped the floor with both of them. He looked forward to that time. But today wasn't the day. He had to take Emory's safety into account.

"Walk, huh?" Norman glanced up at the sky and held out his palm to catch snowflakes. "Don't look to me like this is gonna let up any time soon." He scratched at something in his beard as he looked over his shoulder toward the truck. "For me 'n' Will the walk wouldn't be nothing. Even in this shit weather. 'Cept..."

He gestured behind him at the pickup.

———

Emory watched through a sliver of space between the window frame and the muslin curtain as the man she had tried unsuccessfully to seduce worked the combination on the padlock, went through the gate, and crossed the road to the wrecked pickup, where the passenger door stood ajar.

He bent down, looked inside, appeared to be speaking to someone. After a sixty-second conversation, he turned back to the two men. His expression was dark and dangerous. Tight-lipped, he said something to the pair, then strode through the gate and across the yard toward the cabin, leaving the gate open.

She backed away from the window as he burst through the door. "Stay out of sight, but keep an eye on them. Tell me what they're doing." He went to the end of the sofa, lifted it, and moved it several feet, then knelt and flipped back the corner of the carpet.

"What's going on? Who are those men?"

"The brothers Floyd. Norman and Will."

"Are they asking for your help with their truck?"

"It's beyond help. They want a ride."

"To where?"

"Their place. What are they doing?"

"Helping someone out of the pickup. Who's that?"

"Their kid sister."

During this terse exchange, he'd pulled up a section of the wood flooring. In the rectangular cavity under the floor was a metal locker like the one she'd found beneath the bed. He flipped the latches and raised the lid.

Firearms. Many. Of all types.

He lifted out a handgun, checked the clip, then tucked it into the waistband of his jeans and pulled down his sweater and coat to conceal it. While Emory stood there, mute with astonishment, he closed the trunk, replaced the flooring and the rug, and moved the sofa back into place.

He said, "Secret's out," and motioned down toward the hidden armory. "If the need arises, help yourself. Do you know how to shoot?"

She gaped at him as he went to the bed and stripped the pillowcase off the pillow. Then he picked up her shoes and tossed them into the pillowcase. "If you should run out of firewood before I get back—"

"*Back?*" she exclaimed. "You're not seriously thinking of going with them?"

But apparently he was, because the trio outside were making their way toward his pickup. The one toting a shotgun looked eager to check it out. He went ahead while his brother, with noticeable impatience, ushered their sister around the icier patches in the yard.

"As I was saying, firewood is stacked on the outside of that wall." He raised his chin in the direction of the wall that held the bookshelves. Patting his coat pockets, he located his gloves and pulled them on. He dropped his cap and scarf into the pillowcase, gathered the top of it in his fist, and tossed it over his shoulder like a Santa sack. "I won't be long."

She planted herself between him and the door. "Are you crazy? They look dangerous."

"They are."

"Then—"

"I'll be okay."

"How do you know?"

"Because I know."

"That's no answer."

"Move, Doc."

"They could slit your throat."

"Not their style."

"What do you know about their *style?*"

"More than I want to."

"You've had confrontations with them before?"

"Not exactly."

"What does that mean?"

"I knew who they were, but until today, we hadn't met. They're my neighbors."

"Which you claimed not to have."

"Yeah, well, I lied about that."

"How close do they live from here?"

"I don't have time to go into it now. Move out of my way before they come to see what's taking me so long."

He tried to go around her, but she side-stepped to block him.

"You've been using the icy roads as your excuse for keeping me here."

"They're still treacherous. Which is why that damn heap crashed into the tree."

"Then why are you driving them home?"

"Because it's too far for the girl to walk." He reached behind her, lifted his key ring off the hook, and dropped it into his coat pocket.

She grabbed his sleeve. "You can't leave me here."

For the first time since coming back inside, he paused to really look at her, then, with a sudden move, dropped the pillowcase and closed his hands around her head. He ran his gloved thumb across her lower lip.

"I swore to myself I wouldn't touch you. But I wish like hell I'd fucked you anyway."

Then he bracketed her hips between his hands and forcibly moved her aside. "Stay out of sight until we're gone. If they come back in place of me, shoot the sons of bitches and ask questions later." In one fluid motion, he bent to pick up the pillowcase, opened the door, and left.

Following his interview with the detectives, Jeff was banished to the chaotic lobby, where the floor had been tracked with muddy, melting ice. He'd eaten a snack from a vending machine and washed it down with bitter, tepid coffee, also from a machine. He'd then claimed a vacant chair and camped in it, so to speak, while he waited for something to happen.

The longer he sat there, the angrier he became.

He had called in sick to his secretary earlier, but he was re-considering whether or not he should notify his boss and tell him where he actually was and what was going on. But he talked himself out of that, deciding there was no sense in sounding an alarm until the situation called for it.

Alice had been worried about Emory yesterday afternoon. By now, she would be climbing the walls. He knew he should call her, but talked himself out of that, too. It would look bad if Knight and Grange discovered that he'd contacted his illicit lover while his wife was unaccounted for.

He read the *Wall Street Journal* and played a game of Scrabble on his phone, all the while stewing in resentment over being ignored. An hour crawled by. When he couldn't stand the in-activity any longer, he took to swearing under his breath, and, when he got truly fed up, he risked losing his seat by leaving it to go to the reception window and demanding that the deputy seated there summon Sergeant Detective Sam Knight immedi-ately.

A few minutes later, Knight came through the connecting door, seeming to be in no apparent hurry, uselessly trying to tug his off-the-rack trousers up over his belly. "Must be mental telepathy, Jeff. I was just about to come get you. Come on back."

He was *Jeff* now?

Knight held the door for him. The lady with the collapsed barn roof was no longer in the squad room. Personnel were talking to one another or on their phones. Some were at their computers. But no matter how they were engaged independently, they simultaneously paused to follow his progress over to Knight's desk, where Grange was already waiting, looking as dour as an undertaker.

"Oh God," Jeff moaned. "What's happened?"

Grange answered by pointing him into a chair.

He remained standing. "Damn you, answer me."

"Nothing's shaking so far," Knight replied as he lowered himself into his desk chair. "Sit down, Jeff, please."

"That's all you people seem capable of doing. Sitting. Why aren't you doing something constructive to find my missing wife?"

"We're doing everything we can."

"You're just sitting here!"

Realizing he had called even more attention to himself, he sat down—hard—and glared at the two detectives.

Knight said, "It wouldn't do any good for us to go chasing around, burning up fuel, when we don't know where she went after she left the motel."

"What about her credit cards? Wasn't Marybeth—"

"Maryjo."

"Whatever. Wasn't she supposed to be checking on charges and ATM withdrawals?"

Grange joined in. "It would have speeded things up if you'd had Emory's credit card numbers."

"I explained that," Jeff said, practically having to unclench his teeth to get the words out. "Emory has her accounts. I have mine. She pays her bills—"

"Actually she doesn't."

Jeff looked from Grange to Knight. "What's he talking about?"

"The accountant who keeps the medical clinic's books also pays Emory's personal bills. He charges her a small stipend each month. He gave us her personal account numbers."

"Great. Fantastic. Did Maryjo follow up?"

Knight said, "Friday afternoon shortly after leaving Atlanta, your wife gassed up her car using a credit card at a service station. We've got that transaction on security camera video. By the way, she was dressed just like you described."

"Why would you think she wouldn't be?"

"Could be she'd stopped somewhere between your house and

the service station and...you know...switched clothes." Before Jeff could respond to that inanity, Knight went on. "Anyhow, she charged her motel room to the same card and used it again to pay for her dinner on Friday night. None of her cards has been used since."

Jeff gnawed his lower lip. "Since Friday night?"

"Do you know how much cash she had on her?"

He shook his head, then cleared his throat and said, "But I doubt it was much. She isn't in the habit of carrying a lot. It's sort of a joke between us. She never seems to have any cash."

After a lapse of several moments, Grange said, "We've also retrieved her cell phone records. Last call she made was Friday evening." He smiled, but it wasn't a friendly expression. "To you."

"She called to let me know she'd made the trip without mishap, that she was already in bed and about to go to sleep." He leaned forward, placed his elbows on his knees, and covered his face with his hands. "None of this is good news, is it?"

He heard Knight's chair squeak, then the detective's hand landed heavily on his shoulder. "Hang in there. It might look like we're not doing much, but we're pulling out all the stops to find her."

As he escorted Jeff back to the lobby, Knight casually asked if he could take a look at Jeff's handgun. "Standard procedure. You understand. If you'll give me your car keys, I'll send a deputy out to get it so you won't have to go out in that mess."

Jeff doubted the weather was the reason Knight didn't want him to retrieve the gun himself, but he surrendered his keys without argument.

Having been assured that he would be the first to hear any updates, good or bad, he was again abandoned.

His chair had been claimed by a biker-looking type with a braided goatee that extended almost to his waist. While Jeff paced, he checked his phone for missed calls. One of Emory's girlfriends, whom he'd called the night before, had left a voice message telling him that she hadn't talked to Emory for more than a week.

A client had left a message expressing his displeasure over the dive the stock market had taken and asked Jeff if he had any ideas on how to make up for the loss. His tailor had called to inform him that his alterations were ready. There were two missed calls from the clinic's main number, but no one had left a message.

Alice, of course, knew better than to call his cell phone.

He spent an hour on futile pacing and was seething with frustration when Grange bustled into the lobby, wearing a hat with ear flaps and zipping up a quilted puffy jacket as he walked toward him.

"They found her car."

"Only her car? What about Emory?"

"They're looking."

"Where?"

"Nantahala."

"Where's that?"

"You're in it. National forest. Knight and I are rolling."

Grange was nearly out the door before Jeff processed all that and reacted. He jogged to catch up and followed the deputy. No sooner had he cleared the exit than Sam Knight pulled a tricked-out SUV to the curb. Grange opened the passenger door and climbed in. "Stay put. We'll be in touch."

With that, he closed the door and the SUV sped away, leaving Jeff staring after it through the snow.

―――⊶⊷―――

It didn't take long for Emory to deduce why he'd taken her shoes. She couldn't leave in stocking feet. He'd guaranteed that she would remain trapped here until he returned. But she'd be damned before she became part of the spoils claimed by the red-neck duo if they, not he, came back.

He'd moved the sofa with ease. It took more effort for her, and it was even harder to pry up the section of flooring, but she managed with the help of a screwdriver she found in the drawer where he kept the smaller one with which he'd repaired the toaster.

She chose a pistol at random and set it on the end table with care.

Soon after they'd married, Jeff had introduced her to a small handgun he owned and had given her a rudimentary lesson on how to fire it. But she never had. It had been a revolver. This one had a cartridge. Recognizing the difference was almost the sum total of what she knew about firearms. But having one in reach was good for her peace of mind.

She also felt more secure once she was fully clothed. As soon as her running clothes were completely dry, she changed into them.

Left with nothing else to do, she restlessly prowled the cabin. She pawed through the contents of drawers she hadn't explored before, but found nothing that gave away anything about her host—no journal, correspondence, receipts, not a single scrap of paper with enlightening information on it.

That itself was a reveal. He was scrupulously careful. He kept nothing that could identify him.

Going over to the shelves, she ran her index finger along the book spines, noting that the titles had been alphabetized. She thumbed through several of them, looking for loose sheets or no-tations handwritten in the margins. After a time, she concluded that the shelves he'd installed himself held nothing except books.

In desperation, she held her hands palms-down on the cover of the laptop, mentally willing it to give up its secret password like a Ouija board. It didn't.

She added logs to the fire when it burned down. She paced,

frequently looking out the window, hoping to see the approach of the pickup. As aggravating as it was to admit, she was worried about him. The two men had looked disreputable enough to kill him for his boots, much less for his truck. Perhaps the "kid sister" had been a lure. Maybe they had deliberately crashed their dilapidated pickup into the tree as part of an elaborate scheme to rob him.

He'd told her he hadn't met the brothers until today, but he had admitted that he knew who they were. He knew that slitting his throat wasn't their *style*. What was that about? Her imagination expanded on several themes, all of them catastrophic, all ending badly not only for him but also for her.

It was an appalling thought, one she hadn't allowed herself to contemplate before now: She might never get home.

By now Jeff would have notified the police, but would he know where to tell them to start searching? She'd talked about her destination, but had he paid close attention or retained a thing she'd said? Even she couldn't remember how specific she'd been when she'd shown him the map of the national forest on which she'd marked her trail. But even with only a general idea of where she had set out that morning, a search would be under way.

She would get home. Of course she would. And then—
What?

The crystal ball was as murky on her future from that point as it was on her immediate situation.

When she and Jeff reunited, they would be glad and relieved to see each other. But their quarrel would only have been suspended, not settled. The wedges between them would still be firmly lodged. Assuming he was having an affair, upon her safe return, would he end it strictly out of a sense of obligation? That would serve no purpose other than to keep everyone unhappy.

In fairness, how could she blame Jeff for having a lover when a stranger's embrace and near kiss had made her burn hot?

Yes. There was that.

Her attempt to be a femme fatale had ended on an ironic twist: it was she who'd been seduced. She had put on that mortifying display, but when he began caressing her, she stopped playacting. He'd pulled her to him, and she'd felt him hard and insistent against her, and the truth had been undeniable. She'd wanted him.

Every feminine urge had sprung to life, and it wasn't just the long dormancy that had made her sexual desire so acute. It was him. She wanted to experience him, every rough surface, every gruff word, his outdoorsy scent, the whiskey taste of his breath, the arrogant jut of his penis. She had wanted the totality of him with a reckless disregard for what was right and proper for Dr. Emory Charbonneau.

If he hadn't ended it in that insulting manner, she would have made a further fool of herself.

Thinking about it agitated her and increased her anxiety, so that when she heard the pickup pulling into the yard, she retrieved the pistol, cradled it between her hands, and aimed it at the door.

He stamped in, looking more forbidding than she'd ever seen him. The pistol didn't disconcert him in the slightest. He took one derisive look at it, then tossed the pillowcase containing her shoes over to her. It landed on the floor at her feet.

"Put your shoes on. We're leaving."

"Where are we going?"

"I'm taking you down the mountain, and I'm in a hurry."

Chapter 12

Come October, the heating system in Jack Connell's apartment building was cranked up to somewhere around eighty-five degrees, and it stayed at that setting until May. After coming in from a frigid wind that whipped through the brick-and-mortar canyons of Midtown Manhattan, he exchanged his suit and overcoat for shorts and a Jets T-shirt, opened a beer, and carried it with him into his home office, a small room sparsely furnished with a desk—a door suspended between two sawhorses—and a secondhand chair on casters, one of which wobbled.

He called the number Greer had given him for the television news reporter who'd covered the protest march on the state capitol building in Olympia, Washington.

The phone rang several times, and when it was answered, the background noise was deafening. After several false starts, the young man explained that he was out, having happy hour drinks with friends. On the West Coast, happy hour apparently began at three thirty.

Jack shouted, "You talked to my colleague earlier today. Wes Greer."

"Oh, the FBI agent?"

"Right. You told him that the group featured in your story's video had come by bus from Seattle to participate in the demonstration. Were they isolated people with a common passion or an organized group?"

"A group. With a name. Can't remember it now. It's in my notes. When do you need it?"

"Yesterday."

"Oh. Can I get back to you? I'll have to call the newsroom and have somebody go over to my desk."

Jack gave him his cell number. While waiting for him to call back, he went into the kitchen and made a sandwich of stale rye, hot mustard, and deli roast beef that hadn't gone completely green, opened another beer, and was halfway through each when the reporter phoned.

"The group is Citizens Who Care. CWC."

"Is there a contact person?"

"The guy who started it. A relative of his—I think it was his nephew—was shot and killed while buying a Slurpee at a convenience store. He got in the way of an armed robber. Anyway, this guy's an uber-activist. He has a long name, like a Polish hockey player or something. Ready?"

The reporter spelled it out, and the letters were mostly consonants. Jack asked if he had a phone number for him.

"Figured you'd want that, too." He read it out. "Say, why're you trying to track him down? Is there a story here?"

The poor sap had no idea.

Jack made up some mumbo jumbo about the "Bureau's interest" in any group or individual supporting either "stricter gun laws" or any "opposed to government's suspension of personal liberties."

"Oh, that's been done to death." The reporter sounded bored and ready to return to happy hour with his friends. "But keep my number and call me if you come across anything newsworthy. On the QT, of course. I'd never reveal you as my source."

Jack made a promise he never intended to keep, thanked the reporter, and hung up. Switching to a burner phone, Jack called the man with the odd name, and the gentleman himself answered.

He sounded like a nice enough guy, which made Jack feel bad for lying to him. But not too bad. He used a fake name to introduce himself. "I'm not taking a survey or trying to sell you anything. I'm looking for a long-lost classmate."

He launched into a whopper about an upcoming high school reunion. "I'm in charge of finding people the class has lost track of. You'd think it would be easy, the Internet and all. But some have slipped through the cracks.

"Last night, me and the wife were watching the news, and, swear to God, I think I spotted Becky Watson in your group that marched on the state capitol. Even in high school Becky was politically active and a crusader for causes like gun control. Which, so am I, by the way."

"Becky, you said? We don't have a Becky in CWC."

"Maybe she goes by Rebecca now."

"Nope, sorry. Nobody named either Rebecca or Watson."

"Gosh, I was positive that was her. The white spiky hair was exactly the same."

"That sounds like Grace."

"The lady I'm talking about was wearing a red coat."

"Her name's Grace Kent."

Jack, heart bumping, scribbled down the name. He wanted to probe the gentleman for information about his fellow demonstrator: What does Grace do for a living? Does she have a daughter around twelve years old? Does she have a brother who visits her regularly? You can't miss him. Big, tough-looking, dark hair, light eyes.

But he resisted the temptation to ask. He didn't want the

man's curiosity aroused. He might feel obligated to alert Grace Kent that someone had called inquiring about her.

He sighed with exaggerated disappointment. "Oh well, not our Becky then. But it was worth a shot. Sorry to have bothered you. Thank you for your time."

"No problem. Good luck with your class reunion."

Jack's fingers couldn't move fast enough on his keyboard, but for naught. No one with the name Grace Kent was listed in the Seattle phone book. He ran a Google search, didn't find anything. So he called Wes Greer and put him on it, then sat there and absently finished his sandwich, chewing mechanically, thinking.

It took him less than two minutes to make up his mind, then he was on the phone again, booking an early flight, arranging for a car service to take him to LaGuardia at six o'clock in the morning, and reserving a rental car in Seattle. As he packed a roll-aboard suitcase, he acknowledged that the trip would probably turn out to be the last in a long line of wild-goose chases.

The last one being to Salt Lake City, preceded by Wichita Falls, Texas. Before that, Lexington, Kentucky. Seemingly random places and individuals, unrelated except for a single commonality—one man.

He was already in bed but not asleep when Greer—who, it seemed, never slept—called back. "I have an address. Grace Kent actually lives across the Sound, not in Seattle proper."

"How do you get over there?"

"Ferry."

Wonderful.

Jack typed her street address into his phone, gave Greer his basic itinerary, and closed by saying, "For the time being, nobody needs to know I've gone. In fact, I'm out sick with the flu."

"Got it."

As he lay staring at his bedroom ceiling, he placed odds on the likelihood of Grace Kent being Rebecca Watson. He was going on nothing more than Rebecca's friend, Eleanor Gaskin, who hadn't laid eyes on her in four years, picking her out of a jostling crowd in a news video of mediocre quality. Based on that alone, he was making the cross-country trip.

Would it be asking too much that he catch a break and the picket carrier turn out to be Rebecca? Dare he hope that she would cooperate and tell him where her brother was? As long as he was fantasizing, why not imagine that her brother was visiting her, and that he would answer the door when Jack rang the bell?

He could trust Greer's discretion, so at least if this turned out to be another false lead, another dead end, no one would regard him as a complete fool.

Except himself.

And he was used to that.

"When will we be there?"

"When we get there."

Emory clutched the edge of the seat as he steered the pickup around another hairpin curve. The headlights had been their only source of light since the abrupt departure from the cabin. If there was a moon, the cloud cover obscured it completely.

They hadn't passed a dwelling or structure of any kind. Nothing. It was as remote a road as she'd ever been on, and certainly the most hazardous. As feared, there were icy patches beneath the accumulation of snow, invisible until the truck lost traction.

As they took the turns, the headlights swept over unforgiving rock formations that rose straight up out of the narrow shoulder, some encrusted with ice where waterfalls had frozen. Where there weren't rock formations there was forest. The massive tree trunks wouldn't have yielded to a tank. Or, most terrifying of all, the lights cut into black nothingness. One skid and they could plunge over the edge into the void.

She wanted to shut her eyes so she wouldn't see the hazards that threatened, but she didn't dare because of the ridiculous assumption that strictly by her will to live she could help keep the truck on the road.

He'd told her that he was accustomed to these mountain roads with their curves and switchbacks, but he drove with single-mindedness, not nonchalance. His gloved hands gripped the steering wheel, his eyes never left the road.

Answers to her questions about the Floyd brothers had been brusque and monosyllabic, if he answered at all. She had stopped asking. Whatever had happened between him and his unkempt neighbors had prompted him to take her home, or at least to drop her somewhere so she could get home. That was all she cared about.

She *told* herself that was all she cared about.

"What are all the guns for?"

"What are guns usually for?"

"To shoot...things."

He shrugged as though that's all the debate the issue warranted.

"It's dangerous to have them around. What if I'd accidentally shot you?"

"It would have been a miracle."

"You're a large target. At that range I couldn't have missed."

"Probably not, but there wasn't a cartridge in it."

"It wasn't loaded?"

He came as close to smiling as he ever did. "Doc, a word of advice. If you aim at somebody with the intention of shooting him, make sure the weapon is locked and loaded, ready to fire. If you don't intend to shoot him, don't point the thing at him in the first place."

"You sound like an expert on the subject."

He didn't say anything in response to that, nor did he say anything as he navigated the next series of switchbacks.

Finally, she asked. "How much farther?"

"A few miles."

"Do you mind if I turn the heater up a bit?"

"Go ahead."

Before leaving the cabin, he'd draped a coat of his over her, telling her that her running clothes wouldn't be sufficient to ward off the cold. The coat swallowed her, of course, but she was grateful for it and pulled it more closely around her now.

"I really would be cold without your coat. Thanks."

"You're welcome."

She didn't want to distract him with conversation, but she was desperate to know what lay in store. "Will you...What will you do?"

"When?"

"When we get there."

"You'll see."

"Can't you just tell me, so I'll know what to expect?"

"It won't be long now."

Indeed, over the next half mile the steep grade leveled out and they began to pass houses. They were spaced widely apart, but they were the first signs of civilization she had seen in four days. Coming around a bend, the headlights caught a small city limit sign.

She turned to him with surprise. "This isn't Drakeland."

"No."

"Is Drakeland farther on?"

"It's in the other direction. This road doesn't go there."

"I thought you were taking me to Drakeland."

"What made you think that?"

What *had* made her think that? He hadn't told her that was their destination, but since it had been her starting point, she had assumed he would take her back there.

The town through which they were driving now barely qualified as such. It had two caution lights, one at each end of the narrow state road that bisected the town. On one side of it were a bank, a service station, and a double-wide serving as the US Post Office. A café, taxidermy, and general store were on the other side. All were closed for the night.

Emory had anticipated being returned to someplace with lights, activity, people. Batting down a flutter of panic, she asked, "Are you going to leave me here?"

"No."

His terse response did little to assuage her misgiving.

At the second caution light he turned right, drove two blocks, then turned right again into an alley that ran along the back of a cluster of what appeared to be small businesses and offices.

"What are you doing? Where are we going? Are we meeting someone here?"

"We're making a quick stop, that's all." He pulled up to the back door of a single-story brick structure, turned off the head-lights, and cut the engine. "Sit tight for a sec."

He got out and stepped around to the bed of the pickup. Looking through the rear window, she watched as he raised the lid of a tool box attached to the cab and took out a tire iron with a socket wrench at one end and a sharp, double-pronged hook at the other.

He carried it to the rear delivery door of the office. Before Emory could fully register what he intended to do, he'd done it. He used the tool to pop out the doorknob, including the entire locking mechanism, leaving a neat round hole in the metal.

He came back to the truck and returned the tire iron to the tool box, then opened the passenger door, unbuckled Emory's seat belt, closed his hand around her biceps, and hauled her out.

"You're up, Doc. Hustle."

At first she'd been too dumbfounded to react. Now she did, frantically pulling against his grip on her arm. "What are you doing?"

"Breaking and entering."

"Why?"

"To steal what's inside."

"Are you insane?"

"No."

"You're about to commit a felony!"

"Uh-huh."

His reasonableness astonished her. It terrified her. Crazy people often appeared perfectly sane until they...weren't. She wet her lips, took quick shallow breaths. "Listen, I'll give you money. You know, you said I had gobs. I...I'll give you all you want, just—"

"You think I'm after money? Jesus."

The man who'd taken a tire iron to a locked door for the purpose of breaking in and stealing actually looked affronted.

"Then why in God's name—"

"This is a doctor's office."

A new light dawned. "Drugs? You want *drugs*?"

He sighed and propelled her toward the door. "We haven't got time for this bullshit."

She dug her heels in. "I won't be any part of this." She swung at him with her free fist, but he dodged it. "Let go of me!"

"Quiet!" Gripping both her arms now, he looked around to see if her raised voice had roused anyone, but the alley remained dark except for a lone street light at the end of the alley, and somehow, impossibly, it beamed into his eyes as they bored into hers. "The girl in the pickup?"

"The F-Floyds' sister?"

"She's in a bad way and needs your help."

"What's wrong with her?"

"I'll explain on the way back."

"You can't be serious."

"We're going back to help her."

"I'm not going back." She tried to push away from him and began struggling again.

"Emory."

What stilled her wasn't so much the little shake he gave her but the use of her name and the authority with which he spoke it. "We can stand here arguing and risk getting caught and going to jail, or—"

"*You'd* go to jail. Not me."

"Or you can hold to your Hippocratic oath, get in there, and gather up what you'll need to treat her."

"I won't commit a crime."

"Not even for a good reason?"

"Nothing could compel me."

"You'll soon be eating those words." He pulled her toward the door of the office. "You're reputed to be a do-gooder. Here's your chance to do some good."

Chapter 13

———◦◉◦———

Jeff had watched daylight turn into a short-lived dusk. Darkness fell fast.

He killed time. He wanted to kill Knight and Grange for not keeping him updated as promised. Instead, he'd sat and watched the wall clock tick away the afternoon without a clue of what was happening beyond the sheriff's office lobby.

As it neared closing time at the clinic in Atlanta, he called the main number.

"This is Jeff Surrey. Are the doctors still there?"

"Oh my God, Mr. Surrey." The dulcet tones with which the receptionist had answered gave way to a voice that wavered with emotion. "I've left you messages asking if there's been any word about Dr. Charbonneau. We've all been sick with worry. Please tell me she's all right."

"Let me speak to the doctors, please. Either one."

"Dr. James is standing right here."

He heard the receiver being transferred from hand to hand, then, "Jeff?"

"I'm afraid I don't have much to tell you, Neal. They located

Emory's car early this afternoon. But only her car. That was the last report I got."

"Hold on. I'm gonna put you on speaker. Everybody wants to hear."

Jeff could picture the clinic staff clustered around the desk phone as he related what little he knew. "I looked up that national forest on the Internet. It covers thousands of square miles, most of it mountainous, some of it referred to as 'wilderness.' The terrain isn't for the fainthearted."

"I've camped in that area," the doctor said. "And she's lost in it? Christ."

"Fortunately, as you know, Emory is very fit and has incredible stamina."

"Isn't it snowing up there and the temperature well below freezing?"

Leave it to Neal James to paint the bleakest picture possible. "Yes, the weather is impeding the search for her."

Several questions were hurled at him at once. He interrupted them. "I'm sorry. I don't know anything else. The deputies haven't returned, and they haven't called in. Or if they have they haven't spoken to me. It's been hours since they left, and I'm as much in the dark as you are. It's frustrating as hell."

"Do you want me to drive up there?"

The doctor was extending the offer for Emory's sake, not Jeff's, and he was glad he had a valid reason to decline it. "There's nothing you could do. Until I know something conclusive, I'm thinking positive and holding out hope that Emory is all right and simply unable to reach me."

The clinic staff endorsed that view, but their voices were subdued, a few tearful, as they said their good-byes.

He then called his office and left a voice message for his secretary, telling her only that he had a family emergency and wouldn't be in again tomorrow. Just as he disconnected, Knight appeared.

When Jeff saw him, his heart skipped. "Emory?"

Shaking his head, he said, "The search continues. I'm sorry."

He motioned Jeff to join him, and they took the familiar route through the warren of desks in the large squad room. Grange was seated at Knight's, a cup of coffee cradled between his hands, which looked red and chapped. His cheeks were ruddy with cold.

Jeff took the chair he'd sat in before. "How long have you been back?"

"Only long enough to grab some coffee," Knight said. "You want a cup?"

Jeff shook his head, then looked back and forth between the two. "For God's sake, tell me something. *Anything.* I've been dying here."

Knight scooted aside his coffee mug and picked up a rubber band, which he popped against his fingers. "Sad truth is, Jeff, we don't know shit about where Emory's at."

He looked over at Grange, who gave a solemn nod of confirmation.

"Her car...?"

"Was the only one in a parking area that accesses a scenic overlook and several hiking trails. Those trails branch off every which o' way, then each one has arteries that go up, down, all around. I wrote down the names of some of the trails. Take a look, see if one sounds familiar."

Jeff took the sheet of paper Knight passed him and read down the list. "They all sound the same. Indian names. Nothing jumps out at me. The trail she took might be here, but... I'm sorry. I just don't remember."

"Well, all of them were being searched till it got dark. Up to that point there'd been no sign of her."

Jeff let the sheet drift down onto Knight's desk, then bent his head low and massaged his eye sockets. The two officers gave him several moments to absorb the implications of what they'd told him. Finally he raised his head and dragged his hand down his face. "Her car didn't provide any clues?"

"It was glazed with a thin layer of ice, covered in snow, but otherwise didn't seem to have been touched since she left it. No tracks around it either, indicating nobody else has been up there since she parked."

"What about inside the car? Any sign of a struggle?" He swallowed. "Foul play?"

"That's the good news. No sign of struggle," Knight said, smiling at him kindly.

"Thank God."

"Looked to us like she parked and walked away on her own. No flat tire. She didn't leave the key, of course, but after the, uh, crime scene guys—"

"Crime scene?"

"We're treating it as such till we know better. Anyway, after they got finished with the car, we checked it out. It started right up. No engine trouble. In the trunk we found the boots she was wearing on Friday and a duffel bag with an ID tag on it."

"A gold leather fleur-de-lis with her business card inside."

Knight nodded.

"She has a set of those," Jeff said.

"We brought the duffel to the office here and want you to go through it, see if you notice anything unusual. But we already checked inside and saw nothing but normal stuff. Change of clothes, underwear, toiletries."

"She would have been traveling light. She intended to stay away two nights at the most."

"There was also a laptop in it," Grange said.

"She never goes anywhere without that."

"We can't crack it without the password. Do you know it?"

"Her mom and dad's names, only backward."

Grange jotted down what he spelled out. "They're waiting on this." He got up and disappeared down a hallway, where

Jeff supposed personnel would begin exploring the contents of Emory's computer.

"We didn't find her cell phone."

He came back around to Knight. "She carries it in a fanny pack when she runs. In case..." He paused on the stammer. "In case she has trouble."

"Well, she still hasn't used it. We checked. And it's not emitting a signal."

Grange returned and said to Knight, "They'll let us know."

"Who'll let you know what?" Jeff asked.

Grange was characteristically laconic. "Our computer geeks. They'll let us know if they find anything useful on her laptop."

Jeff had kept a lid on his frustration for as long as he could. "Meanwhile my wife is still missing. Isn't anybody actually looking for her?"

"Lots of folks are, Jeff. But it's dark. The roads up there are damn near impassable, but we've got officers driving 'em anyway. Snowfall is a lot heavier up there than it is down here. Tomorrow, if the weather clears, we'll put up a chopper, but the forecast isn't promising. The search will continue overland, but that's slow going because of the terrain. If it's feasible, we'll get a canine unit to—"

"Bloody hell." He stood up and walked away, grinding his fist into his opposite palm. "'Tomorrow.' 'If.' 'Canine unit,' for chrissake." He stopped pacing and turned back to them. "Where's this parking lot? How far from here?"

"A piece," Knight replied.

"Oh, that's helpful."

"Jeff, sit down."

"My ass has grown carbuncles from sitting! I'm going there myself."

"That wouldn't be too smart."

"Oh, while to you *smart* means getting the password to Emory's computer?"

Knight sighed. "Criticize our efforts if it makes you feel better, but if you go stumbling around up there, we'd soon need a search party for two people instead of one."

Jeff stood there, rocking back on his heels, fuming. "What about the FBI?"

"We could pull 'em in, but they'd be doing what we are."

"Which is precious little."

"Look, Jeff, I know it seems like nothing's being done, but—"

"Goddamn right. That's exactly what it seems like."

"I understand how frustrating that must be."

"Like hell you do. Has anybody you love ever gone missing?"

Properly put down, Knight quietly admitted that he hadn't experienced that misfortune.

"Then don't pretend to know what I'm feeling right now."

"Okay, I'll stop with the banalities if you'll sit down and let us talk through some things with you."

Jeff didn't comply immediately, but ultimately, realizing the futility of having a temper tantrum, he returned to his seat. "Talk through what things?"

"Well," Knight began, "as I said, it appears that Emory parked and walked away from the car under her own power. No sign of her being assaulted or dragged off, anything like that."

"Which means that she likely had a mishap in the frigging wilderness. She's still out there while we sit here where it's nice and cozy and the coffee's hot."

"Could she have met someone?"

"No," Jeff replied curtly. Then, after a beat, he looked at Grange, who had asked. "Like who?"

"There are marathon clubs. Sometimes the runners train as a group."

"Emory trains alone."

"Always?"

"Yes. If she's a member of a club or something, she's never

mentioned it to me. She doesn't go to meetings or anything like that. Have you checked with any such clubs?"

"Maryjo did. None had Emory on their membership roster."

"Then why did you bring it up?"

"Double-checking," Grange said, remaining unflappable. "It's unlikely, but Maryjo could have missed one."

Knight said, "My wife walks every morning with a group of women in the neighborhood. No power walk, you understand. More like a stroll that gives them time to gossip about anybody who isn't walking." Looking at Jeff, he asked, "You're sure Emory doesn't have a running buddy?"

"I'm sure. I don't know of anyone she would have been meeting. Besides, the reason she came up here on Friday was to be alone."

"Why did she want to be alone?" Knight asked.

"So she could focus. Running is like therapy to her. She uses it to sort things out, get her head on straight. It's like...like *church* to her. It gives her a spiritual high."

"I've heard of that." Knight looked over at Grange and nodded sagely.

"Still, she must be awfully committed to drive over a hundred miles to train alone on a mountain trail."

"She challenges herself," Jeff said. "She sets tough personal goals."

"Overachiever?"

"And then some. She's a perfectionist. If she commits to something, it's forged in steel."

"Including marriage?"

Grange's out-of-left-field remarks were beginning to grate on him, and he let it show. "Pardon me?"

Knight, in the tone of a wise grandfather or a priest, asked softly, "Is she faithful to you, Jeff?"

He saw red and shot each of them a glare. "I know what you're thinking, and you're wrong."

"What do you think we're thinking?"

"That Emory rendezvoused with a man up here. That I'm a chump, the last to know that my wife is cheating."

"Not possible?"

"No. Absolutely not."

"All right," Knight said. "I warned you that we'd have to ask some tough questions. If you say everything is rosy on the home front, then…" He extended his hands at his sides, letting the gesture speak for itself.

"I didn't say it was rosy." Jeff lowered his gaze to the floor, and when he raised his head, both deputies were looking at him expectantly. "Emory and I had a quarrel on Thursday night."

"The night before she came up here?"

"Yes."

"Over what?"

"It started out small. I didn't want her to come up here. I thought the trip was absurdly unnecessary. Why couldn't she do a distance run closer to home, someplace that didn't require an overnight stay and which was, frankly, less dangerous? One thing led to another, the argument escalated. Both of us vented some spleen.

"We went to bed angry. Friday afternoon when I saw her off, there were still bad feelings on both sides. Neither of us apologized or took back anything we'd said the night before."

Knight grimaced. Grange didn't even blink.

After several moments of weighty silence, Knight asked, "During that argument, what did you vent about?"

"Generally, the time she spends running. Specifically, this upcoming marathon. She's spent over a year organizing it. Big charity event. She's pledged a bundle if she finishes. This will be the first one she's run since injuring her foot. The training has been rigorous. More than I believe is healthy or wise.

"I urged her to go only half the distance, but she wouldn't hear of it. How would it look to all the other runners if the organizer failed to finish? I said that was ego talking and referred to her commitment as an obsession."

Knight whistled.

Jeff said, "I'll admit, that was hitting below the belt. She stormed out of the room, and I was too angry to go after her. The quarrel ended on that note."

"What did she vent about?" Grange asked.

Jeff took his time before answering, weighing how much he wanted to disclose, and decided to be forthright. "I was passed over for a promotion to partner in my firm. Not because I hadn't earned it, but because of inner-office politics. Which is galling. I was disappointed, disenchanted, and, I confess, Emory bore the brunt of my dissatisfaction."

"How so?"

"I've been moody and withdrawn. Admittedly, not much fun to live with. I rebuffed her attempts to cheer me and bolster my self-esteem." He raised his shoulders. "Thursday night, months of frustration came to a head. We both said things."

Grange just sat there looking at him. Knight asked, "No abusive language? Did the fight ever get physical?"

"Good God. No! We're not white trash. Raised voices was the extent of it."

Knight nodded. "My wife and I had a fight this morning over a wet towel I left on the bathroom floor. She yelled at me, asked why I didn't pee on the floor while I was at it. You never know what's going to set a woman off."

The comparison left Jeff too affronted to speak.

Knight stood up, and, as though he'd given Grange a silent signal, he did likewise. Knight said, "Anything turns up tonight, we'll let you know."

Jeff looked at them with incredulity. "That's it? You're closing up shop and going home?"

"Don't worry. We've got people working different angles."

"What people? What angles?"

"Angles. In the morning, we'll get an early start. Might actually help to have you come along, Jeff."

"I'd like that very much. I don't think I could endure another day of just sitting around."

"Good. You can ride up there with us."

In that rigged-out SUV? Not likely. "I'll follow you in my own car."

"Naw, let's all go together," Knight said, settling it and leaving no room for argument. The detective lifted his quilted coat off the back of his chair and pulled it on. Eyeing Jeff's overcoat and Burberry scarf, he said, "You'll need different clothes."

"I packed a ski jacket."

"You packed?"

Jeff turned to Grange. "Sorry?"

"You packed before leaving Atlanta to come up here?"

"I brought some things, yes."

"How come? Did you count on being up here for a while?"

"I *reasoned*," he said, emphasizing the word, "that when I joined Emory, it was unlikely that we'd drive back before Monday morning. I came prepared to spend at least one night."

Grange registered no reaction to the explanation.

Knight pointed Jeff toward the exit. "Tomorrow morning we'll pick you up, say...seven? Is that too early?"

"I'll be ready. I only hope the motel can accommodate me for another night."

"Taken care of," Grange said. "We called and booked the room for you."

Chapter 14

Emory clutched the strap above the passenger window as the pickup took a curve. They were on the same dark and icy road as before, this time ascending, which made the navigation even more difficult. But in addition to the perilous roadway, she worried about being pursued.

They'd been in and out of the doctor's office within five minutes. The man who had engineered the break-in had held a flashlight and monitored not only what she was doing, but had kept watch through the windows to make certain that no one had been alerted to the break-in.

She'd collected instruments, supplies, and medications she thought she might need and had placed them in a plastic trash can liner to bring with her. No one accosted them when they left. They drove out of town the same way they'd driven in: unobserved.

Or so she hoped. The third time she turned her head to look out the cab window at the road behind them, he said, "Relax, Doc. There's no posse chasing us."

"Since I'm new to thievery, I'm a bit nervous. How did you know there wasn't an alarm system in the doctor's office?"

"I didn't."

Stark with disbelief, she said, "What would have happened if an alarm had sounded? We would have been caught."

"No we wouldn't."

"You think we could have slipped out of that sleepy little town in this large and conspicuous pickup truck?"

"Yes."

"Impossible."

"No it isn't. I've done it."

She didn't know whether to be shocked by his admission or comforted to know he had a knack for eluding capture. "I still can't believe that you—that *I*—broke the law."

"Don't beat yourself up. You've more than compensated for our minor B and E tonight."

She gave him a pointed look, and he answered her unasked question.

"There's a lot online about your philanthropy."

"Is that why you called me a do-gooder?"

"You don't need to go to Haiti or organize fund-raisers to help someone in need. You've got a girl right here."

"If she's as you described, she needs an ER."

"I offered to take her. She refused to go."

"Why?"

He concentrated on climbing a steep grade, downshifting and steering with care, but Emory thought he used that as an excuse not to answer her.

"Why did she refuse?" she repeated.

"She's scared."

"Of what? Doctors? Hospitals?"

"When we get there, you can ask her."

"When we get there, I'm calling nine-one-one."

"Good luck with that."

"You'd stop me?"

"They would."

"The brothers?"

He muttered what sounded to her like *fucking hillbillies.*

"If that's your opinion of the Floyd family, why did you get involved with them?"

"Would you rather the girl suffer?"

"Of course not." Knowing she was treading on thin ice, she said, "But I think the situation with her has given you a valid reason to engage with them. It's an opportunity you didn't expect, but you're seizing it. Tell me if I'm getting warm."

His gloved fingers flexed against the steering wheel before resuming their grip, but he didn't say anything.

"You've locked horns with them before."

"No. I haven't."

"I don't believe you. You said—"

"Look, Doc, you could speculate till you turn blue, and you'd still be wrong. All you need to know is that I gave Lisa my word that I'd bring back help. I keep my word."

"You gave me your word that you'd take me back, yet here I am."

"I'll see you safely back. Just not tonight."

"No, tonight you were too busy burglarizing a doctor's office and making me your accomplice."

"I forced you to at gunpoint."

"Not exactly."

"Close enough. If the need ever arises, you can lay all the blame on me."

"How? I don't even know your name."

He glanced at her. "You're beginning to catch on."

He spoke rather tongue-in-cheek, but there was truth in the statement. When she did go home, how would she ever explain him, explain any of this? Everything that had taken place since she regained consciousness in his rustic cabin seemed beyond the realm of possibility.

These kinds of adventures simply didn't happen to people like her. In her wide circle of acquaintances, no one she knew had experienced such an unthinkable departure from their world and their ordered life within it. Was bizarre the new norm? It seemed so, because reality had become surreal.

Or was this reality? Had she really burglarized a doctor's office? Was her fellow criminal a man who'd admitted to being in hiding from the authorities? Had she eaten from his table, used the bar soap in his shower, worn his clothes, come perilously close to making love to him?

Or would she soon wake up and find herself lying next to Jeff in their well-decorated, climate-controlled bedroom where the temperature remained constant year-round, where one day and night were more or less the same as the ones before and the ones after, where nothing too cataclysmic ever happened? Would she shake him awake, and laugh, and say, "You won't believe the wild and woolly dream I had."

But that scenario was difficult to envision. She couldn't pull it into sharp focus. Details of it—the texture of her favorite sheets, the color of the bedroom walls, the sound of Jeff's soft snores—were disturbingly indistinct, while the profile of the man beside her was shockingly familiar.

She couldn't call him by name, but she could describe the crescent-shaped scar above his left eyebrow. His silver-threaded hairline, the lines bracketing his mouth, the ever-changing facets of his eyes—these were only a few of the many aspects of him that had become well known to her.

His voice, which at first had seemed without inflection, could be very expressive if one knew the nuances to listen for. He could whisper, when one would think that a man of his size was incapable of speaking that softly. He never failed to fold the dishtowel after using it. When he sat in his recliner to read, he mindlessly stroked the corner of his lips with his thumb, and after adding a log to the grate, he always dusted his hands on the seat of his jeans.

He'd turned her into a criminal tonight. A week ago, she would have been flabbergasted by the prospect of such a thing. But as she considered it now, she realized she wasn't as scandalized as she should be.

When they came around a curve in the road and there was the familiar split-rail fence, the gate, his cabin, the thought that flitted through her mind was, *We're home.*

She was accepting of and comfortable with the outrageousness of her situation. That, more than anything, should have frightened her.

He slowed down. "Should we stop? Is there anything you need from inside?"

"I don't think so."

For days she'd wanted to escape his cabin. Now anxiety tugged at her as they drove past the relative safety it represented. "Regardless of my objections, I want you to know that I do think it's noble of you to help this young woman," she said. "I even admire the extremes to which you've gone in order to help her."

He didn't respond, sensing there was more she had to say.

"But this isn't my specialty and I'm ill-equipped. And if her condition is as serious as you indicate, despite her scary brothers, despite *you*, I'll do whatever is necessary to get her to a hospital."

"She won't go, Doc. I told you. She was in Drakeland this morning. She could have gone to any number of clinics. She didn't. She called her brothers to come get her and bring her home. They were on their way when they wrecked the truck."

"Are the brothers expecting us?"

"I got their grudging consent to bring back a doctor. Took some persuasion from their mother."

"There's a *mother*?"

"She introduced herself as Pauline. Don't hold the sons against her. She's pathetic, beaten down. She's very worried about Lisa."

Up ahead she caught a glimpse of lights through the trees. "Is that it?"

"That's it."

"So they *are* close neighbors."

"I already admitted to lying about that. Now, pay attention. This is important. I can't turn my back on those guys. So if I say 'git,' you go, understand? No questions, no arguments, no hesitation. You just do what I say, when I say."

"Are they really that dangerous?"

He clenched his jaw, and the ferocity of his expression was chilling. "They're stupid and mean, and that makes them dangerous." He patted in the vicinity of his waist. "I've got the pistol handy."

"That's supposed to make me feel better?"

"What should make you feel better is that I won't hesitate to use it."

He stated it unequivocally, and she believed him.

"You'll be okay," he said, as though sensing her mounting apprehension. "One more thing, though. They don't know that you're my... guest. Better that they don't know you're staying under my roof."

"Better for whom?"

He braked. The truck skidded several yards before coming to a stop in the center of the road. Laying his arm along the back of the seat, he turned to her. "Better for *you*," he said angrily. "Don't use them to get away from me."

In a small voice, she said, "I was joking."

"It's no joking matter. Do not ask for their help."

"I won't."

"Swear it, Doc."

"I won't. I swear."

He continued to stare hard at her, then lifted his foot off the brake and drove on. A quarter mile farther, he turned into a drive that was rutted and strewn with junk of every description.

Even the softening effect of the snow didn't hide the ugly scars of neglect and disrepair. Lights were on inside the house, but nothing about the property looked inviting.

Especially not the dog that charged out the front door and set up a ferocious barking. He looked like a guardian of hell as he came up on his hind legs against the passenger door of the pickup, his nails scratching against the metal. Only the window separated Emory from his bared, snapping teeth. Breathless with fear, she flattened herself against the seat.

"Oh, I forgot," he said. "There's also a mean dog."

———◦———

She hadn't screamed, or even yelped, but she looked petrified. Disregarding the frenzied dog, he put the truck into gear and executed a three-point turn so the vehicle was facing out.

Moving only her head, she turned to him, a question in her eyes. He said, "A precaution. In case we need to leave in a hurry."

A piercing whistle brought the barking to an abrupt stop. The elder brother had come out onto the porch. The yellow light bulb shining down from under the eaves cast deep shadows on his face, emphasizing his glower.

"That's Norman."

Responding to another sharp whistle, the dog backed off, but it retreated only a few feet and stood just beyond Emory's door, rigid and alert, ears twitching, as though anticipating a command to tear their throats out.

He leaned across Emory and pressed his hand against her thigh for reassurance as he shouted through the passenger window. "Call off your damn dog."

Norman shaded his eyes against the porch light glare. Seeing Emory, he said, "Who the hell is she? You were supposed to be bringing a doctor."

"This is Dr. Smith."

Norman clumped down the steps and sauntered over to the pickup. Through the window now smeared with canine slobber, he gave Emory a once over. "She's a doctor?"

"She is."

Smirking, Norman drawled, "Too bad I ain't sick."

To her credit, Emory didn't flinch or give any other indication of fear. But the contempt in her voice could have chiseled ice. "I understand that you neglected to get medical treatment for your sister. So I came to see about her. But I'll leave right now if you don't restrain that animal."

Amused by her feistiness, Norman gave her his stupid grin and said, "Yes, ma'am, doctor ma'am," then turned and took the dog by the collar. He dragged it over to a tree and clipped a chain to the collar. "Lay down," he commanded, throwing in a kick that sent the dog sprawling in the muddy snow. It sprang up immediately but stayed where it was, sitting on its haunches and panting hard.

Emory turned her head and spoke in an undertone that Norman would be unable to hear. "Are you sure your gun is loaded?"

"Always." After a beat, he added, "I've got your back, Doc. You can count on it. I would kill them before I let them touch you."

Their faces were very close, so he could see the bewilderment with which her eyes searched his. Then she assumed an expression of determination. Turning away from him, she opened the passenger door and got out. "Where is Lisa?"

Norman bowed from the waist and swept his arm wide toward the house. "Back bedroom."

The dog growled as they filed past. They trooped up the steps and across the porch and went inside, stepping directly into a living room. He'd seen it this afternoon when he brought them home. Nighttime hadn't improved it.

It was filthy from the moldy ceiling to the stained rug. Sections of wallpaper had been peeled away, exposing the Sheetrock. A tent made of newspaper was acting as the shade for the floor lamp, the stand of which was bent.

Will was sprawled on the sofa watching a wrestling match on TV. The shotgun was propped, barrel up, against the cushion beside him. Upon seeing Emory, he raised his eyebrows. "You shittin' me? What the hell's goin' on?"

His brother said, "Neighbor man here brought us a lady doctor. Ain't that a stitch?"

Norman's moniker grated on him, but he let it pass because he wasn't about to tell the Floyd brothers his name. Furthermore, they were appraising Emory like hungry jackals, which made him feel all the more protective of her.

Ignoring the uncouth pair, he took Emory's arm and guided her toward the bedroom where he'd left Lisa earlier. Her mother was standing in the open doorway of the room, twisting the hem of the soiled apron tied around her waist.

Pauline Floyd was skinny to the point that her shoulder bones poked up like drawer pulls against her faded dress. Her hair was so thin that scalp showed through the frizzy gray tuft on top. Her face said that she'd seen plenty of hard times, and that this was another of them.

"Pauline," he said, "this is Dr. Smith. Dr. Smith, Mrs. Floyd."

Emory murmured an acknowledgment to the introduction.

Pauline addressed her anxiously, "Can you help my girl? She's carrying on something awful. Says her belly hurts, and she's bleedin'."

Emory looked into the room toward the bed, where the small mound beneath the frayed bedspread lay perfectly still. "I hope to help her. Where can I wash my hands?"

The old woman tilted her head quizzically. "The bathroom, I guess." She hitched her thumb.

Emory excused herself and followed the direction Pauline had indicated.

The old woman watched her until she disappeared through a doorway, then came back around to her neighbor. "How long you been living down the road from us?"

"A while."

"By yourself?"

"Yes, ma'am."

She glanced toward the bathroom. "She a real doctor?"

"She's an excellent doctor."

"I don't know of any lady doctors 'round here. Where'd you get her at?"

"In town," he said, hoping that would be all the explanation required.

Emory emerged from the bathroom looking pale but full of resolve. She walked past him and Pauline into the bedroom. They followed her over to the bed. Lisa lay on her side, knees to chest.

Emory took a box of latex gloves from the trash can liner she'd carried in with her, pulled on a pair, then touched the girl's shoulder. "Lisa? I'm Dr. Char—Smith." She applied gentle but insistent pressure until the girl rolled onto her back.

She was very pretty, with delicate features and silky blond hair. By contrast, her eyes were so dark, the irises were indistinguishable from the pupils. Looking beyond Emory toward him, she smiled shyly. "You came back?"

"I promised you I would. I brought the doctor."

She shifted her gaze to Emory. "It hurts."

Emory patted the girl's slender hand. "I hope to relieve that soon, but first I'll have to examine you. All right?"

Lisa glanced at her mother, then tentatively nodded.

Emory straightened and turned. "We'll need privacy."

He said, "I'll be right outside the door." But when he motioned for Pauline to go ahead of him, she protested.

"She's my daughter. I've saw everything."

"Dr. Smith will call us as soon as she's completed her examination. Right, Dr. Smith?"

"Certainly," Emory replied.

Silently she telegraphed to him the urgency of the situation. No longer giving Pauline a choice, he took her arm and propelled her toward the door. When he looked back, Emory was bending over the bed, talking softly to her patient.

He closed the door and put his back to it. Pauline told him that she would be in the kitchen and headed in that direction. She walked with the skittishness of a mouse, keeping close to the wall as though afraid of being seen and raising ire. She disappeared through an open doorway.

Will hadn't moved from his place on the sofa. On the TV, two women wrestlers were throwing each other against the ropes, but the volume had been lowered. Norman sat in an upholstered chair that at one time had matched the sofa, but it was now haphazardly striped with silver duct tape that held together rips in the stained fabric.

He had their undivided attention.

Norman said, "Sit down and take a load off."

"I'd rather stand, thanks."

"What's your name, anyhow?"

"What difference does it make?"

Norman copped some attitude. "You're messing in our business, that's what difference it makes."

"All I'm doing is getting medical treatment for a sick girl."

"Sick my ass." Will rolled off his spine, picked up a can of beer from the scratched and rickety coffee table, and took a swig. "She should've known better than to get herself knocked up."

Earlier, when he'd first seen her in the wrecked truck, he'd noticed that Lisa's lips were white with pain, but when he'd asked her the nature of her ailment, she hadn't been forthcoming with an answer.

Since her brothers had seemed indifferent to her condition, he'd consented to drive them home. He'd helped Lisa into the house and, after making a hasty explanation to Pauline as to why he was there, he and the old woman got Lisa into the bedroom.

Sensing the girl's reluctance to discuss her problem with members of her family, he sent Pauline out of the room to get Lisa a glass of water. Only then had she told him in confidence that she had miscarried. Shamed, she begged him not to tell her mother.

"You shouldn't go through this alone. Have you told anyone?" he'd asked.

"My aunt and uncle—I live with them in Drakeland—or did. They kicked me out of the house when I told them what was happening. I had to tell my brothers so they would come get me. But I don't want my mama to know."

She had started to cry and had been so distraught, he'd given her his word that he wouldn't tell her mother, but he had impressed on her that if she was in that much pain, she should be seen by a doctor. Either he would drive her or she could call nine-one-one. "The EMTs will keep it confidential. They have to. They're professionals."

She wouldn't hear of it. That's when he'd offered to bring medical help to her. Knowing what the frightened girl had suffered—and continued to—physically as well as emotionally, her brother Will's "knocked up" remark infuriated him. He curbed the impulse to yank the younger Floyd off the sofa by his stringy hair and throw him through the window.

He asked, "How old is Lisa?"

Will shrugged and looked over at Norman. "How old is she? Fourteen?"

"Fifteen."

Will turned back to him. "Fifteen."

"She and your mother seem to have a close relationship."

"You know women," Norman said with a snort. "They stick together."

"Then why is Lisa living with relatives in Drakeland?"

"None of your friggin' business," Will said.

Norman replied more civilly. "Better schools down there."

"Lisa's in high school?"

"'Course," Norman said. "What do you think, she's a retard or something?"

"I was just wondering if the father of the baby she lost is as young as she is."

"She works at a Subway on weekends," Will said. "Who knows who all she's fucked." He took another slurp of beer, eyeing him over the top of the can as though hoping he would take umbrage.

He did, but he kept his expression impassive and addressed his next question to Norman. "Have you lived here all your lives?"

"Yep. Well, 'cept for a time a few years ago. Me and Will heard about work up in Virginia. Went up there for a spell."

"How'd that go?"

Norman scratched his armpit. "Not so good. No sooner got there than the economy went to shit. We both got laid off."

"That's too bad."

"Not really. Mama wanted us back home, and anyway Virginia ain't all it's cracked up to be."

"What kind of work did you do up there?"

Norman's eyes narrowed. "What's it to you? In fact, what's with all the questions about our family?"

"Just making friendly conversation."

"Well, make it about something else."

Will said, "What we need is a change of subject." He snapped his fingers. "I know. Let's talk about *you*."

The feral gleam in the younger Floyd's eye put him on guard, but he kept his tone neutral. "What about me?"

"How come you keep so to yourself?"

"I like my privacy."

"You like your privacy," Will repeated, as though pondering the reply. "You a homo?"

Norman snickered then laughed behind his fist. Will gave his brother a self-congratulatory wink.

He let their levity run its course, then said, "No, Will, I'm straight. Sorry. I hate to disappoint you."

It took a few seconds for Will to process the implication. When he did, he lunged off the sofa and came lumbering toward him. Norman stuck out his booted foot and planted it directly in his brother's path. Will tripped over it and fell face first onto the filthy rug. He came up hurling curses. Norman physically restrained him.

"Calm down, Will. He's just egging you on. And you asked for it, after all."

Will's stream of profanity continued as he tried to wrestle free of his more level-headed brother. Pauline came in to see what the commotion was about, but after taking in what must be a familiar scene, she slunk back into the kitchen unnoticed.

While Norman was still trying to talk Will out of ripping his fucking head off, the door behind him opened. Emory glanced toward the wrangling brothers, but another problem superseded them. Low but insistently, she said, "I need to talk to you."

Keeping his eye on the Floyds, he backed into the bedroom and shut the door, then dragged a straight chair over to it and secured it beneath the doorknob. He didn't need to ask about Lisa. Emory's demeanor spoke volumes.

She said, "This isn't a miscarriage."

He glanced toward the bed, where Lisa lay, crying softly. Emory had stripped the surgical gloves from her hands. She was holding them inside out, but he saw that the fingers of them were stained dark. "Then what's the matter with her?"

"She's in labor."

Chapter 15

Jeff read the name of the caller on his cell phone and considered not answering. Speaking to Alice directly wasn't the best of ideas. But then, everyone knew her to be a friend to him and Emory as a couple. Naturally she would be worried and calling him for information and to offer every means of support.

He clicked on. "Hi."

"Jeff, what the hell is going on?"

"Emory is missing."

"Tell me something I don't know. It's already gone viral on social media."

"Shit. The clinic staff?"

"The clinic per se hasn't issued a statement. But individual staff members have been telegraphing it. Some of Emory's friends, too, who say you began yesterday calling around looking for her."

He swore under his breath. "I knew that sooner or later there would be a social media blitz, but naively I hoped to have more time before the onslaught."

"I've been out of my mind with worry. Talk to me."

He spent the next ten minutes detailing the situation without any interruption from her beyond spontaneous exclamations of dismay and empathy. He wound down and finished with, "First thing tomorrow morning, I'm going with Knight and Grange to the place in the mountains where they found her car."

"This is unbelievable."

"I know. It's like she was beamed up by aliens, and that's the least horrible thing I can think of. The ghastly alternatives—"

"Don't. Don't do that to yourself. You could drive yourself crazy with speculation."

"I'm halfway there already. Crazy, I mean. The two detectives urged me to remain positive, but let's be realistic, Alice. It's been too long since she was seen or heard from. No matter how angry she was when she left, if she were able to contact me, she would have by now. This can't be good."

"I'm afraid you're right."

She was too practical a woman for lying either to him or to herself.

"It will be on TV tomorrow," he told her. "Probably as early as the morning newscasts. News outfits get most of their leads from social media now. Once the sheriff's office confirms that she's officially missing, reporters and camera crews will flock up here."

"Emory is so well known and has such a high public profile."

She said it without jealousy or rancor. One thing about Alice that he appreciated most was that she was well aware of Emory's many accomplishments but wasn't threatened by or resentful of them. Emory had a competitive nature. Not so Alice, who was unlike her in every regard and quite comfortable with paling in comparison to his wife's stellar brilliance.

Which was precisely why he was with Alice.

He said, "Because of Emory's notoriety, Knight told me to brace myself. He warned that this might be my last night of peace until she's found. Once the word is out, I'm likely to be besieged by media.

"In Knight's opinion, that won't be all bad," he went on. "He says it's usually a good idea for a family member to make a public appeal, to go on camera and ask for help or information. You've seen them on TV, sobbing parents, distraught spouses, begging for the safe return of the missing loved one. I never thought I'd be one of those poor slobs."

"Will you be comfortable doing that?"

"It won't be easy, but I'll do whatever is expected or required of me."

"You sound exhausted."

"It's been a shitty twenty-four hours."

"What prompted you to drive up there yesterday?"

Leave my bed and drive up there. She didn't say that, but it was implied.

"As you kept pointing out to me, it was unlike Emory to go so long without calling, out of courtesy if for no other reason. I still didn't believe anything catastrophic had happened, more like she was punishing me for our argument.

"I drove up here expecting to find her sulking in her motel room. I planned for us to make up, or at least to call a truce until we could get home and sort things out. Who in hell could have foreseen *this*?"

She made soothing sounds. He imagined her hugging his head to her pillowy breasts, running her fingers through his hair, and stroking his cheek. He'd never required or particularly enjoyed cuddling, but it was essential to Alice. Her body, lushly proportioned, seemed to demand that she make good use of what it had been designed for.

As though following the track of his thoughts, she said, "I wish I were with you."

"Wouldn't do."

"I know. That doesn't stop me from wanting it. Where are you now?"

"Some crappy motel. I don't even know the name of it."

She suggested that he find better accommodations. As he explained how he'd come to be in these particular lodgings, he went over to the window and peeped through the split in the tacky drape, halfway expecting to see Grange and Knight sitting in their SUV with the darkly tinted windows, keeping vigil on his room through night vision binoculars.

"Putting me here and covering the bill is their subtle way of telling me that I'm not free to come and go, like they've got to keep an eye on me."

"That's not so surprising, is it? Naturally they're worried about you, your state of mind. And if there's a sudden development, they need to know where to find you in a hurry."

"Maybe."

"Jeff? What?"

She'd picked up on his vexation, and he welcomed the opportunity to unload. "It's almost like they think I had something to do with Emory's disappearance."

"They can't possibly think that!"

"Oh, they can. It's always the husband, isn't it?" He didn't say "cheating husband," but Alice was smart enough to infer the adjective.

In a small voice, she asked, "Have you told them about us?"

"God no. Hell no. I owned up to the fight Emory and I had on Thursday night, but...I don't know. Maybe I'm just being paranoid, but it seemed to me that they read more into it than it actually was. Knight even had the gall to ask if our fight had turned physical."

"It's their job to be suspicious."

"Grange certainly is. He pounced when I mentioned packing a bag before leaving Atlanta, asked if I had counted on staying a while."

"Did you explain how fastidious and persnickety you are about your wardrobe?"

He took that as a rhetorical question. "The two of them also have this good cop/bad cop routine that's so transparent it's almost funny."

"Except that it's not funny, Jeff. None of it. Your wife, my friend, is missing."

"Yes, she's missing. She's missing because she went to a place where she—or any woman—should never have gone alone. I should have kept my mouth shut about it. Trying to talk her out of this trip only made her more determined. You know how strong willed she is. Now we're all suffering the consequences for her bad choices."

"Jeff," she chided softly.

"I'm sorry. That sounded terrible. I'm not myself."

She was quiet for a time, then, "These two detectives said there was no indication that she'd been accosted."

"Not where her car was parked, anyway."

"Which doesn't rule out something dreadful happening to her while she was running, either foul play or an accident that impaired her."

"That's what I keep harping on to them, but..." He hesitated, debating whether or not to bring this up, then said, "They posed another explanation for her disappearance."

"What?"

"It's absurd, but they suggested that Emory met someone up here, a man, and that she's on a lover's getaway. Knight asked me outright if she was unfaithful."

"Do you have reason to suspect that?"

That wasn't the reaction he had anticipated, and it caused him to sputter a laugh. "Jesus, Alice. Not you too? What's good for the goose?"

Apparently she was thinking precisely that. The extended silence at the other end was weighty with implication. Finally she said, "Knowing Emory—"

"It's out of the question."

"I was about to say that it seems highly unlikely."

"If she has another love interest, it's her damn marathons. Not a man. But to her, running is just as orgasmic as fucking. More so, if you want to know the truth."

"I *don't* want to know. I told you from the beginning, Jeff. We can talk about anything, no subject is off-limits, except your personal life with Emory."

"Alice—"

"I never want to hear how wonderful, or lousy, or mediocre the sex is. I don't want to hear about it at all."

"All right! I heard you!" Jesus! Wasn't anybody on his side?

Suddenly she was contrite. "I apologize. The last thing you need is for me to lash out at you."

"Look," he said brusquely, "I need to go."

"Jeff."

"You shouldn't have called. I'm glad you did. But we've talked too long. If anyone checked my phone I'd have to explain this call. I'll be in touch when I can. Good-bye."

"Jeff, wait."

"What?"

"Have you considered..."

"Spit it out, Alice. What?"

"Maybe you should have an attorney present when you talk to them."

Again, not a comment he had anticipated from her. "That's all I need. A lawyer advising me not to answer their questions. That wouldn't appear at all suspicious."

"I just think it would be wise to—"

"No, it would be stupid. Because if these two detectives have got into their pea brains that I'm culpable, retaining a lawyer would seal it. No, Alice. No attorney."

"I'm only trying to help."

"Which I appreciate. But I've got to handle this my way."

"I understand. But please don't shut me out. What can I do?"

He thought about it, then said coldly, "You can stop calling me."

"*Labor?* She told me she'd lost the baby."

He spoke in a hush, but his alarm was apparent. Keeping her voice low, Emory said, "She has." Taking a deep breath, she organized her thoughts into an explanation.

"Lisa estimates that she conceived four and a half months ago. But two *weeks* ago, she miscarried. Being at least sixteen weeks along, she should have consulted a doctor, who would have prescribed medications that cause and accelerate the elimination of tissue.

"It may require several weeks for the body to rid itself of it. Often, if the pregnancy is as advanced as Lisa's was, a D and C is performed. It can be a heartbreaking, even traumatic, time for the patient, but there are no residual health issues."

Apparently uncomfortable with the subject, he pushed his fingers through his hair. "But she didn't see a doctor."

"No. She's suffering now because not all the uterine material was discharged naturally when she miscarried. She didn't receive treatment, or the medications, or a D and C. Her body is trying to expel a sixteen-week fetus on its own, and the contractions are so strong, it's essentially like being in labor."

"Christ." He looked aside before coming back to her. "You're sure there's no longer a baby?"

She was touched by his apparent concern. "I'm sure. She had profuse bleeding, today as well as two weeks ago. And the size of her uterus isn't nearly as large as it would be if she was almost halfway into a pregnancy." She looked over toward the bed. Lisa had stopped crying, but she'd laid her arm across her forehead. "She says she's glad it died."

"How long has this been going on?"

Emory came back around to him. "Today's bleeding? It woke her up this morning and became so significant, as did the cramping, she was forced to tell her aunt and uncle."

"Kindness personified, from what I understand."

"She told you they kicked her out?"

He nodded.

"Leaving her no choice but to call her two cretin brothers and ask them to come get her."

"How long will it take to, uh, get it out?"

"I don't know. I could use the instruments I brought to scrape the uterus, but I'm reluctant to. First, because that's not my area of expertise. Secondly, these are less than sterile conditions. The threat of infection would be too great."

He mulled it over for several moments, then said, "Okay. Bundle her up. We're taking her to the hospital."

"Wait." She placed her hand on his arm. "I also have the emotional stability of my patient to consider. She insists that no one else learn about the baby. When I suggested that you and I drive her and her mother to the nearest medical facility, she threatened to kill herself."

"She was hysterical."

"She was perfectly rational. How willing are you to take a chance on her meaning it?"

He swore under his breath and then released a long breath. "What do you suggest, Doc?"

She looked at her wristwatch. "I suggest we let nature take its course. It's almost two o'clock. The road will present fewer hazards in daylight. Let's reassess at dawn. Maybe between now and then, I can calm her down enough to accept the situation and talk her into telling her mother what's actually going on."

He inched closer and lowered his voice, so there was no chance of Lisa's overhearing. "Come on, Doc, don't you think Pauline knows? She's coarse and uncultured, but she's not stupid."

She gave him a wan smile. "I'm almost certain she knows. And more than likely Lisa knows that she knows. But denial is the only way she can cope right now."

He looked over at the bed, his forehead creased with worry. "She's not in danger of dying, is she?"

"Believe me, if I thought it was an emergency situation, I'd bundle her up and drive the truck myself. But it hasn't reached that level. Her blood pressure is a little high, but her distress is probably the explanation for that. Her bleeding is what is to be expected. I'm monitoring her temperature. It's normal."

To further assuage his worry, she said, "She's frightened and uncomfortable, but her body is responding as it should. Women in third world countries endure this without medications or clinical procedures, and they survive."

He looked around the bedroom. "This qualifies as third world."

"As a precaution, I'm giving her antibiotics."

He tilted his head toward the bed. "Mind if I talk to her?"

"No. You're a hero in her eyes. She said you were about as nice a person as anybody she's ever met."

"She doesn't know me."

"That's what I said." She smiled to let him know that she was teasing. "Go on. I'll give you two a moment."

"Don't open that door."

She looked at it and shuddered. "I have no intention to."

He went to the side of the bed and knelt beside it on one knee, bringing him eye level with Lisa. Emory couldn't hear what he was saying, but Lisa was listening with rapt attention.

Weariness claimed Emory and, despite the shabby condition of the wall, she leaned back against it and closed her eyes. Her head was aching, but she attributed the dull pain to fatigue more than to her concussion. The space between her shoulder blades burned with tension. Considering the events of this night, was it any wonder?

Not too long ago, within a span of time that could be measured in hours rather than days, she'd thought that waking up in a stranger's bed, not knowing where she was or how'd she got there, was the most bizarre thing that could ever happen to her. How wrong she'd been.

"How are *you*?"

Roused by the familiar scratchiness of his whisper, she opened her eyes and was momentarily disoriented. "Gosh, I must have dozed off standing up. I haven't done that since med school."

"Tired?"

"Exhausted."

"Crime takes a toll."

She gave a soft laugh. "Felony for the sake of a patient. There's a first for everything." Then she added, "I better understand the gray area of your morality now."

"*Dark* gray," he said, and she smiled. "Are you hungry?"

"Yes, but I wouldn't eat anything that came out of this house."

"Some water?"

"If you wash the glass first and you're the only one to handle it."

"I wouldn't have it any other way." He moved the chair from beneath the doorknob and was about to open it when she stopped him with a question.

"The brothers were fighting when I came out to get you. What was that about?"

"Me."

"You?"

"Will asked me if I was a homo."

"How crass. What did you say?"

He looked at her for a moment, then removed his hand from the doorknob, placed it around the back of her neck beneath her hair, and pulled her up to receive his kiss—his open-mouthed, exploratory, evocative, and unshy kiss, which started out slow but soon acquired an urgency that was barely contained.

He kissed her like he meant it, like this kiss was going to be the last thing he ever did on earth, and he was going to do it right, thoroughly, and leave nothing wanting.

But she was left wanting, and judging from the rapid rise and fall of his chest and the fever in his eyes when he jerked his head back, he'd been left wanting, too.

Roughly, he said, "I told him no."

The crisis came a little after four o'clock. Lisa gripped her lower abdomen and cried out.

"I know it hurts." Emory had never experienced anything worse than mild menstrual cramps. She'd never conceived, never miscarried, and, if she had, she would have gotten immediate and ideal medical care. The girl's evident suffering affected her beyond her professional objectivity.

After her second cry, the bedroom door was flung open and Pauline marched in. "Mr. Whatshisname there wasn't going to let me in, but short of hog-tying me, he couldn't keep me out."

He who'd been standing guard outside the bedroom looked at Emory with chagrin. "I swear to you that I wouldn't hesitate to hog-tie Norman or Will, but I'm no match for Pauline. I'll be right outside the door." He stepped back and pulled it closed.

When Lisa saw her mother, a look of relief washed over her face, as though she'd been excused from having to make a difficult decision. "Mama?"

She extended her hand. Pauline gripped it as she sat down on the edge of the bed. Looking up at Emory, she said, "I was the eldest, and all my brothers and sisters were born at home. I ain't squeamish. I can massage her belly."

Twenty minutes later, Emory left mother and daughter alone. Pauline was cooing to the girl, her calloused and unmanicured hand amazingly gentle as she smoothed back Lisa's hair from her forehead.

Emory went to the door and opened it. He was there as he'd said he would be, standing sentinel. The brothers were asleep.

Will snored from the sofa. Norman was in the recliner, his head resting against his shoulder, a string of drool dangling from his lower lip.

Emory had the plastic trash can liner, now closed with a tightly tied knot at the top. "This needs to be disposed of. I suggest burning it."

He took it from her without a qualm. "How is Lisa?"

"Much better. I'm close to convincing them that she should have a follow-up physical examination. But I think she'll be all right. I'd like to stay with her for a while longer, just to make sure."

He nodded and turned away to do his chore.

Shortly after that, Emory and Pauline gave Lisa a sponge bath and changed the bedding. The fresh sheets were dingy but clean. Pauline carried out the soiled ones and told Emory she was going to make coffee.

Emory took Lisa's blood pressure, but even before she'd removed the cuff, the girl's head was sunk deep into the pillow and her eyes were closed.

Arching her back to work out the kinks, Emory walked over to the window and looked out. She thought her eyes were playing tricks on her. The sun wasn't up yet, but there was enough predawn light for her to make out a large form, kneeling down beside the dog, stroking its head, and talking to it with words she was certain didn't matter to the abused animal. It was responding to the first kind touch it had probably ever experienced. It ate a morsel of food from his hand, then licked his palm in gratitude.

"Is he your boyfriend?"

Emory looked over toward the bed and was surprised to see that Lisa was awake and observing her. "No. We just met."

"What's his name?"

"He's a very private man."

Lisa studied her for a moment, then said, "You don't know it either, do you?"

She gave the intuitive girl a rueful smile. "No."

"I've seen him working in his yard when we've driven past his place. He always scared me."

"Why?"

"For one thing, he's so big."

"He is."

"And kinda broody looking. I never saw him smile before last night."

"He's not inclined to very often."

"He smiles at me, though. And at Mama. And at you."

She had the knowing look of a woman, and Emory realized that she must have witnessed the kiss, the kiss that caused a curling sensation low in her belly every time she thought about it. The kiss that had lulled and electrified her at the same time. She had never felt safer or more endangered.

The emotions were conflicting, yet on one point she was crystal clear: She hadn't wanted it to end. Despite the situation and the squalid surroundings, she had longed to experience more of his lips, his taste, the bold trespassing of his tongue.

Lisa startled her out of her reverie when she said, "One time, when my brothers dumped a barrel of trash right outside his gate, I told them they were crazy to rile him."

"I think you're probably right." She hesitated, not wanting to place Lisa in an awkward position, but feeling pressured to ask. "Do you know if the three of them have tangled before?"

"Before what?"

"Before he became your neighbor."

"No. I'm sure of that. I've heard Will and Norman talking about him, wondering who he is and what he's up to. Mama reckons he's hiding from the law."

Emory said nothing.

"Or, Mama said, maybe he's hiding from a wife and kids he ran out on."

No bride. No wife. Not ever.

"But I don't think that's it," Lisa said. "I'd sooner believe he was an outlaw than a man who deserted his family."

Emory looked over at her. "Why would you think that?"

"He just don't seem the type. But something's going on there. It's invisible, but you can tell he carries it around with him."

Silently, Emory agreed.

"If I was guessing," Lisa continued, "I'd say he has a mean streak a mile wide. He keeps it under control. But if he ever let it loose, look out."

Without realizing how disturbing her observations were to Emory, she added, "But he's been awful nice to me, from right off when he looked into the truck and saw that I was ailing. He's treated me nice, and not like he expects anything in return. If you know what I mean."

Emory nodded understanding.

Lisa thoughtfully plucked at the frayed hem on the top sheet. "I don't think he's the kind of man who'd mess with me. Take advantage of a woman. You know?"

"No, I'm certain he's not that kind of man." Emory had been with him for three days, and he hadn't taken advantage, even when she'd thrown herself at him. *You almost got me, Doc.*

"What do you make of him, Dr. Smith?"

Emory turned back to the window and watched him scratch the dog behind its ears. He unhooked the chain from its collar. Nuzzling his hand, the dog happily fell into step beside him as he turned and headed back toward the house.

"Honestly, Lisa, I have no idea what to make of him."

Chapter 16

"You warm enough back there?" Sam Knight looked at Jeff through the rearview mirror.

Riding in the backseat of the SUV, with its official markings on the door panels and light bar of the roof, he felt like a caged animal in a circus parade, part of the sideshow, but disliking it intensely. "I'm fine. Thanks."

"Still cold as a witch's tit this morning. But at least the snow has stopped. Let me know if you need more heat."

"I will."

"There's Buddy."

Knight pulled off the road and up to the entrance of a local bakery, where Grange was waiting out front. He was holding a flat box and a white paper sack in his gloved hands, stamping his feet to stay warm. As soon as the SUV came to a stop, he climbed into the passenger seat.

"Lord! It's cold."

"Thanks for volunteering to get our breakfast," Knight said. "Coffee smells good. Pass a cup on back to Jeff. What kind of doughnuts did you get?"

"An assortment."

Knight drove back onto the highway but stayed in the outside lane, driving with care. With so much care, in fact, it was maddening to Jeff.

Grange distributed the coffee and passed the box of doughnuts around. Knight, fortified with a bite of his, addressed Jeff in the mirror. "Dr. James called us this morning."

Grange corrected him, mumbling around a bite. "Dr. Butler."

Knight turned to his partner. "Huh?"

"Dr. Butler's the lady. Dr. James is the man."

"Oh, right," Knight said. "I keep getting their names mixed up. Anyhow, Jeff, she called."

"She called me, too."

"Did she?"

He nodded as he blew on his coffee. "To let me to know that the clinic is offering an award for information."

"That's something, isn't it?" Knight exclaimed. "Twenty-five grand."

Jeff said, "I'm humbled by their generosity. To think that Emory's associates would do that for her. For me."

"Speaks well of both y'all."

"Emory is highly regarded among her colleagues."

"I read about her going to Haiti after the hurricane," Knight said. "Volunteered for weeks at a time."

"She's made three trips and is planning to go again when she can work it into her schedule."

Grange wiped sugar glaze off his fingertips with a paper napkin. "What does she do about her practice when she takes off like that?"

"Other pediatricians cover for her, and they're glad to do it because she never forgets a favor and always returns it."

"Sounds like she's got a kind spirit," Knight said as he reached into the box for a second doughnut. "A genuine humanitarian."

"She is, which is just one of the reasons why I love her. But with all due respect," Jeff said as he folded his half-eaten doughnut into a napkin and replaced the cap on his Styrofoam cup of coffee, "you're telling me things about my wife that I already know. When are you going to tell me something that I don't know? Like why you can't find her and what's being done to remedy that."

"We're working on it."

"So you've said. Dozens of times. But I see no evidence of it."

"There weren't any developments overnight. We're hoping for better luck today."

"You're depending on *luck*? Jesus."

He turned away from the rearview mirror, choosing to look out the window rather than into Knight's woeful eyes. They had exited the main highway and were now on one with only two opposing lanes and an occasional passing lane. It was a twisty road, the curves coming so frequently that the backseat ride was making Jeff carsick.

"Don't be discouraged," Grange said. "We're working on other angles."

"You mentioned those last night," Jeff said. "You failed to specify what those angles are."

"Well, for one, there's the money."

Jeff's head snapped around to Grange, who was watching him over the back of his seat.

"Emory's money," the detective clarified, as if Jeff didn't know to whose money he referred.

"Your wife is loaded," Knight said. "Family fortune. She could up and quit and never have to ask another kid to say 'aah.'" He laughed. "If I was that rich, I'd never turn a lick."

"That's offensive," Jeff snapped.

Knight looked at him in the mirror. "Sorry, Jeff, I didn't mean—"

"Emory would be sorely offended by remarks like that. She works harder because of her inheritance."

"Is that right?"

"She never mentions her wealth, much less flaunts it. In fact she's almost apologetic about it."

Grange said, "Which explains why she gives so much of it away."

"She's pledged two hundred grand to an upcoming marathon." Knight addressed the information to his partner, but Jeff realized the older man had said it for his benefit. "Might take some time," he went on, "but I guess if she applied herself to it, she could eventually give *all* her money away."

"Which wouldn't leave any left over for her beneficiary." Grange looked back at Jeff. "Which happens to be you, doesn't it?"

He gave the smug deputy an icy glare. "I believe you already know the answer to that."

"Well, Jeff, we have to check these things out. It's routine when a spouse goes missing."

The folksier Knight's tone became, the less Jeff liked and trusted it. Didn't they realize that he was smart enough to know when he was being played? He said, "If you've checked out Emory's finances, then you know that I don't manage her portfolio. In fact, all her investments are with another firm."

"Yeah, the top guy at your place of business told me that."

He gave Knight a sharp look in the rearview mirror. "Excuse me?"

"You had led your company to believe that she would turn all her money matters over to your firm when y'all got married. But she didn't. That's what your boss told me anyway."

"He told *you*?"

Knight nodded. "When I called him yesterday and asked him who held the reins for Emory's fortune."

It crawled all over Jeff to learn that yesterday, while for hours on end he'd been cooling his heels in the lobby of the Hicksville sheriff's office, he was being investigated and talked about within his firm.

Which meant that his coworkers knew it wasn't sickness that had kept him out of the office. They'd known the nature of the "family emergency" even before they'd heard about Emory's disappearance on the news this morning. These yokels had made him out to be a liar to his firm's senior partner, and that made him livid.

"You don't manage her money," Grange was saying, "but you get it if she predeceases you, correct?"

"If you had asked me, I would have told you that," Jeff said, barely keeping his fury under control. "You wouldn't have had to call my firm and bothered my coworkers with questions that have nothing to do with Emory's disappearance."

"We've got to cover every angle," Grange said.

"Speaking of," Knight said, "what's the name of that drug you wanted Emory to endorse?"

"How did you know about that?"

"There were a lot of e-mails on her computer about it. Back and forth, between you, the pharmaceutical company, your wife. Going back more than a year. What was that all about?"

"Since you seem to already know, why don't you tell me?"

"Be easier if you'd just put it in a nutshell for us," Knight said. "We've got nothing else to do while we're riding."

It occurred to Jeff that perhaps he had underestimated these two. By an act of will, he brought his temper under control, and, when he spoke, he made himself sound bored. "The company had gone through all the steps with the FDA—and there are many—and had received approval to conduct patient trials."

"What was the drug for?"

"To help prevent obesity in children who are genetically predisposed. Emory was invited to be one of the participating physicians."

Grange said, "But when the trial was over, she didn't endorse it."

"In her opinion, the side effects weren't worth the benefits derived from the medication."

"In other words, it did more harm than good."

"Those other words are yours, detective," Jeff said. "Not Emory's."

Knight said, "You had encouraged clients to invest heavily in this drug."

"No," Jeff said, drawing out the word. "I encouraged clients to invest in a company that is on the leading edge of pharmaceutical breakthroughs that target current medical problems, like childhood obesity, which affect millions of people globally, not only healthwise, but in every other way. Culturally, socially, financially, and so on."

Knight chuckled. "Skim off the BS, Jeff. The SEC's not eavesdropping. Translated, a high sign from your wife would have gone a long way toward helping make your clients, and thereby you, a lot of money."

"Emory hasn't yet given the drug either a thumbs-up or a thumbs-down. She merely withheld her endorsement pending further study."

Knight and his partner exchanged a look that indicated further study of this issue was also pending. Jeff looked away as though unperturbed.

"Oh, by the way," Knight said, "would you mind if we sent some guys over to the motel to take a look inside your car?"

"My car? What the hell for? Do you have a warrant?"

"Do we need one?"

"No. Search all you want. Strip it. While you're at it, search my house, too. Send cadaver-sniffing dogs. Be sure to check the pine grove at the back of our property. That's an excellent place for a grave."

Knight looked over at Grange. "Told you he'd be upset."

"I'm not upset."

But to Jeff's own ears, he sounded upset. Rather than give them the satisfaction of watching him seethe, he turned his head to stare out the window. For the next half hour, they drove with only the two in front occasionally exchanging a few words. Nothing important was discussed.

The gaining altitude and curviness of the road increased Jeff's carsickness. The drop-offs where there were no guard rails made him more anxious than he already was. He wished he hadn't agreed to come along. The day had started off badly.

He hadn't slept well and had gotten up before his alarm and turned on the TV. As expected, all the Atlanta stations covered the story of Emory's disappearance. Within minutes of the broadcasts, his phone had begun to ring. Acquaintances—some he barely knew—were clamoring to know more. He'd answered only a few of those calls, letting most go to voice mail.

While waiting for Knight to pick him up, he'd ruminated on everything that had been said and tried not to put too much stock in the detectives' apparent suspicion. By Knight's own admission, putting the spouse under a microscope was routine. If he let their insinuations rattle him, they would assume he was guilty.

But with all this talk of Emory's finances, and now the search of his car, he was second-guessing his decision not to retain an attorney, as Alice had suggested.

She had also called this morning in spite of his telling her not to. They'd kept the conversation brief, but he was angry at her for defying him, and even angrier at himself for giving in and answering when her number came up on his phone.

He was angry at the pair of small-time detectives who apparently thought he was too dense to see through the ludicrous law-and-order charade they were playing with him.

Mostly, he was angry at Emory. It was her fault that he was being made to suffer through this.

<hr />

"Know what I can't get over?" Norman, who'd been eating a bowl of cereal at the dining table, tipped his chair on its back legs. "What I can't get over is you being so stingy with your name. Guess I'll just keep on calling you neighbor."

"Your mother called me Dr. Smith's guard. Guard, neighbor, whatever is fine with me." He had accepted Pauline's offer of a cup of coffee because the water to brew it had reached a boiling point and he'd washed the cup himself. Under Norman's thoughtful stare, he blew on the hot coffee and took a sip. "But don't think too hard about it, Norman. You might strain something."

With a good-natured grin, Norman picked up his bowl and spooned another bite. "What I figure is, you're a fugitive from justice."

"Is that what you figure?"

"Me too," said Will, who glowered at him from what seemed to be his permanent place on the couch.

"You can tell us," Norman said in a wheedling tone. "We've had brushes with the law ourselves."

"Have you?"

"You wouldn't believe some of the stunts we've pulled."

"Shut the hell up, Norman," Will said.

But Norman was in an expansive mood. "I did three months in county for lifting an old lady's purse out of her shopping cart in the grocery store."

He didn't react.

"Another time, we stole some retreads from an old guy who runs the junkyard out on sixty-four. Then—swear to God if this ain't the truth—we sold 'em back to him a week later for twenty bucks profit. Old coot never knew he was took."

He drew a deep breath as though singularly unimpressed.

"Will got into a fight with this guy over a poker game. We lit into him good. Took four men to pull us off him. I got probation. Will served a few months for assault. But the other guy is still regrettin' calling my baby brother a cheat. Right, Will?"

"And we ain't done with him either," Will said.

"Is that right?" he asked, arching an eyebrow, feeling it was time to exhibit some interest in their exploits. "What do you have planned for him?"

"None of your damn business."

"Don't be so touchy, Will," Norman said. "He's just making friendly conversation, remember?" Then, coming back to him, he said, "Turnabout's fair play. Come on. You can tell us. What'd you do?"

He drank from his cup of coffee.

"Did you—" Holding his bowl in one hand, Norman aimed his other index finger at him and mimicked firing a pistol. "Put somebody's lights out?"

"Your cereal is getting soggy."

From the sofa, Will said, "Aw hell, Norman, he ain't gonna confess anything to you. Besides, I'll bet there's nothing to confess. He's not near as tough as he makes out."

"Maybe you're right." But Norman continued to regard him speculatively as he held the bowl against his chest and shoveled cereal into his mouth.

Staring into his coffee, he asked, "What about you?"

Norman stopped chewing. "Whut?"

He raised his head and included Will in the look he divided between them. "Either one of you ever killed anybody?"

Norman shrugged. "Never had to."

"Yet," Will added.

"Well, I wouldn't be too eager to if I were you."

"Meaning you have." Norman chortled. "See, Will? Told you."

"He's just talking big."

Norman, eyeing him up and down, said, "I've known a lot of people who needed killing."

"So have I."

"But you don't recommend it. Why's that?"

"Killing isn't all it's cracked up to be, like you said about the state of Virginia." He'd dropped the bait. He wondered if they'd bite. With seeming nonchalance, he wandered into the kitchen and poured himself a refill. "You never told me what kind of work you did up there."

"Worked for a freight company. Long-haul trucks."

"Were you drivers?"

"Naw." Norman wiped milk off his lips with the back of his hand. "Worked the warehouse."

"Crap job," Will contributed. He'd been channel surfing the muted TV. Finding a station rerunning an episode of *Gilligan's Island*, he settled in to watch. The shotgun was now propped against the arm of the sofa, barrel up, close to Will's head.

Norman picked at a cereal flake that had dropped onto his shirt and stuck there. "That company where we was working made history, though."

With slow, measured motions, he returned the coffee carafe to the hotplate. "How so?"

"It was in Westboro. You ever heard of it? The shooting there? Guy with a grudge comes into the place, blasted it all to hell, killed a bunch of people."

He turned back around and nodded at Norman. "I heard about it."

"Well, we was laid off not more'n a week before it happened. Missed all the excitement."

"You ask me, all the men on that island were pussies," Will scoffed. "I'd've nailed Ginger soon as we got to dry land." He switched channels.

Norman slurped milk directly from the bowl. "If I'd been ol' Gilligan, Mary Ann's ass wouldn't've stood a chance."

Will hooted from across the room. "You always did prefer the back door."

"I'd like to go in through Dr. Smith's back door."

Both brothers eyed him, smirking, waiting to see how he would react. Rather than be goaded, he ignored them, and instead he looked out the grimy window above the kitchen sink as though checking the weather. Then, carrying his coffee with him, he headed for the bedroom.

"What's going on in there, anyhow?" Norman asked, nodding toward the door, which had remained closed throughout the night.

"Your sister's being seen to."

"We know that," Will groused. "What's taking so friggin' long?"

"Have we worn out our welcome?"

"Far as I'm concerned, you weren't never welcome."

"We'll be on our way before long," he said. "Oh, Norman?"

"Huh?"

"Better watch that chair."

"Huh?"

He kicked the back legs out from underneath the chair. Norman went over backward, landing hard and splashing his enraged face with what was left of the milk in his cereal bowl.

Will, reacting too quickly to think about the shotgun, rolled off the sofa and came up like a sprinter leaving the blocks.

He dropped his cup of coffee in time to catch Will's chin with an uppercut that sent him staggering backward. Moving quickly, crushing the coffee cup beneath his boot, he grabbed the shotgun, swung it up, and aimed it at the brothers, freezing them in their tracks as they were lunging for him.

Emory opened the bedroom door. "What's going on?"

Keeping his eyes on the brothers, who were still poised to attack, he backed his way over to Emory where she stood in the open door. "You feel okay about leaving Lisa for the time being?"

"Yes, I think she'll be all right."

"Good."

"Sure as hell, I'm gonna kill you," Will said through his clenched teeth.

"Not today, you're not."

He took the pistol from his waistband and passed it to Emory. "If either of them moves, don't stop to think about it. Pull the trigger. Got it?"

———

Dumbfounded, she nodded her head once. He slipped past her into the bedroom.

Norman and Will stood facing her, breathing hard with wrath, reminding her of snorting bulls. Norman said, "Who is that son of a bitch?"

"I don't know."

"Bull. Shit," Will said. "You two are in cahoots. Barging in here like you own the damn place. What are you up to?"

"All I did was come here to take care of your sister."

"She would've done all right without you."

"Possibly, but I'm glad I could help."

Norman asked, "You really a doctor?"

"Yes."

"Yeah, well I think you're lying," Will said, pugnaciously raising his chin where a fist-sized bruise was forming. "What's his story?"

The subject of the question moved up behind her, closed his left hand around her biceps, and pushed her forward. "Don't let go of that pistol." Emory kept her eyes forward as he propelled her across the living room and out the door. "Get in the truck."

Before releasing her arm, he gave her a little push and she started down the porch steps. She heard Will say, "He's stealing our shotgun!"

Beneath the tree, the dog stood up and wagged his tail. Apparently she'd become his friend by association. When she reached the pickup, she opened the passenger door and looked back to see him still on the porch, watching her while guarding the door with the shotgun.

"Why aren't you coming?" she asked. "What are you going to do?"

"Get in the truck and don't get out."

She hesitated.

Enunciating, he said, "Get in and shut the door."

She climbed in and pulled the door closed. He waited until he was sure she would stay, then turned and disappeared through the front door. A few seconds later, there was a shotgun blast that sounded like an explosion in the morning air.

It was followed by a second.

Chapter 17

Emory pushed open the door, leaped from the truck, and ran toward the house, colliding with her scowling protector as he came down the steps. "Dammit, I told you to stay in the truck." He spun her around and thrust her in that direction.

"You shot them!"

"No I didn't."

No, he hadn't.

Because she could hear the Floyds' obscenity-laced tirade, then both burst through the front door. Fury made Will clumsy as he tried to reload the shotgun. Norman, in stocking feet, slipped on one of the porch steps.

Emory was hoisted none too gently into the cab of the pickup, then its owner came around, got in, and started the engine, every motion efficient and controlled, as though he didn't have two bloodthirsty men on his heels.

He accelerated so hard that the tires spun before gaining traction. They sped out the drive, leaving the Floyds shaking their fists and yelling threats.

Emory was paralyzed with disbelief. They rode in silence for the brief time it took to reach his cabin. He got out and opened the gate, then drove the truck to its usual parking space. Getting out again, he went over to a chopping block and worked the ax blade from the heavily notched surface.

She tracked his progress across the yard, back through the gate, and across the road to the pickup truck with the listing tree still embedded in its grill. He went around to all four tires, methodically hacking great gashes in them.

Then he came back through the gate and latched the padlock, testing it with a sharp tug to make certain that it was secure. After replacing the ax in the chopping block, he came back to the truck, opened the passenger door, and reached inside.

Instinctively, she recoiled. He frowned at her. "I want my pistol back."

She'd forgotten she still had it. Her right hand was clutching it in a cold death grip. "Are you going to shoot somebody?"

"Not before breakfast."

This time when he reached for it, she let it go. He stuck it back into his waistband as he turned and started toward the cabin.

She stepped out of the truck and looked back at the gate, considering if she should climb the fence and take off running. He had lied about having neighbors. In addition to the Floyds, surely there would be others reasonably nearby.

But the road was steep, with too many switchbacks to keep count of. It intersected with other rural roads that were similarly daunting. Her right foot was throbbing from having stood at Lisa's bedside most of the night. Her head was muzzy from lack of sleep. The temperature had to be well below freezing. Which probably wouldn't be a problem because he could catch her before she'd gone fifty yards.

Realizing the foolhardiness and futility of even attempting to escape, she followed him inside.

He was crouched in front of the grate shoveling cold ashes aside. He laid kindling and, when it caught, added logs. "It'll take a while to get warm in here. Till it does, you'd better keep the coat on."

His coat. She had removed it in order to treat Lisa but had put it back on shortly before they left. Suddenly it felt heavy and cumbersome, but she was still glad for the warmth and sense of protection it provided.

He replaced the fire screen and turned to face her. "Are you still hungry?"

"Hungry?" She stared at him with bewilderment. "I don't get you at all. You commit burglary in order to help a young woman you don't even know. You're gentle enough to convert a vicious dog into a pal. But then you fire a shotgun at two men, unprovoked."

"It wasn't unprovoked."

"When we left, you definitely had the upper hand. You didn't have to go back inside at all."

"Yeah, I did."

"Why?"

"Because of you."

"Me?"

"They'd made some crude references to you."

"You should have ignored them."

"I didn't want to."

"What did you expect? Refinement? They're ignorant and scurvy, and—"

"They're shit is what they are."

"Okay, they're lowlifes. Does that justify shooting at them?"

"I didn't shoot at them. If I had, they'd be dead."

"Then why fire the shotgun at all?"

She tried to stare him down, but, to her consternation, he turned away. "Do you want to use the shower first, or should I go ahead?"

Furious over his being so indifferent to her outrage, she went after him and grabbed his sleeve, bringing him around. "Damn you, answer me!"

"What?"

"Tell me why you fired the shotgun. And don't claim it was self-defense."

"I wasn't going to."

"Then why'd you do it? Just to make a point?"

He remained immutable.

"Tell me!"

"*I shot out the TV!*"

Stunned by both his shout and the explanation, she fell back a step, having a wild compulsion to laugh. "The TV? Why?"

He pulled his sleeve from her grip. "So they wouldn't see your picture on it."

———◆———

By the time he emerged from the bathroom, freshly showered and wearing clean clothes, she was serving up the scrambled eggs and bacon she'd prepared. After all, it was morning. Most people were having breakfast at this time of day. Breakfast was the one conventional thing in this otherwise Looking-Glass universe in which she was now living.

As though he hadn't dropped a bombshell before retreating to the bathroom, he thanked her for the plate of food she set down on the table in front of him. As he tucked in, she motioned toward a plate stacked with slices of toast. "The toaster works better. It popped them up."

"Good. The repair saved me from having to buy a new one."

Performing ordinary tasks like making toast and placing the stick of butter on a dish had given her a self-delusional sense of control over her situation. She knew he noticed the dish as he knifed a pat of butter and spread it over his toast. He acknowledged it with a glance toward her but didn't comment.

Halfway through the meal, he asked if she wanted another cup of coffee.

"If you're getting up, please."

He came back to the table with their refills, then sat down, straddling the seat of his chair in the way of a man. Any man. A normal, nonviolent man. A man who hadn't shot out the TV of his redneck neighbors at dawn.

No longer able to hold back the question, she blurted, "My picture was on TV?"

"I saw it on our way out. That's why I had to go back inside and take care of it."

"Were they saying—"

"I don't know what they were saying. The audio was muted." He took a sip of coffee, watching her through the steam rising out of the cup. "But in big yellow letters across the bottom of the screen was a notice of a reward. Twenty-five thousand."

"Who put up the reward? Jeff?"

He shrugged. "But I couldn't let the Floyd brothers see that. God knows what they'd have done in order to claim the reward."

"Why didn't you explain this to me right away? Why did you let me go on the way I did?"

He leaned back in his chair. "I wanted to learn what you really think of me. Now I know. You have a very low opinion."

"That's not true."

He made a scoffing sound.

"Well, can you blame me? Pauline, who only met you last night, conjectured that you're a fugitive."

"She tell you that?"

"Lisa did."

"That seems to be the consensus among them. Norman bragged about his lawbreaking and urged me to swap stories with him."

"What did you tell them?"

He didn't answer.

"Nothing," she said, guessing but knowing she was correct.

He asked, "Lisa tell you anything else?"

She related the context of their conversation about him. He didn't comment on the girl believing him to be an outlaw over a wife deserter, nor did he say anything in response to her qualifying him as a man who wouldn't expect sexual favors in exchange for kindness.

"She holds you in high esteem," Emory said. "But you remain a puzzle to her. She asked me what I made of you."

He waited, unmoving and expressionless.

"I'll tell you what I told Lisa. I don't know what to make of you."

He kept his level gaze on her a few moments longer, then got up and carried his empty dishes to the sink. They worked side by side to clean the kitchen. It was amazing to her that, given the events of the last twelve hours, the scene they were now enacting was so commonplace. They could be any couple anywhere, going about a morning routine.

Except that established couples knew what to expect from each other. There might be an occasional surprise, but typically one didn't astonish the other with extraordinary acts of kindness followed by outbursts of violence.

And established couples usually didn't kiss with the blatant eroticism with which he'd kissed her last night. Not unless the partners were skin to skin, and the kiss was a prelude to the lovemaking it intimated.

When the last dish was put away, she said, "If you don't mind me borrowing another shirt..."

"Help yourself."

On her way to the bathroom, she took a shirt and a pair of socks from the chest of drawers. Her running clothes smelled of the Floyds' house. It was a relief to peel them off. She put them in the sink to soak while she showered and washed her hair. The goose egg was barely a bump, and, except for a little tenderness, she wouldn't have known the cut was there.

He'd said it wouldn't require stitches in order to close, and she wondered now how he had known that. Maybe he'd planned it that way. Maybe he had struck her just hard enough to knock her unconscious, but not so hard as to cause a gash that required stitches.

She wondered where he'd hidden the rock.

She wrung out her clothes and took them with her into the main room. As before, she moved one of the dining chairs near the hearth and draped the garments over the rungs of the ladder-back. She sat on the hearth and finger-combed her hair until it had partially dried.

"I should dry it completely," she said. "But I can't hold my head up any longer."

He marked his place in the book he'd been reading and set it on the table. "I'm whipped, too." He left his recliner and went to each window, pulling down shades behind the muslin curtains, making the room darker, leaving the end table lamp and the fireplace the only sources of light.

"How do you know the Floyds won't come here seeking retribution for their TV?"

"If they planned to attack today, they'd already be here."

"They're on foot."

"That's not what's holding them back. Underneath all the swagger, they're cowards."

"How do you know?"

"I know the type."

"You know *them*. From somewhere. From something." She waited for a second or two, then prodded him for a response. "Don't you?"

"Go to sleep, Doc."

Too weary to engage in an argument with a stone wall, she got into bed and pulled the covers over her. He returned to his recliner, switched out the lamp, and covered himself with a quilt. Ponderous minutes ticked by. As tired as she was, she couldn't relax. Every muscle of her body remained rigid, her mind in turmoil, her emotions clashing.

She knew that he wasn't sleeping either. If she opened her eyes, she would no doubt find his on her: ever watchful, penetrating in their intensity, remarkably still except for the flickering reflection of the firelight.

Had he not shot out their television, the Floyds might have noticed the bulletin, called the police, reported her whereabouts, and collected their reward. By now she would have been in familiar surroundings, reunited with Jeff and resuming her ordinary life.

Instead she was snuggled into the bed of this unnamed man, who by turns mystified, aroused, and appalled her.

Regardless of her intention to keep her eyes closed, they opened of their own accord. As expected, he was looking directly at her. "Before we left, you went back into the bedroom."

"I wanted a private moment with Lisa."

"What for?" When he didn't say anything, she came up on her elbows so she could see him better. "What for?"

He took a long time to answer. "I asked which of her brothers had fathered the baby. She told me it could have been either."

Chapter 18

It rained a lot in Seattle. What a hell of an understatement that was.

Special Agent Jack Connell's flight out of LaGuardia had been delayed for several hours due to sleet, snow, and high winds. He almost preferred that wintry mix to this weather. His experience with it so far—and he was just now driving the rental car off the lot at Sea-Tac—led him to believe that the whole damn Pacific Northwest was underwater.

Driving from the airport into the city, he kept one eye on the rain-washed freeway while trying to find the defroster switch on the unfamiliar dashboard. Miraculously, without killing either himself or another motorist, he made it through downtown and to the ferry pier.

Any scenery he might have enjoyed on a sunny day was ob- scured by a downpour and dense fog. The city was swallowed by it within minutes of the ferry's departure, and what lay ahead was as much of a great unknown as the Atlantic Ocean had been to fifteenth-century sailors.

He'd never much cared for boats. Boats chugging through fog

he cared for even less. It was an hour and a half before his destination port was announced, and he was relieved to drive back onto terra firma. Or what would have been firma if it hadn't been waterlogged.

He checked into his hotel and, without even taking the time to settle into his room or unpack his suitcase, he braved the weather again. Using the car's GPS he drove straight to the residence of one Grace Kent.

It was a two-story house, white clapboard with gray shutters flanking the windows on both levels. The front door was red, and on the exterior wall to the side of it was a brass mailbox.

He considered going up to the door and checking to see what kind of correspondence had been delivered to her that day. But discretion being the better part of valor and all that, he decided against taking the risk. He instead drove to the end of the block, where he parked beneath the rain-laden branches of a giant conifer.

More than three hours elapsed. Just before six o'clock, a minivan pulled into the driveway and into the garage, which was opened with a remote. The door was lowered before Jack could see who was inside the van.

But a few minutes later when the front door was pulled open, he grabbed his camera and focused the telephoto lens on the woman who came out to get her mail.

Grace Kent was Rebecca Watson. No question.

This wasn't a baby step closer to his quarry. This was a giant leap.

———

Sam Knight leaned far back in his desk chair and stacked his hands on the top of his pot belly. "What do you think?"

Without so much as a blink, Grange replied, "Guilty as hell."

They were both weary from spending an entire day actively

involved in the search for Emory Charbonneau. Most of the time had been spent outdoors fending off the cold, or in the SUV trying to warm up while listening to Jeff Surrey cast aspersions on their aptitude.

They'd dropped him at the motel, another source of complaint, and had returned to the office to assess the day's lack of progress before heading for home and grabbing a few winks before resuming in the predawn hours.

"He's guilty, all right," Knight said. "But being an asshole isn't a criminal offense."

"They should pass a law just for him."

Knight chuckled, though it wasn't a laughing matter. He picked up a rubber band and began stretching it around his fingers. "You think he killed her and hid the body."

"Instant divorce. A lot less hassle, especially when there's a sizeable estate involved."

"Which he would inherit."

"That would be sufficient motive, but maybe not his only one."

"Okay, I'll bite."

Grange was eager to expand. "She didn't move her pot of gold over to his money management firm when they married. Nor has she endorsed that drug, which he's talked up to his clients as a sound investment."

"From a professional standpoint," Knight said thoughtfully, "that's two strikes against Jeff. She's made him look bad and might have cost him a partnership."

"On a personal level, it's just as bad. She outshines him on every front. She's well known for her philanthropy. In all the write-ups about her, his name is always a footnote. She's beloved by her patients, but his clients blame him if the economic news isn't good."

"He's jealous of her success as a human being."

"Resentment in addition to the money angle." Grange shrugged. "Seems a no-brainer."

"The no-brainer part bothers me," Knight said. "It's almost too obvious. Plus, we don't have a body, a smoking gun, or the suspect's opportunity to do her in. Last time I checked, stuff like that comes in handy when you go to a DA and try to get somebody indicted for wife-killing. Until we get more, we essentially don't have anything. We may never get anything either." He looked at the large map on the wall and sighed. "She could be anywhere."

The media had called the search for Dr. Emory Charbonneau a "coordinated effort," which was a misnomer to many, and a joke to Sergeant Detective Sam Knight. Coordination was almost nonexistent because every law enforcement agency within a tri-state area was involved, and each had its own agenda, personnel problems, budget considerations, and general stupidity. There were many dedicated and determined officers, but their efforts were often undermined by those not so sharp or dutiful, of which there were also many.

Then there were the hundreds of volunteers, each with a reason all their own for joining the search, not the least of which was the twenty-five-thousand-dollar reward. Knight was just jaded enough to believe that had induced many to sign on.

But even if the volunteers' willingness to withstand hostile terrain and subfreezing temperatures was purely altruistic, one had to worry about one of them stumbling over Emory Charbonneau's body, literally, and compromising a crime scene.

Given all that, the margin of error was oceanic in scope, and snafus were virtually guaranteed.

Meanwhile, Grange was convinced the husband was the culprit and that her remains wouldn't be found until Jeff gave up and told them where to look. Unhappily, Sam conceded that his partner was probably right.

"His Saturday is iffy," Grange said. "Where was he all day?"

"You heard the man. He puttered around the house, then ran some errands."

"Somehow puttering and Jeff Surrey just don't jibe. Also, he can't produce anybody with whom he came into contact," Grange reminded him. "Not for the entire day. Nobody like a barber or a merchant who would remember him. Then on Sunday, he's also underground until midafternoon when he started calling around and leaving messages, asking if anyone had heard from Emory."

Knight picked up the thread. "He becomes the troubled husband, but only after a significant amount of time had elapsed."

"Playacting. All for show."

"So how'd he do it?" Knight asked. "When?"

"Mind if I take a stab?"

Knight gestured for him to surmise out loud.

"Okay, Emory does her run on Saturday, as scheduled. She lets Jeff know she's staying over. He drives up here, and they meet at a prearranged place and time. He lays it on thick. 'Honey, I'm sorry. I should have been more understanding about your marathon training schedule. Let's kiss and make up.'"

"All the while, he's waiting for the moment to whack her by whatever method."

Grange nodded. "He disposes of the body, then goes back to Atlanta. Next day, Sunday, he starts calling around for her, then returns to Drakeland and puts on the concerned act at the motel, the café, and on his first visit to this office. 'My wife hasn't come home. Somebody help me.'"

"And he didn't even say please," Knight said.

"If he had, we'd have known right off that it was all an act."

The rubber band was getting quite a workout by Knight's fingers. "Sounds good, but it's hot air in terms of evidence. The crime scene unit went over every millimeter of his car."

Jeff had seen through their "it's just routine" ruse. He'd balked, but not as vociferously as Knight would have expected, and most of his protests centered around the damage likely to be done to his custom leather interior. He was assured that the department was bonded to cover any unlikely damages.

Then, as though it had been his prerogative to refuse them access, he'd said, "Fine, search it. It's a waste of time and manpower, but I've got nothing to hide."

And possibly he didn't. Nothing incriminating had been found. No blood, fibers, hair, chemicals, chemical smell to indicate that he'd cleaned up after himself, or a bad smell like that of a dead body.

They were relieved that they'd found nothing to indicate that bodily harm had been done to Dr. Charbonneau. At the same time, it had been a letdown to come away empty-handed. All their questions remained unanswered.

Knight said, "Bother you that he didn't demand a lawyer, a search warrant?"

"It bothers you, obviously."

"It does. A guy like him, cool as a cucumber, you'd've thought he'd've lawyered up at the get-go."

"But he's savvy enough to know that would sharpen our interest in him."

"Maybe. But what it says to me is that he knew we weren't going to find anything in his car. So, if he did kill her, he left her at the scene. Also—"

Grange groaned at the thought of there being another out for Jeff Surrey.

"Also," Knight continued, "he handed over his cell phone."

"He quibbled."

"Not much. Mostly facial expressions showing his displeasure. He didn't give us as much argument as you'd expect from a man who's got the murder of his wife to cover up."

"So what's that mean?" Grange asked.

"It means he's either innocent and just looks guilty or he's goddamn smart."

"I'm thinking the latter."

"Me too. But we've got to crack him."

Grange tapped the eraser end of a pencil on the desk. "Could it be that *Alice* is better friends with him than with Emory?"

Knight popped his rubber band against his fingers. "An affair? Jeff?"

"You think it's beyond him?"

"No, I just can't imagine him working up enough emotion or blood flow to get hard."

"For some men getting hard isn't about flesh."

Thinking about it, Knight tilted his head to one side. "I guess. Power. Control."

"Cruelty."

"I'm old-fashioned. I like flesh."

Grange smiled, then turned serious again. "Over the past couple days, there were"—he paused to check his notes—"five calls back and forth between the two of them."

"She's a good friend and client."

"That he talks to late at night? First thing this morning?"

"He explained those calls. Alice is concerned about Emory. 'Extremely,' to quote him."

Grange nodded. "She would be either way, though."

"Either way?"

"If she's a friend to both, then, in these circumstances, naturally she would be concerned about them both. Extremely. But she would also be concerned if her lover had gotten rid of his wife—with or without her prior knowledge—in order to clear the way for them to be together."

Knight mulled it over for a ten count. "Tomorrow, while I'm babysitting Jeff, you drive down to Atlanta, canvass her neighbors, ask if she had any visitors on Friday and Saturday while Emory was out of town."

Grange grinned. "Bet you a twenty that there will have been sightings of Jeff's fancy car with the custom leather interior."

Chapter 19

⫷⫸

D_{oc?"}

Emory tilted her head down to the hand resting on her shoulder and rubbed her cheek against the back of it.

"Are you going to wake up or sleep through?"

"Hmm?"

She came awake slowly and opened her eyes. The hand she was resting her cheek against was attached to a long arm covered in ivory cable knit, attached to a broad shoulder that blocked her view of the ceiling.

He was bent over her, his face close. Firelight cast his features in sharp relief, highlighting his cheekbones and strong chin, accenting the silver strands in his hair but etching deeper the lines bracketing his stern lips and making mysterious lairs of his eye sockets.

She wanted desperately for him to kiss her.

He withdrew his hand and backed away from the bed. She sat up. The window shades were still down, but there was no daylight limning the edges of them. Groggy and disoriented, she asked, "What time is it?"

"Six thirty. You pretty much slept the day away."

"I can't believe I slept that long."

"You had a rough go of it last night. I didn't know whether to wake you or not."

"I'm glad you did."

"Your tights." He passed them to her.

She threw off the covers, got up, and went into the bathroom. She used the toilet, pulled on her tights, rinsed her mouth out, and ran a hand through her hair, which had dried crazily and in tangles because she had gone to bed with it damp.

When she came out of the bathroom, he was standing in front of the bookshelves, perusing the titles. She went over to the fireplace and checked her running top and jacket. "Still damp," she said. "I'll have to wear your shirt for a while longer."

He didn't say anything. There was a broodiness to his silence that compelled her to fill it. "In fact, I'm a right mess. No moisturizer for three days. My hair a riot. If you ever saw me looking like my normal self, you wouldn't recognize me."

Keeping his back to her, he said, "I'd recognize you."

His somber tone and standoffishness implied a subtext to his simple statement, and when she realized what it was, dejection settled over her as heavily as his coat had felt earlier. "But that will never happen, will it? Once I go home, we'll never see each other again."

"No."

He didn't elaborate. He didn't make it conditional. He declared it as a foregone conclusion.

She didn't know what to say, and even if she had, she wasn't sure she could speak. Her throat was tight with an emotion she shouldn't be feeling. At the prospect of returning home, she should be experiencing a sense of relief and happy anticipation. Instead, she felt desolate.

Of course, once she resumed her life, she would get over this silly and inexplicable sadness. She loved her work and her patients. She had the marathon to look forward to. People were counting on her. Once she got home, she would have no time to waste. She would need to plunge right in and make up for lost time, for the time she'd spent here.

Soon, these past few days would seem like a dream.

But why did she feel as if she were waking up before the dream reached a satisfying conclusion?

Breaking into her thoughts, he said, "If you want something to eat, help yourself."

"I'm not hungry."

Apparently he wasn't either. The kitchen area was dark. He pulled a book from one of the shelves and carried it with him to the recliner.

She said, "Perhaps you aren't as confident of the Floyds' intentions as you wanted me to believe."

When he looked up at her, she nodded down at the pistol that was on the end table, the lamp shining down on it, well within his reach. "No sign of them," he said. "But I might have been wrong."

She sat down on the sofa. "How did you know it was Lisa's brothers?"

Absently, he ran his fingertips over the title embossed on the book cover. "I didn't until she told me. She was so dead set against anyone knowing about the baby, even though she'd lost it. I guess any fifteen-year-old in that situation would be afraid of being found out. But she was particularly insistent that Pauline not know about it.

"Meanwhile, those two jackasses were drinking beer and actually seemed amused over her situation. Suddenly I realized why. It was their inside joke. I hoped I was wrong. But when I asked Lisa straight out, she started crying and told me."

Emory hugged her elbows. "Was it an isolated incident?" she asked hopefully.

"No. Been going on for a long time, she said."

"How could Pauline be blind to it?"

"She knows, Doc. Of course she does. She hasn't acknowledged it, probably not even to herself, but she knows. Why do you think she sent Lisa to live with her sister and brother-in-law in town?"

Emory propped her elbows on her knees and held her head between her hands. "It's obscene. You read about it, hear stories about it on the news, but it's hard for me to believe that things like this actually happen."

He gave a mirthless laugh. "Oh, they happen. Worse than this. Your nice, sanitary world protects you from the ugly side of our society."

She lowered her hands. "Don't you dare do that."

"What?"

"Insult me like that."

"I wasn't—"

"Yes you were." She stood up. "I can't help it that my parents were affluent. I didn't ask to be born into a nice, sanitary world any more than Lisa can help the circumstances of her birth."

He set his book aside and raked his fingers through his hair. "You're right. I was out of line. I apologize."

"Don't patronize me either."

"I wasn't."

"Next you'll be calling me a do-gooder again."

He came out of the chair. "All right, then tell me something I can say that won't piss you off."

Still angry, she asked, "What will become of Lisa?"

"Hopefully the aunt and uncle will take her back."

"They don't sound like the most generous of hearts. A foster home might be preferable."

"Foster home?"

"CPS could place her—"

"CPS?"

"Child Pro—"

"I know what it is," he said, vexed. "But to get them involved, Lisa would have to report the sexual abuse."

"Of course she'll report it!"

"She hasn't up till now."

"But she will. Those two degenerates need to be in jail."

"Yes. But it'll never happen. It *should*. But it *won't*."

"What are you talking about?"

"I know the mind-set, Doc. It's a clannish mentality. They protect their own, no matter what. Pauline has ignored and denied it up to this point. She'll go on the same way. She'll handle it, but outside the law and without government interference."

"If neither she nor Lisa reports it, if *you* don't, then I will."

"You would do that to Lisa? Put her through the fallout, which could involve harsh reprisal from Norman and Will on both her and her mother?"

"So we're supposed to look the other way and let them get away with rape?"

He didn't say anything, but Emory shivered at the look that came over his face.

"What are you going to do?" She looked down at the pistol. "You can't kill them."

He held her gaze for a moment, then walked over to the fireplace and began shifting the logs with the poker. "Not your problem."

"You made it my problem."

"Well, it won't be from here on."

She was about to launch another volley when she noticed the controlled actions of his strong hands. Not a single motion was wasted, each was deliberate. She experienced that misplaced constriction in her throat again. "You're taking me back."

He didn't say anything, only stared into the heap of embers.

This accounted for his mood since he'd awakened her. She swallowed. "Tonight? Now?"

"Whenever you're ready. The roads are clear enough."

"We should go now then," she said, although it hurt her throat to speak. "People are out in the cold, looking for me."

"Not tonight."

"What?"

"I went online and checked the news while you were asleep. They suspended the search until daybreak tomorrow."

She glanced over at the laptop that she'd noticed earlier on the kitchen table.

"What are they speculating happened to me? Did you read anything about Jeff?"

"I only read the bullet points, not the details." He kicked at an ember that had fallen just outside the grate. "What will you tell him about your time here?"

"I haven't the slightest."

His head came around, his right eyebrow slightly arched. The expression was so familiar to her now. He wanted an answer but didn't want to come right out and ask for it.

"I have no idea what I'll tell Jeff. Or anybody. I don't remember what caused my concussion, so I can't describe it as either an accident or an attack. I don't know where we are, exactly. What can I tell them about you when I don't know anything? Not your name or... or even why you brought me here."

He cursed on a soft expulsion of breath as he braced his hands on the mantel and dropped his head between his arms. He remained staring down into the flames for several moments, then added logs to them and replaced the screen. He dusted his hands on the seat of his jeans.

Then he turned to her. "Well, I can clear up that last uncertainty for you. Why I brought you here. I found you on the trail. What I did for you, sheltering you, feeding you, providing first aid—"

"You would have done for any stranger in need."

"Hell I would," he said harshly. "Yeah, I would have taken an injured person to an ER, dropped them off, and driven away. No risk, no involvement, no chance of exposure. But you, the most serious threat of all to—" He looked around at the interior of the cabin. "To everything. You, I wanted to hold on to for just a little longer."

He held up his hand and closed it into a fist, as though demonstrating. "You'll never appreciate the risk I took to keep you here. You sure as hell can't identify with the struggle it's been to keep myself off you." He walked toward her, and when there were only inches separating them, he asked, "You still scared of me?"

"Very."

He took another step. "But you're not running. How come?"

"Because I do identify with that struggle."

The sound he made was part groan, part growl. "You'd be smart to stop this now, Doc."

He gave her time, but when she didn't move, he reached around her with one hand and splayed it over her bottom. It seemed the heat of his hand dissolved the fabric of her running tights as he brought her up against him. He slid his other hand under her hair and curved it around the back of her neck, as he had done the night before.

"Last chance."

She placed her palms on his chest and then slid them up onto his shoulders.

"Okay. I warned you. I told you that if I ever got my hands on you again—"

"You'd put them all over me."

"That's not all I said I'd do."

He covered her lips with his and unleashed the hunger he'd restrained the night before. Nothing was tempered, not the introduction of his tongue, not the need with which her mouth opened to him, not the darkly erotic words that he whispered when he finally broke the kiss and released her, but only so he could hastily undo the buttons of his shirt she wore.

He opened it and looked at her, his gaze scorching every place it touched on. He caressed her tummy with the backs of his fingers, gauged the narrowness of her rib cage by bracketing it between his hands, then plumped her breasts in his palms. She leaned into them and made small wanting sounds when his fingertips charted the tapering shape of her breasts all the way to the tips which hardened beneath his caress.

"Damn," he murmured.

Taking her hand, he towed her over to the bed, where he pushed the shirt off her shoulders so he could continue to look at her while he pulled his sweater over his head and threw it aside.

Then his hands went to his fly and deftly unbuttoned it. His eyes never breaking contact with hers, he slid one hand inside the vee of soft denim and made an adjustment that caused her breath to hitch.

"I won't last long."

"You won't have to." She lay back on the bed and scooted up to make room for him.

He got onto the bed on his knees, leaned over her and peeled off her running tights, then positioned her bent legs on either side of his hips. He looked down at her with such avid interest, she went hot all over.

Swearing with impatience, he worked his jeans down, then did as he'd said he would: he put his hands on her. First insistently against her inner thighs as he spread them, then tenderly when he stroked where she was wet and achy, then aggressively beneath her ass as he tilted her up. He pushed into her in one, purposeful glide.

"Jesus, Doc," he groaned, "I promised you it wouldn't hurt."

"It won't."

"It might."

Flexing his hips, he seated himself even deeper, then stretched out above her and began moving. Mating. All raw, male power and surety. Unapologetic, dominant and possessive.

Encircling her wrists he raised her hands above her head. Looking directly into her eyes, he slid his other hand between their bodies and touched her with such carnal precision, she arched up into his hand, rubbing herself against it in a silent plea that he press, circle, stroke. And he did. Again and again. He lowered his head to her breasts, sipped at her tight nipples and flicked them with his tongue.

Her orgasm was shattering.

With a snarled obscenity he pulled out barely in time and imprinted her body with his.

Writhing and straining, they wrung out every ounce of pleasure, and when he came, the pulses were strong and intense. Then they seemed to melt into each other, spent. It was a long time before he released her hands and moved off her.

When she finally had the wherewithal to open to her eyes, he was lying beside her on his stomach, cheek resting on his stacked hands, black lashes casting long shadows on his cheekbones.

There was a sheen of sweat on his back. The skin was smooth, the slopes and hollows of his musculature beautiful. His jeans rode low, in the seductive territory where the dip in his back swelled into his ass.

Feeling her stare, he opened his eyes. It was like twin lights coming on inside a blue glass bottle. His attention was drawn to the semen on the flannel shirt that was now hopelessly twisted around her. His eyes moved back to hers. Sounding defensive, he said, "You sorry yet?"

By way of a reply, she reached out and brushed her fingers across the small of his back. Then a bit lower. Then her fingertips ventured beyond his waistband and flirted with the shadowy cleft.

"You keep doing that, I'm gonna have to roll over."

With a touch as light as a breath, she traced the groove as far as she could reach.

Grunting with a mix of discomfort and arousal, he rolled to his back and kicked off his jeans.

The human body held few mysteries for her. She'd seen hundreds, thousands, of bodies. Every shape and size. But she was awestruck by his. And actually a bit shy of its uncompromising maleness—his overall size, the fan of hair that spread over his chest, the lightning bolt tattoo just above the crease where his thigh met an abdomen corded with well-defined muscles, his sex, tight and full again with want of her.

Impatiently he rid her of the shirt, then placed his hand on the back of her head and pulled her toward him. He kissed her long and deep, his tongue repeatedly plumbing her mouth. When he finally broke the kiss, he set her just far enough away from him so that he could study her, which he did with a boldness that thrilled and excited her.

He placed his hand around her breast and gently squeezed the nipple between his fingers. His voice a sexy rasp, he said, "You're not gonna go run screaming from me?"

In a sublime state of arousal, she smiled and shook her head no.

"Then make memories for me, Doc."

"Memories?"

Leaving her breasts tingling, he skimmed his hand down over her belly. He contemplated the architecture of her hipbone as though it was a marvel. Then he brushed the backs of his fingers over the soft hair. "Make memories for me to take out and play with when you're gone."

"What kind of memories?"

Her question ended on a surprised inhale when he deftly relocated and moved her thighs far enough apart to accommodate his wide shoulders. She could almost feel the probe of his hot gaze as he slid his hands under her and pulled her closer. She definitely felt the first sweep of his tongue, then his lips moving against her as he whispered. "Dirty ones."

Chapter 20

Something woke her, and she came awake knowing that she was alone in the cabin.

She lay cocooned beneath the covers, but the bed had begun to cool without his body heat.

Maybe he'd stepped out to get firewood.

But she knew she was deceiving herself. It was more than the empty place beside her that let her know he was gone. Just as he seemed to fill the room with his sheer presence, his absence created a vacuum.

She dreaded learning what her solitude indicated.

But she must.

She sat up, hugging herself for warmth. Her nipples contracted in the cold. They were sore. A thousand other effects of their lovemaking combined to create a general achiness all over her body.

To feel this way was shocking and wonderful and she couldn't conjure up a shred of remorse for it. Indeed, she hoped the twinges and stings, these sweet reminders of their ardency, would stay with her for a long while.

He'd left the space heater on in the bathroom, but with the flame turned low. She didn't switch on the light, not wishing to have a clear reflection of herself in the mirror. She didn't care about her dishevelment. What she didn't want to see was the forlornness of her expression. It was one thing to feel sorrow; seeing evidence of it in her eyes would make it worse.

She showered quickly. When she came out of the bathroom, she got a fresh shirt from his drawer, then went to one of the front windows and raised the shade. It was still very early. Wispy clouds hovered above the distant peaks like a sheer stole. Otherwise, for the first time in days, the sky was clear and promised to become blue as the day progressed.

The yard was empty. His pickup wasn't in its parking spot.

Listlessly, her hand dropped to her side. The muslin curtain fell back into place.

She turned. That's when she noticed that on the dining table, where she couldn't fail to see it, was her fanny pack. The two twenty-dollar bills, her driver's license, credit card, and her marked map were inside. Beside it were her sunglasses.

Her running clothes, including her gloves and headband, had been folded neatly. Her shoes had been placed beneath the table, side by side, heels and toes aligned, socks stuffed into them.

The array signified that it was time for her to go.

Her limbs felt as though they weighed a thousand pounds apiece as she removed his shirt and draped it over the ladderback chair. She dressed mechanically and collected her belongings. When she was ready, she sat down on the sofa to wait.

Last night he'd said, "When you're ready." Clearly she hadn't been ready to go, nor had he been ready to return her. During the night, they'd whispered and sighed the urgent language of lovers, but they hadn't spoken once of the life to which she must return, or of the *something*, which even Lisa had intuited, that made his anonymity necessary. Each had known that last night represented a King's X. They had taken a time-out.

But with morning—

Her eyes strayed to the end table. Conspicuously missing from it was the pistol.

She jumped to her feet. "Oh God. Oh *no!*"

In three strides, she made it to the door and yanked it open. The cold air took her breath, but she practically hurdled the porch steps. She slipped on a patch of ice on the flat rock embedded in the ground, but the skid only served as impetus. She pounded across the yard, climbed over the gate, and started running full out in the direction of the Floyds' house.

It was uphill all the way, but she ran it as though it were level ground, fearing that, if she slowed down even a little, she would be too late. Her best effort might not be enough. She might not make it in time to prevent—

There! The tin roof line with its lightning rods appeared above the treetops. Rather than letting up, having her destination in sight spurred her on. She was heaving each breath when the trash-strewn drive came into view. Then she saw his pickup. And saw him.

Her breath stopped, trapped between her lungs and her throat, which froze up with dread, so much so that she couldn't even call out to him as he took the porch steps two at a time, practically ripped the screened door from its hinges when he pulled it open, then kicked the front door so hard it swung wide into the room and banged against the inside wall. He disappeared into the house.

Seconds later Norman was hurled out of the house with such force that the screened door didn't impede his headlong plunge across the porch and down the front steps. He somersaulted and wound up on his back only a few yards away from her.

He clambered to regain his footing and defend himself against the man who followed him out of the house. He was carrying the familiar shotgun, but he tossed it aside and jumped the steps, bearing down on Norman and hitting him in the face with a fist that had the impact of a sledgehammer.

Bone and cartilage crunched as Norman's nose was ground flat into his face. Tissue liquefied. Blood spurted. He yelled in pain but got several rapid punches to the gut before he fell to the ground.

Emory covered her cry of dismay with her hand.

The mistreated dog was running circles around the two men, barking maniacally.

"Sic him, you goddamn mutt!" Will shouted as he came crashing through the screened door wearing only his pants.

He lunged for the discarded shotgun but caught a boot in his crotch before he'd cleared the steps. He dropped to his knees, screaming and clutching his testicles, but he wasn't spared another boot, this time to the face. It demolished his cheekbone. A slug to his jaw relocated his chin to beneath his ear and ruined his lupine leer forever.

He went over backward, his head landing on the lower step with a sound like clapping two-by-fours, but not so hard as to knock him unconscious. He howled in agony.

Norman wasn't finished. By now he'd regained some of his wits. Despite the blood running down into his beard from the mess that used to be the center of his face, he somehow staggered to his feet and took two wild swings that were easily ducked. His right fist was caught in midswipe and used to whip him around.

Placing his lips a breath away from Norman's ear, he said, "You only thought you missed all the excitement of Virginia."

Then he shoved Norman's hand up between his shoulder blades. Emory heard the sickening sound when the ball joint popped from his shoulder socket. His scream became a strangled whine as he took a blow to the kidney. When his dangling arm was released, he fell like a ragdoll.

"This one's for the dog, you cock-sucking son of a bitch."

Emory was certain that the kick he gave Norman's ribs left several of them broken.

The victor was seemingly unaffected except for being slightly winded. He backed away from Norman, walked over to Will, and surveyed the damage, apparently finding it sufficient because he didn't touch him, only said, "If you lay a hand on Lisa again, I'll come back and break your neck."

He picked up the shotgun, removed the shells, then carried it over to a stout tree, and swung it at the trunk again and again until the stock broke away from the barrels. He collected the two pieces from off the ground and tossed them into the bed of his pickup.

The dog came over to him, tongue lolling, tail wagging. After getting a pat on the head and a scratch under the chin, the animal went over to its place beneath the tree and plopped down with a sigh of canine gratification.

Emory ran over to Norman.

Or tried. Her arm was hooked, and she was jerked to a stop. "Don't touch him."

"We can't just leave them like this."

"Hell we can't," he said and propelled her toward the truck.

"*I* can't." She dug her heels in.

"You are."

Before she could protest again, she noticed that Pauline, huddled inside a moth-eaten cardigan, had come out onto the porch. He turned to see what had drawn her attention, then went around to the driver's side of the pickup and took a brown paper sack from the floorboard.

He walked back to the house and leaned forward over Will to pass the sack up to Pauline. "There's a coffee cup inside to replace the one I broke. The cash should cover the cost of a new television."

Looking baffled, she said, "Thanky."

"How is Lisa this morning?"

"Good. Sleepin' sound." Looking down at Will, who was loudly moaning, she added, "Was, anyhow."

"Pack up her things, and yours. I'll come back for you later."

With even more perplexity than she'd shown before, she looked around, taking in the dilapidation of her house, the shambles of her life. When she came back to him, she said, "I can't leave my home."

He looked about to speak, then sighed with resignation. "Have Lisa ready."

He walked back to the pickup, and this time when he opened the passenger door, he said, "We're not arguing about this, Doc."

Seeing it would be pointless to try, she got in. What other choice did she have?

"Did I wake you up?"

Sam Knight rolled onto his back and fumbled his cell phone closer to his ear. "She found?"

"No," Grange said, "but Jeff's mistress caved."

Knight sat up and shook off his grogginess. "That was fast."

"I drove down to Atlanta early, skipped interviewing the neighbors, and instead was ringing her doorbell before dawn. Woke her up and took her off guard."

"Aren't you a go-getter?"

"At first, she was defensive and evasive, but when I pretended that we know more than we do about her relationship with Jeff, she started crying. Broke down, admitted to their affair."

"Huh." By now Knight was trying to pull on his socks using only one hand and mimicking drinking a cup of coffee so his wife would take the hint and bring him one. "She say how long it's been going on?"

"Six months. Since Memorial Day weekend. Emory got an

emergency call, had to meet a patient at the hospital, left a cook-out at Alice's place early."

"And the minute her back was turned..."

"To bed they went. From the start Alice has been afraid Emory would find out. Never meant for it to happen. Never intended to hurt anyone. Just one of those things. Nobody sees it coming."

"So to speak."

Grange was too excited for the double entendre to register. He kept talking. "She blubbered the typical guilt-trip stuff that people blubber when they're screwing a friend's spouse."

Knight blew an air kiss to his wife, who'd brought him coffee. "So what about the spouse, our dear Jeff?"

"I asked her if she thought he had something to do with Emory's disappearance. She jumped all over that."

"Which direction?"

"Shot down the notion. Adamantly. Said it was unthinkable. Besides, she says he couldn't have done it. She claims they were together from Friday evening till Sunday daytime."

"Where?"

"Her house. They always shack there. She's his client, which gives them a plausible out if Emory ever catches them."

"Stop. I'm getting an image of him doing her taxes while naked."

Grange laughed.

Sam thoughtfully sipped his coffee. "She says they were together all weekend, huh? Convenient, wouldn't you say? Could be she's only providing him with an alibi."

"Could be, but I believed her, Sam. By that time, she was making me coffee. She was shaken and eager to cooperate."

"Okay, so they were keeping the sheets hot till Sunday. Till how late in the day on Sunday?"

"After a late breakfast. Not too long before Jeff started making his round of calls."

"Hmm. This isn't good for us, Buddy. It doesn't fit the Saturday night scenario we discussed last night. Either Alice is lying about him being with her all that time, or, if she's telling the truth, when did he kill Emory?"

Grange thought about it. "He admits to driving up here on Sunday. Maybe he met Emory somewhere along the way. They set up a place to hash things out. Wherever that place was, he left her body, then drove on up here and did the woe-is-me."

"Doesn't work. Doesn't for Saturday, either. *Because*," he stressed, "Emory's car was in the parking lot on the mountain, preserved in two days' worth of ice and fresh snow. Came to me in the middle of the night. She didn't leave the mountain. Not in that car."

"Shit."

"We gotta put Jeff on the mountain, and so far we ain't."

"Double shit. But the thing is, Sam, I think he did it."

"I think he did, too," he grumbled.

Each contemplated the dilemma, then Grange said, "The extramarital affair, plus the money, plus his being a prick, gives us reason enough to hold him and buy ourselves a little more time to either break him, break Alice, find Emory's remains, or come up with a piece of physical evidence."

"You're expecting a miracle?"

"They happen."

Knight mulled it over and reached a decision. "Where you at?"

"In my car on the way back. About an hour out. I let you sleep in."

"Thanks." Knight consulted his wristwatch. "We're supposed to pick Jeff up at nine."

"I'll make it back well before then."

"So let's pick up Jeff half an hour early, take him by surprise, and hit him hard with his infidelity. You know the drill."

"I get to be the bad cop?"

"See you in sixty."

"For God's sake, Alice, would you please get a grip?"

"I don't think you understand the implications, Jeff."

"I understand them perfectly. I just don't think we should panic simply because—"

"Because the detectives have somehow learned about us, when already you think they suspect you of harming Emory? You don't think that's cause for panic?"

"I'll grant you it's cause for *concern*, but let's not blow it out of proportion. Now, take a deep breath, and tell me everything Grange said again."

She talked him through it, but the repetition didn't improve the message.

"He showed up at my door before daybreak, Jeff. The timing of his visit alone implies that they're taking this—our affair— seriously. They see it as a significant factor of Emory's disappearance. Forgive me, but that's a bit unsettling."

He didn't dispute that. Grange had driven all the way down to Atlanta, which indicated that he and Knight's random speculations had begun to solidify and actually take shape. Jeff feared that his designation as "frantic husband" might soon be traded for "person of interest."

If that happened, media cameras would photograph him being escorted into the sheriff's office by badged personnel with stern faces. Interviews with him would then become official interrogations, and there was a distinct difference. During the former, investigators were deferential and polite. The atmosphere was sensitive and sympathetic.

An interrogation was just the opposite.

He would be forced to retain an attorney, and that was as good as an admission of guilt. There would follow a massive groundswell of distrust and disdain toward him. Nothing he said would be believed. He would be reviled by complete strangers and close associates alike. His clients would question his integrity and take their portfolios to another money manager.

The thought of being subjected to such humiliation caused him to break into a cold sweat. Using a corner of the sheet, he blotted at the trickles of it running from his armpits down his ribs. However, the sour stench of it worked like smelling salts, jolting him back to his senses.

He was getting way ahead of himself. No one had accused him of anything yet. They knew he and Alice were lovers. So? Adultery was a sin, not a crime.

Nevertheless, in the minds of many it would be a serious sin to commit against Emory Charbonneau, champion of the downtrodden, sweetheart of the dispossessed. It was time for him to take preventative measures before he was hung out to dry in the arena of public opinion, where already his wife outscored him by a wide margin. If his infidelity came to light, he might be publically scourged. They'd sell tickets.

Abruptly, he said, "You shouldn't have called me, Alice. That was the worst possible thing you could have done."

"Would you rather I let the detectives show up and arrest you without any warning?"

With diminished patience, he said, "They're not going to arrest me. They have absolutely no basis on which to arrest me. They can't put me in jail for sleeping with you. Which, under the circumstances, must stop. I've got to be an ideal husband, the kind Emory deserves. You and I shouldn't have any further private contact."

"Until when?"

"I don't know."

"Jeff, please. Let's talk this through."

God, he hated her whining. And hated even more that he heard a car pull up just beyond the motel room door. "Don't call me again." He clicked off.

Far less confident of avoiding arrest than he'd let on to her, he moved quickly to the window and peered through the crack between the drapes. Knight and Grange were climbing out of their SUV, and they weren't delivering doughnuts and coffee.

Why were they here a half hour early?

His phone vibrated. "Dammit!"

Knight shouted through the door. "Jeff? You up?" He sounded all business and by no means folksy.

Jeff's phone continued to vibrate. Cursing under his breath, he answered in a whisper. "I told you. Do *not* call me again."

Knight pounded on the door. "Jeff, open up. Now."

In his ear, "Jeff?"

A key rattled in the lock. *Knight had a key to his room?*

Through the phone, "Jeff?"

A shoulder was put to the door and, when it came open, the two deputies practically fell into the room. Grange's hand was on his gun holster. Both drew up short when they saw him standing there shivering in only his underwear.

He felt clammy, lightheaded, and breathless as he smiled and extended his cell phone to Grange. "It's Emory."

Chapter 21

———— ⊰◈⊱ ————

He pretended to be one of the volunteers who'd been searching for Emory.

He blended in with them, dressed as most were in heavy outdoor gear. His scarf—the one she'd knifed—covered his chin. He had turned up his coat collar, too, so it covered a good portion of his face. His cap was pulled low. He was wearing dark sunglasses to help hide the scratch she'd inflicted on his cheekbone. It was healing but still visible.

Most of the marks she had left on him weren't. They were deep inside where wounds were never superficial and scars had significance.

For a city the size of Drakeland, her disappearance and recovery were major events. Upon hearing that she was back in the fold, and feeling the flush of success even though she hadn't exactly been *found*, a hundred or more of the volunteers had congregated outside the local hospital to give her a hero's welcome.

Now, as the sheriff's office SUV pulled up to the emergency room entrance, it was swarmed by cameramen and reporters, most of whom were up from Atlanta. Gawkers, who had no idea what was going on but were drawn to the spectacle, elbowed for space and a more advantageous view. Uniformed officers were trying with limited success to control the pandemonium.

He stood head and shoulders above everyone in the crowd, but the chance of Emory spotting him was remote. She wouldn't be looking. This was the last place she would expect him to be.

It was the last place he expected himself to be.

He continued to ask himself why he'd come. The answer continued to elude him. Halfway home after delivering her, he had felt the compulsion to make a U-turn, and he had. Some things one just did and never came to terms with *why*.

So here he was: the reason for her absence, a witness to her homecoming.

A potbellied man in uniform alighted from the driver's side of the official vehicle, opened the rear door, and assisted her out of the backseat. With a heavy blanket draped around her shoulders, she looked small and overwhelmed. She was wearing her sunglasses, so her eyes were concealed, but her mouth was unsmiling. Her sneakers were muddy from running the mile between his cabin and the Floyds' place.

He hadn't counted on her waking up and realizing where he'd gone in time for her to get there and witness the beating he'd given them. He'd left her snug beneath the covers of his bed, rosy and warm, doped by sex, sound asleep. The next time he saw her, she was standing in the Floyds' yard, breathless and aghast.

The Floyd brothers were the reason he'd come to North Carolina. He had vowed to seek retribution, vowed to get it. He just hadn't counted on things happening how they had, or when they had.

He'd considered postponing taking action until Emory was no longer under his roof and compounding the danger. But after the incident with Lisa, after he and the brothers had declared themselves enemies, he couldn't predict what they would do.

He'd felt he couldn't delay, that he had to act before the opportunity was lost.

Only a vow as binding as the one he'd made himself regarding Norman and Will Floyd could have dragged him from beneath the soft weight of Emory's arm across his belly.

He hadn't seen her until he pitched Norman through the front door and followed him out. She had looked at him with stark horror, but he had gone there with a purpose that even her revulsion couldn't check.

The deed was done, and it was too late now to call it back. He wouldn't reverse it even if he could. He didn't regret doing it. He only regretted her having seen him do it.

That would be her last impression of him. Fresh blood on his hands. An indelible stain darker than that on his soul.

After leaving the Floyds' place, he'd stopped at the cabin only long enough to go inside and retrieve Emory's belongings. He'd set the fanny pack in her lap without so much as a blink of acknowledgment from her.

During the long drive down to Drakeland, she had only stared straight ahead, her hands tightly clasped, probably fearing that if she uttered a peep, she would rile the beast she'd seen unleashed.

On the outskirts of town, he'd pulled the pickup to the shoulder of the highway and put the gear in park. "About a half mile up ahead is a gas station. You can call somebody to pick you up there."

He reached across her knees and opened the glove box, where he'd placed her phone. Earlier, as he'd silently moved about the cabin collecting her things while she slept, he had considered including her phone. He'd spent a night with her that he would die remembering. He would revisit it a million times in his fantasies.

But mistrust was second nature to him. He had decided to hold on to her phone until the very last minute.

Handing it to her, he'd told her that he'd charged the battery.

"But I would appreciate it if you didn't make that call until I get a few minutes' head start."

She'd looked at the phone as though not recognizing what it was, then she raised her eyes to his. "You completely confound me. I don't understand you."

"No way you could. Don't even try."

"You went there expressly to fight them."

"Yes. And I think they were expecting me. Norman was asleep in the recliner, but he had the shotgun across his lap."

"He could have killed you."

"He didn't react fast enough."

"You said something to him. You said he only thought he'd missed the excitement in Virginia. What were you talking about?"

"Nothing that concerns you."

"It does concern me! I watched two men get beaten to within an inch of their lives."

"They had it coming."

"Perhaps for Lisa, but—"

"Let it go, Doc."

"Give me *something*." Her voice had cracked on that. "Some explanation."

The silver trinket had burned like a live coal deep inside his jeans pocket. She still hadn't missed it. It was too small and worthless for her even to have noticed it was gone, but it was a treasure to him. Part of her, now his.

Wasn't it only fair that he give her something in return? But what she'd asked for—an explanation—he couldn't give.

After a long moment of silence, tears had welled in her eyes. "Who *are* you?" By her tone, he'd known that she was demanding to learn more than his name.

He'd turned away and looked out the windshield, wanting like hell to touch her just one more time, to feel her mouth open and soft under his. But if he had, it would have been harder to let her go.

So he called up the numbness with which he armed himself to get through each day. When he'd reached across her again, it was to pull the door handle. He opened it with a shove. "Bye, Doc."

She continued to look at him with incomprehension. He kept his expression shuttered. Eventually, she'd climbed down out of the truck and closed the door. He'd driven away.

He guessed she'd done what he'd asked and hadn't called anyone immediately because it was a good hour before the news bulletin came in over his truck's radio that she'd been recovered.

He was taking a huge gamble by returning to town. She could have given the authorities the make and model of his truck. Maybe she had even memorized the license plate number and handed it over.

But he didn't think she'd give him away, not particularly because she wanted to protect him, but to protect herself from scandal and embarrassment. The more she told about him, the more she would have to reveal about herself and their time together, and he didn't believe she would publically divulge that.

But he wondered how much she would tell her husband in private.

The potbellied deputy who'd helped her alight was joined by another who'd been riding shotgun in the SUV. They flanked her, protecting her as they made shuffling progress through the throng toward the entrance to the ER. She kept her head down, her face averted from cameras. She didn't even glance his way.

If she *did* happen to see him, would she point him out and accuse him of being her captor? Or would she pretend that he was just another face in the crowd, a face she didn't know, one she hadn't kissed, clasped to her breasts, pressed between her thighs as she came?

He would never know because she didn't look his way before being ushered through the automatic double doors and out of sight. He continued to stare at the empty space where he'd caught his final glimpse of her until the crowd of onlookers began to disperse, eddying around him as he stood rooted to the spot.

News teams began ambling back toward their vans. Then a shout went up. "Mr. Charbonneau! Mr. Charbonneau!" And suddenly he was being buffeted by reporters and cameramen as they rushed past him back toward the SUV.

Climbing from the backseat was Emory's husband, easily recognizable from pictures of him on the Internet. Having been identified, Jeff Surrey was now surrounded by media. A sound bite from him was the next best thing to one from Emory.

Jeff ran slender fingers through his fine, fair hair as though preparing himself to appear on camera. He was dressed in dark slacks, a turtleneck, and a black quilted puffer jacket more suited to a ritzy ski resort than to a rural town in the foothills.

"It's Surrey," he said into the first of many microphones thrust at him. "My name is Jeff Surrey."

"Is your wife okay?"

"Has she told you what happened?"

"Where has she been, Mr. Charbonneau?" asked one, who'd missed or ignored his corrective disclaimer.

Jeff held up his hand for quiet. "Presently, I know little more than you do. A short while ago, Emory called me from a service station on the edge of town. As it so happened, I was with personnel from the sheriff's office when I got the call. I, along with Sergeant Detectives Knight and Grange, rushed to the site immediately."

Questions were hurled at him, but the one he addressed was why Emory had been brought to the hospital. "She has suffered a concussion. Self-diagnosed. Other than that, she appears not to have any serious injuries, but I insisted that she be brought here and examined to make certain of her condition."

In response to the next barrage of questions, he said, "It's my understanding that a representative from the sheriff's office will conduct a press conference at the appropriate time, after officers have had a chance to talk to Emory at length. Now, if you'll excuse me." He began pushing his way through them.

As Jeff Surrey neared the hospital entrance, he came within ten feet of the tall man in the watch cap, who felt nothing but contempt for the one in the slick ski jacket. He'd quickly formed an opinion of Emory's husband. He was a vain, smug bastard, full of self-importance. What had she ever seen in him?

Trying to find an answer, he closely scrutinized Jeff from head to—

His heart clutched, then went stone cold. Inside his head a clamor began. *Fuck me, fuck me, fuck me!*

But he remained silent and dead still and let Jeff Surrey walk past, never guessing the avalanche he'd incited. Arrogance intact, Emory's husband strode into the ER. The glass doors slid closed behind him.

In them, the reflection of a man appeared. He saw himself, gloved hands clenched into fists at his sides. His jaw granite, his stance combative, a stag eager to butt heads, a gunslinger itching to draw. He looked fearsome even to his own eyes.

And he realized how conspicuous that would make him if he lingered.

He hovered on the brink of indecision for a few seconds more, then turned away from the building. He hunched his wide shoulders inside his coat and merged with a group of volunteers who were discussing the miracle of Emory's survival, the fortunate outcome that just as easily could have been disastrous, and the relief her husband must be feeling to have her back safe and sound.

He peeled off from the group without ever being noticed and walked the several blocks to where he'd left his pickup in a busy supermarket parking lot. He got in but sat behind the steering wheel, banging it with his fists and swearing.

He'd thought that when he'd said good-bye to her, he had cut himself free, that he could move on, adrift and unhappy, but at peace for knowing that he'd done the right thing.

Hardly.

Jack Connell awakened hopeful that morning. But one glance out his hotel room window, and he knew he wouldn't be completely drying out anytime soon. The rain continued. In torrents. He couldn't even see the marina across the street through the downpour.

It took him ten minutes to shower, shave, and dress. Twenty more, and he was back on the street where Rebecca Watson lived. He parked at the opposite end of the block from where he'd been yesterday.

He'd seen Rebecca only that once, when she came out onto the porch to get her mail. He never caught sight of her daughter, Sarah.

Munching on peanuts saved from his flight, he'd watched the house through the dinner hour and into the rest of the evening. Night fell. Through the fogged windshield, he'd kept surveillance on the house until all the lights inside were out, then he'd stayed for another hour. Nothing happened. No tall brute sneaked into the house under cover of darkness. Drat the luck.

On his return trip to the hotel, he'd picked up a heart-attack-in-a-sack at a fast-food drive-through. He'd eaten the meal while catching up on e-mails, then went to bed.

Now he was back, anxious to see what the day would bring.

At seven forty-two, the garage door came up and the minivan was backed out. The door went down. The van came in his direction and drove past. In the passenger seat was a preteen girl, texting on her cell phone. The driver was a blur through the rain-streaked windows, but the white hair was unmistakably Rebecca's.

He waited until they had rounded the corner and then followed, keeping several cars between them.

After a short drive, Sarah was dropped off at a parochial middle school. The girl stopped texting long enough to lean across the console and kiss her mother's cheek before getting out.

From there, Rebecca drove to a Starbucks. She went inside with her laptop tucked under her arm. A few minutes later, he saw her sit down at a table near a window. Observing from a parking lot across the street, his mouth watered for a hot cappuccino, but he didn't want to chance going into the store and being recognized by her.

She remained engrossed in whatever was on her laptop. No one joined her at the table. A few minutes to nine o'clock, she left, taking a coffee with her.

The town center reminded Jack of New England villages. Trendy shops and restaurants occupied older buildings that had been attractively renovated. Rebecca Watson's shop was one such enterprise.

At nine thirty, she flipped the OPEN sign on the glass door of Bagatelle.

Jack called Wes Greer. After exchanging good mornings and giving each other recaps of the previous day, he asked if Wes had obtained the information he'd requested.

"She does all right with the shop," his colleague reported. "Especially in the summer months during tourist season. It slows down this time of year, but she enjoys a brisk holiday season. And June's good."

"What happens in June?"

"People get married."

"Huh. What does she sell?"

"Stationery, glassware and china, gifts. Like that. Stuff your wife clutters up the apartment with."

Jack wouldn't know. He didn't have a wife.

Not for lack of trying. Although his ex-fiancée would dispute the effort he'd put into nurturing the relationship. Vehemently. *You're not even trying to make this work, Jack. If I left, it would take days for you to realize I was gone.*

It had taken three.

Before hanging up, Jack asked, "Anything else shaking?"

"Pretty quiet. How's the weather out there?"

"It sucks."

Despite the rain, Bagatelle did a respectable weekday business. All except one of the customers were women, and the sole male who went into the store wasn't the one Jack sought.

By twelve thirty, his bladder was bursting and he was hungry. He pulled his jacket up over his head and dashed to a deli he'd made note of earlier. He ordered a sandwich, then went into the bathroom and peed a quart, at least. He returned to the car with his food and drink. After eating, because of yesterday's long flight and short night, he struggled to stay awake as the afternoon progressed.

For stimulation, he opened the file and reviewed material he already knew by heart.

Physical description: six-four, two hundred and twenty-five pounds, dark hair, blue eyes, crescent scar above left eyebrow, one tattoo on lower abdomen. DOB: February 3, 1976. POB: Winston-Salem, North Carolina. Education: Bachelor of Science degree, Constructional Engineering, Virginia Tech. Military Service: Army. Criminal history—

Jack glanced up in time to see the subject's only known relative flip the sign on the door to her shop. She'd waited until straight up five o'clock to close, although she hadn't had a customer in more than an hour. She was as disciplined as her brother.

Jack let several vehicles go past before he pulled out into traffic behind her. He followed her home, not turning the corner onto her street for a good five minutes after she had. He drove past the house. The garage door was down. She hadn't come out to get her mail yet. There was a magazine sticking out the top of it.

He drove to the end of the block and parked under the conifer, put his camera within reach, and yawned broadly as he settled in for another hours-long vigil.

It lasted only a couple of minutes.

Rebecca came out onto the porch, but she didn't stop at the mailbox. Instead she popped open an umbrella, strode down the front walkway, stepped off the curb, and—

Oh *shit!*

She marched down the middle of the street straight toward him, and she was steamed.

Chapter 22

don't know."

The semicircle of faces around Emory's hospital bed registered varying degrees of the same expression—disbelief. Jeff's was tinged with consternation. Drs. Butler and James exuded a sympathetic bedside manner. The two detectives regarded her with skepticism.

She repeated, "I don't know. Not his name. Not the location of his cabin. I'm sorry. I know you were expecting me to give you a full explanation, but the truth is that I don't remember much."

Jeff leaned down and whispered in her ear. "This isn't a test, Emory. Don't become upset. If you can't remember, it's okay. What matters most is that you're back."

"Your husband's right, Dr. Charbonneau," said Sergeant Detective Sam Knight.

He had introduced himself as the lead investigator on her missing person case. He had a grandfatherly countenance and a laid-back manner. Because she had liked him immediately, she hated lying to him. Although, stripping the facts down to their bare bones, she didn't know the name of the man she'd spent four days with. Nor could she lead them to his cabin or locate it on a map.

Knight gave her an encouraging smile. "Take your time. We're in no hurry. Let's take a different approach. How 'bout telling us what you can remember, not what you can't."

"I remember parking my car near the overlook on Saturday morning and setting out to run. But beyond that, my recollections are indistinct. I don't even know if they're sequential. They're piecemeal.

"I remember waking up with an excruciating headache. I was dizzy and sick to my stomach. I threw up at least once that I remember. But time had no relevance. I drifted in and out of consciousness. Until I woke up this morning."

That was a lie, and everyone must have suspected it was because no one spoke for several moments.

Then Knight said, "Going back to Saturday, you told us you ran the Bear Ridge Trail. Any particular reason why?"

At least she could answer this one truthfully. "I'd marked it on a map I had of hiking trails. The map showed it to be winding but eventually ending at an overlook on the other side of the peak. That was to be my turnaround."

"Bear Ridge branches off into others. Might be helpful for us to see your map, so we'd know exactly where you went."

"I'm not sure I took the path I charted. As it turns out, my map wasn't that reliable or accurate. It designated Bear Ridge as being paved. It was, but badly. Long sections of it are reduced to little more than a gravel path. I think I must've fallen in loose gravel and hit my head on a rock or boulder."

Jeff gave her hand a squeeze. "It's a miracle that you survived."

Unanimously they had marveled over her basically sound physical condition. She had assured them that being admitted to the hospital was unnecessary, but her protests had been overruled. The detectives, Jeff, and the ER personnel had insisted that she have a brain scan, and when it confirmed that she'd suffered a concussion, it was decided that she be kept overnight for observation.

She had disagreed, but by then the two doctors with whom she shared the clinic in Atlanta had arrived, and they concurred with the local medical staff. She was staying in the hospital overnight. Period.

The cut on her head had been examined. It was healing. Nevertheless, it had been thoroughly cleaned with a strong antiseptic, and she was given antibiotics to counter any incipient infection.

Her sprint to the Floyds' house had aggravated her stress fracture. She explained it as an unfortunate outcome of her strenuous run on Saturday. An ice pack had been strapped to the foot and it was now elevated on a pillow.

She was getting fluids through an IV. That precaution was entirely unnecessary, but she couldn't refuse it without assuring them that she'd been adequately hydrated for the past four days.

She didn't have to fake her headache. She wasn't suffering the stabbing pain of her recent concussion, but the dull throb of a classic tension headache, one exacerbated by intense and contradictory emotions. At her request the window blinds had been closed. She'd said that blocking out the light helped relieve the headache, when actually she feared the sunlight beaming in would spotlight her lies.

Lying went against her nature. Being untruthful to her colleagues and to the detectives shamed her. It was even harder to lie to Jeff. From the moment he'd entered the service station and taken her into his arms, he'd been reluctant to let her out of his sight even long enough for her to receive medical treatment.

He reached down now and stroked her cheek with the back of his hand, not knowing that it evoked a memory of another man's touch.

Doc? Are you going to wake up or sleep through?

Unable to handle both that recollection and her husband's adoring smile, she looked toward the foot of the bed where her associates stood shoulder to shoulder. "Jeff told me about the award you offered."

They believed it to be news to her. It wasn't, but having known about it since yesterday didn't diminish her gratitude. "I can't..." Her throat grew so thick she could barely speak. "I don't know how to thank you for your willingness to do that."

Dr. James said, "We would have doubled the amount in order to get you back. As it is, in celebration of your safe return, we're donating the original twenty-five thousand to Doctors Without Borders."

Completely overcome with emotion, she sniffed. "I need a tissue." Jeff grabbed the box off the side table and extended it to her, then kept his hand on her shoulder while she blotted her leaky eyes. After a moment, she gave an embarrassed laugh. "I'm not usually such a waterworks."

"The emotions you've kept pent up over the last four days are just now surfacing."

How wrong he was. Over the past four days, she'd had numerous outbursts of widely varied emotions, all of them passionately felt. But she gave him a weak smile. "I'm sure you're right."

Knight waited for her to compose herself, then said, "Would y'all please give us a few minutes alone with Dr. Charbonneau?"

"What for?" Jeff asked.

"We just need to clear up a few details for the paperwork we've gotta file. Also, the department's PIO is waiting for clearance from us on the statement he'll give to the media, and we need her input on that. Don't want to say anything that's incorrect. Shouldn't take long."

His rambling was a non-answer, but short of challenging the officer, Jeff had little choice except to comply. He leaned down and kissed her forehead. "I'll be in the hallway if you need me. I love you."

"I love you, too."

He shot the two law officers his frostiest and most disparaging look, then joined her two associates as they filed out.

Knight remarked on Jeff's disdain. "He doesn't regard us too kindly."

"Can you blame him? You suspected him of God knows what."

"Were we that obvious?"

"Apparently so. He told me you treated everything he said and did with suspicion." During a private moment in a curtained-off area of the ER, while waiting for her CT scan to be assessed, Jeff had told her about the detectives' preoccupation with him while she remained missing in a frozen wilderness.

"Well," the older detective said now, "I'll admit that Grange and me bounced around some theories. In situations like this, it's often the significant other that's the culprit. My apologies to both y'all."

He pulled a chair nearer her bedside and sat down. Grange remained standing at the foot of the bed. He wasn't as gregarious as his partner, but he made up for it by being extremely observant, which put Emory on guard.

Knight began. "We don't know much more than we did while you were missing, Dr. Charbonneau."

"I realize how frustrating that must be for you."

"Let's start with the man you can't name."

The mention of him filled her with such despair, she feared it would be detectable.

Knight said, "He told you he came across you laying on the trail, out cold."

"While he was hiking."

"And he carted you off to his cabin."

She nodded.

"You can't direct us to it?"

"No. For four days my universe consisted of a bed behind a screen."

"Screen?"

"A folding screen of louvered panels. He set it up to give me privacy."

"Decent of him."

"Very."

"But you don't remember much about him?"

"Only that he treated me with extraordinary kindness."

"Like a Good Samaritan?"

"Yes, whatever I needed..."

Sorry, Doc.

For what?

Keeping you awake.

I haven't complained.

So, you don't want me to stop?

No.

Don't stop this?

No. God no. Don't... don't stop.

You'll have to be the one who says you've had enough.

I'm not there yet.

Good. Because I can't stop.

The deputies were looking at her curiously. She cleared her throat. "He was very thoughtful. Considerate."

Neither of the men said anything.

She wet her lips. "He took care of my needs. I was aware. But not. Do you understand? Most of the time, he left me alone. To... to recover."

Knight folded his arms across his sizeable middle. "In all that time, he never offered to call nine-one-one?"

She rubbed her forehead. "I don't think so. Maybe. I don't remember. Wasn't there a storm? Fog? Weather that made the roads impassable?"

"Uh-huh."

"He told me—he promised—that he would deliver me safely back once the roads cleared."

"But he didn't," Grange remarked. "Most of the roads were clear yesterday."

"I'm certain he would have if I had felt better."

Jesus, you feel good. Sweet. Perfect.

Buying time before continuing, she reached down to reposition the ice bag on her elevated foot. "But I wasn't up to it yesterday. Then I woke up this morning. My head was clear. I asked him to drive me here, to Drakeland, and he did."

"Actually he dropped you outside of Drakeland," Grange said. "Why?"

"I don't know."

"Why not drive you to the sheriff's office?"

"I don't know."

"He could have collected the reward."

"Maybe he didn't know about the reward."

Grange shifted his weight from one foot to the other. Knight ran his hand over his face. Grange said, "What kind of truck was he driving?"

"A pickup."

"I mean Ford, Chevy, Ram . . . ?"

"I didn't notice. I don't know much about pickups."

"Color?"

"Blue. Sort of silvery blue. And . . . tall."

"Tall?"

"High off the ground," she said.

"What about him? He tall, too?" Knight asked.

"I described him to you earlier."

"Yeah, but in all the confusion, you might've forgot something."

At the combo service station/convenience store, the scene had been chaotic. Her reunion with Jeff. The excitement among the personnel running the place. Customers taking pictures of her on their cell phones. A man delivering tobacco products trying to get a selfie with her.

Amid all that, the two deputies had pressed her for an explanation as to how she'd come to be there, and, when she told them that a man had dropped her off a short distance away, they'd naturally wanted to know his name. Since she couldn't provide them with that, they'd asked her for a general description. She'd been inordinately general: Caucasian male.

"Hell, that circus going on at the Chevron almost made me forget what Miz Knight looks like." Knight's broad smile did little to put her at ease. "Let's start with the basics," he said. "Like his age."

"He was old. Ish. There was gray in his hair."

"Height? Weight?"

"My perspective wasn't good. I was lying down; he was standing."

"Not even an estimate? Taller than me or Grange? Noticeably shorter?"

"Not shorter. Slightly taller than Sergeant Grange."

By a head, at least.

"Good," Knight said. "We're getting somewhere. He have a belly like mine?" he asked, patting it. "Or was he more of a hard body like my partner?"

"Somewhere in between."

He repeated the words in a mumble, as though committing them to memory. "Distinguishing features?"

"Like what?"

"Big ears? A wart on his nose? Facial hair, scars, tattoos?"

Keep kissing my lightning bolt at your own risk, Doc.

Why? What happens?

It strikes my cock.

She looked away from Knight's perceptive gaze. "No distinguishing features that I recall."

"Approaching town, which direction were you coming from?"

"The north, I think. I'm not sure. We took a lot of turns."

"Huh."

A short silence ensued then Grange said, "Since we now know for certain which trail you were on Saturday morning, several deputies have been dispatched to see if they can retrace your steps."

"Why?"

"In the hope of locating this man who took care of you," Knight said. "To thank him and such."

She didn't believe for a moment that was the reason they were trying to retrace her steps. Her heart began to thud. "I don't think he would wish to be thanked."

"How come?"

"He impressed me as someone who would shun the limelight. He was...shy."

"Huh."

Knight's repetitive use of that single syllable was most eloquent. It implied he wasn't believing what he was hearing.

Grange was more direct. "You perceived a character trait like shyness, but you aren't clear on his height or general body build?"

She divided a look between them. "Why are you so interested in him?"

"No reason in particular," Knight said. "Just seems strange that after he sheltered you for four days and nights, took such good care of you, that he'd just drop you on the side of the road instead of delivering you into the arms of your husband or turning you over to an officer of the law."

She scrambled for an answer which, if not probable, wouldn't stretch plausibility too far. "You referred to the circus at the service station," she said. "He realized that my reappearance, my reunion with my husband, would result in exactly that kind of scene. Obviously this man values his privacy. He's reclusive and wishes to remain so. I think everyone should respect that and leave him in peace."

"So he knew that you had a husband crazy with worry over you."

She looked at Grange, realizing that she'd trapped herself. She truly was a dreadful liar.

When she didn't speak, the deputy continued. "Even if the roads were frozen over and too hazardous to drive on, why didn't he at least call somebody to let them know you were safe?"

"Perhaps his phone was inoperable."

"He had yours, Dr. Charbonneau. It was working this morning."

She couldn't think of anything to say, so she wisely said nothing.

"Why didn't you call your husband?" Grange asked.

"Until this morning, I was drifting in and out of consciousness."

"But you had intervals of lucidity."

"I wouldn't call it lucidity. I was awake, but my thoughts were hazy."

"Too hazy for you to make one phone call?"

"It crossed my mind, of course. But fleetingly. In the abstract. I didn't act on it because my phone was out of reach, and I didn't have the wherewithal to ask for it, or to get up and retrieve it."

"He had your ID. He knew who you were, where you lived. But he never offered to make a call for you?"

"Maybe he did and I don't remember. But again, I—"

"You have hundreds of numbers programmed into your phone," Grange said, pressing now. "A couple of taps on the screen, and he could have notified someone that you were still alive."

She lowered her gaze. For the longest time, neither of them said anything, but she could feel their stares boring into the crown of her bowed head.

Knight was the one to break the tense silence. "You're not being quite up front with us, are you, Dr. Charbonneau?"

"I've told you what I know."

"Well, what you've told me and Grange bothers us."

She raised her head and looked at him. "Why? I'm back. I'm fine. Isn't that all that matters?"

"Well, it would be. Except we've got an individual who interests us. He passed up a sizeable reward and dodged being thanked for his hospitality. We're thinking there was a reason he ducked the media and wanted to remain anonymous, that maybe he wasn't such a Good Samaritan.

"We think maybe your concussion wasn't caused by you falling, and that possibly he didn't *find* you on the trail, but that he *assaulted* you on the trail, banged you on the head, and then, for reasons only he knows, he chickened out on killing you."

The rock.

You weren't supposed to see that. I knew seeing it would upset you.

Chapter 23

———※◈※———

When she didn't speak, Knight leaned forward and propped his forearms on his thighs, inspiring her confidence. "Emory—can I call you Emory? You need to tell us if this man, uh, compromised you in any way."

You sorry yet?

"No, he didn't."

"I understand it might be too painful for you to talk about it to us," Knight said. "If that's the case, we can get a female officer to come over and take your statement. But we need to know if a crime was committed. No matter what he threatened to do if you reported it, you—"

"Sergeant Knight." She held up her hand. "I must stop you there. I was not his victim."

"We've had whack jobs hide up in these mountains before, you know. Good territory to get lost in. Remember the guy who bombed the Olympics in Atlanta?"

"The man in the cabin was perfectly sane."

"See any porno lying around? Videos, magazines?"

"No."

"Women-grabbers often—"

"He wasn't like that."

"Not creepy then?"

"No."

"Any rants against the government?"

"When he spoke at all, he was reasonable and soft-spoken, certainly not ranting. I would describe him as taciturn." She glanced toward the foot of the bed. "Like Sergeant Grange."

"Huh." Knight turned and looked at his partner as though assessing him for the first time. Coming back to her, he took a rubber band from his shirt pocket and began winding it around his fingers. "Did you see anything that looked like bomb-making materials?"

"No."

"Did he have guns?"

"I'm certain he did."

He raised his eyebrows. "How do you know?"

"A deer head was mounted above the mantel."

"In these parts, there are deer heads mounted above nearly every mantel."

"Precisely."

She had scored that point. Following a lull, Grange asked, "Did he demonstrate any violent tendencies?"

"Not toward me." She envisioned Norman and Will Floyd lying where they'd landed, bloody and misshapen, moaning in misery. She also thought of the gallantry extended to Pauline and the wrenching concern for Lisa. "The truth is, gentlemen, this man remains as much a mystery to me as he does to you."

Knight popped the rubber band against his fingers several times. "Guess that says it all. Unless you can think of anything else."

She shook her head. "I'm sorry."

"That doesn't leave much for us to tell the media," Grange said.

She'd momentarily forgotten the upcoming press conference, and she was grateful she wouldn't be called upon to make a statement. "Please keep the explanation to a minimum. I didn't suffer any physical or emotional trauma. I really don't owe anyone an explanation—"

"Well, see, you sorta do," Knight said. "Faking your disappearance. Causing a false public alarm. Those are crimes, Emory."

Her lips parted in surprise. "I didn't fake my concussion."

"No, no, we saw the CT," Knight said. "That part's factual. The rest..." He frowned and seemed in no way forgiving.

She took a swift breath. "I realize how many people were involved in the search for me. An undertaking like that costs time and money, and I intend to donate funds to each county involved to help them recoup that expense. Perhaps to the school systems or to the public health departments."

"Well, that's awful generous of you. A gesture like that would go a long way to keep you in the public's favor. And nobody feels inclined to press charges against you at this time."

Knight was smiling, but Emory noticed that he'd kept open-ended the option to prosecute. "To the best of my knowledge," she said, "I fell on the Bear Ridge Trail. I hit my head, sustained a concussion, and lost consciousness. When I came to, I didn't know where I was, and a combination of unpredictable circumstances prevented me from getting back. I owe my life to the kindness of a man who remains a stranger. After a few days of rest, I should be fully recovered. That's the statement you should give the media."

Essentially it was the truth.

They seemed to think it over. Knight looked over at Grange, and Grange said, "It's the best we've got." As though to soften his obvious dissatisfaction, he politely asked if she would continue her marathon training.

"Not right away." She looked at her injured foot and said ruefully, "I won't be ready for the upcoming one."

"That is a shame," Knight said. "Jeff told us how hard you've worked organizing it, making it an event."

She wondered if they knew about their heated argument on that topic but saw no point to mentioning it now.

Knight stood up, signaling an end to the interview. "Well, don't want to tucker you out."

"Will I see you tomorrow before Jeff and I leave for Atlanta?"

Knight said, "Prob'ly not."

"Then I'll thank you now. I know you put a great deal of time and effort into finding me."

"It's our job."

"Even so, thank you."

"You're welcome."

As he and Grange were about to leave, she said, "Would you do me one final favor? Would you please ask Dr. Butler to come in?"

"Remind me which one that is."

Grange nudged his partner toward the door. "The woman."

When the doctor came into the room a few moments later, Emory was glad she came unaccompanied. As she neared the bedside, Emory reached out and clasped her hand. "First of all, thank you for dropping everything and driving up here today."

"Everyone at the clinic has been frantic with worry. The office staff, nurses. Even patients. Suffice it to say Neal and I have been at wit's end. You're the heart and soul of the clinic."

"I don't know about *that*."

"No false modesty allowed. The practice was your vision, your initiative. Besides that, we all love you."

"As you demonstrated by offering the reward," she said huskily. Then, "Lord, I need another Kleenex." She popped one from the box and dabbed at her eyes.

"Are you sure you're as all right as you let everyone think?"

"I'm all right. I just need to ask you to do something for me, and it's rather sensitive."

"Of course, Emory," she said, moving closer. "Anything."

"Please bring me some morning-after pills." Emory saw her initial shock turn into alarm.

"He *raped* you? The man in the cabin? Have you told the deputies? Did they prepare a rape kit in the ER? What about Jeff? Have you told—"

"I wasn't raped."

Emory's quiet but emphatic tone stopped her. She actually swallowed audibly.

"We were intimate, but the sex was consensual. It was—" Emory stopped before submitting to the sob pressing against the back of her throat.

Rendered speechless by the disclosure, the doctor sank into the chair recently vacated by Sam Knight and for a time simply stared at Emory. Finally finding her voice, she said, "The story you told the detectives, was it all a fabrication?"

"Not the backbone of it." She didn't expand on what had been half-truths and evasions and what had been complete false-hoods. The lies had to be hers alone.

"I remain flabbergasted. I don't know what to say."

"There's nothing to say."

"I beg to differ. It's so...so un-Emory-like to—"

"Have unprotected sex?"

"To have any kind of sex with a stranger. He *was* a stranger, wasn't he?"

"He was four days ago." She smiled wistfully. "Not so much of one now."

Unable to bear her friend's mix of compassion and bewilder-ment, she turned away and looked toward the lavish bouquet of white calla lilies that Jeff had brought to her room shortly after she was checked in.

"It's not as out-from-nowhere as you might expect. I'm almost certain that Jeff is seeing someone and has been for quite some time. I could use that as justification for what I did, but that would be disingenuous and unfair. I didn't do it to punish Jeff. The fact is, I didn't take Jeff into account at all. I wanted to be with this man, and he wanted to be with me, and that was all that mattered."

"Will you see him again?"

"No."

You outdid yourself on the memories, Doc.

They'd exhausted themselves and had been lying spooned, fitted tightly together like two pieces of a puzzle, limbs entwined, hands clasped against her breasts. She'd been on the verge of sleep when he'd rubbed his face in her hair and whispered those words.

Then, *Would have been easier if you hadn't.*

Probably he hadn't intended for her to hear that annotation, or the bleakness that underscored it. He must have felt, as she did now, doomed never to be entirely happy again.

"Who was he, Emory?"

Roused from the bittersweet recollection, she whispered, "I don't know. I wasn't lying about that. I don't even know his name."

"But you slept with him."

"Yes. And I don't, nor ever will, regret it."

She became aware of the tears rolling from the corners of her eyes and hastily wiped them away. "But there are practical matters that must be addressed. As you know, I went off birth control pills six months ago, when I thought that perhaps having a child..."

She stopped and rethought what she'd been about to say, which would have sounded like she was laying blame on Jeff. Whatever else, she must never deceive herself into believing that he was responsible for what she'd done last night.

"The future of my marriage being uncertain, I can't risk adding the complication of a pregnancy."

"No precautions were taken?"

"Precautionary measures, yes, but nothing...scientific. Or reliable." Her face grew hot as she remembered his groaning, *Christ, this is torture*, averting danger with no time to spare.

"Can you bring me the pills? I can't ask the hospital staff here because I can't trust their discretion. I know I can trust yours."

"I'll get them for you, of course. But you know that emergency contraception isn't one hundred percent effective."

"I understand. But the sooner I take the first pill, the better. Which is why I'm asking you to get them for me right away, rather than waiting until tomorrow when I could buy them for myself."

"I'll go now." She stood and headed toward the door, but Emory stopped her.

"Alice?"

She turned and looked back toward the bed.

"Thank you."

Alice shook her head. "It's nothing."

"No, I'm thanking you for your confidence and for being my friend."

Chapter 24

Rebecca Watson, undaunted by the downpour, walked straight to the driver's side of Jack's rental car and rapped on the window.

Lowering it required starting the motor, which took all of five or six seconds, but the delay seemed to make her even angrier. The window came down. Rain blew in. She practically hissed at him.

"Special Agent Connell."

"I didn't know if you would remember me."

Her glower dismissed that statement as ludicrous. "If you had come to notify me that my brother is dead, you would have been straightforward and rung the front doorbell. You wouldn't have been hunkered down here half the night or spent all day spying on me. So what brings you here?"

The fact that she knew about his surveillance told him that she kept vigil herself. She watched for people watching her. He said, "Can we talk?"

"Fuck off."

"Good. You're willing to cooperate."

She gave him a drop dead look.

"I've come all this way. Please?"

She remained unmoved.

He glanced in the direction of the house. "Is he living with you?"

"Have you lost your mind?"

"Is he in this region? Residing nearby? On the next block?"

She didn't say anything.

"If he's not around, then what's the risk in talking to me?"

She didn't say yes, but she didn't say no, and she didn't tell him to fuck off again, so when she turned and walked away, he cut the car engine, got out, and followed her back to the house.

She didn't offer to share her umbrella. He covered his head with his jacket again. When they reached the porch, he shook off what rain he could. She went in ahead of him, but not before getting her mail out of the box.

"There's nothing here for you to get excited about, but knock yourself out." She thrust the handful of mail at him. He caught it against his wet jacket. Without looking at any of it, he neatly stacked it on the foyer table.

She folded her arms across her midriff. "Okay, you're here. What did you come all this way for?"

"Can I use your bathroom?"

She studied him for a moment, as though trying to figure out whether or not he was joking. Deciding he wasn't, she said, "Sure," and motioned for him to follow her down a central hallway to a tiny powder room tucked beneath the staircase.

Going in ahead of him, she lifted the lid off the toilet tank. "See? Nothing in there but the balls and cock, or whatever they're called."

"Ballcock. One word."

She replaced the lid with a clatter of porcelain and pointed to the framed mirror above the basin. "No medicine cabinet for you to inspect. You're free to tear out the plumbing underneath the sink, but if you do, you'll have to put it back together or re-imburse me for a plumber."

"You've made your point, Rebecca."

"Be sure to wash your hands." As she went out, she pulled the door closed with a bang.

He not only washed his hands, but after drying them he used the hand towel to blot rainwater off his face and neck. He straightened his tie and finger-combed his wet hair.

A few minutes later, bladder relieved and feeling presentable, he walked into her living room. She'd switched on the table lamps and was sitting in the corner of the sofa, feet tucked under her. The black, high-heeled pumps she'd kicked off lay beneath the coffee table. Ungraciously, she pointed him toward a chair that looked far less cozy and comfy than the sofa.

They faced off. He was the first to speak. "I like the new hairdo."

"Pink copied it."

"She knows her stuff."

"Enough with the flattery bullshit. How did you find me?"

"Your friend Eleanor."

"Oh." That took her aback. A sadness crept into her expression. "How is she?"

"Good. Expecting her first child in a few months."

"So she married Tim?"

"Last name Gaskin?"

She nodded, and when he confirmed that was Eleanor's married name, she said, "When I last saw her, they were getting serious. Is she happy?"

"Glowing. The baby is a girl." He told her about his visit to the brownstone and described it to her. "Eleanor called me after spotting you in the national news story about the protest in Olympia."

She drew a deep breath. "I saw it, too. I never would have participated in the march if I'd thought I'd be caught on camera."

"You stood out."

She touched her cropped hair. "I didn't think anyone would recognize me."

"Eleanor did. She was certain it was you. I wasn't. Not until yesterday when I saw you come out and get your mail."

"After all these years, you're still looking."

He shrugged. "I haven't found him yet. You're my only link."

"Lucky me."

"I'm not so bad."

She said nothing to that.

He looked around the pleasant room. He didn't know anything about home interiors, what was quality, what was junk, what was current. His apartment was functional, and that was its only boast. But to his unpracticed eye, this room looked tastefully done. Despite Wes Greer's description of the things sold in her shop, the room wasn't cluttered.

Neither was she. She wore a simple black sweater and slender black pants. Jewelry consisted of a wristwatch with a black leather strap and a long single strand of pearls. They were the same color as her hair. On her, the stark contrast worked. The only spot of color, her eyes.

He said, "Your daughter, Sarah, has grown up a lot."

"She's in the school orchestra."

"What instrument?"

"Cello. She's at rehearsal. Another parent is driving car pool today. She'll be home by six fifteen." She looked at her sensible wristwatch. "I want you out of here before then."

"Does she remember Westboro?"

"Of course."

"Does she talk about him?"

"All the time."

"What does she say?"

"That she misses her uncle."

"What do you say back to her?"

"That I miss him, too."

He held her gaze for a moment, then said, "Rebecca—"

"It's Grace now."

He tilted his head to one side. "Why Grace Kent?"

"It was suggested by the forger who made all my false documents. I didn't have another name picked, so I went with his choice."

In spite of her confession to a federal crime, he smiled. "I thought maybe you'd remarried a guy named Kent."

"I don't want another husband."

"After the one you had, I can't say that I blame you."

"Did you tell him where we are?"

Jack was already shaking his head. "And I don't plan to. I'm not here to cause you any grief. Although I could have you arrested for living under an assumed name."

"Some big, bad FBI agent you are," she scoffed. "Don't you have anything better to do?"

"Oh, I'm busy. I'm presently following up on a strange incident that occurred in Utah. Before that, I looked into a curious happening in Wichita Falls, Texas, that to this day, after two years, remains unexplained. First one that captured my interest took place in Kentucky."

Her face became a mask.

"What do you know about a soccer coach in Salt Lake?" he asked.

"That chances are good he's Mormon?"

"He's not. He moved there from Virginia."

"They don't have Mormons in Virginia?"

"The night before a championship game, what would possess a soccer coach to take a baseball bat to his femur and smash it all to hell? At least he *claims* the breaks were self-inflicted."

He let that resonate. Rebecca said nothing.

"What's also strange," Jack continued, "you'd think his team of thirteen-year-olds, their parents, and members of the community would be appalled by this tragedy. But nobody who knows him regrets his forced retirement. He had a winning record, but many questioned the methods he used to motivate his players.

"It's rumored he instilled fear. Any kid who made a mistake was humiliated. I say rumored because the kids themselves were tight-lipped about what took place during practices and after a losing game. One of the dads told me it was like his son was afraid to tattle.

"On the night of the incident, the coach told the emergency responders, his wife, the police, his priest, every-damn-body that he did that to himself. Then he clammed. No details. No reason why. No nothing. As recently as yesterday, he still refused to talk about what went down that night." He gave her a meaningful look. "You see the irony here?"

"How could I possibly miss it? You practically spelled it out in capital letters on the wall. And it's quite a story. However, how it relates to me, I don't have a clue."

"Want me to spell that out, too?"

"If you think I'm guilty of something, then why don't you arrest me?"

"I don't want to arrest you."

"Then what excuse do you have for hiding in the bushes last night and all day today, keeping track of my every move?"

"I don't enjoy spying on you."

"Then stop."

"I will. Tell me where he is and—"

"I don't know."

"Rebecca—"

"*Grace.*"

"Whatever," he said, raising his voice to match hers. "Do you expect me to believe that you haven't had any contact with him in four years?"

"I didn't say that. I said I don't know where he is, and I don't."

"So you *do* have some contact with him. How often? Once

a year, every other month, twice a week? How does he get in touch?"

She stuck out her hands, palms down. "Get out your bamboo shoots. Or does waterboarding work better?"

Frustrated, Jack got up and rounded his chair, placing his hands on the back of it as he leaned into it. He stared her down, or tried. She had the same ability to look through a person that her brother did. Turning away, he muttered, "Goddamn family trait."

"What?"

"Your eyes."

"You're not the first to remark on that. When we were kids—" She bit off what she was going to say.

Jack stepped around the chair and sat down again. "When you were kids, what?"

"Nothing."

"Come on. Tell me something I don't know. One grain of information."

"Mom made pot roast every Sunday."

"Everybody's mom makes pot roast on Sunday. Tell me something about him."

"You already know everything."

"Surprise me with something."

"He actually likes squash. Or did. I suppose he still does."

Jack watched as, in spite of herself, her thoughts turned to times past. Happier times. In a poignant tone of voice, she said, "He was always protective of me. I'm two years younger, and he took the big brother role seriously. For as far back as I can remember, he watched out for me. He wouldn't let anyone pick on me."

"With him as your bodyguard, it would take a real dumb bully to mess with you."

"I stood up for myself, too."

He grinned. "I bet you did. How exactly?"

"I told all the bullies to fuck off."

He'd walked right into that one, and he supposed that to some extent he had it coming. Grin dissolving, he turned his head toward the window; it was like looking through a waterfall. He watched rivulets of rainwater charting their inevitable course down the glass.

Coming back to her, he said quietly, "I'm not trying to bully you, Rebecca. I would if I thought it would do any good, but I don't think even bamboo shoots would get out of you where he is."

"They wouldn't, because I don't know."

"Think of the victims' loved ones." This was hitting below the belt, but he would use any device he could. "They stay in touch with me, you know. E-mails. Phone calls. Heart-wrenching shit, and I know you're not flinching because of the expletive. You know those people want and deserve—"

"Stop!"

She was off the sofa like a flash, streaking with the swift grace of a black cat out of the room. He knew she'd opened the front door because he felt a gust of damp air. Reluctantly, he got up and followed her into the foyer. She was holding the front door open, staring down at the floor between her bare feet, her posture rigid.

When he reached her, she raised her head, glaring with those crystalline eyes. "I've made a good life for Sarah and me here. But I would abandon it all in a flash. I would disappear again. Keep pestering me, and I will. You know I can."

"And you know that I'll keep looking for him until I find him."

"Waste of time. He'll never let himself be found."

"Are you sure? Have you ever thought that it might be a relief to him?"

She gave a bitter laugh. "Come now. Next you'll be telling me that it would be the best thing for him."

"Wouldn't it?"

She didn't maintain her defiant gaze for long before turning her head aside. Seeing a tiny chink in her armor, he took advantage of it. "You know it would be best for him, Rebecca. It would be a hell of a lot better for you, too. You could stop worrying about me spying. You could use your legal name. Wouldn't that be better for everybody?" He took a step closer to her and spoke with urgency. "Help yourself by helping me. Give me a hint, put me on a trail."

"You're asking me to betray my brother."

"He'll never know the information came from you. I swear that." She was listening, so he pressed on. "You don't want to abandon your pretty house here, leave your charming shop. And, even if you did, what about Sarah?"

She shot a look up at him, and he thought, *Aha! A score.*

"She was a child when you left New York, too young to understand the implications. Running away with Mommy in the dead of night was a big adventure. It wouldn't be like that now. She would balk. She wouldn't want to leave her friends. She would resent you for making her."

"It's almost time for her to get home. You have to go."

"Will you tell her that I've been here?"

"Do you think I'm crazy?"

"Then how will you explain being so upset?"

"Don't flatter yourself, Jack. You don't have the ability to upset me."

"That you called me by my first name indicates just how upset you are. Furthermore, you're lying. I think it upsets you a lot to keep your daughter living a shadow life."

He could tell she wanted to kill him for saying that. She was bristling. "Leave."

Their standoff lasted for several moments, neither giving an inch, then he swore under his breath. "All right, I'll go. For now."

"And don't come back."

"No promises of that." He stepped out onto the porch.

"Thanks for the use of your bathroom." He pulled his jacket up over his head.

"Special Agent Connell?"

He turned.

"If you go anywhere near Sarah with the idea of weaseling information out of her, I'll run you down with my car and then I'll castrate you."

Chapter 25

The press conference was conducted in the atrium lobby of the hospital. The SO's public information officer kept his statements short and sweet, providing little more information than that dictated by Emory Charbonneau herself.

Following the official statement, Jeff Surrey stepped to the podium and thanked all the law enforcement agencies and the dozens of volunteers who'd participated in the search for his wife. Then he petitioned members of the press to leave them in peace while she continued to rest and recover.

"She's anxious to return to her medical practice and resume normal activities."

"Does that include running marathons?" asked a reporter.

"Of course," Jeff replied. "But following this experience, she may rethink where she trains." That won him a smattering of laughter. He addressed another couple of questions, both relating to Emory's charitable pursuits. "In fact, this experience has left her more enthusiastic than ever. She has inspired me to accompany her on her next trip to Haiti."

That announcement came as a big surprise to everybody, but none more so than Alice Butler. Knight, standing on the fringes of the gathering, noticed her reaction. He and Grange ducked out as soon as the press conference concluded and returned to the sheriff's office. Grange wandered over to Knight's desk, bringing a saucer-sized chocolate chip cookie for each of them. "This might spoil your supper, but what the hell."

"Not a chance. The missus called a while ago and promised me chicken and dumplings." Knight bit off a quarter of his cookie. "You notice Alice Butler's reaction to Jeff's announcement about Haiti?"

"I was watching Jeff."

"Looked like she'd swallowed an egg."

"Well, the wife has returned. Jeff is showering her with affection and attention. Alice has got to feel slighted."

"I don't doubt that she's glad to have her partner and friend safely returned."

"Me either," Grange said. "But she's human. On the flip side, she has to be relieved that she wasn't drawn into a criminal investigation." He chewed his cookie. "Why do you think she's lying? Not Alice. Emory."

Knight leaned back in his chair, propped his feet on the corner of his desk, and reached for his trusty rubber band. "Because she doesn't want her husband and the rest of the world to know that she was cozied up with some guy while good people were out freezing their asses off looking for her."

"Payback for Jeff's affair with Alice?"

Knight shrugged. "Could be that his affair is payback for one of Emory's. Who knows? Anyhow, she got cold feet when her romantic getaway turned into a missing person case. Smart lady that she is, she decided to get herself on home."

Grange frowned with uncertainty. "I don't think it's as cut and dried as that, Sam."

Knight didn't either. "So talk."

"The concussion was recent," Grange said. "I asked the doctor myself. The wound on her scalp, also recent. During her four-day absence, she sustained those injuries. The *how* is what remains unclear."

"You think she lied about falling and hitting her head?"

"Possibly."

"Why lie?"

"I don't know. But I think it must have to do with the Good Samaritan. How could she stay four days with him and not know his name?"

Knight twisted his rubber band. "Jeff seemed to buy into her story of 'I don't remember.'"

"Making him guilty after all."

"Of what?"

"Stupidity."

Knight laughed. "I said he *seemed* to buy her story. Only way he can save face is to pretend he believes her. He wasn't about to point at her and shout, 'Liar, liar, pants on fire,' in front of God and everybody."

"In my book, he's still an asshole."

"You won't get an argument from me." Knight stood up, stretched his back, and pulled on his coat. "Chicken and dumplings are calling my name."

"So, case closed?"

"The missing person ain't no longer missing, Buddy."

"That much is true."

Sensing his partner's reluctance to call it quits, Knight propped his butt against the edge of his desk. "You want to arrest Dr. Charbonneau for creating a false alarm when she's got two medically documented head injuries?"

"No."

"Good. Because no prosecutor would touch it. Aside from being a lousy liar, she's as stable and sane a person as I've ever met."

"Agreed."

"So what would've been her motive for staging a disappearance?"

"Attention? Celebrity?"

"Doesn't need it," Knight said. "She's already got all the attention in the world focused on her and her good deeds."

"Retribution on somebody?"

"Besides her cheating husband, you mean? And we don't even know if she's onto his cheating. She has no known enemies. We've yet to find anybody who has a bad word to say about her. Even Dr. Butler, her husband's lover, sings Emory's praises. Tell me what she had to gain by pulling such a stunt."

"Not a damn thing," Grange said. "Which makes lying about it all the more peculiar. If she didn't devise this scheme, she shouldn't have to lie. But she is. Why?"

"Shit. Right back to my original question." Knight dragged his hand down his face, and when Grange was about to speak, he beat him to the punch. "I'm with you, I'm with you. We're missing something."

"What do you think it is?"

"Beats the hell out of me. I just hope that when and if it rears its ugly head, it's not *too* ugly."

———

Jeff looked at Emory's untouched dinner tray. "I don't blame you. It doesn't look all that appetizing. Would you like for me to go out and bring something back for you?"

"I'm not hungry, but thank you for offering."

He wheeled the tray aside so he could sit on the edge of her bed. As always he was perfectly groomed, but she could tell that he was almost as weary as she. The past four days had been harrowing for him, although each time she apologized for the hell he'd been put through, he assured her that his tribulations were forgotten the instant he heard her voice coming through his phone and knew that she was all right.

"What about your dinner?" she asked.

"I'll grab something."

"You should have let Alice and Neal take you out before they left for Atlanta."

"I didn't want to leave you alone. Besides, I think they were relieved I didn't accept the invitation. They were anxious to head back before it got any later. Alice was going to follow Neal in your car."

Jeff had asked one of them to drive it back to Atlanta so Emory could ride with him tomorrow.

Before leaving, Alice had sneaked her the EC kit as promised. She'd told Emory she didn't expect her to have any side effects, but got her promise to call if she did. Alice had also tactfully reminded her that while the pills could prevent pregnancy, they didn't prevent STDs.

Jeff snapped his fingers in front of her face. "Are you with me?"

"I'm sorry."

"I was telling you that I remembered to get your duffel bag and boots out of the trunk of your car before Alice left. Everything's in the closet, including your laptop, which the sheriff's office returned. They also gave me my pistol back."

"Pistol?"

"Just a formality, I was told. But I'm sure they checked it for recent firing." He gave a snarky smile. "Joke's on them, isn't it?"

"I fail to see the humor."

"So do I. Thank God this ordeal is over for both of us." He took her hand and clasped it between his. "Emory, I won't press you to know where you were or what you were doing after Saturday morning."

"Jeff—"

"No, don't say anything. I don't want to place you in a position of having to lie to me. The fact is, whatever transpired, I deserved it. I've been a bastard. On the best days, I've been withdrawn. On the worst, I've been difficult and often downright impossible."

He paused as though giving her a chance to dispute that. When she didn't, he continued. "You know how badly I wanted that partnership. There have been other disappointments as well."

"I can't endorse that drug, Jeff. Perhaps—"

"This isn't about that. I swear. What I'm trying to say is that these letdowns are no excuse for the way I've behaved, for the way I've treated you."

"I didn't set out to punish you."

"All right, I'll accept that," he said, but with a notable lack of conviction. "What I want you to know is that it took almost losing you for me to realize how vital you are to my happiness. No, not just to my happiness. To my *life*. I want us to make a fresh start. I want—"

His cell phone rang, interrupting him. He pulled it off his belt, read the caller's name, and muttered with irritation, "Seriously?" He answered. "What is it?"

He listened for several seconds, then said, "I have no idea. Yes, I'll ask her right now. Uh-huh. Okay, good-bye." He clicked off. "That fat detective. Knight."

"What did he want?"

"He asked if you had the hiking trail map you used on Saturday."

"It's zipped into the inside pocket of my jacket."

He got up and moved to the narrow closet where he'd earlier stored her duffel bag. Also in it was the plastic bag containing her running clothes and other belongings, which she'd given over in exchange for the hospital gown. He brought the bag back to the bed and dumped the contents.

"This blue jacket?"

She nodded, then leaned her head back and gazed at the acoustic tiles in the ceiling. "Jeff, why did you announce at the press conference that you planned to go to Haiti with me?"

She had been disinclined to watch it, but a nurse who'd been in the room at the time of the broadcast had excitedly turned on the TV. A portion of it had aired live, a leading segment of the evening news.

He said, "I wanted to go on record that I'm turning over a new leaf."

"It's an admirable gesture. But I can't see you enduring the heat and the squalid accommodations. Doling out toothbrushes to children and instructing them on their use? It just isn't you."

"But I want it to be. I want to become more involved in the things you're involved in, and…Are you sure that map was in this pocket?"

"Yes."

He turned it inside out and showed her. "Not here. I've checked all the other pockets, too."

She raised a shoulder. "That's where I remember putting it. Did Sergeant Knight say why he wanted it?"

"Something about investigators retracing the route you took on Saturday. Said the map you used might come in handy. I'll call him later and tell him we can't find it." He began stashing the items back into the plastic bag. "Who repaired your sunglasses?"

I can be dexterous when dexterity is called for. Feeling the heat of guilt staining her cheeks, she looked away. "One of the nurses, I suppose. There were several in the ER who helped me undress."

"Good thing you've got a change of clothing to wear home tomorrow. These look and smell a little worse for wear. Are you sure you don't want me to toss them?"

"No. They'll wash."

"All right then." He replaced the bag in the closet and sat back down on the edge of the bed. "Now," he said, taking a deep breath, "where was I?"

"Making a fresh start." Before he relaunched the discussion, she said, "But do you mind terribly if we start tomorrow? There's so much for us to talk about, and I'm too exhausted tonight. I'm sorry."

"No, *I'm* sorry. I should have realized." He lifted her, hugging her against him. He ran his hands up and down her back, stroking her bare skin through the opening in the hospital gown.

"There were times during the past few days when I was afraid I'd never hold you like this again. I've missed it...missed this...missed you." He kissed her temple, then her cheek, and then her lips, softly and chastely. Lowering her back onto the pillow, he said, "Now rest."

"I will."

"If you change your mind about wanting something to eat, wanting anything, promise you'll call me."

"I promise. Rest well. I'll see you in the morning."

"Bright and early. I can't wait to quit this town." He blew her a kiss at the door.

After he left, despair descended on her like some dark, malevolent bird, its wings widespread, covering her completely. Would she always feel this miserable with guilt over the lies she had told and continued to tell?

Throwing off the light blanket, she got out of bed. Pulling the IV pole along with her, she went over to the closet and took out the plastic bag that contained her belongings. She pulled from it her left running shoe, and from beneath the inner sole of it, she took out the map.

Knight had forgotten to get it from her before he left. As soon as she was alone in the room, she had retrieved the map from her jacket pocket and put it in her shoe, the only place she could think of to hide it until she was away from the hospital where she could safely throw it away.

She wasn't really concealing anything. She'd been truthful about the name of the trail she'd taken, if not specific about the narrower paths she'd branched off onto, some of which deviated from the trail she'd marked.

All the same, she would hang onto the map, not wishing to make it easier for investigators to retrace her exact route and possibly find something left behind, a clue as to her rescuer's identity or the location of his cabin.

Sam Knight, despite his "aw shucks" manner, was still a lawman. Unanswered questions and missing details nagged him. He'd led her to believe the case was as good as closed. But if that were true, why was he interested in seeing the map? Why were investigators still searching the trail?

The detective remained curious about her Good Samaritan.

Chapter 26

The phone deep inside his coat pocket vibrated.

He took it out, read the LED: BLOCKED CALL.

He answered but didn't say anything.

"It's me," Rebecca said.

He'd lied to Emory about not having a cell phone. He had dozens, off-brands he bought in the supermarket, the kind that sold for practically a dime a dozen, disposable. They were used only to communicate with his sister.

Each time he called her, he gave her the number for the next phone, then destroyed the one he'd just used. That way, she always had an untraceable number to call if she needed to reach him in an emergency.

He braced himself to receive bad news. "What's happened?"

"Special Agent Jack Connell came to call."

He hadn't seen that coming, and for a moment he was speechless. Then, in a stage whisper, "Are you fucking kidding me?"

"I wish."

"When was this?"

"Today."

After four years, Connell had showed up *today*. The day Emory was returned to her husband, when she'd been surrounded by law enforcement officers and media. Coincidence? The two events had occurred three thousand miles apart. What possible link could they have to each other? Only one. Him.

"What did he want?"

"What do you think? You."

"Son of a bitch."

"He's still got the puppy dog eyes," she said.

"Don't trust them."

"Oh, I didn't. Not for a minute. He's as manipulative as ever, but he really needs to brush up on his surveillance skills. He was parked down the street when I came home from work yesterday evening."

"Why didn't you call me then?"

"I thought he would give up and go away."

"Fat chance of that."

"I waited twenty-four hours before busting him."

"He came alone?"

"Yes."

"How long was he there?"

"Here in the house, for about fifteen minutes."

"You let him in?"

"For fifteen minutes," she repeated testily. "Then I sent him packing."

"Doesn't mean he's not still watching you."

"I don't think he is."

He had to trust her on that. She was savvy and elusive. Or had been until now. He asked the most pertinent question. "How did he track you all the way to Seattle?"

She explained how her former coworker at Macy's had spotted her on a newscast. He began to relax a little when he realized that there was no connection between Emory and the FBI agent's unheralded visit to his sister.

"It was stupid of me to participate in the protest," she was saying. "I realize that now, but I never thought it would merit national news coverage."

"But you've changed your appearance."

"Not enough to fool Eleanor, it seems."

"I remember her. You two were close."

"She had a mad crush on you, I think. Before..."

What she'd been about to say was *before Westboro*. Everything had changed after that, but it was a waste of time to discuss what they both already knew, and prudently they shouldn't talk too long. Especially in light of Jack Connell's recent reappearance. "You didn't leave him alone, did you?"

"Only to go to the bathroom, and—before you panic—I listened at the door. He peed and washed up. He wasn't in there long enough to do anything else. But I thoroughly checked the room after he left anyway."

Good girl. "What did you two talk about for fifteen minutes?"

"He mentioned Salt Lake City. Texas and Kentucky, too."

"I don't suppose they were vacation destinations on his bucket list."

"Don't be cute. He asked what I knew about a soccer coach. I played dumb, but of course he didn't buy it."

No mention of North Carolina or even the region. No mention of an Atlanta physician who'd gone missing for four days. Breathing more easily, he switched subjects. "How's Sarah?"

"We'll get to her. How are *you*?"

"All right."

"No you're not."

"Yes, I am."

"What's happened?"

"Nothing."

"Don't bullshit me! You don't sound right. Are you sick?"

"Healthy as a horse."

"Then what's going on?"

Rebecca had always been able to detect an evasion. A lie she could spot from a mile off. He should quit while he was ahead. "Look, I'd better go. Thanks for the heads-up about Connell."

"I had to warn you. He's still on your trail."

"If he was hot on it, he wouldn't be pestering you. One thing, though. You're sure it was your friend who put him on to you? He might have been lying about that."

"He wasn't. I checked. After he left, I called Eleanor." Rebecca was scrupulous about covering her tracks, and thereby his tracks. It took him aback that she had reconnected with her friend in New York.

"She verified that Connell had come to see her and only after she had called him." Sounding defensive, she added, "I enjoyed talking to her. She's married now. Pregnant with her first child. It was good to hear her sounding so happy."

He bowed his head low, tucking his chin into the collar of his coat, pained that his sister felt it necessary to make an excuse for enjoying a chat with an old friend. Her loyalty to him had cost her dearly. He probably knew of only a fraction of the sacrifices she had made, and was still making, in order to protect him.

"I'm glad you called," he said thickly. "Thanks. I'll be in touch."

"Don't you dare hang up!"

"I've talked too long already."

"You asked about Sarah."

His heart hitched. "She okay? Jesus, Connell didn't—"

"No. I threatened him with emasculation if he went near her."

"And then I'd have to kill him."

"Unnecessary for the time being. In answer to your question, Sarah is doing great."

"Still playing the cello?"

"There's a recital in a few weeks. I wish you could be here for it."

"I wish I could be too." A silence followed, and it stretched out until it took on more significance than merely a lapse in conversation. "What aren't you telling me, Becs?"

When she was twelve and he was fourteen, she'd smacked him every time he'd taunted her with the pet name. Over time, however, she'd come to like it, even though his using it usually signaled a shift in the tenor of their conversation. It was the verbal equivalent of getting to the heart of the matter, of the kid gloves coming off.

"Sarah and I like it here," she said. "She loves her school. She has tons of friends. The shop is doing well. Outperforming my projections. We've made a home here. If I were to uproot us again—"

"I didn't ask you to uproot the first time."

"No, it was my decision alone to leave New York. But as long as Jack Connell had me on his radar, he was going to be a pest, and I hated having my life monitored.

"Then, too, Sarah and I needed a fresh start, away from that jerk I was married to. I don't regret leaving Manhattan."

She paused to take a breath. "But moving to a different city now, assuming another name, having to lie to everyone in order to establish a new identity, I don't want to do it again."

"I don't want you to either," he said, meaning it. "Stay where you are, Becs, and live your life. Don't consider me every time you make a decision. Your happiness and well-being, Sarah's, that's all that you should take into account."

"But now that Jack Connell knows where I am—"

"You can't betray me to him because you don't know anything."

"He doesn't believe that. He's certain that I know where you are."

"Then he's wrong, isn't he?"

"And so are you."

"Am what?"

"*Wrong.* Something's going on. What?"

God, she was tenacious. "Don't worry about me. I'm fine."

Ever attuned to the slightest nuance, she asked, "What did you do this time?"

"You know better than to ask."

"Just tell me so I won't have to worry."

He hesitated, then said, "I got crosswise with my neighbors." Experience had taught her to read between the lines. She wouldn't guess that, this time, he was speaking literally.

"Plural?"

"Two of them."

She made a small sound of regret. "How *crosswise* did you get?"

"They're still breathing, if that's what you're asking."

"Don't get nasty. I just want to know what happened."

"Actually, Becs, you don't. If you don't know, you won't ever have to lie about it."

"For God's sake, when will you stop?"

"When I'm finished."

"Or until someone finishes you."

"There's always that possibility."

She gave a huff of mirthless laughter. "But I'm not supposed to worry?"

He didn't have a response for that.

"If you're done there, wherever *there* is, you'll be relocating now."

He looked at the building across the street from where he was leaning against a utility pole. Visiting hours at the hospital were over, so there weren't as many people coming and going as there had been earlier.

The two men who'd escorted Emory into the ER earlier in the day had driven away in their SUV. The news vans had departed after the press conference. Shortly after ten o'clock Jeff Surrey had left in a late-model European car.

Somewhere in that building Emory was alone, and would be for the rest of the night. That should relieve his mind. It didn't.

To his sister, he said, "I can't relocate right away."

"You always do. Immediately."

"Not this time."

"What makes this time different?"

He couldn't tell her or she would be even more worried and afraid than she was. If he told her about Emory, she would advise him to turn his back, walk away, leave it alone, and do so tonight, *now*. He didn't want to hear it from Rebecca. He knew it already.

"I have to wrap up something here before moving on, that's all."

"You're not going to tell me, are you?"

"No."

"Does it have to do with Westboro?"

"No. This is something else." Before she demanded to know information he wouldn't share, he gave her the number of another burner phone. "Same rules. Call it only if you have to."

"I will. Will you call me?"

"Sure."

After a beat, she said, "You're taking on more trouble, aren't you?"

He didn't say anything.

"Swear to God," she said, "if I knew where you were, I would call Jack Connell right this minute and tell him."

"No you wouldn't."

She blew out a gust of breath and, with defeat, said, "No, I wouldn't. But he did say something about you today that I can't get out of my head."

"This ought to be good."

"He said that it might actually be a relief to you if you were found."

"A *relief*?"

"That was the word he used."

"Then he's full of shit. If he comes around again, tell him to fuck off."

She laughed. "I couldn't have said it better myself."

Her laughter was a good note on which to end the call. Before either of them became maudlin, before they had to actually say good-bye, he disconnected. Then he removed the battery from the phone and ground the phone itself beneath his boot until it was broken into bits.

He knelt and swept all the pieces of the phone off the ground into his hand and dropped them in his coat pocket to dispose of later. Then he dug into his jeans pocket and took out the tiny silver trinket, the token that he'd kept as a tangible link to Emory, not realizing until today what vital importance it had.

Thoughtfully rubbing it between his fingers, he gave the hospital one last look, and, convinced that nothing untoward was likely to happen tonight, he started back toward where he'd left his truck. He had a lot of work to do tonight. Busy work. Tasks that should keep his mind off Emory.

But wouldn't.

For four years, he'd lived with loneliness and had even reconciled himself to it.

But in only four days his tolerance for it had expired. It had begun to hurt.

Chapter 27

Emory sat bolt upright, gasping.

Wildly, she looked around, expecting to see the log walls, the lamp with the burlap shade, him.

But he wasn't there, and this wasn't the cabin, and the Floyd brothers weren't about to barge through the door with a loaded shotgun.

She was in her hospital room, safe and secure.

So why was her heart racing? Why was she so oxygen-deprived that her hands and feet were tingling?

She recognized the classic symptoms of a panic attack, but for the life of her, she didn't know what had brought it on. A bad dream? Deep-seated guilt from having lied to law enforcement officers?

Either would do it.

But she sensed the reason for her acute anxiety was something more imperative. She got out of bed and dragged the IV pole with her over to the door. Opening it only a crack, she stuck her head through and looked in both directions. The corridor was empty. No one lurking outside her room. None of the nursing staff in sight. Nothing threatening.

She backed into the room and closed the door.

She went into the bathroom to use the toilet and bathe her face with a damp cloth. The tile floor was cold against her bare feet. On her way back to the bed, she retrieved the bag containing her belongings from the closet and carried it with her to the bed. As she rummaged through it looking for her socks, she conceded that Jeff was right. Her running clothes did smell rather—

Suddenly prompted by intuition, she upended the bag and shook the contents into her lap, convinced that the answer to what had caused her panic attack was something within that bag.

She rifled through the articles rapidly, then more slowly, handling them individually, taking them into account one by one.

When realization struck, the shock was electrifying.

She sat for a moment trying to decide what to do, then, with trembling hands, she punched in a number on her cell phone, and waited anxiously for the call to be answered.

After several rings, a sleepy voice said, "Emory? Is everything okay?"

"Alice! I apologize for waking you."

"Are you all right?"

"I'm fine. I mean I'm not, or I wouldn't be calling you at— What time is it?"

"Doesn't matter. What's wrong? You sound frantic."

She forced herself to calm down and take deep breaths. "I need to ask you something, and I didn't want to wait until morning."

"I'm listening."

"Today, when all of you were in my hospital room and I was describing the fall I took, and hitting my head, all that, did I mention breaking my sunglasses?"

"What?"

"Think back, Alice. Please. It's important. Did I refer to breaking my sunglasses?"

"I don't remember. Why?"

She swallowed with effort. "Because Jeff asked me earlier tonight who had repaired them. I told him that one of the nurses must have, when actually it was the man in the cabin."

"Okay," Alice said slowly, clearly mystified.

"How did Jeff know my glasses had broken when I fell?"

Alice took time to think it over. "You repeated your story several times throughout the afternoon. You must have mentioned the sunglasses at one time or another."

She gnawed her lower lip. "I don't think so."

"Are you implying... What are you implying?"

"Just hear me out, please. Since our reunion this morning, Jeff has been like a different person. He's hovered. He's been protective, loving, even contrite. Not at all like him, as you know."

"Emory—"

"I know what you're going to say. You're going to say that would be normal penitential behavior for a man who's been having an affair."

"That's exactly what I was going to say. In light of your close call, he feels truly rotten and wants to atone for straying."

"That makes sense, and I would agree, except that his coddling feels phony and forced. Like he's putting on an act. I don't feel comfortable around him. He's made me very ill at ease. I know it sounds crazy."

"It doesn't sound crazy. It does, however, sound like it's coming from someone who took a hard blow to the head. Did they give you a sedative tonight? It could be affecting—"

"This isn't medication talking. I'm not delusional. I'm not hysterical."

Alice's silence on the other end indicated that perhaps she did sound hysterical. She rolled her lips inward to prevent herself from saying anything that would affirm it.

Alice said, "Let me be sure I understand. You're suggesting that Jeff was there, that he had a hand in the injury that caused your concussion?"

"If he didn't, how did he know about my sunglasses?"

Alice took a deep breath. "All right, say he did incapacitate you. Then what? He left you for this mountain man to kidnap? Do you think Jeff and he were in cahoots?"

"No. Impossible."

"More impossible than what you're alleging?"

"I'm not alleging anything. I'm just—" What *was* she doing?

"Have you told the two detectives about this?" Alice asked.

"Not yet."

"You should."

"I considered calling Sergeant Knight, but I wanted confirmation about the sunglasses first. I hoped you would tell me yes I definitely referenced them, or no I definitely did not."

Softly Alice said, "You didn't. Not in my hearing."

Emory expelled her breath in a gust. "Thank you."

"But how many times had you told the story before Neal and I arrived?"

"Several. Fragments of it anyway."

"Can you absolutely swear that you didn't at some point mention your sunglasses?"

When she looked back over the day, it was a jumble of incomplete impressions, as though someone had made a jigsaw puzzle of it, then tossed all the pieces into the air and let them fall.

She'd been suffering the impact of her reentry into normal life and concentrating so hard on not trapping herself in a lie, perhaps she had referred to her sunglasses and simply didn't remember doing so.

"No," she admitted softly. "I can't absolutely swear to it."

Alice waited several moments, then said, "I believe you took something Jeff said in passing and blew it out of proportion."

"I'd like to think so. Truly I would. But I have such a strong gut feeling that something isn't right."

"May I offer a couple of explanations for why you feel that way?"

"Please."

"You've been through an ordeal that packed a wallop, emotionally as well as physically. You suffered a brain injury, a mild one, but a brain injury nonetheless. You slept with a stranger. In terms of Emory Charbonneau's comfort zone, that's outside the stratosphere. Naturally, you're feeling a bit fragile, insecure, even frightened."

"I hear what you're saying, Alice. But when have you known me to let my imagination run wild, or to go all aflutter in a crisis situation?"

"Never. But this was no ordinary crisis. This was *your* crisis."

She sighed. "All right, that's one explanation. You said you had a couple."

"Guilt, perhaps?"

Emory thought about it. "I'm finding fault with Jeff to assuage my own guilt for sleeping with another man?"

"I'm no psychiatrist, but that kind of transference seems logical, doesn't it?"

"I suppose."

"You don't sound convinced."

She wasn't. She had done the exact opposite by resolving not to blame Jeff for her adultery. "It's not entirely unthinkable that Jeff was somehow involved. The detectives suspected him."

"He was cleared."

Yes, Emory thought, *but only because I showed up alive.*

Alice was saying, "Jeff isn't the warmest individual, and, in fact, he can be a self-centered son of a bitch. But during one of our conversations while you were still missing, he told me he wanted to be an ideal husband to you, the kind that you deserve." She paused, then added in a heartfelt whisper, "I swear to you, he couldn't have harmed you."

Panic attacks were sparked by traumatic events. Just as often they were brought on by imagined or manufactured terrors. Clearly Alice believed her suspicions were groundless. And perhaps they were. "I apologize for waking you up."

"You know I'm here for you," Alice said. "But I need to beg off. I have two scheduled C-sections tomorrow."

Emory apologized for keeping her on the phone for so long.

Alice was still reluctant to hang up. "Are you sure you're all right?"

"Yes, I'm fine. Thanks for listening."

"We'll talk again tomorrow. Get some rest. Things will look better in the morning."

But in the morning, they didn't.

She was dressed and waiting when Jeff arrived. He pushed through the door and exclaimed, "You look gorgeous!"

She forced herself to smile. "Hardly, but I made a few improvements."

"That's always been one of my favorite outfits."

"It's jeans and a sweater."

"It's *you* in jeans and a sweater." He bent down and brushed his mouth across hers. "How did you sleep?"

She didn't tell him about her panic attack or her conversation with Alice. But after it, while lying sleepless and agitated, she had made up her mind *not* to live in doubt and fear. She refused to harbor doubts about the man to whom she was married. She would ask him straight out how he knew about her sunglasses. She hoped he would have a logical explanation that would eliminate her misgivings and make her feel ridiculous for entertaining them even for an instant.

Briskly, he rubbed his palms together. "Got everything? Ready to roll?"

"As soon as they bring a wheelchair. You know, hospital rules. While we're waiting, I want to ask about something that's been nagging me."

His smooth forehead furrowed. He took her hand and massaged the back of it with his thumb. "Judging by your expression, it's something serious. What is it?"

Gathering her courage, she said, "Jeff—"

Her cell phone rang. Earlier she'd transferred it from her fanny pack to her handbag. She took it out, read the LED, and answered. "Sergeant Knight?"

Jeff dropped her hand, muttering a swear word.

"Hey, Dr. Charbonneau," the detective said. "How're you doin' this morning?"

She was on the verge of blurting out *You may have been right about Jeff after all*. But instead, she said, "I'm feeling much better, thank you."

"Glad to hear it. Is your husband with you?"

"He's standing right here."

"Good. That's good. Listen, something's come up. Me and Buddy Grange would like to drop by the hospital before y'all leave for home. Is now a good time?"

The nurse appeared in the doorway, pushing a wheelchair.

Emory held up an index finger, asking her to wait for a moment. "What's come up, Sergeant Knight?"

"Rather not go into it over the phone."

Jeff. They'd discovered something that implicated Jeff.

"We'd rather talk to y'all in person," Knight said.

A bit breathless, she said, "No need for you to come to the hospital. We'll come to you."

Chapter 28

Knight and Grange walked them through a squad room that Jeff had described to her in disparaging detail. "I hoped never to see this place again," he said to Emory under his breath. "He didn't give you a hint as to what this is about?"

"Only that he didn't want to discuss it over the phone."

They followed the two detectives down a short hallway and into an interrogation room. "It'll be quieter in here," Knight said as he held a chair for her. "Jeff, you take that seat. Can I get y'all something to drink?"

They declined in unison.

Knight sat down across the small table from her. Grange propped himself against the wall, one hand in his pants pocket, the other holding a manila envelope against his thigh. He looked casual and relaxed.

Emory wasn't deceived.

Knight began. "You got a good night's rest?"

No, I had an epiphany. She hedged. "You know how it is in a hospital."

"They wake you up to put you to sleep."

"Something like that."

"Can we please get to the reason we're here?" Jeff said. "We have the drive to Atlanta ahead of us." He looked impatient, like he would very much like to be anyplace other than here.

Knight grimaced. "We've inconvenienced you and then some, Jeff."

"Inconvenienced? Try insulted."

"Right." Knight sighed. "And Grange and me have both told you we're sorry. We say so again. Our apologies." When Jeff didn't respond, Knight went on. "Reason I called y'all this morning, reason I asked about your wife's rest, I thought maybe something had been jostled loose during the night."

"You make it sound like teeth," Jeff said.

Knight grinned with good humor. "I was thinking more along the lines of a memory that had slipped her mind yesterday. Thought something might've worked itself free overnight."

Under the circumstances, the detective's perception was extraordinary. She glanced nervously at Jeff before coming back to Knight. "The deputies who were going to retrace my route, have they discovered something?"

"Not yet. That map of yours ever turn up?"

"You have maps of the park," she countered. "Probably much more detailed than mine, which I printed off the Internet. How could it possibly help?"

"Well, so we'll be sure you didn't take a detour or make a wrong turn. Because—here's what's so darn bedevilin'—nobody can pinpoint the spot of your mishap, whatever it was. Any idea how far you'd gone before it occurred?"

"I estimate that I'd been running for about an hour. I never reached my turnaround."

"You're sure of that?"

"Yes."

They looked doubtful, but she couldn't tell if it was over her not reaching her turnaround or her inability to remember if she had. She shifted in the chair, which had probably been designed for discomfort. "Believe me, I want to know what happened up there as much as you do."

Knight exchanged a look with Grange before coming back to her. "You're sure you don't have anything to add to what you told us yesterday?"

She would rather not bring up her sunglasses until after she learned what they had to share, the matter too sensitive to discuss over the phone.

"Nothing? Aw-right then." Turning to his partner, Knight asked, "Is it ready?"

Grange pushed himself away from the wall. "All set." A laptop sitting on the table had been turned away from her. Grange pivoted it until the monitor was facing her.

Jeff, who also had a vantage point to see the screen, said, "What the hell is this? Home movies?"

Knight said, "Kinda like that."

"This was brought to our attention this morning." Grange tapped the play icon in the center of the screen, and the video began.

The picture quality wasn't good, it was dark and grainy, but Emory recognized the room instantly. Her stomach dropped. Behind her eardrums, her blood surged like water from a breaking dam.

She watched as she walked into the frame, her back to the camera. When she turned, a beam of light shone directly into her face. She raised a hand to shade her eyes. "Lower that, please. It's blinding me."

She remembered him moving the flashlight a few degrees to the right, but she was still visible to the camera as she took in her surroundings. "This is his office. There won't be anything in here. We need to find an examination room, a storage closet where he keeps supplies and meds."

"Lead the way, Doc."

She walked out of frame. The room went black, and so did the computer screen. Then a menu materialized, giving the viewer the options to replay, pause, or exit.

Grange paused it and returned to his place against the wall.

Emory sat as though petrified. She could feel Jeff's incredulous gaze. After a few ponderous seconds, he stood up and moved to stand behind her chair, gently placing his hands on her shoulders.

"Emory, who was that? *What* was that?"

Through her sweater, his hands felt damp. Or, more likely, it was her body that had broken a sweat from sheer mortification.

Knight placed his hands on the table. She noticed that a rubber band was wrapped tightly around two of his fingers. He was plucking at it, making light snapping noises.

"Dr. Charbonneau? Emory?"

She quit her study of the rubber band and looked him in the eye.

"Dr. Cal Trenton was in Coral Gables, Florida, with his wife to celebrate their fortieth wedding anniversary. He gave his whole staff the week off. They didn't reopen till yesterday. When they did, they discovered that the office had been burglarized, and everybody went into a tizzy. It wasn't until this morning that the doctor remembered the nanny cam he'd put in his bookcase a few months back.

"Seems he keeps a bottle of hooch in his bottom desk drawer, and he suspected the after-hours cleaning ladies of helping themselves. He hoped to catch them at it. But," he said with a wave that dismissed the backstory, "in the long run, he just replaced them with a crew of teetotalers.

"He didn't know if the camera was still recording. It was on one of those cycle-timer things. A loop, I think somebody called it. Anyhow, he took out the disk and brought it here to the deputy who'd investigated the break-in yesterday." He raised his beefy shoulders in a shrug that was almost apologetic. "He recognized you right off, of course. Called me at home."

She was looking at him, but her eyes had glazed, thinking of the catastrophic damage this had done to her credibility. She was armed with nothing more than an unexplained reference to sunglasses. The authorities had a video of her burglarizing a doctor's office.

Knight spoke her name, softly but with a definite prod behind it.

She brought herself out of her daze. "Will I go to jail?"

Knight looked over at Grange, who seemed to share his senior partner's dismay. When Knight turned back to her, he said, "That's all you have to say?"

"Yes."

"No explanation?"

"Is one necessary?"

"Emory, don't say another word until we get an attorney here," Jeff said. He tugged on the back of her chair as though expecting her to stand up and leave.

"You can play it like that," Knight said.

"I should have played it like that when you started questioning me about her disappearance. We know how wrong you were then, and I'm certain that Emory has a logical explanation for this…" At a loss, he motioned toward the laptop. "But she won't say anything else until she has a lawyer present."

Knight patted the air. "Calm down, Jeff. We don't want to book Dr. Charbonneau just yet. We feel sure there were extenuating circumstances, and we'd like to hear what they were. While we get some clarification from Emory, why don't you wait outside?"

"Why don't you kiss my ass?"

"Jeff." She turned in her chair and looked up at him. "You're probably right about having defense counsel. I'm sure our business lawyer could refer someone. Would you please deal with that for me?"

"And leave you in here alone with them?"

Grange stepped away from the wall. "Actually, it's not up to you to decide who stays and who goes. We can have you escorted out."

Before the situation got entirely out of hand, Emory clasped Jeff's arm. "Call our lawyer and get that process started. I'll be careful of what I say."

He glared at the two detectives. "If this ever results in an arrest or trial, I'll testify that you denied my wife an attorney's presence when you questioned her."

"Duly noted," Grange deadpanned.

Jeff bent down and kissed her temple, whispering, "Why didn't you share this with me?"

"I couldn't."

He hesitated, obviously wanting to know more. Then he gave her shoulders a reassuring squeeze. "I believe in you."

"Thank you."

He stalked out and slammed the door shut behind him.

A tense silence ensued. Finally Knight said, "Well? Care to share what you were doing in that video?"

"Isn't it apparent?"

"You don't want to tell us why you burglarized this doctor's office?"

"No."

"You holding a grudge against Dr. Trenton?"

"I've never met him. I didn't even know his name until you told me."

"You picked his office at random?"

She didn't answer.

"You were just cruising through that one-horse town, spotted his office, and decided to bust the lock on the back door and help yourself to some medical supplies?"

She remained silent.

Knight leaned forward. "Emory, let's cut this BS. Excuse the French. Why'd you break into that doctor's office and take—"

Grange stepped forward and extended him a sheet of paper he withdrew from the manila envelope. Knight shoved on his reading glasses. Reading aloud, he itemized the things she had collected into a plastic trash can liner for easier toting, which had been her accomplice's idea.

When he finished, she said, "Plus a box of latex gloves."

Knight shook the paper in his hand. "Why'd you take these things that you could've gotten from your own office?"

"I was more than a hundred miles away from my office."

"And you needed this stuff right that minute?"

She said nothing.

"Did you need these things to treat a patient?"

Again, she remained silent.

"Yourself? Were you treating yourself? Don't look at me like I'm loco. Did you need these items for yourself?"

"No."

He sat back, took a moment. "Okay. The man with the flashlight, he called you Doc, suggesting some level of familiarity. Is he the man from the cabin, who took good care of you but whose name has escaped your recollection?"

"It hasn't escaped my recollection. I don't know it."

"He was your partner in crime, and you don't know his name?"

Without admitting to the commission of a crime, she said, "I don't know his name."

Knight and Grange looked at each other. Grange raised his eyebrows expressively. Knight glanced toward the door, then, lowering his voice, asked, "Emory, is he a boyfriend you met up here for the weekend?"

"A boyfriend?" It was a laughable term when applied to him. "No. I'd never seen him before."

"Before what?"

"Before I regained consciousness inside his cabin."

Still speaking in a hushed voice, Knight said, "We don't want to cause a rift between you and Jeff. Y'all will have to sort out the marriage angle on your own. But you need to tell us who this burglar is."

She looked at each of them in turn. "If you want his name from me, you had just as well save your breath and put me in jail now. I don't know who he is."

Knight released a long sigh. "Technically you committed a Class H felony, which, if convicted, is punishable by several years in prison. However, in North Carolina we have structured sentencing, and we use a point system to rank a crime, taking into account the severity of it, the perp's motive, and previous criminal history."

"I'm not sure what—"

"What that means is," he said, cutting her off, "nobody wants to lock you up. This was no crash and grab. There was a bank envelope with a couple hundred dollars of petty cash in the office manager's desk. It's still there.

"A locked cabinet containing painkillers, uppers, and downers, which would have sold on the street for a bundle, was left untouched. Well, not untouched, exactly. The lock on it was broken, but nothing was taken except for two weeks' supply of antibiotics, which, I'm told, in Europe you can buy at the CVS or whatever."

He let all that sink in before continuing. "Dr. Trenton said it looked to him like the missing articles had been shopped for, so to speak, by a professional. A medical professional, not a professional thief. He said the only things taken were what would be needed for a procedure. Say, the termination of a pregnancy."

He'd been cataloging her reactions, and when she cast her eyes down she cursed herself for being so transparent.

Knight sat forward again, all earnestness and compassion now. "Did that man force you to steal that stuff and get rid of a problem for him?"

She said nothing.

"Emory?"

She refused to respond.

As though receiving a silent signal from Knight, Grange pulled out a chair and sat down with them at the table. He had lived up to Jeff's description as the "bad cop." She prepared herself for some arm-twisting.

He said, "Sam and I don't believe you got it into your head to commit a B and E and steal some country doctor's plastic gloves. Dollarwise, the medical equipment stolen didn't add up to much. If Dr. Trenton is reimbursed for it, I doubt he'd want to see an esteemed colleague like you charged, much less tried. Granted, the medications that were stolen are controlled substances, but somebody could get a lot higher on a bottle of NyQuil."

He paused. "Sam and I think you were forced or coerced into committing that burglary. What we don't get is why you're protecting *him*, the guy we can't see. The guy with the raspy voice. Who is he, Dr. Charbonneau?"

"I've told you, I don't know."

"Well, we may be able to help with that."

Surprised by that statement, she watched Grange remove a map from the manila envelope. He spread it open. It was a duplicate of the map she'd used to chart her run on that otherwise innocuous Saturday when, without any foretelling, her life had turned upside down. If the last five minutes were any indication of things to come, it appeared likely that her life would never be right side up again.

Someone had drawn a star in red ink on the map. Grange put the tip of his index finger on it. "This is the parking lot where you left your car. Your starting point, right?"

She nodded.

"The Chevron station where you were dropped off yesterday is here at this crossroads." He pointed it out to her. "And here's the town where Trenton's office is."

"What we did," Knight said, "was sorta connect those dots to form a circle. Then we started checking arrest records, looking for anybody with priors who lives within that circle or close enough."

Grange said, "Several names popped up."

She held her breath.

"One was a guy who is currently serving time for armed robbery," Grange said. "Another's wife killed him eight months ago, so he's not our man. But we got several other names." Knight smiled at her. "And one in particular looks real good to us."

Chapter 29

Emory thought she might throw up. She lowered her head and cupped her hand around her mouth.

Was yours a violent crime?

Extremely.

"Name's Floyd."

Her head snapped up. "What?"

"There are two of them, actually," Grange said. "Brothers. Norman and Will Floyd."

It was an effort not to give away her relief.

"Will, the younger, is particularly ornery," Knight said. "Dropped out in tenth grade, and nobody in the school system was sad to see him go. Always in trouble. Noted bully. Ne'er-do-well. He has a couple of B and Es to his credit. Vandalism. Shoplifting.

"Last summer, he harassed a young woman at a baseball game, got rough with her in the parking lot, but she got cold feet about pressing charges, so he was released. Here's his mug shot. Look familiar?"

He withdrew a rap sheet with Will Floyd's photo. In it he looked like the belligerent, depraved individual he was.

"And this is his big brother, Norman, who has a similar rap sheet."

Knight passed it to her. "Take a good look at them. But before you say anything, you should know that we already sent a deputy up there to question these boys."

Her burble of elation was replaced by dread. It seeped through her like a paralyzing poison.

"What we heard back from the deputy? He was informed by their mother that her sons are presently sharing a room in the county hospital. The deputy went to see them there. Will is real bad off. He has a…mandi…mandubur—"

"Mandibular fracture," she said quietly.

The detective nodded. "That's it. His jaw's wired shut with rods sticking out his face. The deputy described the apparatus as looking like something out of a torture chamber.

"Norman's face looked like 'a hunk of pork gone bad that had been run through a sausage grinder anyway.' That's a quote. Plus he's got four broken ribs, a dislocated shoulder, and a kidney that has turned his urine red. The deputy took his word for that."

Grange picked up the thread. "But when he wasn't wheezing in pain, Norman could talk, and before his brother wrote down on a piece of paper for him to shut the eff up, he alleged it was their neighbor who inflicted the injuries.

"He claimed they'd never had any trouble with him until night before last, when he and a lady doctor, a Dr. Smith, intruded on what should have been a private family matter and made a house call to treat their ailing sister, Lisa."

After a time, when she still didn't speak, Knight said. "Emory? This guy who lives down the road a piece from the Floyds, we're bettin' he's the man in the video. Correct?"

Both settled gazes on her, but it was Knight whom she addressed. "Was Lisa there?"

"At the house? No," Knight replied. "Mrs. Pauline Floyd told the deputy that somebody came early this morning, before daylight, and took her."

"Took her?"

"Yes, but she wouldn't say who."

"Don't forget about the dog," Grange said.

"Oh, yeah," Knight said. "He also drove off with the family pet."

At the tender memory the dog evoked, she smiled.

Grange said, "That's funny?"

"No." Feeling weary, she pushed back a strand of hair. "I assure you that the situation in the Floyd household was no laughing matter."

Grange pounced on that. "So you were there? You were Dr. Smith?"

Declining to answer that, she asked, "Was Pauline all right?"

Grange held her gaze, as though considering how much to tell her. "Depends on your viewpoint. She was fine. But she frustrated the deputy by claiming not to know the individual who thrashed the living daylights out of her sons, although according to them she witnessed the altercation.

"The deputy described her as uncooperative because she flatly refused to answer his questions about the unnamed someone who carted off her daughter, saying only that he was a 'right decent sort.'"

He'd won Pauline's loyalty by treating her with respect and dignity, probably one of the few people in her whole life who had.

Knight was saying, "Those boys told the deputy that relatives in town had been persuaded by Pauline to take Lisa back. Whatever that means. We got the name of Mrs. Floyd's sister and called. She confirmed that the girl and dog were dropped off at her place around dawn by a man driving a pickup truck. He didn't stick around. Left his passengers at the curb and drove away. Exactly the way it was with you yesterday."

She didn't address his last statement. She was thinking about Lisa's welfare. "Has anyone spoken to Lisa?"

"Not yet. We will."

"Send a female officer to question her. She should be gently dealt with."

After a short but telling pause, Grange asked, "Was she raped?"

Emory said, "She's fifteen."

"Did you terminate her pregnancy?"

"That's privileged information."

"Did the mystery guy get the girl pregnant and—"

"No."

"How do you know?"

"Again. Privileged."

"The Floyd boys don't share their mother's opinion of this man. Before pulling the dumb act, Norman referred to him as a brute."

She snuffled with disgust. "Norman would know."

After a short pause, Knight tried again. "Emory, did you witness the beating he gave those boys?"

"I want my lawyer."

Knight leaned toward her again. "You scared?"

"Of arrest?"

"Of *him*?" he asked with annoyance.

"No."

Knight angrily popped his rubber band. "What gets me, is all y'all refusing to talk about this guy. The deputy told us that no sooner had Norman mentioned him than Will went bonkers right there in his hospital bed. He was mm-hmming and shaking his head, best he could with those rods sticking out his jawbone.

"Then he motioned for paper and pen and scribbled that note for Norman not to say any more, and Norman heeded the warning. Went mute from there. It was like they were scared, and these two have never been timid a day in their lives, and they don't frighten or back down easily."

She just looked at him.

He exhaled heavily. "I'll repeat one of the questions I asked you yesterday, Emory. While this man held you captive, did he threaten you, harm you?"

"I wasn't held captive."

"He never restrained you?"

Let go of my hands.

No, Doc.

Please.

No.

But I want to touch you, too. Let go.

Un-huh. This is the only way I can control—

What?

Myself. If you touch me, I'll come inside you.

Huskily, she said, "I wasn't restrained."

Knight looked over at Grange, and Grange shrugged. Knight came back to her looking thoroughly exasperated. "Okay. We learned from the Floyds where he lives." He scraped his chair back and stood up. "We thought we'd take you up there."

"What?" she exclaimed in alarm.

"Yep. I'm betting that when you get there, things you can't remember will start coming back."

———※———

He couldn't believe it.

He fucking *couldn't believe it.*

No wonder Emory's body hadn't been found. She wasn't fucking *dead*!

Cell phone to his ear, Jeff paced the lobby of the SO. That smelly, grimy, unsightly hallway in which he'd spent countless hours already had become a metaphor for his life. Everything about it sucked.

Emory lived.

"Mr. Surrey, are you still holding?"

"Yes," he shouted into his cell phone. "Did you tell him who was calling?"

"I did." The law firm's receptionist apologized again for the delay. "He's with another client. If you'd rather hang up and let him call you back when—"

"I'll hold. Put a note under his nose. Tell him it's urgent."

"Is it regarding Dr. Charbonneau?"

"Yes."

"We heard she was returned safely yesterday."

Yes, about twenty-four hours ago. When Jeff heard her voice coming through his phone, what whizzed through his mind was the irrational thought that she was speaking to him from the other side.

But no, she wasn't channeling from the land of the undead. At the moment Knight and Grange had barged into his motel room, prepared to arrest him for her murder, she proved herself to be very much alive.

And what a life she had been living!

When he'd placed his hands on her shoulders in a seeming gesture of concern, he'd wanted instead to wrap them around her neck. Who would have blamed him? How much could a man be expected to take before he snapped?

His fury barely under control, he said into his phone, "Get him on the line."

He was put on hold again. As if the indignity of having to arrange for a defense lawyer for Emory wasn't bad enough, he was having to wait for the privilege.

When her body wasn't discovered after the first twelve hours of the search, he'd started rehearsing how to play the aggrieved widower. He'd ranted. He'd stamped and stewed and made a nuisance of himself, pressuring them to find her, when, actually, the longer she remained lost, the better.

Just as he was growing accustomed to her being dead, she had turned up alive.

The receptionist came back on. "He'll speak with you now, Mr. Surrey."

The attorney addressed him brusquely. "What's so urgent, Jeff?"

He couldn't bring himself to explain Emory's escapade in any detail. "Emory didn't come away from her harrowing experience unscathed. She needs a good defense lawyer, she needs one immediately, and money is no object."

After agreeing to a retainer's fee, he got their business lawyer's promise to hop right on it. He was just concluding the call when Grange surprised him by entering the lobby through the front door, not from the squad room. Beyond him, Jeff could see the SUV parked out front.

Grange said, "We're going up there."

"Up where?"

"Are you coming or not?"

Chapter 30

———◦◉◦———

With head-spinning expedience, Emory was hustled outside and into the SUV. The seating arrangement was as it had been yesterday on the way from the gas station to the hospital. Knight was behind the wheel, Grange also in front, Jeff seated in the back with her.

Today, however, the mood inside the vehicle was considerably different.

When Jeff got in, he reached across the backseat and took her hand. Speaking in an undertone, he told her about his brief conversation with their business lawyer. "He's retaining someone who handles criminal law cases." He winced on the word *criminal.*

"Thank you for doing that."

He said nothing more, but, feeling his censure, she turned her head away and stared out the window. *Gorgeous scenery up here.* She tried to empty her mind of everything except the landscape as they wound their way into the mountains.

On a clear day, the vistas would have been breathtaking. Today fog blanketed the valleys. The highest peaks were obscured by low-lying clouds. She recognized the turnoff she'd taken into the national forest last Saturday morning, but they drove past it without anyone remarking on it.

In fact no one spoke for the entirety of the trip. Then they rounded a bend. "Look familiar?" Knight asked over his shoulder as he applied the brakes and the SUV slowed down to go through the open gate. "That's the Floyds' pickup across the road. All the tires have gashes in them."

She wasn't asked what she knew about their wrecked truck; she didn't volunteer anything.

In any case, she was feeling such a surge of emotion, it would have been difficult for her to speak. The split-rail fence had been strung with crime scene tape. The yard was crowded with official vehicles bearing the insignias of various agencies. Personnel, bundled up in winter gear, were poking about, drinking from thermoses, talking among themselves. Two emerged from the shed, one carrying a paint can, the other a spool of wire. The door to the cabin was standing open.

Knight got out and handed her down from the backseat. "This the place?"

What would have been the point of lying? But she didn't vocally confirm it either. She asked the question she'd been dreading most. "Is he in custody?"

"No."

Her knees went weak with relief. Jeff stepped to her side and cupped her elbow for support. "This is a bad idea. She's not up to it."

"No, I'm fine, really."

He seemed on the verge of arguing when his cell phone chirped. "It's Alice," he said after checking the caller. "How much do you want me to tell her about this?"

"Nothing yet."

He gave a curt nod of agreement. "I'll think of something."

Raising the phone to his ear, he walked away from them. She

was glad. She didn't think she could have borne his being inside the cabin. Knight and Grange ushered her up to the door and motioned for her to precede them.

The charred logs in the fireplace had gone cold. On the hearth, the wood box had been emptied and upended. His books, once neatly arranged alphabetically, lay in one large heap on the floor as though ready for a bonfire.

In the center of the floor, the hidey-hole had been exposed and the foot locker removed. It stood open and empty. The lamp remained on the end table, but the burlap shade had been removed, exposing the bare bulb. Men in uniform were searching drawers and cabinets. The mattress on the bed had been stripped and pulled aside.

Knight was saying, "When our people got up here, there was no sight of him and the cabin was mostly empty. Cleaned out. He didn't leave behind a single scrap of paper. Nothing. But we'll find him."

She didn't think so. He always did as he said. As promised, he had returned her unharmed. He'd rescued Lisa from her brothers' abuse. He'd left the Floyds alive but not before getting more than the pound of flesh he felt was due for whatever grievance he bore them.

He had also told her that they would never see each other again. He would hold to that, too.

A deputy came in from outside. "Found these in the shed. Somebody asked what the bar was for." He dropped the heavy articles onto the floor and stamped out.

Emory looked from the pair of gravity boots to the worrisome suspension rod overhead and gave a half laugh, half sob.

Knight mistook the sound for one of distress. "Does this bring back painful memories, Emory?" He looked up at the bar in the ceiling. "Was he into kinky stuff? Did he hurt you?"

"How many times must I tell you? No."

He studied her for a moment, then summoned over a deputy.

"Keep the husband distracted," he said. "In fact, why don't all y'all take a ten-minute break outside?"

The room emptied except for her and the two detectives. Knight said, "Let's sit." He sat down with her on the leather sofa.

Grange pulled up one of the dining chairs, and as he sat he motioned toward the foot locker. "Reeks of gun oil."

They looked at her. She kept her expression neutral. When it became obvious that she wasn't going to reveal anything voluntarily, Knight asked, "How many firearms did he have?"

"I never counted them."

"What kind were they?"

"I wouldn't know one from the other."

"Handguns? Rifles?"

"Some of both."

The men consulted each other with a glance, then Knight said, "You say he didn't hurt you."

"He didn't."

"Okay, but based on what he did to the Floyd brothers, it's clear that this man is capable of violence. He also motivated you, if not coerced you, to commit a felony. Now, Emory, looking at it strictly from a law enforcement standpoint, don't you think it's *feasible* that he attacked you on that trail?"

"For what purpose?"

Grange said, "Maybe just for the hell of it."

She looked toward the kitchen area where the drawers had been opened and rifled. She thought of how tidy he'd kept it and how meticulously he'd performed every task, such as repairing a toaster. "Whimsy? No, Sergeant Grange. He would never do something just for the hell of it. Besides, I've told you that he treated me kindly."

"I wouldn't call turning you into a thief a kindness," Knight said. "But just for the sake of argument, let's say that break-in was for a good cause. Let's say it was necessary in order for you to help a girl in need of medical treatment. Let's also say that those Floyd boys deserved the whipping they got. Going by their rap sheets, that's not a stretch."

"Then why are we here and having this conversation?"

"Because I still believe you were a hostage of sorts, not a willing participant in that burglary. Buddy and me don't want to see you punished for something you were forced to do under duress."

He leaned toward her, getting to the crux of his argument. "Even if you can't remember it, it's reasonable, isn't it, that this guy clouted you over the head and hauled you off that trail? Any way you look at it, that's assault and battery and kidnapping."

"I don't believe he's guilty of those crimes."

"If he's not guilty of something, why didn't he bring you into town and make himself known?"

She opened her mouth but had no words with which to respond.

However, as though she had spoken, Knight said, "Exactly. Staying under the radar was worth twenty-five grand to him. Which leads us to believe that he's a fugitive. You need to help us catch him."

"Why do you need me? You've searched every inch of this cabin."

"Which doesn't belong to him. It's a rental."

"Oh."

"You sound surprised."

She glanced toward the denuded bookshelves. "He treated it as an owner would. But if he's a renter, then surely his name is on the lease."

"Rent's paid by a lawyer in Seattle."

"Seattle?"

"On behalf of an LLC, and the general partner of the LLC is a corporation. We're trying to cut through all the red tape necessary to get to a human being behind the corporation, but in the meantime, our suspect is getting away."

Grange joined in. "The Floyd brothers claimed not to remember what he looks like. Their mother, too. The description Lisa gave the deputy could've been of me or Beyoncé. We find it real hard to believe that their powers of recall are that imprecise. And we think you remember him in a lot more detail than you gave us."

Knight said, "That could be construed as obstruction of justice."

"How could you prove what I do and do not remember about him?" she challenged. "I had a concussion and a CT scan that shows it."

In frustration, Knight switched tactics. Sighing as though in resignation, he said, "We're getting nowhere fast. I can hear your husband arguing with the deputies outside, and I sympathize with his impatience. He's had it up to here with us.

"And, pardon me for saying so, Emory, but you're looking peaked. Maybe you shouldn't have checked out of the hospital so soon. We should've thought twice before hauling you up here.

"But since we made the trip, tell us one thing. Just one thing that'll help us. Then we'll go back to Drakeland, see that you're put up someplace nice and made comfortable so you can rest."

She waited out the inanities, then said, "Please stop talking to me as though I'm an imbecile."

"Last thing I think is that you're an imbecile."

"I'm not infirm either. I am, however, tired of your hounding me to give you information that I don't have."

"I think you do."

"Then you think wrong."

Grange said, "We could charge you with aiding and abetting a criminal."

"You don't know that he's a criminal."

"We've got video of him committing a burglary."

"No you don't. You've got video of *me*."

"Did he threaten you and the Floyds not to reveal his identity?"

"I don't know his identity."

"Every minute you sit here and refuse to cooperate—"

"I'm not refusing."

"—he's getting farther away."

"Tell us his name."

"I don't know it."

"Emory—"

"I don't know his name!"

"Hayes Bannock."

"What about him?" Jack asked.

"His fingerprint was lifted off a kitchen sink faucet in North Carolina."

Just before six fifteen yesterday evening, Jack had left Rebecca Watson's house wanting to throttle her.

Except for locating her, the trip to the West Coast had been a total bust. Reasoning that there was no sense in hanging around and placing his manhood in jeopardy, he'd gone straight from her house, all the way back across the water on the damn ferry, through Seattle proper, finally reaching Sea-Tac in time to claim one of the few remaining seats on the red-eye to New York. He killed time in the airport by reading a bad novel about a good cop, until the flight's departure, which was delayed by an hour and a half. It had been bumpy to the degree that food and beverage service had been limited and passengers were required to stay buckled in their seats.

Then, because of weather, the flight was kept in a holding pattern for hours until finally getting clearance to land. He'd waited in the half-mile-long taxi line at JFK, stamping his feet and trying to keep his back to a polar wind. He had just now trudged into his apartment, trailing his roll-aboard, and feeling grimy, gritty, and generally like hammered shit.

He'd almost ignored Greer's call. Now he let go of the handle of his rolling suitcase. It toppled. "Say again?"

Greer repeated the stupefying statement.

Jack stood perfectly still, waiting for the punch line, for the second shoe to drop, for the "Gotcha!"—although he couldn't imagine his trusted associate pulling a dirty trick like that on him.

After fifteen seconds of stunned silence, Greer said, "Jack?"

"Yeah, I'm here." His heart began to beat again. He found some oxygen. "When?"

"When did they lift it? Some time this morning. It was copied in an e-mail to you. Came in about three minutes ago. I thought you'd've seen it."

"I was dealing with the taxi and getting into the building. Keep your phone in your hand."

Jack clicked off and accessed his e-mail. The most recent in his inbox was from a Sergeant Detective Sam Knight. He tried to read it so quickly the message would just as well have been written in Zulu. He started with the salutation and began again, forcing himself to go slower.

Words leaped out at him. Breaking and entering. Assault and battery. Kidnapping. Statutory rape. "Jesus." He called Wes Greer back.

Greer said, "Left me speechless. What about you?"

"When he resurfaced, he sure as shit didn't soft-pedal. How soon can you get me down there?"

"You just got off a red-eye. Take today to—"

"No, *now*. I'm gonna shower. Let's talk again in five minutes."

He was clean and shaved and hurriedly switching the dirty clothes in his suitcase for clean ones when Greer called back. "I e-mailed your itinerary."

"Any flight delays expected?"

"Not here. Your connecting flight may get held up in Char-lotte if the fog in Asheville doesn't lift."

"Fog? Doesn't Asheville have mountains?"

Flying into mountains in fog held even less appeal than fog-shrouded ferry rides. He really needed to catch this mother-fucker.

On the cab ride to LaGuardia, he punched in the contact number at the bottom of the e-mail he'd received. The call was answered by a gravelly voice with a noticeable drawl. "Sam Knight."

They exchanged perfunctory introductions, then Knight said, "We just got back from up at his place. I put in the e-mail every-thing we know at this juncture."

"No sign of him?"

"Not since he dropped off Lisa Floyd at her aunt's house this morning, and nobody can or will describe his pickup."

"What do you mean by 'will'?"

"All the Floyds are as stupid on the subject of him as Dr. Char-bonneau. Beats all I've ever seen. Like he sprinkles people with amnesia powder instead of fairy dust. Is he a Charles Manson type? A Jim Jones?"

"I wouldn't describe him as such. But he does hold sway," Jack said, thinking of Rebecca's blind devotion to her brother.

"Apparently. We're about to issue a BOLO."

"Hold up on that."

"Hold up?"

"Once he knows you're onto him, you won't have a prayer of finding him. Believe me, I know."

"For my guys only then, what's he look like?"

Jack gave him a description, receiving a series of harrumphs in response.

At the end of it, Knight said, "Six four, two twenty-five, dark hair, unusual blue eyes, and he was tough to remember or de-scribe?"

"He inspires loyalty."

"Or fear."

"Or fear," Jack conceded.

"Who is this guy? What'd he do? When we ran that print, we struck. But all his files are sealed, classified except for your office. Why's that?"

Jack didn't want to divulge that until he had the measure of this man, Sam Knight. Even if he trusted him implicitly, he didn't trust other personnel, and the mention of Westboro would spread through small-town officers' ranks like wildfire. That would be cataclysmic.

"Don't issue any bulletins yet," he said. "I'll explain everything when I get there."

Or maybe not. Depending on how things unfolded, it would be just as well if Sergeant Detective Sam Knight never knew the identity of the man he was seeking.

Before ending the call Jack inquired about the weather conditions there.

"Dense fog and snow showers. S'posed to get worse before it gets better."

Chapter 31

A felony, Emory. A *felony?*"

"You don't have to shout, Jeff. I heard you the first dozen times."

"I doubt you'll be charged, but...for chrissake. Think of the negative publicity."

"I apologize for any embarrassment I have caused or will cause you."

He stopped pacing and turned to face her. "Don't make me out to be the bad guy here."

"I'm not. I didn't mean it sarcastically. You have every right to be upset."

He had been humiliated, and she deeply regretted that. Throughout the day, he'd remained stoic and publically supportive. But now that they were alone for the first time since the burglary video had come to light, he was venting justifiable outrage.

It was a befitting note on which to end a day that had begun with her in the throes of a panic attack. She'd convinced herself of Jeff's culpability, only to discover that it was she, not he, who might have to face criminal charges. On the bright side, she wasn't spending the night in jail.

Upon their return from the cabin, Sergeant Knight had made it clear that she was still a suspect—or, at the least, a material witness—but he had grumbled about the "shit that would hit the fan" if they put her in lockup until they had all their *t*'s crossed and *i*'s dotted.

Lisa Floyd had been questioned by a female deputy, and it was reported to Knight and Grange that the girl had praised "Dr. Smith" to the hilt. It was only after learning that Lisa had told the deputy the nature of her medical crisis that Emory confirmed it to the detectives.

"Her condition wasn't immediately life-threatening, but it was traumatic, and she was in a great deal of discomfort. I did what I could."

"Those are what I'd call mitigating circumstances," Knight had said. "Why didn't you explain all this as your reason for breaking into the doctor's office?"

"It would have been a breach of patient confidentiality."

"That the only reason? Or are you still protecting your accomplice?"

She'd said nothing to that.

"Who got Lisa Floyd pregnant?"

"That remains confidential."

"Him?"

"No. Lisa will tell you the same. He had never even met her until that day."

The defense attorney arrived from Atlanta late in the afternoon. After being fully apprised of the situation, he'd insisted that Emory be detained no longer.

"It's the mystery man from the cabin we want, not you," Knight had told her as, with obvious reluctance, he escorted her out. "We'll resume tomorrow. Right now I've got to drive halfway to Asheville and pick up a fed from New York who got himself lost in the fog."

"A fed from New York?"

"That's right. Seems this FBI agent has been after Hayes Bannock for several years."

"Who is Hayes Bannock?"

"As if you don't know."

"I'm sorry, I don't." Then her lips had parted in wonder. "Is that his name?"

Reading her reaction, Knight propped his fists on his hips. "Well, I'll be damned. You honestly didn't know his name, did you?"

Hayes Bannock. She had tried it out and decided that it fit him to a tee. Then the rest of what Knight said had sunk in. "He's wanted by the FBI?"

"Looks like. Special Agent Jack Connell can't wait to get here and join the chase."

With that troubling thought prevailing, she had hoped that a long soak in a hot bath would relieve her anxiety, but with Jeff's pacing and haranguing, she could barely hear herself think. Relaxation was out of the question.

He was saying, "Last night you let me go on about turning over a new leaf. I owned up to having been difficult to live with. I waxed poetic about how vital you are to my life. All the while I was babbling about fresh starts, little could I guess the surprise you would spring on me this morning."

"I didn't spring—"

"During my mea culpa scene, how did you manage to keep a straight face?"

"Jeff, nothing I did was done to spite you."

"Perhaps not, but the net effect is the same. How am I going to explain this to my clients? To the partners of the firm?"

"They won't hold you responsible for my actions."

"The hell they won't. And what about *your* associates? I put

Alice off, telling her only that you were clearing up paperwork. But how are you going to explain your criminal activity to her and Neal? To your patients? Your behavior has placed the future of your precious clinic in jeopardy."

"I'll explain it to them just as I explained it to the detectives, to you, and to the defense lawyer. I did what was necessary to treat a patient. Even if no one else understands that, I'm confident that Neal and Alice will. They would have done the same."

"At the risk of a malpractice suit? I don't think so. Neither of them would be that foolhardy."

"I didn't take potential lawsuits into account. Not at any time. I was concerned only about Lisa's welfare."

"Oh, it's a compelling argument. I'll hand you that. The lawyer can make a case with it. He'll probably even spin the burglary till it looks noble and just."

"Then why are you so angry?"

"Because, as your husband, I'd like to know what happened in those four days that changed you from the reasonable, rational adult who left Atlanta on Friday into a hillbilly outlaw."

"Isn't that a rather ridiculous overstatement?"

"Not from where I'm standing. The Emory I know—*knew*—would have taken the girl to the emergency room if she were that concerned about her condition."

"Lisa refused to go."

"This mysterious man, Bannock, he didn't factor into your decision to treat the girl at home?"

"He pleaded with her to call nine-one-one. He offered numerous times to drive her to an ER, despite the icy roads. It was only after she refused that he...involved me."

"You're a terrible liar, Emory."

"Yes, I know. But that happens to be the absolute truth."

He snorted with skepticism as he walked over to the bar that separated the living area from the kitchen.

They had rented a suite in a chain residence hotel that didn't meet Jeff's standards, but which he deemed a huge improvement over where he'd spent the last several nights, courtesy of the sheriff's office. The suite was bi-level, with the bedroom and bath upstairs.

On the way there from the sheriff's office, he'd stopped at a liquor store and bought a bottle of the single malt scotch he preferred. He poured himself three fingers' worth.

"Want one?" he asked.

"The Emory you know doesn't like scotch."

He frowned at her drollness. "This qualifies as an emergency. Can I get you anything from the minibar?"

"No thank you."

"Let me know when you get hungry. I'll have to go out and bring something back. No one in this town has heard of room service." He sat down in an easy chair and placed his feet on the matching ottoman. Pressing his thumb and middle finger into his eye sockets, he sighed. "Jesus, what a nightmare. But stay tuned. There's more to come."

Emory, semireclined on the sofa, hugging a throw pillow to her chest, watched him. It disturbed her to realize that she was looking for dishonesty or perfidy, which, under the circumstances, was unfair. And yet...

"Jeff?"

"Hmm?"

"How did you know that my sunglasses got broken when I fell?"

He lowered his hand from his face and looked over at her. "What?"

"Last night, you asked me who had fixed my sunglasses. How did you know they'd been broken?" He looked stumped. She repeated, "How did you know they'd been broken?"

"Because of the sloppy repair job. You were wearing them on Friday when you left the house. They were fine. Yesterday, when you were changing out of your clothes in the ER, an orderly, someone, handed your things over to me. I had to sign an inventory form. As I was putting everything into the plastic bag they provided, I noticed that one of the stems on your glasses had been glued together."

"It's hardly noticeable."

"I noticed. You know I have an eye for detail."

She nodded.

"Anything else?" he asked tightly.

"Actually, yes. Are you having an affair?"

He seethed for a moment, then turned to the end table at his elbow and decisively set his glass of whiskey on it. "Let me get this straight. You're the one who went missing without explanation, and, as it turns out, went on a crime spree with a man of mystery under whose roof you spent four nights, and *I'm* the one being put on the defensive?"

"Are you having—?"

"Yes!"

She took a deep, stabilizing breath. "Since when?"

"Makes no difference now. It's over."

"Oh?"

"I called an end to it."

"I repeat, since when?"

"Recently."

"How recently? Since my disappearance?"

"Well, it wouldn't have been seemly, would it, to be dallying with a lover when the fate of my wife was unknown."

"Do the detectives know about it?"

"They discovered it, yes."

"While investigating you?"

"That's right. They were delighted to find you alive, but I think they, particularly Grange, were disappointed that they couldn't charge me with murder."

"What about you?"

"What about me?"

"Did it delight you that I turned up alive? Or not?"

The skin covering his face actually tightened. "I'm not even going to honor that with a reply."

"Which is not an answer, is it?" she murmured.

If he heard her, he didn't acknowledge it. He reached for his drink and sipped at it again.

"Who is the woman?" she asked.

"Doesn't matter."

"It does to me."

"She's unimportant, Emory. I didn't begin the affair because of burning desire or unrequited love."

"You wanted to hurt me."

"I suppose so."

"Why?"

"Quid pro quo. You have your other loves, and they consume you. They're all more important to you than I'll ever hope to be. Your medical practice, your patients, your marathons, your charities."

"It had nothing to do with the drug trials and my lukewarm opinion?"

"No more so than anything else."

"Oh, I see. There are more offenses I'm not even aware of."

"That's precisely the point. As my wife, you should be aware of them, shouldn't you?"

She was about to speak, but he held up his hand.

"I began the affair because you had turned me into a cliché. It chafed, Emory. I resented the role of underappreciated hanger-on, a shadow in your dazzling presence. I went in search of attention and affection." He slammed back the rest of the whiskey. "And enjoyed a lot of both."

"Then why did you end it?"

"Dealing with your little escapade has kept me busy. I've hardly had time to think about her, much less screw her."

The snide words were intended to wound. They were lancing,

but they didn't pain her as much as they might have even a week ago. She also should have felt gratified or vindicated by his confession. Oddly, she didn't. It only made her feel more alienated from him. Truthfully, she hadn't slept with someone else out of spite. But Jeff had.

His resentment didn't come as a surprise. She'd felt it on occasion. But she hadn't known until now how deeply embedded it was. She couldn't help but wonder just how far his hostility toward her extended.

She actually started when the doorbell rang.

Jeff got up to answer, momentarily disappearing into the small entryway of the suite. Emory heard him say, "Who's this?"

"Special Agent Jack Connell. Federal Bureau of Investigation."

Chapter 32

Upon hearing the man introduce himself, Emory's heart sank like a stone. She stood up, facing the entry, as Jeff led Sam Knight and the newcomer into the living area.

Jack Connell was of average height and weight, in his midforties. He was dressed in slacks, sport jacket, and overcoat, but in place of a tie, he had a wool scarf around his neck. His hair was reddish brown. There were dark crescents beneath his brown eyes. He looked road-weary.

Sam Knight said, "He insisted on coming to talk to y'all right away." The detective sounded no happier about this meeting than she was. "Grange's kid is sick, so I told him he could skip."

"Dr. Charbonneau." The FBI agent crossed over to her, removed his leather glove, and extended his right hand. "Jack Connell."

"How do you do?" They shook hands. "I understand you got lost in the fog."

He smiled with a chagrin that made him human and likable. She resisted the appeal of those traits. She didn't want the man hunting Hayes Bannock to be engaging.

He said, "I was afraid I would drive off a cliff, so I pulled over at a roadside stand that sells boiled peanuts. Just a lean-to and a chicken wire fence securing the cauldron. There was no one around, but I stayed put until Sergeant Knight met me and guided me in the rest of the way."

"I know firsthand how impenetrable the fog in the mountains can be."

"I want to hear about that."

They remained in an awkward tableau until she invited everyone to sit down. The two arrivals discarded their outerwear. With a noticeable lack of cordiality, Jeff offered them something from the minibar. Jack Connell declined refreshment. Knight asked for a Diet Coke, adding, "And are there any peanuts or a snack of some kind?"

Emory returned to her place on the sofa. Connell took the easy chair recently vacated by Jeff but moved aside the ottoman. Yielding the floor to the federal agent, Knight carried his canned drink and a bag of cheddar-flavored popcorn to the dining table. Jeff sat down beside Emory. She caught herself moving her knee from within touching distance of his.

Connell began. "Sergeant Knight provided me an overview of your experience. As soon as I read his e-mail, I traveled straight here. That fingerprint is the first tangible—"

"Excuse me. Fingerprint?"

He explained to her how it had been retrieved. "It's the first tangible lead I've had on Bannock in years."

"What did he do?"

"We'll get to that, Dr. Charbonneau. And, by the way, we here in this room, and Sergeant Grange, are the only ones privy to this information, and for the time being I want it kept that way. Can I count on your discretion?"

Jeff said, "What's the big secret? This individual is a fugitive or you wouldn't be here."

Connell said, "It's sensitive," then dismissed Jeff and directed his attention to Emory. "I'm very interested to hear firsthand about the time you spent with Bannock. Start from the beginning and tell me everything."

She did so—omitting the personal aspects. "I assume you know about his altercation with the Floyd brothers?"

"Sergeant Knight filled me in," Connell replied. "Bannock left them in bad shape."

"After leaving their house, he drove me into Drakeland and let me out near the Chevron station."

"Did he say why he let you out on the roadside?"

"No. But he...he did ask me not to call anyone until I reached the gas station."

"Giving him a head start," Connell said.

She didn't tell him those had been Bannock's words exactly.

"How'd he look?" the agent asked. "I mean overall. Healthy and fit?"

"Yes."

"Did he seem depressed?"

"I wouldn't call it depression."

"What would you call it?"

She searched for a word to describe Hayes Bannock's reticence. "Introspective."

"Hmm. Was he hostile?"

"Toward the Floyds? Yes."

"Toward you."

"No."

"Toward anything else?"

"Such as?"

"The government."

She shook her head. "Not specifically."

"What was his attitude about life in general?"

Again, she took time to find the right word. "He seemed resigned."

The agent nodded as though he understood her meaning. "What did you two talk about?"

"Nothing substantive. Until a few hours ago, I didn't even know his name."

"What did he tell you about himself?"

"Virtually nothing. I guessed that he'd been in the military, and he more or less confirmed it. He didn't say where he served or in what capacity, but I got the impression he saw combat."

"He did."

"On the subject of war, he said he didn't recommend it."

"He wouldn't. He served in Afghanistan. Two deployments. Hard-core army. Did he mention his family?"

No bride. No wife. Not ever. She cleared a sudden hoarseness from her throat. "He told me he wasn't married."

"No, but he has a sister and niece in Seattle."

Seattle, from where his rent was paid. "How old is the niece?"

"Twelve."

Remembering how he'd been with Lisa, she thought he could probably easily win the affection of a twelve-year-old niece. And his sister? "Are he and his sister close?"

Connell grimaced. "Like you wouldn't believe. In fact, just over twenty-four hours ago, I was in her house, trying to pry, cajole, wring information from her. She claimed not to know where he was."

"Perhaps she didn't."

The agent shrugged, indicating it was no longer an issue. Bannock had been found. Or as good as.

"What else can you tell me about him, Dr. Charbonneau?" he asked.

He has a thunderbolt tattoo just above his groin. When I traced the design with my tongue, he warned me of consequences. I didn't heed his warning.

"He keeps his promises," she said softly. "He reads a lot. He repairs things." She looked at Jeff. "He glued the stem of my sunglasses back together. He also builds things." She described the bookshelves, the unfinished shed.

Connell said, "He holds a degree in constructional engineering."

Beside her, Jeff had begun to fidget. "This is all thoroughly captivating, Mr. Connell. But does it have a point? What does any of this have to do with what Bannock did to Emory?"

Connell jumped on that. "You're assuming that he knocked your wife unconscious and carried her away."

"Aren't you?"

"I would be very surprised," the agent replied. "Shocked, actually."

That took Jeff aback. Emory as well. She looked over at Knight, whose hand had been arrested in midair between the bag of popcorn and his open mouth.

Connell remained focused on her. "Is that what you believe happened to you that day on the trail?"

"When I woke up in his cabin, not knowing where I was or how I got there, my initial reaction was to be afraid of him. And for the first two days, I remained wary and cautious. I even made a couple of futile attempts to leave."

"He stopped you?"

"Circumstances did. The weather. Then the situation with Lisa."

"Okay. You were saying?"

"Over time, I came to believe that he hadn't harmed me and didn't intend to."

"Truly, Dr. Charbonneau, I believe you were safe the entire time you were with him," Connell said. "It would have been totally out of character for him to see a woman alone, or anyone with whom he didn't have a quarrel, and attack them. He's not a sexual predator either. That's not what he's about."

"Then what *is* he about?" Knight asked.

"Punishment. I suppose some would term it *vengeance*, but it's less personal than that."

"I believe the Floyd brothers would take personally what he did to them," Jeff said.

"Actually punishment fits," Knight said. "The deputy who interviewed Lisa speculated that her brothers had been messing with her and that's how she got pregnant."

They all looked to Emory, who said nothing. But her pained expression must have given her away.

Jack Connell sighed as he dragged his hand down his face. "That would light Bannock's fuse, all right. But his grudge against the Floyds goes back farther than the abuse inflicted on their sister."

Looking at Emory, he continued. "His moving to the mountain wilderness wasn't coincidental. He tracked Norman and Will Floyd here. He was out to wreak havoc on them and was only biding his time. Did he tell you that?"

"I inferred it, and when I asked, he didn't deny it, but he also didn't explain what he held against them."

"We'll get to that, too. First I want to ask you about his cache of firearms. Knight told me Bannock shot at the Floyds."

"He didn't," she said. "He had a pistol, but he never used it. He never even took it out."

In his own defense, Knight spoke up. "Norman Floyd told our deputy that Bannock fired both barrels of a shotgun at them."

"That's a lie," Emory said with emphasis. "It was their shotgun, not his, and he used it to shoot out their TV." The three men registered astonishment, prompting her to relate the circumstances.

"That doesn't make sense," Knight said. "He wanted to keep them from collecting the reward, but he didn't collect it himself."

"He's not about money either," Connell said.

"Wouldn't it be far more enlightening if you told us what he *is* into rather than what he *isn't?*"

Connell looked at Jeff, but didn't acknowledge his catty remark. Coming back to Emory, he began asking her all the questions the detectives had already covered, but she answered them patiently. She apologized for not knowing the make and model of his truck.

"Don't feel too bad," the agent told her with a wry smile. "He would have ditched it by now anyway. Did he mention leaving?"

"Leaving town?" she asked.

"Leaving the area. Moving on, relocating."

She shook her head.

"Did he mention a soccer coach in Salt Lake?"

"No."

"A priest in Kentucky who resigned his parish and the priesthood, some believe under threat of death?"

"No."

"A hairdresser in Wichita Falls, Texas?"

Emory shook her head in bafflement. "Why are you asking? What do these people have in common?"

The agent sat forward and propped his forearms on his thighs, speaking to her directly, as though they were the only ones in the room. "They have two things in common. Hayes Bannock." He paused, took a breath. "And a mass shooting in Virginia that left eight people dead."

You only thought you missed all the excitement of Virginia. His words to Norman Floyd.

Emory's stomach lurched. Without even excusing herself, she shot off the sofa and took the stairs in record time. Upon reaching the bedroom, she slammed the door behind her and leaned against it as though to keep out the horrific thoughts assailing her.

Mass shooting. Eight people. Dead.

Feeling faint and needing air, she staggered to the sliding glass door that opened onto a narrow balcony. She went to the railing and gripped it, impervious to the biting cold of the metal.

Eight people. Dead.

She breathed deeply of the icy air. The vapor of her exhales blended into the fog swirling around her.

Suddenly sensing a presence, she turned her head.

Only a few feet away from her, standing on the neighboring suite's balcony, was…

Hayes Bannock.

Her heart clutched with terror. And leaped with inexplicable joy.

"Don't scream." He spoke in the familiar whisper that always came as somewhat of a surprise. "Don't do anything until you've looked at this." He held out his hand. In the palm of his glove lay a silver trinket. She recognized it instantly.

"Where did you get that?"

"From underneath you where you supposedly fell." He gave her a mere few seconds to assimilate that, then, "Are you staying with them? Or coming with me?"

Chapter 33

———◦◉◦———

In advance of the meeting, Sam Knight hadn't had much good to tell Jack about Emory Charbonneau's husband.

"Suspecting him of instant divorce, Grange and me did him a disservice. But he's got an ego on him. Haughty, too. When we show up unannounced, you can count on him being a jerk at best."

Jack had gone in with low expectations, and everything Jeff Surrey had said and done since their arrival had lived up to Knight's characterization. Jack hadn't warmed to the man, and it was clear that the feeling was mutual.

Emory's abrupt departure upstairs, the slamming of the bedroom door at the landing, had left the three men suspended in a taut silence. After several moments passed and no one moved, Jack looked over at Jeff. "Is she all right?"

"Did she seem all right to you? After the bombshell you just dropped, would you expect her to be all right?"

"Maybe you should go up and check on her."

Jeff expelled his breath. "Let's give her a moment." He got up and went over to the bar. "She declined a stiff one before you got here. She might have changed her mind." He poured a whiskey and stared into it thoughtfully as he swirled it in the glass.

"Since you know your wife better than anyone," Jack said, "I—"

"Possibly I don't know her at all."

"How do you mean?"

Jeff came around to face him. "I mean that I never would have thought she and I would find ourselves in such sordid circumstances. Emory is nothing if not stable and reliable. This Bannock must have worked some powerful mojo on her. She's not at all herself."

"In what way?"

"Ways, plural. Ordinarily, she's confident and strong-willed. Now, skittish as a rabbit, nervous, agitated. She's distracted, forgetful, absent-minded, when usually she's centered. Almost to a fault. Shall I go on?"

"I'm listening."

The man needed no further encouragement. "Emory is a forward-thinking person. But now she seems stuck inside that damn cabin with Hayes Bannock, still caught up in the distasteful situation he dragged her into with that family of rednecks.

"Whatever she witnessed and experienced up there maintains a grip on her. It's changed her. I hope to God the effects aren't irrevocable. If she doesn't revert to the Emory Charbonneau everyone knows, the fallout from all this could be catastrophic. For both of us. Even more than it already has been," he said, shooting a glare toward Knight.

Coming back to Jack, he added, "Of course, your appearance has been a major setback to her recovery and return to normal life. Thanks for that, Special Agent Connell."

Using that as his exit line, he took the glass of whiskey with him and climbed the stairs. At the top, he tapped on the bedroom door. "Emory?" Getting no answer, he turned the knob and pushed open the door, closing it softly behind him as he entered the room.

Knight dusted popcorn salt off his fingers. "Told you he was a jerk."

"You were being generous. It's all about him, isn't it?"

"Pretty much, yeah."

"He didn't show any compassion toward her for the ordeal she's been through."

"Oh, yesterday, he was all over that," Knight said. "But after seeing the burglary video this morning, he—"

"She's gone!"

Jeff's shout from the landing brought them instantly to their feet.

"What?"

Jeff looked down at Knight with scorn. "What part didn't you understand? She's not up here," he shouted, flinging his arms wide. "Anywhere. The balcony door is open."

The first thing that sprang to Jack's mind was suicide. Even a jump from a second story could be fatal if it had enough purpose behind it. He charged up the stairs, pushed Jeff out of his way, and crossed the room in only a few strides. He stepped out onto the balcony and leaned over the railing, checking the parking lot below.

"I've already looked," Jeff said. "She's not down there. If she jumped, she survived."

Knight, having run out the front door and around the unit, came into view, huffing with exertion. "See anything?"

Jack scanned the parking lot and beyond, looking for a telltale motion, when the whole damn landscape was a kaleidoscope of snow and shifting fog. "Dammit!" He banged his fist on the railing, then turned away to reenter the room. In the act of doing so, he noticed that the door to the neighboring balcony was also open. The room beyond it was in darkness.

"Cover the front," he yelled down to Knight.

Throwing his leg over the low stucco wall separating the two balconies, he approached the dark bedroom, wondering if he was about to intrude upon someone who liked to sleep with the window open even with a stiff north wind blowing.

But the bed was neatly made and appeared untouched.

He entered the suite, which was a mirror image to the one occupied by Emory and Jeff. He went through the bedroom, walked out onto the landing, and flipped on the light fixture above the staircase, ready to ID himself as a federal officer if he surprised someone below. But the lower floor was vacant, too, and the door to the suite...

The locking mechanism had been popped out and lay on the floor.

"Same trick as on the door to the doctor's office," Knight said as he pushed open the door from the other side and walked in, having approached the suite from the front.

"Son of a bitch! Son of a *bitch!*"

Jeff came up behind Knight, but Jack noticed that he'd taken time to put on his jacket before joining them. His eyes on Jack, he said, "That's all you have to say? Son of a bitch? What page do you find that on in the FBI training manual?"

Having had enough of him, Jack closed the distance between them. He poked Jeff in the chest with his index finger, the blow only barely buffered by the thick quilted fabric of his fancy jacket.

"Listen, asshole, if you'd gone up there immediately to see about your wife, chances are very good that she'd still be here."

"You can't blame this on me. It's apparent that your fugitive has kidnapped Emory for the second time."

"Nothing's apparent. While we try to find out what happened to her, there's something you should keep in mind."

Jeff arched a brow. "Oh?"

"If Hayes Bannock has your wife, you probably top his shit list. Be afraid."

Hayes had helped her over the low wall separating the balconies. They'd scrambled through the neighboring suite and out the door.

She was almost giddy with disbelief over what she was doing. She was fleeing into the unknown with a man being sought in connection with a mass shooting. Yet she felt much safer with him than she had with the law enforcement officers who were now kowtowing to Jeff for having suspected him of murder.

Placing her hand in Hayes's and escaping with him had been instinctual. She had no reason whatsoever to trust that instinct, but she did. She ran with it. Literally.

Silently, and half blinded by blowing snow, they sprinted between buildings and across streets. Finally, they left the commercial area and entered a residential neighborhood that was notably run-down. Dogs barked at them from behind chain-link fences, but no one came out to check on the nature of the disturbance.

They didn't slow down until they reached a midsize sedan parked at the edge of a rutted street. The model of the car was too old for a remote. Hayes used the key to unlock the passenger door. Without questioning him, she slid into the seat and buckled herself in as he rounded the hood and got in behind the wheel.

As Connell had predicted, he'd ditched his truck.

Staying off the main roads, keeping to streets that wound through neighborhoods, he drove carefully and within the speed limit, gradually increasing the distance between them and the suite hotel.

He'd told her he'd been successful at evading capture, and once again he was proving himself to be true to his word.

"Is this a stolen car?"

"Nope. Bought and paid for, registered in a fake name, and stored in a mini-warehouse for just such an occasion as this."

"Why'd you leave it in such an unsavory neighborhood?"

"That's why. It's unsavory. Lots of drug dealers in that area. Meth labs, I'd guess. To survive, everybody minds their own business. They see nothing; they report nothing. Main reason, somebody had busted the security camera mounted on the light pole."

She was no longer shocked by his unique power of observation and knowledge about such things. "They know who you are, Hayes."

Upon hearing his name, he jerked his head around and looked at her, then pulled the car to the shoulder, braked hard, and left the engine idling. For a panicked moment she feared he was going to force her to get out.

"They've already searched your cabin."

"Then it seems I cleared out just in time."

"They lifted a fingerprint from it. You were identified by an FBI agent."

The opal fire in his eyes sparked. "FBI agent?"

"He came straight from New York."

"*Shit!* Special Agent Jack Connell."

"You know him by name?"

"Unfortunately. He's been on my tail for four fucking years."

"He wants you in connection with a mass shooting in Virginia. I heard you mention the excitement in Virginia to Norman Floyd."

He studied her for a moment, then said, "Knowing that, you still came with me tonight, no questions asked?"

Huskily, she replied, "So it seems."

He continued to look at her through the mingling vapor of their breath. Then he lifted his foot off the brake pedal and steered back onto the road.

Just outside Drakeland's city limits, he took a state highway and made several turns onto roads that became progressively narrower and more winding. She didn't inquire where they were going. He obviously had a destination in mind. It turned out to be a mobile home, situated semipermanently on a concrete slab fringed with dead vegetation. It was set back from the road but still in sight of it. They would be warned of anyone approaching.

He kept the headlights on as he got out and went up to the door, opening it with a key and switching on an interior light before coming back for her and turning off the car.

She climbed the three steps and entered the main room of the rectangular structure. It was small, compact, sparsely and inexpensively furnished.

"I hope you weren't expecting fancy," he remarked from behind her as he closed the door and slid the bolt. "Heat works, though. You won't be cold for long." He reached out and brushed melting snow off the shoulder of her sweater.

She turned her head and looked at his hand where it rested there. "I didn't even realize until now that I left without my coat."

"Adrenaline."

"I suppose."

His gaze remained steady on hers. "Why didn't you give me away?"

"You told me not to."

"I've told you not to do a lot of things. You've done them anyway."

"I trusted you."

He stroked the side of her neck with his thumb, then quickly withdrew his hand and took a step back. He removed his outerwear and piled the garments on the small dining table.

"A dangerous business, Doc. Trusting me."

"You talk about dangerous? There were two armed men just downstairs, either of whom would gladly have taken you into custody. You took a huge risk to get me out of there."

"I had to get you away from him."

"Jeff."

"Your husband," he said with palpable disgust. From his jeans pocket, he fished out the silver trinket. When he'd showed it to her on the balcony, there had been no question as to whether she would stay with Jeff or flee with Hayes.

She took the charm from him and rubbed it between her fingers. "You had it all the time I was with you?"

"Found it underneath you when I picked you up off the trail."

"Why didn't you ever ask me about it? I could have identified it immediately."

"I was afraid you'd want it back." He seemed embarrassed to have admitted that and made a defensive rolling motion of his shoulders.

"You wanted a keepsake of me? Very sentimental. And very unlike yesterday when you opened the door of the truck and said a terse good-bye. You seemed eager to get rid of me."

"I was. Short of killing the Floyds, I'd settled my score with them. I should have left yesterday as soon as I delivered Lisa to her relatives. Driven away and not looked back."

"Instead...," she said.

"Instead I joined the crowd outside the hospital."

That astonished her. "You were there?"

"Making myself as inconspicuous as possible. You were escorted inside. Jeff was detained by reporters seeking a sound bite. Didn't look to me like he minded the attention. All pumped up and full of himself, he walked right past me. Close enough for me to get a good view of the zipper on his slick ski jacket."

"You noticed it was missing the pull."

"And I realized what I had." He let that settle. "I don't know one designer's emblem from another's. At first I assumed it had come off the zipper of your running jacket. Yesterday, I knew otherwise. It fell off Jeff's jacket when he attacked you."

"And left me for dead." Even though she'd come to suspect that Jeff was somehow involved, it was dismaying and painful to accept he could have been so cold-blooded, heartless, and deceiving. By contrast, Hayes had risked everything to protect her.

Looking into his eyes, she said, "You came after me."

"I couldn't leave you to him. It was hard enough taking you back before I knew he meant to kill you."

Jack Connell might just as well have saved his breath. What he'd told her about Hayes Bannock had no effect on her yearning for him to pull her against him and steal the very breath from her with one of his kisses. She took a step toward him, but he staved her off.

"You and me, it still can't happen." A second elapsed before he added, "If it could, I'd already be on you." He spoke in a low rumble that was rich with carnal implications.

Her own voice was heavy with emotion. "Connell asked me if you had mentioned leaving."

"He knows me. Nothing's changed. I'll disappear again. But not until I'm sure this murderous bastard is nailed." He motioned for her to sit. "Let's talk."

She backed up to the built-in sofa and sat down on the edge of the cushion. He pulled a chair from beneath the dining table, positioned it in front of her, and straddled it backward.

"Must say, you didn't seem a bit surprised to learn that Jeff is the culprit."

"He tipped his own hand. Last night, he asked me who had repaired my sunglasses." She told him about her panic attack and the conversation she'd had with Alice. "I had retold the story several times. I began to doubt my recollection. Alice reasonably pointed out that I was exhausted, on medication, and she swore Jeff couldn't have harmed me. But it continued to nag me. Tonight I confronted him with it. His explanation for knowing the glasses had been broken was plausible, but he became defensive."

"Defensive how?"

"I've long suspected that he is involved with someone else. I asked him point blank if he was having an affair, and he admitted it. He also confessed to resenting me. Not without some basis," she added. "But to a much greater degree than I realized."

Hayes frowned. "Problem is, resentment is a motive, but it isn't proof."

"The trinket is."

He shook his head. "You could have taken it off his jacket yourself and made Jeff out to be the bad guy as payback for his cheating. Or do the investigators know about his affair?"

Regretfully, she nodded. "If I raised the question of his missing zipper pull, it would be my word against his as to where he'd lost it and when."

"Then it's a damn good thing I kept that rock."

"I'd forgotten that!" she exclaimed. "You still have it?"

"Oh yeah. A hard fall could have caused a concussion. Even the gash. But you took a blow that left strands of hair on the rock. That bothered me, enough so that I thought I'd better hold on to it. That's also one of the main reasons I didn't drop you at an ER when I found you. If that rock had been a weapon, whoever wielded it—"

"Remained a threat."

"Correct. As it turns out, my hunch was right. Jeff was a threat up until you took my hand on that balcony."

"Why didn't you share your apprehensions with me immediately when I regained consciousness? Why didn't you explain then why you were reluctant to take me to an ER?"

"The shape you were in, would it have calmed you down if I had started asking who in your life might want to kill you?"

She had the grace to look chagrined.

"If there was a villain, I was the logical choice," he said. "Then you found the damn rock, and that cinched it."

"It looked so menacing," she said, remembering her fear when she saw it. "Can fingerprints be lifted off a surface like that? What can it prove?"

"Your blood and hair will be typed."

"A prosecutor will still have to prove how they got there. An accident? Or with intent?"

"I don't know what good it will do, but it's better to have it than not. Who investigated your disappearance?" After she told him about Knight and Grange, he asked, "How much confidence do you have in them? Even with two pieces of evidence that raise questions about your 'fall,' will they take you seriously or dismiss you as a jealous and vindictive wife?"

"I'm not sure," she replied honestly.

"Before you stick your neck out, you gotta be sure of them, Doc."

"Neither likes Jeff, but they've been deferential and apologetic for suspecting him. I lost a lot of credibility when they saw that video."

"Video?"

"Oh! You don't know about that."

By the time she'd finished, he was shaking his head with self-depreciation. "I was worried about an alarm system, motion detectors, and security cameras, but a freaking nanny cam never occurred to me. I'll have to remember that."

"For the next time you commit a Class H felony."

He arched an eyebrow. "You've learned a lot today."

"More than I wanted to. Where was I?"

"You lost credibility."

"They wanted to know who my accomplice was, and they didn't believe me when I couldn't name you. They questioned the Floyds, even Pauline and Lisa. They all came down with amnesia about you, too, which was very frustrating to Knight and Grange." She told him about their excursion to the cabin.

"I'm sorry you were put through that."

She smiled sadly. "The worst part about it was seeing your cabin ransacked."

"It's just wood and metal, Doc."

"I know, but it had...significance. I was glad Jeff never went inside."

"Afraid he would have seen your guilt?"

"I don't feel any guilt," she replied calmly. "I didn't want him to taint my memories of our time together."

They held each other's gaze for a moment before she continued. "Throughout the day, he pretended to be a pillar of support for the wife-gone-bad. Tonight when we were alone for the first time, he vented his anger."

"What he's really angry over is that you showed up alive. He's out millions."

"I don't think it's about my inheritance. That's almost too hackneyed for him. It's about pride."

"What about the other woman?"

"Jeff didn't tell me anything about her except that she's inconsequential."

"Do you believe him?"

"Oddly I do. I can't see him being governed by passion." Looking down at her hand, she turned her wedding ring around her finger. "Love wasn't his motivation for trying to kill me. I'm not sure love was ever in the equation between us."

He didn't press her for an explanation, but his silence invited her to provide one if she wished.

"I told you how dear my parents were to me. I mourned their deaths for a long time. Even after becoming established in Atlanta, I was still vulnerable, a bundle of raw emotions. When we were building the clinic, my friend Alice introduced me to Jeff.

"He was charming and urbane, but also the epitome of pragmatism. Controlled, cool-headed. Even when I was seized by a crying jag or homesickness for my parents, he didn't buy into my grief. He kept himself apart from it.

"At the time, I told myself he was exactly what I needed, someone who would make me bear up, carry on, get over it. I told myself that if he tried to comfort me, I would reject his attempts as insincere.

"But he never tried. He never offered a single word of consolation. I see now that his detachment wasn't out of consideration for me, but because he simply couldn't be bothered." She gave a rueful laugh. "The qualities that initially attracted me to him are the qualities that are so repellant to me now."

She waited several seconds, then looked at him directly. "It seems I prefer my emotions raw. I didn't realize how much until that night with you." She reached across the space separating them and laid her hand on top of his, where it rested on the back of the chair. "Despite what Agent Connell alleges, I don't believe you killed eight innocent people."

Chapter 34

W‍ere you still up?"

"Jeff?" Alice said a bit groggily. "Up? No. I was in bed, but not asleep."

He didn't care if he'd roused her from a coma.

"You sounded strange when I called earlier," she said. "Why didn't you call me back? I thought you'd be coming by to get Emory's car. Did you make it back to Atlanta okay?"

"Nothing's okay."

"What's going on?"

"I don't even know where to start. But the upshot of it is, Emory is gone again."

"*Gone?*" Suddenly she sounded wide awake.

Half an hour earlier, Sergeant Grange had joined the party. Using cop-speak and acronyms, Knight and Jack Connell filled him in on the latest development. Meanwhile, dozens of other officers were outside trying to pick up Emory's trail. Snow was beginning to accumulate, making the search for tire tracks and footprints even more difficult.

They had, however, discovered two sets of prints just beyond the front door of the neighboring suite. The imprints of Emory's riding boots didn't indicate there had been a struggle or even any hesitancy on her part. Gauging by the distinctive outlines of the soles of her boots, Knight's assessment had been that she had gone willingly with the much larger set of prints, and Connell had agreed.

It was requiring every ounce of cool reason and self-control for Jeff not to pound something or tear his hair out. But he couldn't allow rage to overtake him. He must continue to think calmly and practically.

Almost without their taking notice, he'd excused himself to call Alice. "If Emory contacts anyone, it will be her," he'd told them. But Alice's astonishment had doused that faint hope.

"About half an hour ago, she split. We believe she went with that man from the now-famous cabin. His name finally came to light. Hayes Bannock."

"Oh, Jeff."

Her soulful groan set his teeth on edge. People were saying the dumbest, most unhelpful things to him tonight. "You don't know the half of it. She and this man were accomplices in a crime." He told her about the burglary.

"I can't believe that of Emory!"

"I wouldn't have either if I hadn't seen it with my own eyes."

"Did they charge her?"

"No. They figure she was coerced to participate, though I'm not convinced coercion was necessary. There was this girl." He went on to tell her about the family of Floyds and how they factored in.

"This is all so bizarre," Alice murmured.

"Even more bizarre is where these people live, although *subsist* would be a more accurate word." In disparaging terms he described the state road by which they'd reached Bannock's cabin. "*Backwoods* is an understatement of how rustic it is. The Floyds are his nearest neighbors and that isn't by happenstance. Apparently Bannock already had the brothers in his sights over some past grievance. God knows what. Some tawdry mess, I'm sure. Connell said—"

"Who is Connell?"

"Oh, that's the best part. He's the effing FBI."

"How did the FBI become involved?"

"Hayes Bannock has been eluding Connell for years. Something to do with a mass shooting."

"You're not serious."

"I'm afraid so. His fingerprint was lifted in the cabin. Connell was notified. He rushed right down. Twenty minutes after meeting him and telling him about her mountain adventure, Emory bolted, almost surely with Bannock, and, as we speak, their trail is being obscured by snow." He paused and took a breath. "I think that's everything."

His recitation was followed by a lengthy and teeming silence. Then Alice drew a shaky breath. "Jeff, this is a tragic turn of events."

"You think?"

"Don't get smart with me."

"Then say something less banal."

"Very well." After a beat, she said, "It's obvious to me that Emory has lost her grasp on reality."

He sensed a ponderous footnote left unspoken. "Alice? Dear? Do you know something I don't?"

"I'm not sure it's relevant."

"Tell me and let me decide its relevance."

"I can't betray Emory's confidence."

"Your loyalty to her is admirable, but if you keep something from me and the authorities, you're fostering her bizarre behavior. She's sacrificing her reputation and jeopardizing the future of the clinic. Her career—as well as mine, yours, and Neal's—are at stake. Not only that, her life could be in danger.

This man she's with is a violent criminal. My God, Alice, screw confidentiality and tell me what you know!"

She inhaled a deep breath. "She called me from the hospital last night. Actually early this morning. She seemed on the verge of hysteria. She was breathing erratically, like she was having a panic attack."

"What brought it on?"

"Her sunglasses. She asked me if I remembered her mentioning at some point during the day that they'd been broken."

"She called you in the wee hours to talk about her sunglasses?"

"Because you had asked her about the repair."

"Jesus, she's really hung up on that. She brought it up to me tonight."

"She wondered how you knew they'd been broken when she fell."

"I didn't. All I knew was that when she left home on Friday, the stem was intact. Yesterday I noticed it had been glued together." He waited a ten count, then said, "Alice, what was she... Why did she call you in a panic over something so innocuous?"

"It wasn't innocuous to her. She thought that your question about them might have been a slip of the tongue. That by asking it, you had implicated yourself."

"Good Christ," he exclaimed in a stage whisper.

"I told her that she wasn't thinking clearly, that she was letting her imagination run wild, but even as we hung up, she sounded uncertain."

"She's the one stealing and keeping company with a wanted man, but she implicated *me*. Unbelievable."

"I didn't know about the break-in and all the rest last night when I spoke to her. But even then she seemed irrational, and I told her so. I said that perhaps she was transferring her own guilt onto you."

"Her guilt over the burglary?"

Alice didn't respond.

"Guilt over something else?"

"Jeff, I can't—"

"She slept with him, didn't she?"

Alice held her tongue.

He sneered, "Ah, the resonate silence of a confidante and friend."

"Not that good of a friend," she said with contrition. "I'm sleeping with her husband."

"She knows."

"Oh my God," she wailed.

"Relax, Alice. For God's sake. I didn't name you, but I did confess."

"Why? Why *now*?"

"Emory backed me into a corner. Even after today's shocking disclosures, she had the gall to ask me outright if I was having an affair. In anger I admitted it but didn't tell her with whom."

Speaking in an undertone, she said, "It might be a relief for her to find out. Keeping the secret has been torture."

"No one would doubt your loyalty to her, although you should have contacted me immediately after your conversation with her last night. I should have known about her suspicions regarding me."

"I chalked them up to exhaustion, medication, a residual fear after what she'd been through. Emotional upheaval and—"

"I understand. But you should have told me, Alice. Had I known, things might have gone differently today."

"How so? What would you have done?"

"For starters, I wouldn't have been so eager to take her home. I would have recommended that she stay in the hospital and be kept under observation for another couple of days."

"Seen a psychiatrist, perhaps?"

God bless Alice. He forgave her the previous banalities. She was saying all the right things now. "Yes. I blame myself for not suggesting a psychiatric evaluation yesterday when she seemed unable to remember specifics about how she sustained the concussion and the time she spent in that cabin. Of course, given what we know now, how were we to distinguish between faulty recollection and sheer fabrication?"

"We must get help for her."

"We have to find her first. I only hope she survives this villain. Connell said he wasn't a sexual predator, but... well, he's already seduced her, hasn't he?" He let his voice crack emotionally on the last two words, and Alice's response to it was instantaneous.

"It's difficult to be angry with her and worried at the same time, isn't it?"

"That describes exactly what I'm feeling."

She was silent for a moment, then, "What does all this mean to us, Jeff? To our relationship?"

"I've already told you. We can't go on seeing each other. Emory has to be my sole concern now. I don't say that to hurt you."

"Nevertheless, it does."

"I'm sorry. We both went into this with eyes wide open, neither predicting a happy ending." Then, "I'd better go now, check in downstairs and see if any progress is being made."

"Should I keep this latest incident under my hat?"

"Please. Let's get through the night, see what tomorrow brings."

"All right." Her good-bye was tearful and subdued.

He disconnected and grinned at himself in the dresser mirror. "That went well." Had he scripted Alice, he couldn't have put better words in her mouth.

If Emory survived this second misadventure with her criminal boyfriend, her mental stability would be brought into question. She would be denounced and ridiculed. Perhaps the end of her star-kissed life would bring too much pressure for her to bear. She might very well break under the strain of losing everything she had worked so hard to achieve, and, when she did, God knows what she would do to herself. Suicide would be credible.

As he was leaving the bedroom, he glanced toward the bed where he'd tossed his ski jacket when he came upstairs. He had noticed yesterday that the trademark zipper pull was missing. He didn't know how and when it had become detached, and a search among his belongings hadn't produced it.

It was a small thing. But wasn't the devil in the details?

When Jeff excused himself to go upstairs to call Alice, Jack Connell asked the two detectives, "What's that about?"

Knight, who was halfway through a minibar can of cashews, said, "Dr. Alice Butler. OB-GYN." He explained the three-way medical clinic partnership. "Also, she's Emory's best friend."

"Who's committing adultery with him." Grange tipped his head toward the top of the stairs.

Jack divided a look between them. "Huh. Does Emory know?"

"We don't think so," Grange replied. "She might. She might not care. Would you, if you were her?"

Jack smiled, then asked, "When she went missing, you looked hard at him?"

"Snug as a bug in a rug with Alice Butler from Friday evening till Sunday afternoon, when he became concerned about his wife," Knight said.

Grange expanded on that, recounting the interview he'd had with the other woman. "She confessed, crumbling beneath the weight of guilt. We thought for sure we had Jeff's dual motive."

"Dual?"

Grange told him about Emory's legacy from Charbonneau

Oil and Gas. "She's worth a bundle and then some. We were on our way to apprehending him, but then Emory showed up at the filling station, alive."

Knight said, "The husband's no longer a suspect. Your boy Hayes Bannock stole all his thunder."

"Bannock won't hurt her."

"So you've said."

"I'd stake my career on it," Jack insisted. "Besides, she isn't afraid of him or she wouldn't have left with him tonight."

Grange said, "That's the first thing that crossed my mind when Knight called me and said to get over here. There's a big difference between being unafraid of someone and running off with him. Why'd she go? What did he say to her? What did he do to get her to take off without even getting her coat first?"

Jack said, "I don't know Emory Charbonneau well, but from my perspective, it's just as puzzling. Always before, when Bannock was done somewhere, he split. Like in a matter of hours. After the incident with Norman and Will Floyd, I can't figure why he's sticking around."

"Maybe he's not done with the Floyds. Maybe the beating was only a prelude leading up to a big finish."

Jack pulled the inside of his cheek between his teeth. "I hope not."

"Or maybe we're overlooking the obvious. Maybe Emory's 'he treated me kindly' refrain was euphemistic for..." Knight let his raised eyebrows speak for him, then shook the last of the cashews from the can and tossed them into his mouth. "But whatever he's doing to, or with, or for her, we still want him for assault and battery. So my question to you, Agent Connell, is on behalf of all the men and women we've got out there looking for them. Just how dangerous is this guy?"

"Officers should proceed with caution."

"That's it? That's your only word of advice?" Knight was frowning over the insufficiency. "Word's spread through our department about the Floyd boys. Truth be told, their beating has been toasted by more than one six pack. They're scumbags, and that was the opinion even before anybody knew about them raping their kid sister."

"Have they been charged?"

"Not yet. It's on the DA's desk, but the girl is iffy about bringing it out in the open. You know how that goes."

Jack nodded, and Knight continued.

"In the meantime, everybody's just a tad spooked over the man who whipped the Floyds single-handedly. We found where he stored his weapons, but not the weapons themselves, meaning he could have a lot of firepower with him. Now a fed has shown up hot on his heels. Bannock's taken on a...a..."

"Aura," Grange said.

Knight acknowledged the supplied word with a nod, but he kept his attention on Jack. "I'm asking you as an officer of the law, same as you, to cut the double-talk and basic bullshit and tell us just who we're dealing with here."

"You referenced a mass shooting in Virginia, but you weren't specific." Grange cast a quick upward glance at the closed bedroom door that would prevent Jeff from overhearing. Then, leaning toward Jack and speaking in an undertone, he asked, "Are we talking Westboro?"

Jack looked at them in turn. "You know the story?" And when they nodded in unison, he said, "That was Bannock."

Grange whistled softly.

Knight murmured, "Holy shit."

Chapter 35

At the mention of the eight fatalities, Hayes abruptly got up and replaced the chair beneath the dining table. "You'd better turn in, Doc."

"Turn in?"

"Tomorrow could be a long day."

"I demand an explanation for what Agent Connell told us about you."

"Bedroom's down the hall. Bathroom's on the right. I'll bunk on the couch."

"Hayes?" When he came around to her, she said, "I assume that's your real name. Hayes Bannock?"

He hesitated before giving her a brusque nod.

"I'm glad to finally know it."

"Don't speak too soon."

"If I looked you up on the Internet, what would I find? Your army service record? Your degree in constructional engineering? Your sister and niece in Seattle?"

"My, my. Connell was a fount of information, wasn't he?"

"He referenced a soccer coach. A priest. Others in addition to Norman and Will Floyd."

"I take that back. He was a babbling brook."

"All related to that shooting in Virginia."

His eyes turned cold and hostile. "You should go to bed, Doc. Get some sleep."

"I'm not sleepy."

"Okay then, I'll turn in."

He made for the hallway, but she quickly placed herself in his path. "Tell me what all this is about."

"I'm sure you'll find out, in time."

"I want to know now. I want to hear it from your own lips, not from someone else's."

"Why?"

"Because otherwise I'll never believe you were involved in something so heinous."

"Well I was." His tone was curt, matter of fact. "There. That's all you need to know and all you'll get from me. It has nothing to do with the here and now."

"Agent Connell thinks it does."

"Agent Connell can go fuck himself. What happened then doesn't pertain to you."

"But it pertains to *you*."

"It's not my life I'm trying to save! It's yours."

"I don't need you to save me," she said, warming to the argument. "I can go to Connell myself, to Knight and Grange, and—"

"What?"

"Accuse Jeff."

He gave a stern shake of his head. "Not a good plan."

"Why?"

"You don't have any evidence to support your allegations."

She opened her hand, showing him that she had the zipper pull, then quickly snatched her hand back.

He shrugged with indifference. "Useless. Where you got it and when, your word against his, remember?"

"But it and the rock together would—"

"You don't have the rock."

"But you do."

"That's right. *I* do."

"You'd hold it hostage from me?"

"To keep you from barging in and exposing yourself to that slimy son of a bitch you're married to? Damn right, I would."

"Jeff couldn't do anything to me while I'm surrounded by law enforcement officers."

"Which is the only reason I didn't come and get you sooner. I waited outside the hospital last night until I saw Jeff leave and figured you were safe. You spent most of today in the company of men with badges.

"But what happens when they pack up and go home for lack of evidence against him? You'll have played your hand. You will have accused him. How do you think that will sit with him when he was already prepared to murder you?"

It was a valid point. Even if Jeff were now to provide an iron-clad alibi, she would never trust him or feel comfortable alone with him. Ever again. "All right, my plan is flawed. Do you have one? What do you intend to do?"

"With the rock?"

"With all of it. With what you know about Jeff. With me."

"I don't know yet."

She thought of the Floyds, suffering in their hospital beds. "But you'll stay within the law, right?"

"I don't know yet."

Frustrated almost to the point of tears, she said, "Tell me about Virginia."

"No."

"Please."

"No!"

"I want to know what you did!"

"No, you don't!" His shout echoed off the walls of the confined space. A few seconds passed, then he said in a low voice, "Trust me. You don't."

His strained enunciation, his unyielding expression intimidated her. She backed away from him. "Perhaps you're right. Maybe I don't want to know." Looking around frantically, she said, "In fact, why did I even come here with you?"

"That, I *will* answer." He took measured steps toward her. "I didn't drag you off that balcony and force you to come with me. But I would have if necessary." He let that sink in, then took a step nearer and kept closing in until his face hovered above hers.

"If I'd had to, I would have wrapped you in bailing wire and carried you off. Because I'd rather see you shy away from me, rather see you cringing with fright and mistrust like you are now, rather see you any other way except dead."

It wasn't poetry, but it was profound. Her heart expanded with emotion. She reached up to touch his cheek.

But before it could make contact, he caught her wrist and held her hand away from him. When he finally let it go, he motioned down the hall and ordered gruffly, "Go to bed. Lock the door if it makes you feel safer."

He waited.

She didn't move.

She remained staring up at him with eyes that were calm, accepting, trusting. The opposite of what they should be.

"Okay," he growled, "you asked for this."

He clasped her around the waist and turned her to face the wall. He pulled her sweater over her head, then discarded her camisole in the same ungentle manner. Her bra strap fell victim to his jerky impatience. The garment fell forward from her chest. He pushed it off her, then took her hands, placed them flat against the wall, and covered them with his as he crowded in behind her.

He nipped the side of her neck with his teeth, wanting to mark her as his, damn well knowing he had no right to her, no right even to want her. "Scared?"

"No."

"Then I'm not doing it right."

He charted a trail of biting kisses down her throat; she whimpered but with arousal, not fear. He thrust against her bottom, making certain she knew he meant business. "Now are you afraid?"

Rather than recoil, she pushed back, adjusting the fit, increasing the pressure, causing him to hiss through his teeth.

"You're playing with fire, Doc."

When she did it again with a grinding motion, he removed his hands from hers, reached around, and blindly unfastened her jeans. With little finesse, he pushed his hand into her panties and between her thighs, finding her hot, wet, swollen with the same insistent desire that was throbbing through him.

His fingers curled upward, into her. He stroked the magic spot and felt her quicken. Against her ear, he whispered roughly, "I want to be right there. Right now."

He turned her and lifted her against him, carrying her down the short hallway and into the bedroom. He stood her beside the bed, and she began to take off the rest of her clothes as hastily as he began removing his.

He was naked before she got off her second boot. Flinging back the bedspread, he sat down on the edge of the bed and reached for her just as she stepped free of her underwear.

Positioning her between his open thighs, he held her breast and took the nipple into his mouth, tugging at it with hunger, almost desperation, before folding his arms around her, drawing her closer and pressing his face into her giving middle, then lower into the sweet muskiness of her sex.

Nuzzling there, he ran his hands up and down her thighs, then parted them with more mastery than necessary, because it was clear by now that, as baffling as it was, her trust in him was unshakable.

He used his thumbs to spread her, expose her, prepare her for his mouth's assault. He dipped his tongue into her, once, twice, three times, going deep, then applied it to the tender flesh in fleeting strokes, eliciting from her choppy breaths that coalesced into a low moan when he sucked her tight little center into his mouth.

But he didn't want her to come until he was inside her. He guided her down onto the bed, stood on his knees between her raised thighs, and was about to lower himself onto her when she said, "Wait!"

"I can't."

Well, he could—he did—when she angled up, clasped his ass between her hands and took the head of his cock into her mouth. The pleasure was so immense, he clenched his teeth and wasn't even aware of the pressure he was applying to his jaw until the tip of her tongue delved into the groove, found the sweet spot, and he tried to speak. He gasped and groaned and managed to strangle out, "Christ, I thought I'd dreamed the way you do that." A few seconds more and he panted, "Doc, stop. Stop."

He eased her head away, but not before she got in one quick kiss on his tat.

When she lay back, he followed her down and sank into her, pushing until they couldn't possibly be any closer, then he settled his weight onto her and buried his face in her neck. "You'll be the ruin of me. But fuck if I can help myself."

He levered himself up and, eyes focused on hers, began to thrust into her.

And it was incredible, not only because she was so deliciously tight and silky. She was. Not only because she perfectly timed a corresponding motion for each short, quick jab and every long, smooth glide of his cock. She did.

Not only because whenever he all but pulled out, she worked

the tip of his penis with seductive belly-dance motions until he couldn't stand it any longer and had to again sheathe himself completely.

Not only because her hands caressed him with flawless intuition. And not only because, when she climaxed, he felt every convulsive squeeze, but also saw the tears in her eyes that attested to the overflowing emotion behind them.

All that contributed. But what made him come harder, longer, and more meaningfully than he ever had in his life, was that in those moments when he lost himself in her, she closed her arms around his head, and held it close, and said on a sigh, as though it was the dearest word in her vocabulary, "Hayes."

For a long time after, neither of them moved. Eventually, his mind cleared enough for him to have that *oh shit* instant of realization: he'd come inside her without anything between them. Which was also why it had been so good, and why he didn't regret it enough to disengage himself quite yet.

When he finally did move, he came up on one elbow and looked into her face. She smiled drowsily. He cupped her chin in his free hand and kissed her, taking his time, mating his mouth with hers, lecherously and leisurely.

When at last he angled his head back, he said, "Lucky for me, you don't scare easily."

"Lucky for me too."

"But you're still in danger, Doc. So be scared. Just not of me."

"I know."

"Never of me."

"I'm not." She threaded her fingers through his hair. "I don't know everything, but one thing I do know. You weren't responsible for the deaths of eight innocent people."

Like the mellow glow of a lantern suddenly extinguished, his soul became dark and cold again.

He pulled out of her and rolled onto his back. Staring at the ceiling, he said, "You're right. Only seven of them were innocent."

Chapter 36

The aroma of fresh coffee woke her. It was still dark. She switched on the lamp beside the bed. Her clothes, which had been so haphazardly discarded the night before, were folded and stacked on a chair. She gathered them and her boots and slipped into the bathroom.

Ten minutes later when she walked into the main room, Hayes looked up at her from the dining table where he sat drinking coffee. He'd slept beside her through the night, but they hadn't exchanged a word or touched since his startling statement: *Only seven of them were innocent.*

It had created an intangible barrier that neither had breached during the night. It seemed even more impenetrable this morning. As though last night's intimacies hadn't happened, his eyes were flat, his expression impassive.

He said, "Mugs are in the cabinet to the right of the sink."

She filled one with coffee and sat down across from him at the table, pretending there wasn't a pistol within reach of his right hand.

Noticing her damp hair, he said, "Sorry. I don't have a hair dryer."

"It'll dry on its own."

"Did I leave you enough hot water?"

"Yes, thank you. How do you manage to fit into that shower?"

"It's an acquired skill."

So much for small talk. She sipped her coffee.

He said, "I've made a decision."

She looked at him, listening.

"I'm not going to give Connell the satisfaction of catching me."

"You're going to surrender?"

"Not exactly."

He avoided looking her in the eye, and that made her distinctly uneasy. "Then what are you going to do? Exactly."

"Deliver you to him."

Unsure how to respond, she waited to hear him out.

His eyes moved to the row of faint red marks on the side of her neck. "It's up to you how much or how little you tell him about those. And everything else." He motioned toward the bedroom. "Be as graphic or as coy as you want. He'll be discreet. And, anyway, he'll be interested in me, not *us*. He'll question you about my state of mind. Plans. Things like that."

"He already has."

"He'll keep at you to remember the smallest detail. Things I said, things you observed. While he's taking it all in and figuring out his next course of action, I'll be making myself scarce."

"You'll run."

He raised his shoulder, a nonverbal, uncommitted answer.

She stared into her coffee. "You may get away, but you'll never outrun the deaths of those people."

"Well, that'll give you and Connell plenty to chat about."

Voice faltering, she asked, "Why'd you do it?"

He picked up his mug, then returned it to the table without having drunk from it. Disregarding her question, he said, "Tell Connell what you know about Jeff. He'll see to it that he's thoroughly investigated. Hopefully that will result in his cold ass landing in prison."

"How do you know Connell will see to an investigation?"

"He's an FBI agent. It's his duty."

"But it isn't his case. Won't he leave it to the sheriff's office?"

"No."

"What makes you so certain?"

"Because of the message you'll give him."

"Which is?"

"If he fucks it up, and something happens to you, whether in the near or distant future, I'll kill him." He let that register, then, "Where's he staying?"

"So you can dump me there?"

"Where's he staying?"

"Why should I tell you?"

He propped his forearms on the table. It rocked slightly as he leaned across it toward her. "Look, Doc, we can waste time waltzing around this, you can argue it with me up and down, sideways and backward, but it won't do you any good. I'm not gonna let that fed make me the trophy of his career. Besides that—"

"What? Besides that, what?"

"I've got to get the hell lost, and I can't take you with me. You've got a life to lead, and it can't include me. It's been fun, but here's where we say good-bye and part ways, no matter how good we are together in the sack."

"Why are you being like this?"

"Candid?"

"Offensive."

"No, offensive would have been if I'd said you're a great fuck."

Her face grew hot with anger.

He must've have noticed, because he stifled a laugh. "A little late for blushes, isn't it, Doc? You knew what you were signing up for last night, and it wasn't hearts and flowers. The night in the cabin, too. We both got what we wanted. I got laid and you got...how'd you put it? 'Raw emotions'?"

With that he scraped back his chair, stood up, and shoved the pistol into the waistband of his jeans. "Let's go. I want to get there before daylight, and it's a ten-minute drive to the motel."

"Why did you ask me where Connell was staying if you already knew?"

"To see if you would lie to me."

"How did you find out where he is?"

"Not that many choices in Drakeland. I called around until a desk clerk confirmed that he checked in last night."

"You called? I thought you didn't have a phone."

"I don't anymore." She followed the direction he indicated and saw the pieces of a bashed cell phone lying on the end table. As he pulled on his outerwear, he said, "I'll loan you a coat."

"I don't want it."

She went to the door, unbolted it, and walked out, leaving him to follow.

Or to drop dead. She really didn't care.

It had stopped snowing, but the fog was still thick and the air frigid. The interior of the car was slow to warm, even after he turned on the heater. As they approached the city limits, she said, "You didn't secure the mobile home."

"It's served its purpose. I won't be going back."

"You'll just leave your possessions behind?"

"The possessions that count aren't in the mobile home. I'll collect them and—"

"Ride off into the sunrise?"

"Basically."

"You realize that I can describe this car to the authorities."

"Yes."

"You have a backup plan?"

"Always."

They rode the remainder of the way in silence. He pulled to

the curb on a street that ran along the back of the motel and put the car in park. She stared through the streaked windshield. The defroster was just beginning to melt all the frost and frozen precipitation that had accumulated overnight.

She focused on the disintegrating ice crystals rather than on the tightness in her throat. "I'm relieved. And a bit surprised actually."

"By what?"

"I thought you might mete out Jeff's punishment yourself."

His fingers tightened around the steering wheel. "That was my original plan. And nothing would give me greater pleasure. But I slept on it and decided to entrust him to the legal system. Not to save his skin, understand. But mine. Dealing with you and Jeff will keep Connell occupied for a while."

"Giving you a head start."

"Right."

She hesitated, then said, "Fair warning. I'll tell Connell everything about you that I know. I have to. Before, when the only issue was your involvement with those horrid Floyd brothers, I covered for you, because I shared your outrage over Lisa. But I can't facilitate you in escaping justice."

He held her gaze for several seconds, then reached beneath the driver's seat and retrieved a brown paper sack. "Your evidence," he said, passing it to her. "Don't open it. Don't touch the rock. Hand it over to Connell as is. You still have the charm?"

"Yes."

"All right then. You know what to do."

Knowing that her misery was nakedly apparent, but unable to keep it from showing, she spoke his name beseechingly.

"Enough's been said, Doc. Connell is in room one ten. Get on with it."

Mistrusting herself to linger for even a second longer, she got out of the car. She'd barely closed the passenger door when he wheeled away. She watched through tear-blurred eyes as the tail-lights disappeared around the nearest corner.

Once he was out of sight, she trudged toward the motel. It was the one in which Jeff had been hosted by the sheriff's office, and it was as unattractive as he'd described. Its two levels had open breezeways. Guest room doors were alternately painted red, white, and blue. Near the elevator in the center of the building was a communal ice machine. A neon arrow flickered above it.

Room one ten was three doors down from the end on the first floor. She raised her fist, paused, and looked over her shoulder toward the corner around which Hayes had disappeared. He'd made himself a cruelly insulting stranger this morning, which, she realized now, had been his way of coping with the inevitable good-bye.

Heartbreak wasn't simply a byword.

Steeling herself, she rapped on the motel room door with her knuckles.

From within, a sleepy voice called, "Yes?"

"Agent Connell, it's Emory Charbonneau."

She heard the thud of his feet hitting the floor. He parted the curtains only wide enough to peek out and see her, then there was the rattle of a chain lock and the scrape of a metal bolt, and the federal agent, eyes puffy and hair standing on end, yanked open the door. He was wearing plaid boxers, a white T-shirt, and black socks.

"What the hell?" He swept the parking lot behind her with a searching gaze. "Where'd you come from?"

"He dropped me here."

"Bannock?"

When she nodded, he pushed past her and charged outside, running several yards deep into the parking lot, looking frantically about. He headed for the nearest corner of the building.

"Not that way."

He did an about-face. "Then which way?"

She pointed. "He's driving a green car. Older. I memorized the license plate number."

He patted his sides, searching for his phone, before realizing he wasn't even dressed. "Shit! How long ago?"

"Just now."

As he jogged back, he flapped his hands, motioning her into the room. She turned, stepped through the open door, and came up against Hayes, who stood there as solid as an I beam. He lifted her bodily and set her aside.

"Hayes, no!"

But Jack Connell wasn't warned in time. When he crossed the threshold, there was nothing between him and Hayes's fist, which connected solidly with the agent's jaw.

"That's for pestering my sister."

Propelled by the slug, Connell would have reeled backward through the open doorway, but Hayes grabbed a fistful of his T-shirt, jerked him inside, and hurled him toward the bed. As the agent clambered to regain his balance, his shinbone landed against the metal bed frame. His leg gave out from under him and he went down.

Emory made wild grabs at Hayes's coat sleeve in an attempt to restrain him, but he shook her off. He closed the door and bolted it, then bore down on the other man. Connell scrambled to his feet before Hayes reached him. He stuck out his hands at arm's length, palms toward Hayes.

"You want to add assault on a federal officer to everything else?"

The words halted Hayes. He stood, his chest a bellows, glowering down at the agent.

Fearful and furious at the same time, Emory struck Hayes's arm with her fist. "Why did you come back? Why didn't you just keep going?"

"Is he armed?" Connell asked.

"Yes!"

Hayes said, "Be a man, Connell, and ask me yourself." He raised his coat and shirt, exposing his waistband and the pistol tucked into it.

Connell said, "Carrying a concealed weapon. Attacking a federal agent, breaking and entering, assault and battery. What am I overlooking?" His gaze cut from Hayes to Emory. "Kidnapping?"

"He didn't kidnap me."

"You're positive about that?" Connell asked, as though uncertain if she was lying or simply being terribly naive.

"Well, he didn't kidnap me last night," she declared. "I went with him of my own accord."

"And helped him set me up this morning."

"Wrong again, asshole," Hayes said. "I tricked her into setting you up."

Connell looked to her for verification. "I'm sorry," she said. "He convinced me that he was delivering me to you and then making himself scarce. His words."

"Because he doesn't have the guts to say what he's really doing. He's running," Connell said. "Running from what he did in Westboro."

Upon hearing the name of the community that had won infamy in an afternoon, Emory gasped. "Westboro?"

Hayes looked at her sharply, his face a mask, his eyes cold.

Appalled, she backed away from him. "Westboro was *your* shooting?"

All along, her mind had refused to accept that he was connected to any mass shooting. She had certainly never attached him to Westboro, not even when Virginia had been referenced. She looked from him to Connell to various spots in the room, as she collected the scattered facts she remembered about the act of wanton violence. She stopped on Connell, silently imploring him to deny it.

But his eyes were on Hayes, watching him closely. "An angry and bitter young man walked into his place of employment with an automatic rifle and plenty of ammunition. He took up a position that gave him good cover, and calmly and methodically began picking people off."

The images he evoked caused Emory to shudder. She, like most everyone in the nation, had watched the live television coverage as the horrifying drama unfolded. People running for their lives. Bodies lying in pools of blood. Anxious loved ones awaiting word on who had died and who had miraculously been spared, then, in the aftermath, grieving and celebrating in equal measure as names of the casualties were released.

"The melee lasted for almost two hours," Connell continued. "Which was an eternity for those hunkered down, wondering if one of his bullets would find them. Some used their cell phones to call loved ones, made their peace, said good-bye."

She backed into a chair near the window and sat down, rubbing her forehead as though to smudge the terrible images and make them easier to bear. Then, "Wait a minute." She lowered her hand and with puzzlement looked first at Hayes, whose expression remained inscrutable, then at Connell. "I thought...Wasn't...wasn't the shooter killed at the scene?"

Connell nodded, then tipped his head toward Hayes. "Bannock took him out."

Chapter 37

Jack Connell worked his jaw horizontally back and forth as he pulled himself onto the edge of the bed and sat. He shot Hayes a baleful look. "That hurt."

"Meant for it to. Your visit upset Rebecca."

"It upset me, too," Jack grumbled. "Was she lying, or could she have made it easy and told me where you were?"

"She's never known where I was. All your sleuthing was wasted."

"Not completely. I had the pleasure of her company for fifteen minutes or so. I haven't had that much fun since I walked bare-assed through a pit of vipers."

Hayes knew he was expected to smile. He didn't.

"Have you seen her new hairdo? Wicked. Suits her perfectly."

"Just so you know, Jack, this isn't a make-nice reunion. When this mess is over, everything goes right back to the way it's been."

"You'll take off."

"Right."

"Huh. I thought maybe you had come to your senses and

would want to stay put." Connell looked over at Emory, his implication unmistakable.

"I split as soon as I see her husband behind bars."

"Her husband? What did he do?"

"He left her for dead."

Connell took a moment to gauge Hayes's seriousness. "You're not joking."

"Would I joke about that?"

"You wouldn't. You rarely joke, period," Jack said, making a face. "Start at the beginning."

"I was hiking up on a ridge the day Emory went missing. I spotted her through my binoculars. Got curious."

"Why?"

Hayes glanced at her but didn't say anything.

"Well?" Jack prompted, raising his eyebrows.

"She was a blond in black running tights who had a dynamite body, and she was alone."

Jack looked at her again. "Fair enough."

"What's important," Hayes said with impatience, "is that by the time I reached that trail, she was lying in the middle of it, concussed and almost frozen. I gathered her up and took her to my place."

"Why not to a hospital?"

"Several reasons."

"Besides the black running tights."

"I didn't know what had happened to her. If she'd fallen, that was one thing. If she'd been attacked, she was safer with me."

"That's debatable, but go on."

"She recovered enough so that when the weather cleared, I brought her—"

"I know that part. Knight and Grange filled me in. The gas station. The media frenzy."

"I didn't know until after she was back in the fold that I had returned her to her would-be killer."

"Jeff."

"The very one."

"So," Connell said, drawing out the word and nodding as he pieced it together, "you knew she was in mortal danger."

"Yes."

"But being you and wanting to stay under the radar, you couldn't get the world's attention and announce it."

Hayes figured his silence was confirmation enough.

"Instead," Jack continued, "you sent up a smoke signal for me to come running."

"My fingerprint on the faucet."

"A perfect thumbprint in an otherwise pristine cabin," Connell said wryly. "I knew you wouldn't be that careless."

"How long did it take you to figure it out?"

"Five, six minutes tops."

"You're rusty. Or freakin' old."

"Cut me some slack. I'd just gotten off a red-eye from Seattle."

"I was beginning to think I should have been less subtle, done something like paint a red arrow on a signpost pointing you in my direction. TO BANNOCK: THIS WAY, JERK-OFF."

"I realize it would have been boring, conventional, and totally un-Bannock-like, but you could have just picked up the phone and called me."

"And cheat you out of the thrill of the chase?"

"Fuck you."

"And back at you."

Grudgingly, they grinned at each other.

During their bantering exchange, Emory had vacillated between disbelief and fury. Now she confronted them. "You're *friends?*"

Hayes said, "Not even close."

Jack's reply was, "Quasi friends."

"How long have you known each other?"

Jack said, "I recruited him straight out of the army."

"For?"

"My SWAT team."

She looked at Hayes with wonderment. "You're with the FBI?"

"Was."

"You're the unnamed SWAT officer who made the impossible shot and killed the Westboro gunman? You're the legend?"

Hayes didn't respond.

"Answer me!"

He shouted back, "I will when you ask a question that I feel is worthy of an answer."

The sound that broke the resultant silence was Connell slapping his naked knees. "We've got a lot to talk about. Hand me my pants."

Hayes looked behind him where Connell's clothes were piled in a chair, along with his pistol and shoulder holster. "You should keep your weapon within reach, Agent Connell."

"Lesson learned. God knows who's likely to show up and assault me."

Hayes tossed the trousers toward the bed. Connell caught them and shook them out. "Excuse me, Dr. Charbonneau." He stood up and stepped into his pants. As he did them up, he said, "Oh, before I forget."

He took a cell phone from one of the trouser pockets and handed it to her. "Yours. We found it in the bedroom last night after you ran off. I asked if I could keep it, monitor calls you received. Guess there's no need to now."

"Thank you."

"FYI, the battery has run completely out. It needs charging." He finished dressing, including his shoulder holster, and worked his feet into a pair of loafers. "Emory, what Bannock said about your husband, is it valid?"

"Why don't you ask me?" Hayes said.

"Because I'm asking her."

"I believe it's true," she said.

"Based on a hunch or evidence?"

"In all the confusion..." She bent down and retrieved the brown paper sack containing the rock, which she'd dropped on the floor during the tussle. She handed the sack to Connell. After opening it and looking inside, he turned to Hayes. "Her hair and blood?"

He nodded. "Found at the scene, along with a designer logo off Jeff's ski jacket." Jack mulled over that information for several seconds, then said, "Before we get down to business, I could use some strong, black coffee and hot food, and, since I'm the only one here not currently being sought by local law enforcement, I volunteer to go for them."

He gave them time to argue or offer an alternative. When neither did, he put on his overcoat and gloves and scooped the keys to his rental car off the dresser. "Back soon."

He pulled the door closed behind himself, but even the momentary blast of cold air didn't dissipate the tension in the room. Neither she nor Hayes spoke. He walked over to the bed, pulled the bedspread up over the mussed sheets, then sat down approximately where Connell had been. Only then did he look at her.

"How did you get in here so fast?"

His head went back a notch. "Of all the burning questions you must have, that's the one you asked?"

Without even trying to mitigate her anger, she said, "I'm pacing myself."

"I drove around to the other side of the building, ran like hell, and came through the bathroom window."

"Why not just accompany me to the door? He would have been just as surprised."

"I had to make sure of you."

"Of *me*?"

"I had to be certain that you would do what was right and uphold the law."

She gave a harsh laugh. "Do you realize how ludicrous that statement sounds coming from you?"

"It's my choice to bend the law when expedient. But I didn't want to be responsible for your breaking it."

"You made me into a burglar."

"That was an exception. Even you drew the distinction between the episode with the Floyds and lying to a federal agent in order to let a fugitive escape justice."

"So everything you said this morning was to see in what direction my moral compass was aimed?"

"Something like that."

"Well, I'm happy I passed."

"I know you mean that sarcastically, Doc, but I'm happy you passed, too."

"You put me through hell for nothing."

"Not exactly for nothing, but I'm sorry I had to be so hard on you."

"Not hard, horrid."

"I had to push your buttons, or the ruse wouldn't have worked."

"I could happily kill you right now."

"I have that effect on people."

He'd met her charges with calm acceptance, which only made her angrier. "You never planned to drop me off and hightail it?"

"Do you think I'd trust your safety, your *life*, to Knight, Grange, or even to Jack? Hell. No."

"You must trust Connell to some extent or you wouldn't be here. Weren't you afraid he would arrest you on sight?"

"Arrest me? His pursuit is personal, not official. In his book, my only crime was bailing."

"What?"

"I vanished. Disappeared."

"You didn't commit a terrible crime?"

He gave a brusque shake of his head.

"Then what have you been hiding from?"

"From being the *legend* who took out the Westboro mass murderer."

Left speechless, she could only gape. When she was able to speak, her voice was thin. "You did your job."

"True. But I didn't see it as cause for celebration. I didn't think it merited recognition. It was a good day for our team. We did spare lives, no doubt. I wanted it left at that."

"But it wasn't."

"Not by anybody who knew me. Not by anybody, period. The media wanted my name, but thank God nobody on the team, including Jack, leaked it. I'll always be grateful to them for that."

"Remaining anonymous only made you more intriguing."

"I guess," he muttered. "I was the most sought-after interview, one TV station said. Some of the victims' families wanted to meet me so they could personally thank me. I got it. I understood. Closure. An eye for an eye. All that. But I didn't even read the letters they sent Jack to pass along to me.

"The buzz, for lack of a better word, lasted for months. Seemed like every frigging day it was in the news. A different aspect of the incident. I got sick of it and thought, hell, if it won't go away, I will. So I tendered my resignation and took off. Rebecca, too. Jack's been after both of us ever since."

His explanation disarmed her. But considering the closeness they'd shared, physically and emotionally, she felt wounded by his not confiding all this to her sooner. "Why didn't you tell me? Or was that a test, too?"

"Test?"

"To see if I would believe the worst about you and still go to bed with you?"

"No." Then with more emphasis, *"No."*

"Then why didn't you tell me?"

He pushed back his hair with both hands, and when they met at the nape of his neck, he held them there for a moment before lowering them. "I killed that kid, Emory. I put a bullet through his head and he died."

"You did your duty," she said with soft earnestness. "You did it in order to save lives."

"Doesn't make it any easier to accept. He wasn't a criminal or a psychopath or a fanatic with a point to make. He was a victim, too."

He got up and walked over to the window, where he twirled the wand on the blinds to open them. Looking out, he said, "His name was Eric Johnson. Jack referred to him as an angry, bitter young man, but he had just turned seventeen. Seventeen. He was working through summer vacation, about to start his senior year in high school. Most kids would be excited. Not Eric. He couldn't bear the thought of school and more bullying."

"He was bullied by his classmates?"

"By just about everybody."

"His parents?"

"No." He came around to face her, perching on the window sill. "Honestly, I don't think so. He was their only child, and all indications were that they loved him. Maybe they should have sensed his increasing withdrawal and gotten counseling for him, and maybe they didn't read the signs of his impending meltdown, but their negligence wasn't malicious. Besides, by definition, the unthinkable never would have occurred to them, would it?

"They were shattered by what he did and shocked to learn that he had obtained his murder weapon without their knowledge. His dad had never owned a gun of any kind. Eric hadn't grown up around them. He bought his murder weapon online and learned to use it in secret.

"The discovery came too late, when investigators from every branch of law enforcement turned the Johnsons' lives and their house upside down looking for answers as to why he'd done what he did. Pundits aired their theories. But the reason was clear."

"The bullying."

"Yeah. Eric was an overweight, classic nerd. No people skills. No special talents or athleticism. In an effort to get him more involved, his dad encouraged him to attend a soccer camp one summer, and the following fall, he actually made the junior varsity team. In a journal, he described the cake his mom had decorated in the team colors to celebrate that achievement."

Emory swallowed with difficulty.

"It didn't turn out so well, though. He was slow and had no aptitude for the game."

"Then why was he chosen for the team?"

"To be the coach's whipping boy. If they lost, Coach gave the team hell, but he was especially hard on Eric."

She murmured, "The soccer coach in Utah."

"He's not a coach anymore and never will be."

"You saw to it."

"I never laid a hand on him. All I did was hand him a length of pipe similar to the one he'd cracked across Eric's kneecap."

"With an implied threat."

He didn't respond to that. "More often Eric's torment was psychological. He attended a parochial school. It was reported to the headmaster that he'd been caught masturbating in a restroom stall. During chapel the following morning, the headmaster used the incident to illustrate moral turpitude."

Her heart sank with pity for the boy who'd been publically humiliated, and her expression must have revealed the sadness she felt for him. "This headmaster was a priest?"

"Yeah. A man of God," he said with rancor. "When I caught up with him, he'd been reassigned to a school in Lexington."

"I understand that he resigned under…duress."

"I was in the congregation the morning he confessed to his sex addiction from the pulpit."

"He was a sex addict?"

"I don't know, but I made it clear that was the sin he'd damn well better confess to."

"Moral turpitude." She took a deep breath and let it out slowly. "And there were others. Connell mentioned something in Texas. A hairdresser?"

"Vain bitch. She was Eric's barber. He had a crush on her. She made fun of him on Facebook."

"And?"

"A few weeks after I caught up with her in Wichita Falls, she posted a photo of herself on her Facebook page. Shaved head. No makeup." He sighed, said, "You get the idea."

"Their punishment fit their crime."

"Not so much a crime as a transgression against an easy target. But yeah, I make my point."

"The Floyds?"

He smiled crookedly. "That was especially satisfying."

"They beat Eric up?"

"Just a few weeks before the shooting rampage. In fact, they might have been the final straw. They'd been picking on him since he was hired on. During a lunch break, Eric had enough of their torture and took a swing at Norman. That gave them all the excuse they needed to lay into him. Beat him senseless."

"As you did to them."

"Yes." Darkly, he added, "And I wish I had it to do all over again for what they did to Lisa."

"On that, I agree with you."

His eyes found hers with the accuracy and intensity of lasers. "But you don't agree with the rest of it."

She raised her hands, trying to convey the helplessness she felt. "I'm conflicted."

"Because now I'm the bully."

She was glad he'd said it and not she. "Aren't you?"

"This is why I didn't tell you," he said, his tone cold and clipped. "Why I never wanted you to know."

"You would have let me exit your life without ever knowing—"

"Yes. Because you'll never understand."

"Try me."

"Justify my actions to you?"

"No, justify your actions to *yourself*, Hayes. Because I think that's what you're running from."

He was rocking back and forth on his heels, his expression angry and troubled. She discerned that this wasn't the first time he'd grappled with this. He said, "Eric Johnson will be remembered for gunning down seven people. But no one will remember, or even know, the names of the people who put him behind that brick wall that day, fortified with a weapon and ammo and a consuming hatred for humankind.

"The bullies who instilled that hatred were never made to account. I think they should. I think they should because he died that day, too." He poked his chest with his index finger. "And I was the one who had to kill him."

He gave her a hard stare, as though daring her to take issue. Then he pushed away from the window ledge and began to prowl aimlessly around the room, as though he felt caged, perhaps by his own conscience.

"Why do you think Connell has pursued you all these years?"

He made a dismissive gesture. "Hell if I know. Maybe he wants to assuage his own misgivings about how that mission was...resolved. Maybe he hasn't found a replacement for me on his team. Or he's got nothing better to do, or could be he's just stubborn as a damn mule."

"Those aren't the reasons."

He stopped roaming and turned to her. "Okay, Doc, enlighten me."

"He cares about you and hates knowing that you're wasting yourself by living a shadowy, lonely life."

He tilted his head. "Gee whiz. You figured out all that in...what?" He made a show of looking at his wristwatch. "Ten minutes? You must've taken advanced psychiatry classes in med school."

"You're pushing my buttons again."

"Well, you're pushing mine, too. Who says I'm lonely? And you're one to talk about self-imposed loneliness. Married to a man with an icicle where his dick ought to be. And how about your distance running? I'm no shrink, but it seems obsessive. What do you need that you can't find standing still? What are you running to? Or from?"

His intention was to make her angry or to turn the conversation off himself and on to her, but she refused to take umbrage. "I've been asking myself those same questions recently."

"Well keep to them and stop trying to analyze me."

"When did you last see your sister?"

"We talked two nights ago while I was keeping vigil outside the hospital."

"That's not what I asked. She loves you, Hayes."

"How the hell do you know?"

"Connell."

"The man's all mouth."

"Rebecca loves you."

"It's her main character flaw."

"Your niece loves you."

His jaw worked, but he didn't respond except to turn away from her and go over to the dresser. Bracing his hands on the edge of it, he leaned in toward the mirror, although she noticed that he didn't look into it.

"And I love you."

He jerked his head up. Their eyes clashed in the mirror. "Well don't."

"Too late. I do."

She left the chair, and when she reached him, she laid her

cheek against his back and tightly hugged his torso, linking her hands across his chest.

"You're setting yourself up to get hurt, Doc."

"Probably. But that doesn't change how I feel." She rolled her forehead against the hollow of his spine and placed her hand over his left pectoral. "Reasonably, you know you did what you had to do that awful day in Westboro. You just wish Eric Johnson had been someone you could despise and revile, not someone you pity."

He didn't contradict her or argue, so she continued. "You use your size and stern demeanor to keep people at arm's length, afraid of you. But I'm one of the few who's been given a glimpse into your heart." She pressed her hand against his heart, thrilling to the strong beats against her palm. "And I love what I've seen."

She didn't expect an avowal of love or any such romantic profession from him. When he turned in the circle of her arms to face her, he looked as forbidding as ever. "You think you're smart, don't you? You think you have me all figured out."

"I think I'm close, or you wouldn't be angry."

"You want to know why I can't look in a mirror, Doc? Want to know what I'm running from, why I can't get far enough away from Westboro?"

Knowing that they'd reached the bottom of his personal hell, she already knew what he was going to say.

"Because given the same situation, under the same set of circumstances, with Eric in the crosshairs, I would still pull the trigger."

Footsteps approached the door. The key was inserted into the lock. Connell blustered in. She and Hayes quickly stepped apart, but Connell picked up on the charged atmosphere immediately.

"What'd I miss?"

"Shut the damn door," Hayes muttered.

As he reached behind him to pull the door closed, Connell repeated, "What'd I miss?"

"Not that it's any of your business, but I told her what I've been doing since Westboro."

Connell had brought in several carryout sacks. He set them on the table. Addressing her, he said, "He told you about the people on his shit list and why they were on it?"

"Yes."

"Huh," Connell said. "I thought you'd be discussing Jeff."

"In a way, we were," Hayes said. "He's next on my list."

Chapter 38

The two were even more disreputable-looking than Jeff had expected them to be. Their natural raw-boned appearances were embellished by bruises, bandages, and the external rods holding one's broken jaw in place.

They were reclined in side-by-side hospital beds, their swollen and bloodshot eyes fixed on the TV mounted on the wall from which blasted the inane dialogue of a sitcom rerun.

As he strolled into the room, he smiled at them pleasantly. "Hello. My name is Jeff Surrey."

Norman looked him up and down. "So?"

"You're Norman, correct?" Jeff moved to the foot of his bed. "I'd heard it was Will who'd suffered the more serious injury." He looked toward Will with a moue of sympathy.

"You heard right," Norman said. "And my brother likes to do his suffering in private. You ain't a nurse. If you're a doctor, we got enough already. If you're from the billing department, we get all this for free on account of we're out of work and on welfare."

"I'm not affiliated with the hospital."

"Then what the fuck you want?"

"Hayes Bannock."

"What's that?"

"Not a *what*. A *who*. I'm Emory Charbonneau's husband."

The name struck a chord. Apparently they had been watching news broadcasts as well as sitcom reruns. Norman looked over at his brother and ordered, "Shut that off."

Will, who'd been in charge of the control for the TV, fumbled with it and muted the audio. Jeff had won their undivided attention.

"May I sit down?"

Norman made a gesture of consent. Jeff dragged a chair from beneath the window, positioned it between the two beds, sat down, and casually crossed one leg over the other. "I was told about the unusual circumstances under which you met my wife."

"She went by Dr. Smith."

"She lied about her name. She's been lying a lot recently. Ever since she was abducted by your neighbor."

"Bannock, you say? He was stingy with his name. We never knowed it."

"With good reason, as it turns out. He's wanted by the FBI."

"No shit?"

"No shit."

Norman looked over at Will. "You called it right." Norman came back to Jeff. "We had a bad feelin' about him. What the feds want him for?"

"You know how they are about their cases. Very tight-lipped. But I've met with the agent who's been trying for years to capture Bannock."

"Years? Then whatever he did must've been bad."

"I shudder to think," Jeff said. "His attack on you was psychopathically vicious. And now he's kidnapped my wife. For the second time."

Norman turned his head and exchanged a long look with his brother, as though silently consulting with him. When he came back to Jeff, he scrutinized him as he shifted his weight and resettled more comfortably in the bed. Then he flashed a grin, made particularly ugly by the damage done to his face.

"You sure she didn't just run off? 'Cause it didn't strike us that she was with this Bannock against her will."

"He's brainwashed her."

Norman guffawed. "Get out."

"Maybe not in a literal sense," Jeff said, "but something to that effect. I can tell you with certainty that she's not herself. She's behaving irrationally, and . . . and I fear that if she's ever returned, she won't be the woman she was before. The one I knew and loved."

He covered a light cough/sob with his fist and hoped to God the playacting was convincing. He also hoped they understood at least a few of the multisyllable words.

They understood enough of them. Norman was no longer grinning. "He's got our ma and sister all moony-eyed, too. Sum'bitch just sauntered into our house and made himself all cozy in our business."

"That's why I—"

"But truth is," Norman continued, interrupting, "he's meaner'n a snake, and we don't want no more truck with him, especially with him being wanted by the feds and all. We don't need that shit, nor nothing like it. No thank you."

In the next bed, Will confirmed that with as much of a nod as he could manage.

Bolstered by his brother's endorsement, Norman expanded. "Now, I'm sorry about your wife preferring him. That sucks, all right. But it ain't our problem, it's yours. So . . ." He hitched his chin toward the door. "Don't let it hit you in the ass on your way out."

Jeff remained where he was and brushed an imaginary piece of lint off his trouser leg. "Of course my marital issues are entirely personal, and I wouldn't have aired them to you at all, except for the fact that they *have* become your problem."

"How's that?"

"I'm prepared to leave Bannock's fate to the federal government. My wife is my only concern. His influence has turned her into a criminal and made her mentally and emotionally imbalanced. For instance, yesterday she told detectives from the sheriff's office that the baby your sister miscarried was..." He looked away, as though unable to speak the nasty allegation.

"Wuz whut?"

"Was..." He let out a long sigh. "Fathered by one of you."

Despite his broken ribs, Norman jack-knifed up. "Hell you say!"

Jeff raised his hands in surrender. "Not I, Norman. Emory."

"Well that's a damn lie," he said, jabbing the air with his index finger for emphasis.

"I should hope so. The incest notwithstanding, any sexual congress with Lisa would be statutory rape because of her age. As I'm sure you're aware."

Norman looked across at his brother, whose reaction was hard to decipher, but Jeff decided it contained equal portions of fear and fury.

Jeff fed both. "Lisa was questioned by a female deputy. I wasn't privy to that interview, but based on how fondly Emory spoke about your sister, I got the impression that the two of them have forged a strong bond."

"Lisa thinks the sun rises and sets in *Dr. Smith.*"

"Hmm." Jeff tugged his lower lip as though he found that very troublesome. "I guessed as much. I'm afraid your sister will back anything Emory told the authorities about you. Which is why I felt compelled to inform you that while you're sequestered in here, your family name is being maligned. You're being accused of the worst sort of depravity and an egregious crime."

He purposefully used the big words this time. The brothers probably didn't know all of them, but the language tolled impending doom for the Floyd brothers, and that was Jeff's intention.

Norman looked over at Will. "We gotta get out of here. Shut this down before it goes any further."

Will gave his brother a thumbs-up and began bicycling his legs to push the sheet off them.

Jeff stood. "Wait! You can't leave the hospital. Your conditions are far too serious. I wouldn't have told you if I thought—"

"Don't you worry about us, mister." Norman started tearing at the tape that secured the IV shunt to his hand. "Thanks for coming by and letting us know. We'll take it from here."

"Well," Jeff said, "since you're insistent on taking immediate action...It had occurred to me that we could be of help to each other."

Norman stopped pulling on the tape. Will hummed his eagerness to learn what Jeff had in mind. He even made a rolling motion with his hand as though to say, *Let's hear it.*

Jeff kept his expression thoughtful and serious, but up his sleeve he was laughing.

Hayes's statement caused Emory's heart to lurch. "Jeff is next on your list? What does that mean?"

"I know what it means," Jack said. "For God's sake, Hayes, you can't take this matter into your own hands."

Hayes turned away from them and went over to the table. "What did you get to eat?" He removed a sandwich from one of the bags, folded back the foil wrapper, and inspected the ingredients between the thick slices of bread.

"Did you hear what I said?" Jack asked.

"I can't take matters into my own hands."

"Before I'll let you do something stupid, I'll have you thrown in jail for the Floyds. Swear to God, I will."

"Enough with the threats, Jack. Eat."

He sat down at the table and motioned Emory into the second chair. "You take the bed," he said to Jack as he passed him a Styrofoam cup of coffee and a breakfast sandwich.

Emory sat down as instructed but left the food untouched. "You won't do anything illegal, will you?"

"Like tear Jeff limb from effing limb? I would love nothing better. But you said the key word. Illegal. I refuse to give him a loophole to wiggle through in court. Our job," he said to Jack, "is to make damn certain we have a solid case for the prosecutor." Hearing an approaching vehicle, Emory turned to look through the open blinds. The familiar SUV was pulling into the parking space directly in front of the room. "It's Knight and Grange."

"The cavalry," Hayes said.

"They know who you are," Jack said, and in response to Hayes's angry reaction, he added, "I had to tell them. Last night after you snatched Emory off that balcony, every officer in the area was out beating the bushes for you. If I hadn't told them who you were, you could've been shot on sight."

When the knock came, Emory asked, "Should I let them in?"

"The plan was for us to regroup here at eight o'clock," Jack said. "They're right on time. Open the door."

If the situation hadn't been so serious, she would have laughed at the detectives' dumbfounded expressions upon seeing her. "Good morning." She stood aside so they could come in. Both stumbled to a halt when they saw Hayes sitting at the table, his carryout breakfast spread out before him.

Knight was the first to recover his powers of speech. "I gotta say, you two never fail to surprise."

Jack said, "Sam Knight, Buddy Grange, this is Hayes Bannock."

Emory noticed that it was with reverence and awe that Grange approached Hayes to shake hands. "You're the stuff of legends. Never thought I'd have the honor, sir."

Hayes replied with a terse thanks, and, after shaking hands with Knight, continued eating.

"How'd you get the bruise on your chin?" Knight asked Connell.

"I slipped in the shower."

Emory could tell that neither he nor Grange believed that. They both looked toward Hayes, whose only reaction to their speculation was to ball up the empty wrapper of his sandwich and toss it into the sack.

Knight said, "Gotta tell y'all, I'm dying to know how this little get-together came about."

Jack took it upon himself to explain. He gave them a broad-strokes overview, then filled in the details. "When you arrived, we were about to address how solid the case against Jeff Surrey is. You were the first to suspect him. What's your take?"

Knight thoughtfully tugged at the rubber band around his fingers. Turning to Hayes, he said, "We don't have a crime scene, and even if we did, you compromised it when you removed that rock."

"I realize that. I haven't forgotten all my training. But there was weather moving in, which would have compromised it anyway. Or the rock could possibly have gotten overlooked. Jeff could have started thinking about it, gone back to the spot, and removed it. Best option I had was to take it with me. I was wearing gloves, so the last person to touch it was the person who used it as a weapon."

"Why a rock?" Grange asked. "Not a very reliable murder weapon."

"Jeff wanted it to look like an accident," Hayes said. "Like Emory fell."

"Are you sure you didn't, Dr. Charbonneau?" Grange asked.

"No. The first time you questioned me, I told you I couldn't remember specifically what happened, and I still can't. If it came to trial, I couldn't swear under oath that I didn't just fall."

That disturbed the detectives, and Hayes noticed. With discernible irritability, he said, "Show them the thing off Jeff's jacket."

Emory removed the silver charm from her pocket. While the detectives were examining it in turn, Hayes explained how he'd found it.

Knight asked her, "You couldn't have dropped it there yourself?"

"No, and I'm positive about that. The last time I saw it, until last night, it was dangling off the zipper pull of Jeff's ski jacket."

"What happened last night?"

"Hayes showed it to me out on the balcony of the hotel."

"Huh," the older detective said. "So that's what convinced you to hightail it with him."

"Yes. I realized instantly what it signified, and that I was still in danger from Jeff."

Hayes said, "He didn't get the job done up on that trail, but he was there."

"What were you doing up there last Saturday?"

He explained, this time without referring to her black tights. "It took me a while to circle around. By the time I found her, at least a half hour had elapsed, possibly a little more. She was cold."

"Time enough for Jeff to intercept her, do his thing, and get away without you seeing him," Grange said.

"Obviously."

Knight snapped the rubber band. "Okay, let's assume—optimistically, because I'm afraid that a defense lawyer will brutalize that timeline—let's assume that if we can place him on that trail, we've also got a classic motive. You're loaded."

Emory flinched at the word but didn't make an issue of it. "Jeff also has been having an affair."

Grange said, "So you do know about that? We weren't sure."

"I suspected. He's now admitted it. He told me it was over, but I don't believe anything he says at this point."

"The romance might be over, but he still needs her as his alibi. Alice Butler vowed to me that she and Jeff were together from Friday evening until Sunday afternoon."

Later, Emory wondered how she managed not to cry out and give herself away. Without realizing the blunder he'd made, Grange continued talking, but she was deaf to what he was saying and insensible to everything except the soul-crushing betrayal.

She felt the pain of Alice's betrayal even more keenly than Jeff's. Alice was the trusted and admired colleague with whom she'd built a practice. She'd poured out her heart to Alice about Hayes. Worse, she was the friend to whom she'd shared doubts about Jeff's fidelity, the future of their marriage, and her suspicion of his culpability.

As though reading her mind, Hayes interrupted Grange. "Alice knows that Emory suspects him."

Everyone looked to her for an explanation, but when she didn't immediately launch one, Hayes told them about her phone conversation with Alice. "She attributed Emory's distress to fatigue, medications, like that. Poo-pooed her suspicions, said no way could Jeff have harmed her."

"Love can make you stupid," Connell said. "Maybe she truly believes that."

"Maybe. But she's still lying to protect him."

"Up to us to prove she's lying, though," Knight said.

"Put her love to the test. If Jeff is actually arrested and charged, she may rethink her story."

Grange seemed to like Hayes's suggestion. "Let's get a warrant for him and see what happens."

"Do you know where he is?" Jack asked.

"At the suite hotel," Knight said. "We stopped there on our way here, asked him if he'd heard from his wife overnight. We didn't expect he had," he said, dividing a droll look between her and Hayes. "But we wanted to test his reaction. He told us he'd been going crazy with worry all night. So much so that as soon as it got light this morning, he went to the hospital to see if she'd been admitted to the ER as a Jane Doe."

"He's putting on quite a performance," Jack said.

Grange pulled his cell phone off his belt. "I'll get a deputy over to the hotel to watch his room, make sure he doesn't go anywhere while we're waiting on that warrant."

As he turned away to make the call, Knight said to Jack, "If an FBI agent was waiting on that warrant, too, it might add some heft and speed things along."

Jack looked over at Hayes, posing a silent question. Hayes shrugged. "Can't hurt."

"What are you going to do?"

"Stick around here where it's safe."

"We've canceled the BOLO," Knight told him. "Reason we gave was that last night's incident had been a domestic misunderstanding. We didn't let on who you were. Agent Connell here said you'd be royally pissed if word got out and a big to-do was made of you. Anyhow, you're safe."

"I didn't mean safe for me," Hayes said, his lips barely moving. "I meant for Jeff. If I see him, I'm liable to kill him."

At that point Grange rejoined them and reported that a deputy was in place. "He's got Jeff's suite and car in plain sight."

As Connell was pulling on his coat, he said to Hayes, "I'll call when we've got him in custody. What's your current phone number?"

Hayes hesitated.

Connell rolled his eyes. "Look, I know you leave Rebecca a way to contact you."

Hayes pulled a cell phone from his pocket, and when the number showed up on the readout, he held it out for Connell to see and commit to memory. "Got it." Turning to the detectives, he said, "Let's go get this done, gentlemen."

Grange opened the door and stood aside for Connell to go first. "You can ride with us." The three filed out and pulled the door closed. None of them had seemed to notice that Emory hadn't spoken a word since the mention of Alice.

But Hayes had.

Chapter 39

Looking like trick-or-treaters, Will and Norman arrived at their aunt and uncle's house just as Lisa was about to leave for school.

"Ma's sick," Norman announced. "You gotta come home with us now."

"What's wrong with her?"

Bypassing the question, he asked their uncle for the loan of his pickup.

"How did you get here?" the man asked as he reluctantly handed over the keys.

"A friend dropped us."

"You look awful," Lisa said. "Aren't you supposed to be in the hospital for several more days?"

"We'll be okay. Ma might not." Norman took her by the arm and roughly propelled her toward the truck parked in the driveway. Will was holding the passenger door for her. "You're a freak show," she said.

Glowering with more malevolence than usual, he boosted her in.

Once they were under way, she asked, "What's wrong with Mother?"

"That's for us to know and for you to shut up about," Norman snarled as he wove through traffic. "You been talking way too much, little sister."

"You're lying, aren't you? Let me out of here!" She made a grab for the steering wheel.

Will yanked her back and whacked the side of her head with the heel of his hand, then took a bone-crushing grip on both her wrists, pinning her hands together.

Norman said, "You try something like that again, and you'll regret it."

"Where are you taking me?"

"Just like we said. Home."

"But there's nothing wrong with Mother, is there?"

"Besides being old and ugly? No."

Despite the Frankenstein apparatus, Will managed to snicker at his brother's joke.

Lisa hated them, loathed them, and feared them. She knew from experience that she couldn't get free of Will's grasp until he was ready to release her. He had successfully held her down too many times to give her any hope of breaking away from him now. He was weakened by his injuries, but the feverish light in his eyes warned that he had a lot of fight left in him. And even if she could manage to free her hands, how would she get out of the truck?

Her only hope lay in the man who had promised to come to her aid if she ever needed him. All she had to do was wait until they got home and somehow get to a telephone.

But as they approached his cabin and she saw that yellow crime scene tape had been strung around the entire property, she gave a cry of dismay. "What happened?"

"Like we thought, he's a fugitive. He gave you a phone number, right?"

"How'd you know?"

"Didn't," Norman said, flashing her his cagey grin. "But fig-ured. Did he tell you to call him if—"

"If you tried to rape me."

"Yeah, we know that's what you've been blabbin'. Also know you had the backing of your lady doctor friend. But fuck her. She's her old man's problem to deal with."

"She's married?"

"Looks like, but not our business. It's your tall, dark, and handsome we want."

"What are you going to do?"

He steered into the drive of their house and brought the truck to a jarring stop. The chain was still wrapped around the tree. "Damn him, stole our dog, too," Norman muttered as he cut the engine and pulled his cell phone from the pocket of his dirty jeans—the bloodstained ones in which he'd been admitted to the hospital.

"Here's what's gonna happen, little sister," he said. "You're gonna call your knight in shiny armor and tell him that we've brought you home and that you're scared on account of we found out about the lies you've been spreading."

"He knows they're not lies."

"No he don't," he retorted. "He's just taking your word for it. But you tell him that we're good and mad, and that we've threat-ened to make good your lies, and that you'd sooner kill yourself as have us... do that."

Will grunted his approval of the script.

"And then what?" she asked.

"Then he'll come running to your rescue. When he gets here, he'll wish he'd never been born." Norman grinned and bran-dished the phone. "What's the number?"

She sneered. "When hell freezes over."

Will grabbed her by the jaw, digging his thumb into one cheek and his fingers into the other. Although it cost him a grimace of pain from his broken ribs, Norman secured her hands. She bucked and twisted, but the harder she struggled, the tighter they held on. The pain to her jaw was so intense, tears came to her eyes.

"Hurts, don't it?" Norman said.

He'd broken a sweat, and one of the raw patches on his face had begun to leak fresh blood. "You can imagine the suffering Will here's gone through because of your friend. But he's still got the strength to bend a skinny little whip like you. Eventually you'll tell us what we want to know, so you'd just as well save yourself the discomfort."

She squeezed her eyes shut and shook her head.

After a moment, Norman said, "All right, then, we'll try something else."

The sinister quality of his smooth tone caused her to open her eyes. Her mother had come out onto the porch, a dishtowel slung over one shoulder, her holey cardigan crookedly buttoned, and Lisa's spirit crumbled, because she knew she would do whatever they demanded.

"You make that call, little sister," Norman whispered, "and it'd better be convincing. Or on this occasion we tie Ma to a chair and she watches."

———

Hayes waited until the other three men had left, then he said, "You didn't know it was Alice."

Rather than feeling teary, Emory's eyes felt exceptionally dry, as though she hadn't even blinked since learning of her friend's betrayal. "No."

"You never suspected?"

"No."

"You're furious."

"You're damn right I am." She came out of her chair, pushed

it aside, and began pacing the area between the dresser and the foot of the bed. "I'm not jealous. Not even hurt. I'm livid."

"She doesn't deserve the energy that requires."

"I'm more angry at myself than at her."

"For what?"

"For being so naive."

"Trusting."

"Blind."

"Can I throw out another adjective?"

She stopped pacing and looked at him. "What?"

"Indifferent. You made it easy for her. You didn't care enough about Jeff's diddling to find out who was on the receiving end."

She thought about that, then said, "Stop being right and let me rant."

He motioned for her to continue.

"What really makes me angry is that I told her about my night with you. It was the most treasured secret I had, and I wanted to keep it all to myself. But I had to share the most personal aspects of it with her." She explained why, then looked at him uneasily.

He met her gaze and said solemnly, "I hope you did me justice."

It was such an unexpected reaction from him that she laughed. "Connell was wrong. You can joke."

"Wasn't joking."

But he was, and she ate up the sight of his rare grin. He was right, Alice didn't deserve the energy it took to be angry. Besides, her heart was too full of another emotion. Softly she said, "I think your friend Jack is onto us."

"He's not my friend, but he is onto us. When he came back with breakfast, he knew he'd interrupted either a fight or foreplay."

"Was it a fight?"

"Sure as hell wasn't foreplay."

Knowing she was venturing into the deep end, she said, "We left that conversation unfinished, Hayes."

Just like that, his mood shifted. He stood up and turned his back to her. "Better that way."

"I don't think so."

"We'll only go round and round on this issue, Doc. It's pointless."

She went to him and forced him to face her. "During one of our first conversations, I said, 'There's always a choice.' And you corrected me. 'Not always,' you said. Remember?"

"Yeah."

"You were right. You did what you had to do in Westboro because you had no choice."

"What you're saying then is that there are dirty jobs, but somebody has to do them."

"Not exactly the phrasing I would use," she said.

"But that's basically where you're coming from."

"Where are you coming from?"

"Same damn place," he said tightly. "But do you understand what that means? It means there's a part of me that doesn't mind being dirty. That scares me. It should scare you."

She could tell by the implacability of his eyes that her arguments hadn't made a dent. "You're going to disappear again, aren't you?"

"Why do you sound surprised? I told you I would."

"You also told me that nothing has changed. You're wrong, Hayes. Everything has changed. Damned if I'm going to let you deny it."

She reached up, cupped the back of his neck, and pulled his head down so she could reach his lips. He resisted and tried to angle away until she traced the seam of his lips with her tongue, then he not only weakened to allow the kiss, he took command of it.

Suddenly the aggressor, his mouth slanted over hers and feasted on it. He put his hands under her ass and lifted her onto his thighs, then carried her as far as the nearest wall and pinned her there with his body. Her legs went around him, securing him in the cove of her thighs.

With no space between them to allow for thrusts, he applied a firm and insistent pressure that she met with yearning undulations. Their craving for each other was matched only by their frustration, hampered as they were by clothing, by time and place, and by circumstances.

Tearing his mouth free of hers, he buried his face in the ell of her shoulder and neck, his breath fast and hot against her skin. "Yeah, okay, something has changed. When I'm by myself in the night, I'll want you."

He dipped his head and found her nipple through her clothing, moving his mouth across it as he hoarsely whispered broken phrases. "Sleeping between your thighs, finding your breasts in the dark, listening to your breathing, and smelling your hair on my pillow. I'll want all that, damn you. Damn you, Doc. You won't be easy to let go."

"Then stay with me."

"I can't."

"You can."

"I—"

His cell phone chirped. Once, twice, three times. Then it stopped.

They froze, panting, waiting, and when it began chirping again, she lowered her feet to the floor. He released her and stepped back, his hand going straight to his crotch and massaging it, cursing lavishly as he fished the phone from his jeans pocket.

He answered with, "Good timing, Jack."

As he listened, his expression changed from supreme annoyance to alarm. "Lisa? Can you speak up?" He mouthed an obscenity. "Where? Is your mother there?" A moment later, he hissed another curse, then said, "Do what you can to stay away from them. I'm on my way." He clicked off.

"What?"

"Her brothers picked her up and took her home. She's locked herself in the bedroom, but they're threatening to make good on the *lies* she's been telling about them."

Emory groaned. "Pauline?"

"You don't want to know."

"I'll call the sheriff's office."

"Don't," he said. "They'd go, Lisa would accuse, the brothers would deny, they'd leave. She'd still be stuck there with them. No, this is one of those dirty jobs. I gotta finish it."

"This is a matter for the authorities."

He gave it a few second's consideration. "All right. Give me ten minutes' head start."

"Hayes—"

"Ten minutes." He moved toward the door.

"I'm going with you."

"Hell you are. I can't fight them and protect you at the same time."

"You did before."

"Not this time. Besides, you need to wait for Connell's call about Jeff. Don't forget to charge your phone." He nodded toward a wall outlet where Connell's charger was plugged in. "If Jack can't reach me, he'll call you. He has your number, right? Knight and Grange, too?"

"Yes, but—"

"No buts, Doc. Jeff's secure, which is the only reason I'm leaving you alone. But my business right now is with Norman and Will."

As he pulled open the door, she grabbed his arm. "You said you wouldn't kill them."

"They don't know that."

In a week full of surprises, Jeff received the most unpleasant one of all when he pulled open the door of the suite to find Alice standing on the threshold, fist raised, about to knock.

"Alice. How untimely. What are you doing here?"

"I thought we should talk."

"Not now. I'm on my way out."

"Now, Jeff." She nudged him aside as she stepped into the entry. Noticing that he was already dressed for outdoors, she asked, "Where were you off to?"

Frowning, he checked his wristwatch. "I'll give you five minutes. People are waiting for me."

"What people?"

"Those hillbilly brothers."

"The ones Emory tangled with?"

"Yes. That lot. Emory and Hayes Bannock are the sister's champions. I thought if anything would lure them out, it would be she."

"What are you talking about? What have you done?"

"Doesn't matter. It's Sir Bannock to the rescue."

"What about Emory?"

"Hopefully she will be with her cavalier. If not, Norman assured me he'll happily work on him until he gives over where he's stashed her. Besides, I think it's time I met her mystery man."

"You described these brothers as reprobates."

"They are."

"But you've cooked up a scheme with them? Have you gone mad?"

"No."

"I think you must have, Jeff. Whatever your plan is, it could go terribly wrong."

"I'm prepared for that eventuality."

He opened his coat and showed her an inside pocket. She gaped at him. "You have a *gun*? You?"

"I have a gun. Me." He removed the revolver from the pocket and balanced it in his palm. "Small but trusty."

She walked over to the sofa and sat down, rubbing her temples as though they ached. "This is insane. If there's any kind of fracas, Emory could be harmed or killed."

"And whose fault would that be?" he said. "Her own. Why does she remain everyone's *cause célèbre*? All of this, everything that's happened, she brought upon herself."

She looked at him, her expression wary and accusatory.

Abruptly he turned away. "I've got to go."

"Where's the charm on your zipper pull?"

He came back around. "What?"

"Last Friday night when you arrived at my house, you were wearing that jacket. I remarked on it, how attractive you looked in it. You bragged on it being new and told me how much it had set you back. Remember?"

"I'm not senile, Alice."

"It had a recognizable designer logo dangling from the zipper. It's not there now."

"I lost it."

"Where?"

"If I knew where, it wouldn't be lost." With impatience, he shifted his weight from one foot to the other. "Anything else on your mind this morning?"

"You and I. We're over?"

"I thought I'd made that clear last night."

"You did. But I wanted to hear it from you in person."

"Consider it heard." He motioned toward the door. "I'll see you out, then I need to get on my way."

She stood up shakily. "I'm not feeling well. I need the bathroom."

He sighed. "Top of the stairs through the bedroom. Hurry, please."

"Go," she said tearfully. "I'll be sure the door is locked when I leave."

Chapter 40

She hadn't actually promised Hayes a ten-minute head start before she called the sheriff's office. He had just assumed she would comply with his request. As soon as he was gone, she plugged her dead cell phone into the charger.

She checked her contacts for Sam Knight's number, but before she could send it through, her phone rang in her hand, startling her. Even more startling, her LED read: *Alice.*

With a resurgence of anger, she answered. "I know, Alice."

Alice made a hiccupping sound. "Jeff told you?"

"No. But it doesn't matter how I found out. The point is, I did."

"Emory—"

"Save it. I can't talk to you now. In fact, I want nothing more to do with you. Ever."

"What about the clinic?"

"Did you take its future into account when you started sleeping with my husband?"

"I deserve that. I deserve your scorn. More. But you must listen to me now."

"Nothing you say will change—"

"I lied to the detective."

Emory stopped herself from disconnecting. "What?"

"I told Sergeant Grange that Jeff was with me from the Friday evening you left for North Carolina until Sunday afternoon."

"He wasn't?"

"He was, except…except that I woke up early Saturday morning to go to the bathroom, and he wasn't there. I thought he'd just decided to slip out, go home, and sleep in his own bed for the rest of the night. I didn't like it. I had hoped we'd have one night to spend—"

Caring about none of that, Emory interrupted. "Where did he go?"

"I don't know. I went back to bed, and to sleep, and when I woke up, he was at the bedside, bearing a tray, serving me brunch in bed. He never mentioned leaving. He didn't know I'd missed him. I never brought it up."

"And you didn't tell Grange."

"No. When he showed up at my house unexpectedly, it rattled me. I owned up to the affair, but the idea of Jeff being implicated in a crime against you was so preposterous, I covered for him. You reappeared that same morning, so my lie was vindicated. Or so I thought. But now I think your suspicions have merit."

Emory's heart rate spiked. "What makes you think so?"

"Things he's said, evasive answers—but I'll save all that for later. There's something more urgent you need to know." In stops and starts, her speech so rapid that words stumbled over themselves, she said, "Jeff has cooked up some scheme with these Floyd brothers, using their sister to lure you and Hayes Bannock out. It's crazy."

"Oh my God. Hayes got a frantic call from Lisa. He's on his way up to their place now."

"And Jeff tore out of here no more than—"

"Where is here?"

"The suite hotel." She told Emory about Jeff's call to her the night before. "I got a sense that he was maneuvering me into thinking you'd gone insane. I drove up this morning to confront him about all this and caught him just as he was leaving. I faked being sick, and as soon as he was gone, I called you."

While Alice had been talking, Emory realized that Hayes hadn't given her the number to his cell phone, an oversight which might have been intentional in order to protect her, but it left her with no way to alert him to the trap being laid for him.

Then she noticed the set of ignition keys on the dresser.

She stopped Alice in midsentence. "Do you still have Detective Grange's number?"

"Uh...I think...yes. He gave me his card. It's here in my bag."

"Call him. Tell him what you've told me. Everything. Tell him to dispatch people up to the Floyds' place. Now. Immediately. Impress on him that Hayes is in danger. In the meantime, I'm going up there to try and head him off."

She unplugged her phone from the charger, swept the keys into her hand, and left the motel room. Outside, she depressed the rubberized button on the remote key. The headlights blinked on a nondescript sedan parked in one of the nearby spaces. She ran toward it.

Her phone rang. Alice again. She answered by saying, "Call Grange! Do it, Alice. You owe me this."

"You're serious about going up there?"

"I'm on my way now."

"Then there's something you need to know. Jeff has a pistol."

That almost slowed Emory down. Almost.

Instead, she clicked off, jerked open the driver's door, and slid behind the wheel of Jack's rental car, the one in which he'd gotten lost in the fog. Which was easily done when it was this thick.

Jeff made it as far as the door to the suite and was reaching for the knob when he thought about Knight and Grange's visit to him this morning.

Just stopped by to check and see if you'd heard from Emory overnight.

That had been Knight's explanation for their unannounced arrival. He'd accepted it at the time, but as he thought back on it, he wondered why Knight hadn't simply telephoned to ask. Had he and Grange been checking up on him? Did they still suspect him of wrongdoing?

Call him paranoid, but...

The door to the suite had narrow glass panels flanking it. Keeping his body out of sight, he peered through one of the panes. On the far side of the parking lot sat an unmarked car, noticeable because it was seemingly so innocuous. The driver's door window had been lowered only far enough to accommodate a cigarette whose smoke curled up into the fog and became part of it.

Amateur surveillance at best. But Jeff still had to get around it. He was deliberating on how to accomplish that when he heard Alice's voice coming from the bedroom upstairs. Maybe she'd called the clinic to check in. Or maybe not.

He crossed the living area to the staircase and climbed the carpeted treads as lightly and as silently as possible. The bedroom door stood ajar. He heard her say in a frantic undertone, "But now I think your suspicions have merit."

Damn her! Damn her and Emory both!

His outrage mounted as he listened to one incriminating sentence after another. She outlined his plan with the Floyds. Then, "Emory? Emory, are you there?" She must have been redialing as she repeated in an urgent whisper, "Come on, come on, answer."

Then, "You're serious about going up there? Then there's something you should know. Jeff has a pistol."

After that, silence.

He put the tip of his index finger to the door and pushed it open, following it as it swung inward until he was standing in the door jamb. She'd been sitting on the bed. When she saw him, she came quickly to her feet, trying but failing to conceal her fear.

"Jeff. I thought you'd left."

"I got sidetracked." He looked pointedly at the phone clutched in her hand and made a tsking sound. His gaze came back to connect with hers. "As I told you earlier, Alice, your visit this morning is very untimely."

Emory's hands soon turned slick with nervous perspiration on the steering wheel.

On her way through town, she searched for a police car, any type of official vehicle which she could flag down and ask for help, but saw none. Dialing while driving was risky, especially in the fog, but she took the chance and placed a call to Jack Connell.

After three rings, his phone went to voice mail. In a rush, she said, "It's Emory. Hayes tore out of here after getting an urgent call from Lisa Floyd. But it's a trap. Jeff set it up with the brothers. Alice is calling Sergeant Grange with details. Also, she lied about Jeff's alibi. But the important thing is, get people up to the Floyds' place immediately. Hayes is walking into danger, and every moment counts. I'm in your rental car on my way up there."

Suddenly she realized that she was talking into a dead phone. She cried out in dismay and checked her LED, which confirmed that her meager supply of battery power had run out. But at what point during her message?

She tossed the phone into the passenger seat and concentrated on driving. Lisa's safety, Hayes's life, depended on her getting there, but the conditions prohibited speed. Since leaving the city limits and taking the mountain road, the fog had grown even thicker. Little was visible beyond the hood of the car. She strained to see through it.

Yesterday, on the way up to Hayes's cabin, she had focused on the view out her window, which benefitted her now. Landmarks and signposts sighted yesterday guided her and kept her on the right road, when otherwise she would have become hopelessly lost. Taking a curve slowly, she saw a familiar row of rural mailboxes. Farther on, the piece of metal yard art shaped like a bear, then the house flying the US flag, the dilapidated and abandoned barn.

She knew she was getting close when she passed a fence lined with hydrangea plants as tall as she. She could imagine a profusion of blue flowers in the summer, but the leafless branches of the shrubs were now ice-encrusted, which was what had drawn her attention to them.

Beyond that fence, how much farther had they traveled before reaching Hayes's cabin? Two miles? Five? She couldn't recall.

She drove as fast as she dared, ever in the back of her mind the malice that Norman and Will Floyd harbored for Hayes. Men who would rape their underage sister wouldn't have any qualms against maiming or killing an enemy.

But Grange would have responded immediately to Alice's call. Deputies would have been dispatched, and possibly some were already at the Floyds' place. Connell would also be on his way to help Hayes. Having just now reunited, Connell wouldn't permit—

The sharp curve appeared suddenly, and she saw it too late to avoid the collision.

The car crashed into the gray wall of rock. The seat belt caught. The airbag deployed. It no doubt saved her life, but the impact was bruising. The interior of the car filled with choking powder.

As soon as the bag deflated, she batted at it and groped

blindly for the door handle. She all but fell out of the car, the hood of which had been squashed against the sheer rock face like a soda can.

The soles of her boots lost purchase and she landed hard on her bottom. While she sat there regaining her breath, the cold and wet of the pavement seeped into the seat of her jeans. The discomfort served to revive her.

Pulling herself to her feet, she rested against the side of the car and took inventory of all her parts. She was shaken, and her sternum hurt where the seat belt had caught it, but no bones were broken.

She pushed herself off the car and set out at a run.

As they exited the courthouse and walked toward the parked SUV, Jack groused, "What kind of freaking policy—"

"He's the judge," Knight said.

Grange got behind the wheel, Knight rode shotgun, Jack climbed into the back. "Buckle up," Knight told him. "We got laws."

Jack clicked on his seat belt and checked his phone, the use of which had been forbidden for as long as they'd been inside the courthouse waiting on the arrest warrant. "Emory," he told the other two as he activated his voice mail. Then, "Oh shit! Oh *shit!*"

"What?" Grange said.

Jack rattled off Emory's message. "Hayes is walking into danger. Then she started breaking up and went away. Check your phone, Grange. She said Alice Butler was going to call you with details. Also, Jeff's alibi was a lie." To Knight, he said, "Get some units rolling toward the Floyds' place, but first see if you can get Emory back. I'll call Hayes, and that son of a bitch had damn well better answer."

Grange, driving with one hand, checked his phone. "No calls from Alice Butler."

"Emory's phone goes straight to her recording," Knight said. "Buddy, keep heading for the suite hotel, but let's amp it up."

Grange turned on the siren and light bar and stepped on the gas.

"Son of a gun. When all hell breaks loose…" Knight muttered as he got on the unit's radio to dispatch.

Meanwhile Jack had put in the call to the burner phone Hayes was currently using. He counted one ring, two, and was just about to give up when Hayes answered. "What?"

"I know you got a call from Lisa Floyd, and that you're running to her rescue. What you don't know is that Jeff Surrey is behind her plea for help."

"How do you know?"

"Emory left me a message."

"How did she know?"

"We think it came from Alice Butler. We're trying to ascertain that."

"*Trying?*"

"I called Emory again," Knight said, speaking over his shoulder. "Got her recording."

"Did you hear that?" Jack asked.

"Yeah," Hayes said. "Her phone battery had to charge."

"She cut out on the message," Jack told him, "but one thing came through loud and clear. You're being set up for an ambush."

"Way ahead of you. I figured as much. I just didn't know Jeff was behind it. Where are you now?"

"On our way to Jeff's hotel to serve the warrant."

"Stay with that. Get that bastard locked up."

"Will do."

"Tell Emory to stay put at the motel. Call the room phone if you can't reach her by cell."

"Roger that. Don't confront those hillbillies alone. SO units are on the way."

"I'll handle the Floyds."

"Hayes, you—"

"I'll handle them."

"That's what I'm afraid of."

"We got here in time to head Jeff off," Grange said as he wheeled the SUV into the suite hotel parking lot. "His car's still here."

Jack relayed that to Hayes, who said, "Save me a piece of him," and then he disconnected.

Jack was still cursing him as he scrambled out of the backseat.

"I'll check with our guy." Grange struck out at a jog toward an unmarked vehicle on the other side of the parking lot.

Knight climbed out of the SUV's passenger side. He sounded winded. "Still no answer on Emory's phone. Got squad cars converging on the Floyds' place, but this goddamn weather..." He didn't need to elaborate on the additional hazards it imposed.

Jack said, "Well, it'll hold up Hayes, too. That's good."

During this exchange, they'd been walking purposefully toward the door of the suite. Grange joined them there. "Deputy says Jeff had company. A lady."

Jack said, "Lady? Emory?"

"No. The deputy didn't recognize her."

"Alice Butler?"

"She'd be my guess," Knight said. He pounded on the door. "Jeff? Open up."

They waited. Nothing.

"Jeff!" Knight called. "This isn't a courtesy call. We have a warrant."

After several more seconds and nothing happened, Knight said, "I've had it with this shitbag." He took his pistol from its holster and shot out the lock.

No one was on the lower floor. Grange headed for the stairs, pistol drawn and aimed at the partially open door at the top. "Give it up, Jeff."

When he reached the door, he stood aside and pushed it open. Nothing happened, so he stepped into the room. Jack slipped in behind the detective. Knight brought up the rear, huffing.

Later Jack would recall him saying, "Aw, now that's just ugly."

Emory hurt all over. It hurt even to breathe.

The foggy air felt full of something invisible but sharp, like ice crystals or glass shards. She was underdressed. The raw cold stung her face where the skin was exposed. It made her eyes water, requiring her to blink constantly to keep the tears from blurring her vision and obscuring her path.

A stitch had developed in her side. It clawed continually, grabbed viciously. The stress fracture in her right foot was sending shooting pains up into her shin.

But owning the pain, running through it, overcoming it, was a matter of self-will and discipline. She'd been told she possessed both. In abundance. To a fault. But this was what all the difficult training was for. She could do this. She had to.

Push on, Emory. Place one foot in front of the other. Eat up the distance one yard at a time.

How much farther to go?

God, please not much farther.

Refueled by determination and fear of failure, she picked up her pace.

Then, from the deep shadows of the encroaching woods came a rustling sound, followed by a shift of air directly behind her. Her heart clutched with a foreboding of disaster to which she had no time to react before skyrockets of pain exploded inside her skull.

She fell, landing hard.

When the worst of the light show subsided, she rolled onto all fours and stayed in that position for several seconds, head lowered between her arms, trying to stave off dizziness. Finally, she raised her head only high enough to bring into view a pair of boots.

She stared at them as they came closer, growing larger until they filled her entire field of vision. When they came to within a few inches of her and stopped, she looked up past knees, torso, shoulders, and chin into a pair of familiar eyes.

"Alice?"

Chapter 41

"Y ou could have saved me a lot of trouble and died the first time," Alice said. "Acute subdural hematoma. I was certain I'd struck you hard enough to cause a slow but persistent bleed, which out here," she said, spreading her arms wide, "would have been deadly. But not to you. Not to the Golden Girl. Haven't you ever, just once in your charmed life, had a streak of rotten luck?"

Emory's brain, not even a week away from the first injury, was feeling the effects of the car crash and now a second blow to her head. She tried to stand, but her legs were too rubbery to support her, so she came off all fours and sat.

She tried to focus on what Alice was saying, but the words made no sense. Her image was wavering, as though Emory were looking at her underwater. The fluidity was making her nauseated.

"What are you saying? What is that in your hand?"

"This?" Alice raised the pistol. "It's known in every ER in the country as a Saturday night special. Your basic thirty-eight-caliber revolver."

Emory was beginning to grasp what was happening. "What are you doing with it?"

"I'm about to kill you, and this time I'll make sure you're dead."

Emory's stomach pitched. Nausea surged into the back of her throat. She was only barely able to swallow it. "Why?"

"It would take forever to enumerate all the reasons, Emory, and it's cold out here. To summarize, Jeff was a louse, but he was *my* louse. At least he was until I made the mistake of introducing him to you. You were a much greener pasture. Pretty. Rich. Coveted virtues to him. But he didn't love you, you know. He never did."

"I realize that now."

"However, he reveled in the affluence and status you lent him. So much so that he would never have left you, no matter how rocky the marriage became. He would always have held on."

"So you had to get rid of me."

"You had obligingly shown me the map with the trail you planned to run on Saturday morning. You went over it with me in great detail."

"But you were with Jeff."

"Who never could smoke weed without passing out afterward. I plied him with two scotches, two bottles of red wine, and a high-quality joint to ensure that he wouldn't awaken until late the following morning.

"I made the long drive, parked at your turnaround spot, which you'd also pointed out to me, walked along the trail until I found a good hiding place, waited until you ran past, then came up behind you with the rock I'd found on the path."

She smiled sourly. "In hindsight, I should have stayed a wee bit longer to make sure you were dead or soon would be. I was afraid to touch you for fear of leaving trace evidence. I didn't touch the broken sunglasses that caused such high anxiety.

"Anyhow, I rushed back to my car, which was still the only one there. I met no one on the road coming down the mountain. I made it back to Atlanta in record time and had brunch in bed with Jeff, who was none the wiser. It was just as I outlined it to you this morning, except I was the one who sneaked out, not Jeff."

"You wanted me dead so you could have him."

She laughed. "Emory, you're thinking far too simplistically. I wanted you dead so Jeff would be blamed for it. Being convicted of your murder would cost him his life, one way or another. Two birds, one stone. You see?" She flashed a smile that was overly bright and cheery, a madwoman's grin of self-congratulation.

Emory concentrated hard on gathering puzzle pieces until they formed a complete picture. "Did you leave the trinket off his ski jacket there?"

"It was found? I wondered. I couldn't ask."

Emory didn't tell her who had found it.

"Everything was going according to plan," Alice continued. "Jeff quickly came under suspicion. He pretended to be distraught over your disappearance, but very quickly he grew fond of the prospect of being a wealthy widower, which, of course, was to my benefit.

"But I couldn't figure out why no one could find your body. How hard could it be? I guessed that you'd regained consciousness and staggered off the path and into the wilderness. After three days, I began to relax, believing that if you hadn't died of the head trauma, surely you had succumbed to hypothermia.

"Then you turned up alive. Saved by Daniel Boone. Unbelievable," she said, shaking her head at the wonder of it. "Who would have guessed that your splendor extended to rising from the dead? And that was only the first of several jolts. Your cabin-dweller was a fugitive being hunted by the FBI. You and he were in a feud with incestuous hillbillies.

"But," she said, smiling again, "I saw a way to turn this mess to my advantage. Worse than anything, Jeff hated being seen as a fool, and your escapades were making him out to be a colossal one. He was rapidly unraveling. All I had to do was keep pulling on the thread.

"Last night he tried to convince me that you had become mentally unbalanced. So, as a friend to both of you, I drove up here this morning to lend support. He outlined his ridiculous plot with that pair of brothers. I pretended to be dismayed, when actually I was delighted. Without any help from me, he was digging himself in deeper. Which I would have been happy to sit back and watch him do. But," she sighed, "at the last minute, he forced my hand."

Emory's blood turned cold. "You're referring to him in the past tense."

Lost in her own thoughts, Alice continued, speaking in a rueful murmur. "Incomprehensibly, he was going to chase up here and reclaim you. Even after suffering the humiliation heaped on by you, he still chose you over me."

"My God, Alice, what have you done? You'll never get away with it, not any of it."

"Oh, getting away with it has ceased to matter. My goal was to have the two of you dead, and I'm halfway there." She aimed the pistol down at Emory. "Any final words?"

"Alice, please."

"No? Okay then."

The shot rang out, and Alice crumpled to the ground, her right leg giving out from under her.

Hayes emerged from the fog-blanketed trees like a specter, his gun hand extended at arm's length. "Drop the weapon or you die."

Emory cried out, "No, no!" But her fear was more for him than Alice.

The bullet had entered the back of Alice's leg and exited the front just above her knee. Her teeth chattered with pain, but she kept her grip on the pistol, which was aimed at Hayes, who made a huge target.

Emory thought her heart would burst from her chest. "Alice, please, listen to me, listen to him. Toss the pistol away. Don't make him kill you. Please don't."

Alice didn't seem to hear. She was focused on Hayes. "Emory's super stud."

"Drop the pistol."

"If you'd wanted me dead," she taunted, "you would have made the first shot count."

"I don't want you dead. But I will fucking kill you if I have to."

"Don't make him, Alice, please, please," Emory sobbed. "I beg you. Don't make him do it. Put the gun down. It's over."

"Over for you." She whipped the pistol toward Emory.

The gunshot wasn't as loud as it might have been on a clear day when the air was crisp. The fog muffled some of the sound.

But Alice was just as dead.

Hayes was beside Emory in an instant, bending down to lift her up and hug her against him. His hands closed around her head as he searched her face. "Are you all right?"

She was weeping. "I didn't want you to have to. I didn't want you to—"

"Shh. Shh. I didn't."

He indicated that she look behind her. Sergeant Detective Grange was standing with one hand braced against a tree, bent at the waist, retching violently. Knight stood beside him, his beefy hand on his partner's shoulder.

Hayes's cabin became headquarters for all the law enforcement personnel and emergency responders who arrived on the scene within minutes.

He had carried Emory in his arms the remaining distance and deposited her in one of the olive-green chairs at the dining table. He brought a quilt from the bed and draped it around her.

"That'll help until the ambulance gets here. They'll have a Mylar blanket."

"I only want you." Emory grasped his hand.

He knelt beside her and threaded his fingers through her hair. "What the hell were you doing on that road on foot?"

"Running to warn you."

He dragged his thumb across her lower lip. "Don't do it again," he said huskily.

"Don't ever make yourself so large a target."

"Not much I can do about that, Doc."

They were still staring into each other's eyes when Jack Connell approached. "Hanging in there?"

Tremulous and tearful, Emory said, "We're alive."

"No small miracle," Connell said. "Knight, Grange, and I came upon your crashed car. *My* crashed car."

"I'm sorry about that."

He made a motion of dismissal. "You weren't injured in the crash?"

"Nothing serious. But Alice..." Speaking the name caused her voice to crack. "She struck me. Maybe with the butt of the pistol. I'll need another brain scan."

"Ambulance should be here in a couple more minutes." He shuffled his feet and divided an uneasy look between her and Hayes. Hayes, getting the message, mumbled that he'd see if there was anything he could do outside and left through the open door. She was reluctant to let him go but didn't call him back, intuiting what Jack Connell was about to say.

"Emory, your husband is dead."

She nodded. "She alluded to it. How?"

"Gunshot. Probably with the same pistol she was going to use on you."

"Was it Jeff's pistol?"

"No. One registered to him was found in an inside pocket of his jacket."

"So she wasn't lying about that. She told me he had a pistol."

"He didn't get to implement his plan, whatever it was, and I guess we'll never know. He was killed inside the suite. Somehow Alice Butler got out without the deputy seeing her. Maybe the same way you and Hayes split the other night through the adjoining suite."

He explained that after discovering Jeff's body, he, Knight, and Grange had left the deputy there to guard the crime scene. "We were afraid for your safety and went looking for you at the motel. When I saw that my car was gone, we figured there was only one place you'd go."

"My phone must have died before you got that part of the message. I told you I was on my way up here to warn Hayes." She was watching him through the open doorway. His back was to her. He was talking to Buddy Grange and Sam Knight. "Alice knew."

"She got here quick. She must've come upon the wrecked car and realized you'd set out on foot. She continued driving till she spotted you on the road, then—"

"Came up behind me, like before."

"Before?"

She related Alice's confession.

"So it wasn't Jeff after all," Jack said.

"Not directly. They both deceived me, and Alice told me he wasn't all that bereaved when he thought I was dead. I believe that."

"Hate to say it, but so do I."

Hayes came through the door and rejoined them. "Ambulance driver is turning around so he can back in."

Connell said to Emory, "I'll pass along to Knight and Grange that Alice confessed." He left them to go outside.

Hayes sat down on his haunches in front of her and took her cold hands between his. "Knight told me about Jeff. You okay?"

"It'll take some time."

"You have time."

Absently she nodded. After a moment, she asked, "What happened at the Floyds' house?"

"Norman and Will were on the lookout for me in front. Forgot to cover their back. They're mean, but not too astute."

"Lisa and Pauline?"

"Safe. I got there before the brothers carried out their wretched threat, which was probably an empty one. They wanted me, not Lisa."

"Are they in custody?"

"They probably are by now. The mountain is crawling with cops of all varieties. I left Norman and Will easy to find, chained to the tree where they used to keep the dog."

"Poetic justice."

"I thought so."

She touched the fresh bruises on his face.

He gave her a wry smile. "They didn't go for the idea at first."

Wanting to smile, needing to weep, she leaned forward and nestled her head against his neck. He wrapped his arms around her and held her close. She could feel his lips moving against her hair, but she didn't catch the whispered words.

They stayed that way until two EMTs wheeled in a gurney.

Hayes tilted her head up and kissed her mouth, warmly and sweetly.

Then he stepped away and gave her over to the care of the EMTs, who insisted on strapping her to a board because of the head injury. As they wheeled her through the doorway and out into the yard, she caught sight of Sergeant Grange. She called his name, and he turned. He looked ashen, his shrewd eyes not as bright as usual.

She mouthed to him, *Thank you.* He acknowledged her gratitude with a quick nod, then cast his eyes down at the ground.

Looking for Hayes, she tried to move her head from side to side, but because of the constraint across her forehead, she couldn't. When she didn't see him, she struggled to raise her head, also to no avail. With mounting anxiety, she searched the yard as thoroughly as her peripheral vision would allow.

Finally she spotted Jack Connell. He was watching her, and in an instant she knew the cause of his bleak expression.

She ceased the struggle to raise her head. She wouldn't find who she had been looking for. The tears that leaked from the corners of her eyes were also futile. That he had vanished should come as no surprise. He had told her he would, and he always did as he said.

Finish Line

All along the twenty-six-mile route through Atlanta, spectators and supporters had cheered on the runners, but those congregated near the finish line were especially enthusiastic.

When Emory ran across it and the announcer boomed her name, introducing her as the organizer of the fund-raising race, she received a roar of approval. She was then thronged by photographers from TV stations and print news agencies, all vying for a sound bite. In her breathless state, she kept them brief.

She received pats on the back and hugs from other runners. One of her patients, a six-year-old boy, shyly approached with his parents and asked for her autograph. A group of war veterans, who'd gone the distance in wheelchairs, lined up to high five and salute her.

Her body was aching. Her right foot was hurting to the point of making her hobble. She was fatigued to near collapse, but she was exhilarated. For so many reasons, finishing this race represented a victory of mind, body, and spirit.

During the past six months, much had changed in her life.

At the conclusion of the police investigation into Alice's last few hours, a family member had claimed her body and had it transported to their hometown in Tennessee for burial. Emory had had no contact with the family.

She'd had Jeff's remains cremated and forewent a service of any kind. An outpouring of grief would have been hypocritical. She received only a handful of condolence cards. Her polite acknowledgments were as obligatory as the cards themselves. His belongings were sealed into boxes and delivered to a refuge for the homeless. The only sadness she felt was for Jeff himself. He had lived—and died—joylessly and lovelessly.

She sold their house quickly and moved into a townhouse in a charming gated community in Buckhead.

She and Dr. Neal James had invited a married couple, he an OB-GYN, she an infertility specialist, to join their partnership. They had been excellent additions; the clinic was thriving.

Norman and Will were charged, tried, and convicted of statutory rape. They received the maximum sentence, due in large part to Lisa's courageous courtroom testimony. She and Pauline had moved into an apartment in Drakeland, paid for by Emory. Too proud to take charity without "chippin' in," as Pauline put it, she worked mornings at a nursing home, helping to prepare and serve the noon meal.

Lisa kept her weekend job at Subway. Her sessions with a counselor who specialized in sexual abuse victims were also underwritten by Emory, who considered the payments an investment in the woman Lisa would become.

She remained near the finish line a while longer, extending congratulations to runners as they came in. She promised an interview to the host of a local TV morning talk show. "I'll have my people call your people," he said, and she laughed.

And then, "Good race, Doc."

She turned, and there he was, standing directly behind her.

The carnival atmosphere at the finish line receded, leaving

nothing in the spectrum of her senses except his voice, his face, and the remarkable eyes, that were, as always, steady on her.

He was dressed in a pair of well-worn jeans and a plain white shirt with the cuffs of the sleeves rolled back. He looked wonderfully, ruggedly beautiful, and she wanted to strike him and climb him in equal measure.

They stared at each other for so long, she became aware of attracting the curiosity of onlookers. "Thank you. It was nice of you to stop and say so." Although her heart was breaking, she turned and started walking away.

He fell into step beside her. "Where's your car parked?"

"A few blocks from here."

"My truck's closer."

Without argument, she let him guide her, still not quite believing that this wasn't a dream.

"Quite a turnout," he remarked as they threaded their way through one of the designated parking areas.

"Since this is the first race benefitting this particular charity, I'm amazed by the support and the numbers of runners we had sign up. We raised seven hundred fifty thousand dollars in pledges."

"Seven hundred fifty-*two*." She looked up at him. He said, "I didn't get my pledge in until this morning."

"Thank you."

"You're welcome. Here we are."

"You're back to driving your pickup, I see."

"Nobody's after me."

He helped her up into the passenger seat, then went around and got in.

She said, "As you leave the lot, take a left."

But he didn't turn on the ignition. He just sat there, staring through the windshield. She would turn to stone before she asked where he'd been, what he'd been doing, so she waited him out, and after a time he turned his head toward her.

"Rebecca told me she'd written to you."

"She got my address from Jack Connell. She wanted to thank me for 'knocking sense into you.'"

He snuffled. "Sounds like her." He arched his eyebrow. "She reached you through Connell, huh? She mention him in her letter?"

"Several times."

"Uh-huh. I get it, too. From both of them. I think they have a thing."

"Really?"

He grumbled a swear word. "That would serve me right, I guess." He waited a beat before continuing. "Sarah's school orchestra performed in the city park on St. Patrick's Day. I went out for the concert."

"I'm sure she was thrilled."

"Seemed to be. I stayed a week. Ate a lot of fish."

"You don't like fish."

"Even less now. I got enough omega-3 that week to last me the rest of my life."

She wasn't ready to smile yet. Keeping her voice curt, she asked, "So you and Connell stay in touch?"

"I think he wants to adopt me."

"He adopted you a long time ago."

"Only good thing about his hovering was that he kept me informed on how it all went down when you came back from North Carolina."

That snapped the rein she'd been keeping on her temper. "Then he's a glorified gossip."

"Practically an old woman."

"If you wanted to know how it was going down, why weren't you here to see for yourself?"

"Look, I know you're pissed. You have every right to kick me in the ass and tell me to get lost."

"If my foot didn't hurt—"

"I couldn't come to you until all that crap—yours and mine—was done with. You can understand that, Doc. I know you can."

Their gazes battled. Hers was the first to fall away. "It took me a while, but I did come to understand it. You would have been an additional complication, something requiring an explanation, when I already had much to explain and deal with."

"Exactly."

"But that also gave you a very convenient excuse to disappear again and stay gone."

"I had shit to work through, too. My reentry wasn't going to be easy, and I didn't want you subjected to the heat."

"I could have helped you."

"No, you couldn't. I had to work things out on my own. First, I had to figure out what I was going to do."

"Return to the FBI?"

"No. Jack asked me, but I turned him down flat."

"So then...?"

"I'm, uh, building stuff. More than bookshelves and sheds. I've affiliated with a group of contractors. We go in after natural disasters. Tornadoes, earthquakes. Like that. We get shelters up fast. Repair homes, schools, hospitals, whatever."

"Build stuff."

"Yeah."

He didn't embellish. The inflection in his voice didn't change much either, but it didn't have to for her to discern that he was excited and gratified. The work was perfectly suited to him. However, she knew better than to make too much of it.

"Sounds good."

"Feels good."

He took another long look out the front windshield. She gave him the time to organize his thoughts, and when he was ready to resume, he propped his left arm on the steering wheel and turned in his seat to face her.

"Sam Knight contacted me through Jack. He told me Grange was going through a hard time because of . . . well, you know why. Last week, I went to see him."

"He was in awe of you."

"Well, he now understands why I didn't like anybody looking to me as a hero. He was pretty eaten up, and at first he refused to talk about what happened up there that day. I know that feeling, and told him I did, and after that he opened up. He said he was finding it hard to live with himself for pulling the trigger."

He paused and looked deeply into her eyes. "And I heard myself asking him, 'Could you live with yourself if you *hadn't?*' " He let the question resonate for several seconds.

"I didn't plan on saying that, Doc. The words came from somewhere other than conscious thought. In fact, I think they came from you. But there they were, and saying them aloud made me realize that I couldn't live with myself if I hadn't pulled the trigger that day in Westboro either. I couldn't live with myself if I hadn't stopped him. And, just like that, after four years I was freed of it. I have you to thank."

For a time, she was too moved to speak. She had to clear her throat before she could. "And the people who bullied him?"

"I'm leaving them to their own miserable selves. Their meanness might catch up with them one day, or not. But it won't come from me."

Her heart swelled with love, but there was still one thing she must know. "That day, that awful last day, before the ambulance arrived and you were holding me, you whispered something into my hair. What did you say?"

"I asked you not to give up on me."

"But then you disappeared, Hayes."

"For the last time. I never will again."

"Do you promise?"

"I promise. If it's left to me, I've spent my last day and night without you. But whatever happens next, it's your call."

She kept him in suspense for all of three or four seconds. "I don't feel like driving. Will you give me a lift home?"

"Happy to." But then he didn't move, just sat there, drinking her in with his eyes.

"Are you going to start the truck?"

"Not yet, Doc." He reached across, cupped the back of her head in his large hand, and pulled her to him. "First I'm gonna kiss you till I can't breathe."

He always did what he said.